I0671275

Whatever
He
Wants

Whatever
He
Wants

Bridgett Henson

Empowered Publications Inc
Leroy, Alabama
www.empoweredpublicationsinc.com

© 2013 Bridgett Henson

Scripture quotations are taken from the King James Version.

All rights reserved.

Cover photos by LCK Photography.

This novel is a work of fiction. All characters are a product of the author's imagination. Any resemblances to actual people or events are purely coincidental.

Published by Empowered Publications Inc.
26812 Hwy 43
Leroy, Alabama 36548

ISBN 978-0-9895857-0-5

Acknowledgements

I could do nothing without my Savior, Jesus Christ. Thank you for saving me, filling me with the Holy Ghost, and giving me a work to do. Make me astonished, Lord.

A special thanks to my husband and children who keep up with my notebooks, steal my pens, bring me headphones, reheat my coffee, and eat leftovers and cold cereal while I'm writing.

There are many who've influenced and helped to make this book possible, but most especially LaShay Long who always encouraged me through the good and the bad.

I want to thank Tyler Chastain and Hope Morris for the long hours spent editing my typos and plot inconsistencies.

Megan Crager, Natalie Napper and Jennifer Dixon, thanks for sharing your testimonies.

Brother Willie and Sister Twila Long, you two have inspired me more than words can say. Thank you for your friendship and your willingness to minister to those in need.

Thank you to all the preachers out there who brought me a word from God, especially Greg & Jessica Adkins, Justin Sullivan, Doug Chapman, Papa Hanks and Lamar Chapman.

And thank you so very much to the Swinnea family.

In loving memory
of
Charles Devin Giles.
July 10, 1988
to
March 25, 2013

Author's Note

Although this is a fictional story, the characters struggle with real life obstacles. I have tried to show their temptation without tempting the reader.

There is no graphic imagery in this novel, but if you are at an age where you haven't experienced temptations of the flesh, please do NOT read this book.

If, however, you have lived long enough to encounter the immorality of this world, this novel gives hope that through the blood of Jesus and the following of the Spirit there is no sin unforgivable nor unconquerable, and God has a specific plan for each of his children.

I love to hear from my readers. Email me at bridgetthenson@millry.net, visit my website www.bridgetthenson.com, or friend me on facebook www.facebook.com/bridgetthenson.

Sincerely,
Bridgett Henson

Chapter One

Hangovers and three-year-olds didn't mix. A lesson James learned a few months back. He dismissed an offer from a girl wearing a silly smile and pushed through the crowd on the porch. After working out of town for five straight weeks, he was anxious to see his son, but on the way to their rental, Isaac's mom had texted him. Despite the car he'd bought six months ago, she and Isaac needed a ride. Her message hadn't mentioned this party.

As he stormed through the front door, a wave of music and smoke assaulted him. Where was Isaac? After last month's fiasco, she knew better than to bring him to one of her drunken bashes. Searching for Kathy's spooky black hair, he weaved through the living room mob and ignored the temptation to pray for Isaac's safety.

A brown-haired girl slouched against some guy on the worn couch. James lifted a rumpled blanket off the recliner and tossed it back down. No Isaac.

In the kitchen, a pixie with pink-tipped hair watched a game of Texas Hold'em. He stooped down and checked under the table. Pausing inside the game room that ran the length of the house, he wiped his brow.

Where was Isaac? And where was his nuisance of a mother?

~ ~ ~

Joni sized up the guys in the room. There wasn't much to choose from. Careful not to chip her professionally manicured nails, she flicked open the aluminum can. Maybe, she shouldn't be so picky. It wasn't like she hadn't considered doing it. She just never had the opportunity. Not with anyone appealing, anyway. The others had made their choices and left minutes ago. She sipped the brew and suppressed a shudder. She'd prefer a cheap wine to the foamy drink, but at least this one wasn't as bitter as the first can given to her by the hostess.

She squinted, momentarily clearing her fuzzy head. Time was short. The fraternity brothers would soon arrive to assist anyone who had trouble finishing the game. One guy in particular gave her the creeps. There was a mean look in his eyes and she had no intentions of being here when he arrived. Maybe she should do eeny, meeny, miny, moe? Or maybe she should admit her mother was right and go home?

No. If she wanted to belong somewhere other than under her parents' thumbnail, she had to grow up. How bad could it be? Other girls seemed to enjoy it. She could do this. Now to find someone to do it with…

If the tall guy in the corner could tear himself away from the Xbox, he might be a candidate. Another wave of dizziness clouded her thoughts. She shook her head and concentrated.

On the coffee table, a simple pyramid design proclaimed the blond architect's stupidity. The stack of cans leaned worse than the Eiffel Tower. She wanted someone with intelligence. The cute poker player in the kitchen needed a haircut, but she doubted a pair of scissors could plow through the gel build up. A guy across the table from him burped. Eeew.

She circled back to the game room. There was a pool shark she wanted to investigate further. If he didn't have dirt under his fingernails, he would do for the night.

~ ~ ~

James shoved his way through the sea of dancers. In a darkened corner, behind the large speaker that divided the room, Kathy lit one end of a rolled cigarette and let the excess paper burn. *She better not be smoking junk around Isaac.* A small crowd gathered. When he rounded the speaker, the music volume dropped. Sounds from the pool table mingled with the chatter of voices. "Where's my son?"

Kathy flinched at his words and then flashed a plastic smile. "At your sister's. The Street Preacher is in town."

He released a ragged breath and ran a shaky hand through his hair. With Sara, the worse place that Isaac could be was in church. Sliding his phone from his back pocket, he cringed at the time. Even a camp meeting service would have ended by now. Though he longed to see his son's sweet face, he'd have to wait until morning. James pocketed his phone and refocused on Kathy. "Where's your car?"

"Stolen."

Laughter came from her other side. James cut his eyes to a guy in a gangster hat. "You think that's funny?" The punk held up both hands and stepped backward. Kathy inhaled and passed the stub to a redhead wearing a skimpy top. Freckles decorated her cleavage. Smoke burned James's eyes and he waved the pungent smell away from his face. "How can you smoke that?"

"Loosen up." Kathy's painted lips twisted into a sneer. "It's natural herbs."

He grabbed her arm. "Where is the—" Hair like spun gold brushed past Kathy's shoulder. A new girl rounded the pool table and stopped. Glossy pink lips sipped from a can and then puckered to a frown. Her sweater was the color of gulf water. It matched her eyes. Dark jeans hugged her curves. A fingernail tapped against the can as she studied some dude shooting pool. Boyfriend? She leaned over and inspected the hand steadying the cue. Her shoulders lifted and fell in what could have been a sigh. No, definitely not her boyfriend.

James's world stopped turning as her eyes greeted his. He treasured the gift of her sweet smile. Lashes fluttered and she glanced at his boots. White teeth scraped across her bottom lip as her gaze swept up his body. He shivered. Jade eyes sparkled, and then darted to his side and rounded. Soft lips parted as she gasped and spun away.

Kathy snatched out of his loose grip. The calculated look on her face put him on guard. She raised a thin black eyebrow. "You want her."

He forced air through his lungs. "The car. Where is it?"

Kathy tilted her head. "Joni!" The golden beauty looked their way and Kathy waved her over. James whispered her name under his breath. It suited her. She was more than beautiful.

The weed had circled. Kathy took another hit and offered it to Joni. Thankfully, she shook her head. Kathy passed it around her. Two dainty thumbs indented Joni's can. Despite the drink she'd taken earlier, liquid spilled over the top.

"You don't normally drink do you?" James swallowed the urge to kiss the pink stain from her cheeks.

Though she smiled, her gaze dove somewhere near his boots and lingered.

Kathy snorted. "Don't worry about James. He's a prude."

If only she wasn't Isaac's mother, then James would be free. "Don't start with me tonight. I'm not in the mood."

"But he's the perfect guy to help you out. If he still remembers how? He's experienced with college life."

Joni's head jerked up. A trembling hand covered her mouth. Face crimson, she abandoned her drink on a small table. "Who told you about that?" Her eyes darted about the room, looking everywhere but at him.

Kathy inspected her blue fingernails and shrugged. "I promised to keep an eye on you."

Joni finally looked his way. "But he's your boyfriend…"

He captured her gaze. "No. I'm not." Eight months ago, when Kathy showed up with Isaac, he'd dropped out of school to become a father, but reconciling his short-lived relationship with Kathy had never been a desire, especially given her drug use. She corrupted everything she touched. James couldn't let her harm Joni. "But whatever you need, you don't want her help. Trust me."

Kathy snorted. "James just pays the bills for Isaac's sake. Besides, you have my permission." She stepped between them and held the roach out to Joni. "Here. Smoke this. It'll relax you."

Over Kathy's shoulder, Joni swayed lightly. "I don't know. I've never—"

"Don't." James shuffled around Kathy. Joni didn't belong here.

He glanced over his shoulder at Kathy. "Quit it. She's barely legal."

"I'm not a child."

He turned his head and stared into glazed eyes. Joni lifted her beautiful chin. "I can do whatever I want, but I don't mess around with that junk." She stumbled and he steadied her.

Kathy snickered. "I thought Little Miss Perfect doesn't do drugs." Laughter flowed from the groupies surrounded her.

Joni shook her head and blinked. "I don't understand. Everything is fuzzy." Dazed eyes frowned up at him. "I barely…"—she fell against his chest— "…sipped." Blood raced through his veins, leaving him winded. "James." On her lips, his name danced like a gentle breeze. He caught her by the waist before they both toppled over.

"You can thank me later." Kathy called over her shoulder as she strutted around them.

"Wait!" He reached out with one hand and spun her around. "What did you give her?"

"Nothing that won't wear off by morning."

His palm itched to slap the smirk off her face. Instead, he let her go as Joni snuggled against his chest. He couldn't stop his smile. "What am I supposed to do with you?"

Laughter spewed from a guy beside him. "Dude, if you don't want her, I'll gladly take her off your hands."

He cringed at the thought. The gleam in those eyes stirred the protector in him. He pulled her around to his side—the side away from the ogling guys leaned against the wall. With Isaac at his sister's, he wasn't concerned about the little boy's safety. Joni, on the other hand, needed his help. "Come on. Let's get you out of here."

She blinked up at him. "Where you taking me?"

He half carried her up the hall toward the front door. "Away from Kathy." Joni needed a place to sleep off the drugs in her system. "Where do you live?"

She stumbled into an ice-filled garbage can. "I'm in between homes at the moment." Her dignified manner contradicted the slur in her voice. "Tomorrow, I move into my own place."

Now what? He couldn't take her to his rental. His sister would preach hell and brimstone if she saw anyone in this condition. James shut the front door and closed out the party. Except for a guy passed out in the swing, the porch was empty. Joni dragged her feet. "Wait!" He let her wiggle out of his arms.

She propped against a column and flipped a piece of paper from her pocket. "I'm glad I chose you. Give me a pen. I need to check you off my list." Head tilted, she blinked twice.

He opened his mouth to ask why he was on a list, but she lost her footing and he grabbed her as the paper floated into the darkness.

"Oh no." Reaching over his arm, she grabbed at the weeds. "My list." Her legs folded and he lowered her knees to the porch. She raised her face and pled. "I don't know… I don't know how…" In the light streaming through a hole in the curtain, a single tear shimmered down her cheek.

"Stay here. I don't want you falling." He released her to the concrete floor. His flashlight app illuminated the white paper against the discolored trash. "I see it."

"Yay!" Joni clapped her hands.

He chuckled at her quick recovery and leapt off the porch. After retrieving the paper, he held his phone near. The note read:

1.   *Go to Party.* A smile punctuated this line and a blue check completed the first task.

2.   *No Phone.* Scribbles hid the second objective and traced a sad face.

3.   *Have Sex.* The huge red question mark confused him.

4.   *Pledge to Kappa.* Now, he understood.

"You find it?" She had crawled to the edge of the porch. The hand on his shoulder tugged.

"If you planned on using me to get in a sorority, you should've stayed sober."

Her lethal smile jumpstarted his pulse. "I'm not drunk."

"You're on something. What'd she give you?"

Long lashes fluttered in rapid succession. "Can I have my list back now?"

He settled on the concrete beside her. "What's the question mark for? Why not a smiley face?"

She snatched the list from his hand and squinted down at the paper. "Oh, I don't know if it's happy or sad." Her voice lowered to a whisper. "I've never had sex." Joni fell against him. "You'll have to teach me how."

James groaned and rubbed his hand across the bridge of his nose. He stood and turned his back on temptation. He wasn't a saint and he hadn't been to church in five years, but even if it wasn't on her wedding night, a girl should remember her first time. Come morning, Joni probably wouldn't recall this conversation.

A bump sounded behind him. Before he could turn, she pounced on his back. He staggered, recovered, and grabbed the backs of her knees.

Her giggle shivered through him.

"Joni, don't do that."

Kisses rained along his jaw. Maybe they should go back in the house. She was wasted, and although his brain said she didn't know what she offered…his body was having a hard time remembering.

"James?"

She was a spunky little thing. He shook his head as he waded through the tall Bahia grass. His truck was parked near the country road. "Yeah, Joni."

"You're my knight in shining armor, sweeping me away from the wicked dragon lady." She waved her arms, throwing them off balance.

Intent on catching her, he twisted his torso and fell back against his truck. She tumbled against him and snaked her arms up his chest. "Oops!" Musical laughter and her lopsided smile mesmerized him.

Shaking his head to clear his thoughts, he caught her roaming hands and opened the passenger door. "Climb in."

Although he had to help her, she obeyed without argument.

He jogged around the hood and slid under the wheel. Joni sat on her knees facing him. The CD played with the ignition and she sang along at the top of her lungs as he drove down the isolated road. He snickered at her slurred version of the lyrics. No doubt she'd sound beautiful sober. He turned left. Low pine branches canopied the dirt road which ended at a large hayfield. The sun would rise in a few hours. Surely by then she'd remember where she lived. He wheeled the truck around and backed to the gate, rolling down the windows before he killed the engine.

In the faint moonlight, she jabbed at the radio buttons. "Stupid thing quit working."

He tucked a silky strand behind her ear. "I turned it off."

She frowned out the windshield. The song of a lonely bullfrog blended with the chirping crickets. "Where are we?"

"Nowhere."

"We're parking?" The hooded look returned and she inched close.

Scrambling out of the truck, he escaped and shut the door, but leaned in the window. "We are not parking. We're waiting for you to sober up."

"Oh." Her face fell. "Figures. I never do anything so…bad." Innocence radiated off her.

Turning from the disappointment in her eyes, he waded through the brush, dropped the tailgate, and lay back on the bed liner. The large duffle bag he used as a suitcase pillowed his head. Counting the stars, he tried to forget her silken touch.

He was a rank sinner for sure, but even James had standards. As long as Joni stayed in the cab, she was safe.

The man in the moon laughed as the passenger door creaked open. A thud followed. Did the fall hurt her? He relaxed when the bushes rustled. There was something special about Joni. He tried to hide his interest at the party, but Kathy saw through him—and when it came to making his life miserable, she was like a dog with a bone.

The tailgate dipped and Joni struggled onto the truck bed. "I couldn't find you." She collapsed across his legs. "You vanished."

"I won't leave you." He tugged on her hand. "Crawl up here. You need to sleep off whatever she gave you."

Her full lips pouted. "I don't have a pillow."

Thankfully, she'd forgotten about her to-do list. James flung out his arm and patted his shoulder. "Here. A special pillow made just for you."

The top of her hair tickled his chin. He smoothed the fine strands while her fingers mimicked a piano along his black shirt. The white tips of her nails glistened in the moonlight. "These hands make beautiful music." Her sultry alto voice hummed a soul-wrenching melody.

He captured her hand and rolled toward her. "Go to sleep, Joni."

"Kiss me goodnight." The trust shining in her eyes blinded him. What could it hurt? Maybe her innocence would rub off on him. He pressed his lips against hers and her sweet perfume intoxicated him. One taste wasn't enough. His hand buried in her golden tresses as he deepened the kiss. Her arm curled around his neck. Struggling for control, he broke contact.

Jade eyes filled with wonder. "Hmm, delicious. Do it again."

~ ~ ~

Ugh! Joni tasted sandpaper on her tongue, and a cotton film lined her mouth. Over the side of a green truck, the sky lightened to a dull gray. The solid shoulder cushioning her head shifted. She caressed the muscled arm encircling her and rolled over.

James. The morning dew glistened against his hair, making it shimmer like sweet chocolate. Whiskers on his jaw sprouted in a hundred different directions. As her forefinger trailed the coarse stubble, his full lips twitched into a devilish grin. He was awake.

Her list was complete. She'd spent the night with a man. The pulse at the base of his throat throbbed. Oh, what a man he was. A solid chest rose and fell in short, quick breaths beneath her. Now, she could join the sorority.

The gaps in her memory frustrated her as she searched his golden-brown eyes. "Last night?" Heat infused her cheeks. "Did I…? I mean, was it…?" Her hand retracted against her heart.

"Never mind." She remembered his intoxicating kiss. Everything else was a blur.

"Joni, nothing happened." The corners of his lips arced into a boyish smile. "You were comatose."

Emptiness engulfed her. She turned away and scooted to the tailgate. How could she have failed? She wrote it down. Her mother would be horrified if she knew Joni had left a task incomplete. Well, maybe not this particular list. What went wrong?

James. She turned and glared at him.

"You're mad because I didn't take advantage of you?" He raised himself enough to prop on his elbows and bend one knee. His mouth hung open. "Seriously?"

Joni brushed her hands through her tangled hair and then hid them behind her back. "Not mad. Just…" She swallowed against her dry mouth. "Disappointed."

One of his eyebrows arched. "I read your to-do list." Muscled legs swung over the side of the truck. "But I'm not a rapist and it's not my fault Kappa doesn't allow virgins."

Dirt covered her new boots. She'd have to send them out to be cleaned. Sucking in a deep breath, she forced her chin up. "You don't have to be crude."

"Believe me, the guys at that party are a lot more than crude, but any one of them would've been happy to…" His arm waved in an erratic motion. "Initiate you."

She turned and blinked away the sting in her eyes. The tailgate slammed. She flinched. He mumbled something behind her.

He was right. The guys at the party were gross.

A gentle hand landed at her waist and he whispered near her ear. "I'm sorry, Joni. I know how important the sorority thing is to some girls, but they can't force you to do something like that. They have governing rules and regulations."

She turned in his embrace and he hugged her close. His steady heartbeat soothed her chaotic thoughts. Kappa wasn't the tea party of her dreams, but her mother insisted the dorms were uninhabitable and Joni desperately wanted to live on her own.

She raised her head. Steel bands tightened around her middle and her feet left the ground as he swung her around. Laughter erupted. Dizzy, she clung to him and caught her breath.

"That's more like it." Over his shoulder a blue tractor sputtered across the field. He released her with a grin. "Uh-oh. Time to go."

He rounded the truck and dove into the driver's seat as she climbed in the other side. James winked and started the ignition. Music played. She'd barely buckled her seatbelt when dust flew behind them. He steered onto the asphalt. "Sing for me. I want to hear you without the drunken slur."

Heat spread up her neck and into her cheeks. She loved to sing when her mother wasn't around. "Did I sing last night?"

He flashed a perfect smile and claimed her hand. Her skin tingled as James tugged her close. He held her fingers against the windshield, and she resisted the urge to snatch them away. The way he studied her hand, she felt like a princess.

"Someday soon, I want to hear you play." Was he teasing?

The haze surrounding last night's memories shifted. She remembered the cushion of his arms and the marble of his chest. Reclaiming her hand, she covered her burning cheeks.

James's thumb beat against the wheel. "Dad taught me piano. Do you play in church?"

Some of the girls in her concerto were Christians, but she failed to imagine James in a steepled building. He was too manly. "I play classical."

A slow whistle emitted from his pursed lips. "Way out of my league." James pulled over at a country store. "Come on. I need some caffeine before I can deal with my sister's preaching."

~ ~ ~

Joni perched on the edge of the restaurant-style booth. The tangy taste of her favorite orange juice quenched her thirst. James tossed a wrapped bundle in front of her and slid in the seat. She scooted over to make room.

Steam rose as he gulped his coffee. "After we pick up Isaac, I'll take you home." James lifted his biscuit with both hands and paused. "Where do you live, anyway? Last night you were a little confused." He bit off a large chunk.

She opened the greasy paper and broke off a small piece of sausage. "My parents live across the bay, but my car's on campus. Isaac is your son, right?"

James wiped his hands on a napkin and held out his phone. "He's a great kid."

A little boy grinned from the screen. If his hair was darker, he'd be a miniature of James. "He's cute. Like his daddy. How old is he?"

"Thank you. He just turned four. He should be awake soon. I can't wait to see him."

Joni waved toward his phone. "Do you mind if I use this? The girls are probably worried. I should've been back by now." Trying to hide her heated cheeks, she nibbled on her biscuit.

When she looked up, sparkles twinkled in James's eyes. "No phone. Was that number two or three?"

She popped his upper arm. "Quit it." A giggle escaped her. "Where is my list anyway?"

He shook his head. "I'll never tell. I'm keeping it for a souvenir. It's not every day I get an offer like last night's."

"I don't normally…I mean, I didn't come out and ask you…" She turned her head and sucked in a breath. Her face flamed. How did she land herself in this mess?

Strong arms wrapped around her waist and his laugh tickled her neck. "So, the offer is no longer on the table?"

Her giggled morphed into a laugh. "I can't believe you." She elbowed his side. "Hush, so I can call Marla." Cutting her eyes at him, she flipped her wrist and held out his phone. "It's locked again."

James tapped the screen in her hand. "What's her number?"

"I forget." Joni gnawed the inside of her lip. "She's listed in my contacts. Maybe whoever has my phone will answer." She dialed her own number and groaned at the voicemail greeting. She redialed while James crumpled their trash and threw it in the garbage. In seconds, they were outside in the sunshine. The backs of their hands brushed as they crossed the pavement. The pads of his fingers danced with hers until he entwined them together.

No one answered the second or third call. Maybe the battery was dead. Releasing a frustrated breath, Joni passed him the phone. "I give up."

He flipped through the screens. "What's your last name? I'm adding you to my contacts."

"Maher." Her stomach flip-flopped at the thought of James calling her. Would he ask her out? She hid her smile and climbed into the truck.

A masculine hand with clean fingernails patted the gray, cloth seat. His calloused palm turned up and wiggling fingers beckoned. Joni scooted close. The chocolate color of his eyes melted the world around them. She wet her lips as his head dipped. When their mouths met, her eyes drifted. Whiskers scraped her top lip and her pulse rate soared.

James pulled back and a gentle thumb caressed her chin. "Sorry. I'll shave before I kiss you again."

"You don't have to. I mean…you can kiss me but…" Joni blinked and gathered her thoughts. "I like your whiskers." She looked down in her lap to escape the intensity of his eyes.

"Good." He cradled her hand and changed the gears with his thumb and forefinger. His baritone blended with her alto. After three songs, a large tent dominated a small roadside park. The blue and white stripes protected hundreds of chairs. He turned down the volume. "That's The Street Preacher's."

Once, at a concert in the park, there had been an old, man shouting into a mega phone. She hoped this wasn't the same man.

"Peter travels the Gulf Coast and holds revivals. He's really a nice guy. Actually, he's my cousin, but don't let that get out. It might ruin his reputation." James parked in front of a small travel trailer. "This belongs to my sister."

Joni slid out the driver's side after him. He reclaimed her hand and whispered, "That's Sara."

The lady hurrying toward them was in her early thirties. Waves of curls, the same brown as James's hair, swayed from side to side. She had the clearest complexion Joni'd ever seen.

"James, what a surprise."

"Don't get excited. We're not here for the service." He hugged his sister and stepped back. "Sara, this is Joni." James pulled her in front of him and rested his chin on the top of her head. His arms encircled her. "Where's Isaac?"

Joni leaned against his strength as a question furrowed Sara's brow. "What do you mean? I haven't seen him in a month, when he was with you at Mom's."

"But Kathy said..." The hands on Joni's waist flinched. He spun her around. "I need to find Isaac." Frantic eyes searched hers. "There's no telling where Kathy left him. Sara will give you a ride to campus." A quick kiss to her lips and he raced to his truck. "I'll call you later!"

Joni's heartbeat hammered in her ears as the truck faded in the distance. She watched the news. When a mother lied about the location of her children, they were rarely found alive.

Chapter Two

Joni bit her lip as the truck disappeared down the street. If anything happened to his son it would crush James. She turned to his sister. "Do you think Kathy would hurt Isaac?"

"I don't know." Sara shrugged with a sad smile. "But Isaac's a tough little guy, and God watches over him."

Joni doubted the god thing, but she hoped someone guarded Isaac. Kathy wasn't her favorite person, but only a monster could hurt the cute little boy in the photo.

A beige sedan followed a blue full-sized truck into the park. Other vehicles streamed in. A door slammed and a male voice shouted, "Good morning, brother." Both men wore suits. Between parked minivans two ladies wearing long flowing skirts and heels hugged. One fingered a frilly bow twice the size of the little girl's head. "Did you make this yourself?"

Notes and chords flowed from similarly dressed musicians gathered under the large tent. Joni glanced at her wrinkled jeans. Church would be like every other thing in her life. She wouldn't fit in.

Sara's beautiful curls swayed as she motioned Joni into the camper. The door silenced the upbeat music. Neat and tidy, the compact interior had more room than Joni would have supposed. "Do you have a bathroom? I want to wash my face and hands."

"Let's say a prayer first." Sara closed her eyes and bowed her head. "Lord, we know you provide all our needs. Please take care of Isaac. Lead James in the right direction…"

Joni didn't know what to do as Sara continued to pray.

She shifted from one foot to the other. One thing was certain. James's sister believed in the words she spoke. Her graceful hand waved in the air. Was she trying to get her god's attention? Tiny sequins flashed on the sleeve of her blouse. If Sara's god was real, he'd find Isaac. Only a thoughtless ogre would dismiss the tears flowing down Sara's face.

Joni silently added a request of her own. *If there is a god listening, take care of James and Isaac.* She bit her lip. *And give me a dress to wear. One like theirs.*

Sara opened her eyes and wiped her face. "Thank you, Jesus." She moved to a closet-sized door and stepped into an enclosed bedroom. "The sink is behind the door on your right."

Joni peeked into the smallest bathroom she'd ever seen. Taking a deep breath, she took one step and latched the door. Sara's rumbling penetrated the thin walls, so Joni turned on the water and let it run. The idea of a toilet and sink this close in proximity threw her off balance. Where were the hand towels?

A knock startled her. She turned off the water and popped the latch. Sara had to step aside before the door would swing open. "Mark and Andrew always leave a few minutes early for service. Don't worry about anyone barging in." She held out a bath cloth and a broomstick skirt the same color as James's hayfield. The evergreen heels hooked on her thumbs matched the tinted splashes in Joni's top. "I hope you can wear a size seven."

Joni stared at the offerings for a full second before she smiled and accepted them. "I have the exact same pair at home. Thank you."

"Here's a comb. I'll wait under the awning while you change." In the doorway, she glanced over her shoulder. "There's a full-length mirror on the outside of the bathroom door."

Joni flipped the lock after Sara exited. The sink in the kitchen area served as her bathing station. The cool water refreshed her, but she wished for the makeup in her purse and her phone. She tightened the string at her waist before strapping on the heels. After combing the tangles from her hair, she turned toward the mirror. Not bad. She pivoted. The lines of the skirt fell to the floor. Definitely better than her wrinkled jeans. No one would guess she spent the night in James's truck. Wait. She stared at the ceiling. Did God provide the clothes she'd asked for? She shook her head but smiled. "If you can hear me, thank you, and don't forget Isaac."

Sara closed a black leather book as Joni stepped out of the camper. "Ready?"

Joni straightened her posture and called on her years of training as a concert pianist. She smoothed her hair and inspected her hands. "Yes."

"That skirt looks good on you."

"Thanks." She trailed Sara around the enormous tent. Hundreds of people of all ages chatted in metal folding chairs. Sara walked under the tent from the right side of the stage. She slipped in beside a man and a little boy, and Joni sank in the seat beside her. A gentleman in the front passed a baby behind him to a young girl on the other side of Sara's husband. The girl passed the baby to a lady in the third row. The baby laughed at each change of hands. A motherly figure finally accepted the wiggling infant and pressed a kiss against rosy cheeks.

A keyboard and drums, along with acoustic and bass guitars, produced winsome music. Two rows separated Joni from the stage. She had performed with an orchestra on plenty of occasions, but nothing like this.

The lady standing at the keyboard fascinated her. Rhinestone pins swept the honey-brown hair off her face, and more pins secured curls behind her head. When she played, joy radiated from her. Who was this man, Jesus, she sang of? Wasn't he the baby born at Christmas? Jesus? He died on Easter, right? Could the mere mention of a name do all the things she claimed? Joni didn't think so, but the lady sang as if she believed it.

She leaned forward and watched the pianist's hands. Flawless, they commanded music from the keys. The melody was like nothing Joni had ever heard. The drummer tipped his head back and closed his eyes, never missing a beat.

The air grew heavy.

Something charged the atmosphere and the bass player threw up both arms.

The man in front of Joni stood, blocking her view. Other people rose from the chairs and lifted their hands. She looked around the man until his wife stood beside him. When James's sister rose, Joni smiled and came to her feet. Now she could see the musicians.

She'd missed something. The bass player paced the length of the stage. He had a wondrous glow about him. "What happened?"

Sara simply smiled at her question.

He grabbed the microphone and sang with the pianist. A loud wail came from his lips before he whispered, "Jesus." Joni shivered as nerves tingled through her body.

"Jesus." The man spoke again and Joni looked up.

A warmth cloaked her.

"Jesus."

Joni titled her face upward. She had no idea what was happening to her, but it was good. Tears threatened to spill. She dropped her head and shook off the feeling.

A tall man in a white shirt and tie stepped behind a wooden podium and spoke into a microphone. "Don't think God doesn't remember His children. Last night, He stepped in and made a way of escape, and today He's given you a bonus. A taste of His presence; His peace. This morning He's asking, do you want more? Ha. Ha. Yes, Lord! Give me more!" The speaker paced back and forth and spoke in a language she couldn't understand.

Joni looked around the crowded tent and whispered to Sara, "Who's he talking to?"

~ ~ ~

Morning light revealed the broken, concrete steps and trash in front of the old wood house. James weaved his way through several beat-up cars and ragged trucks parked in the knee high grass. Without knocking, he stormed through the front door. "Kathy!"

A girl looked up, startled. Her eyes widened as she pressed her lips together. A shaky finger pointed to the master bedroom.

James stomped through the locked door.

A guy he'd never seen before lifted his head from the pillow. "Get out of here, you idiot."

James ignored him and marched to the other side of the bed. He snatched the covers. Kathy's exposed body shivered in the cool morning air. Her sleepy eyes popped opened. "James!" She grabbed for the covers as he jerked her out of the brass bed. She clung to the quilt.

"Where is he?" James swallowed the bile in his throat. "What did you do with Isaac?"

"So you're James?" Covered with a sheet from the waist down, the guy reclined against the headboard and lit a cigarette. A gold watch chinked against the scarred wood. "No need to get upset. We were passing the time while you were off entertaining the lovely Joni."

James dragged Kathy out of bed and across the hardwood floor. His punch landed on Preppy's mouth. Blood and live ashes sprinkled the bed.

Ringed hands slapped at the sheets. "Are you crazy? You set the bed on fire!"

"You can have Kathy, but I want Isaac. Now!" James turned, lifted Kathy by her arms, and shook her. "Where is he?"

She clutched the bedcovers around her.

The fear in her eyes scared him. "If you've hurt him. I swear. I will kill you."

"He's at C-Ci-Cindy's house."

His heart stopped. "Cindy?" He shoved her against the bed. "How could you leave him with that crackhead?"

Kathy rolled her eyes. "She's a good person."

Heart hammering, James ran for his truck. Isaac spent the night with Kathy's dealer.

~~~

A silver, heeled sandal lay on its side. Joni stepped around it and onto the stage as the musicians packed their instruments.

The pianist smiled in greeting. "Did you enjoy the service?"

"Yes. It was a new experience for me." She held out her hand. "I'm Joni. Joni Maher."

The lady ignored the offered hand and pulled her into a warm embrace. "I'm Sister Sandra to everyone here, but if that makes you uncomfortable, just call me Sandra."

Joni nodded. "I'm here with James's sister. I was wondering if you could…well, could you teach me to play like you?"

Gentle eyes widened. "James is my nephew. You're a friend of his?"

Joni's lips curved at the mention of his name and heat climbed her neck. "Sort of."

"I see." Sandra's brief mischievous smile turned serious. "Learning the piano takes years. I occasionally give lessons—"

"No. That's not what I meant." Joni shook off the memory of waking in James's arms. "I know *how* to play. Could you teach me your style?"

"My style?" A thick eyebrow rose.

"Yes. Play something and let me watch. I'll probably catch on." Joni moved beside her. The pianist didn't begin, and she backed away. "I'm sorry. You probably don't have time."

"Wait." James's aunt smiled and stepped away from the keyboard. "You play something for me and then I'll play whatever you want to hear."

Joni glanced around and shrugged. "Where's the sheet music?"

"I don't use any."

Awed, Joni stared at the woman. She'd played all morning without music? Not wanting to appear inferior, Joni thought for something she could play. Could she remember the notes? She stepped up, sucked in a quick breath, and played a small piece from Chopin's "Grande Valse Brillante."

When the last note sounded, Sandra gawked. The Street Preacher joined them at the keyboard. "Who is this talented young lady?"

James's aunt smiled and said, "Joni Maher. James's girlfriend."

Kind eyes studied Joni. "James Preston? His girlfriend plays?

Like this?" He squeezed her shoulder. "Welcome to the family."

Her face flamed. She couldn't let them believe she was James's girlfriend, but she couldn't tell them they'd just met, either. "We're only friends."

The preacher's laugh boomed throughout the tent. "James's running days are about over. Praise the Lord. God is great indeed." He whistled as he walked away.

"Yes, He is." Sandra's hands covered the keys and nodded at Joni. "You could give me lessons. But I'll help, however I can."

Joni smiled at the compliment. "Thank you. Please, play the first song."

Sandra did as requested and Joni paid attention to her hands. "Something's missing. Do it like before, with that extra aura."

Her teacher's brows rose. "An aura?"

Joni nodded.

"Oh. You mean the anointing." Sandra flexed her hands. "You can't decide you want to play anointed. It's a gift given by the Holy Ghost."

"Who?" Her confusion must have shone on her face.

"The Comforter. Sent by Jesus."

"That reminds me of my second question." Joni lowered her voice to a whisper. She didn't want to sound irreverent. "Didn't the Romans kill Jesus at Easter? A dead man can't do the things your song claims."

The aura that was missing in Sandra's song returned in her voice. "Oh, precious girl, that's the best part. Jesus is alive and He wants to dwell within you."

~ ~ ~

The screen door hung on one hinge and the aluminum mesh had several gashes and rips. It shook with each blow of his fist. A sense of déjà vu hit him. How many times had he come here looking for Kathy in the previous months? "Cindy, it's James. I'm here for Isaac."

No response.

Lifting the frame, he pulled it aside. Green paint flaked off in his hand. He pounded on the solid oak. "Isaac!"

Several locks clicked and the door crept open. Cindy's cheeks were sunk in and her jeans hung low on her skinny hips. Hopeless blue eyes peered from an ashen face. She'd gone downhill since he'd seen her a few months ago. "James. What are you doing here? You should know better than to beat on my door like the task force."

He pushed past her. A glass bong in the middle of a scarred coffee table grabbed his attention. Three packs of papers and a half empty dime bag lay between an ashtray and a small glass pipe. A torch cooled on its side. His guts twisted, stealing his breath. Had Isaac witnessed this? Shushing voices came from the back. He snatched open doors and searched past the druggies. One room was dead-bolted. "Where. Is. Isaac?"

She stumbled backward. "I couldn't let him stay here. It's not safe. Besides, a kid is bad for business. I took him to my granny's. She'll take care of him."

Both palms pressed against his temples and slid down the sides of his head. Cindy wasn't a bad person, just desperate to survive. He wished he could help her, but he didn't know how. "Where does your granny live?"

Shaky hands struggled to light her cigarette. "Just down the street."

James turned to go, but paused in the doorway. "How long has Isaac been there?"

"I'm not sure. Time kind of slips away from me." Cindy blew smoke in his direction. "Four, maybe five days."

To prevent himself from strangling her, James stuck his hands in his front pockets. "Which house? What's the address?"

Dragging on the cigarette, Cindy squeaked out a street number.

The ragged screen door scraped over the rotten wood floor. James jumped in the truck and raced down the street."

The four-wheel drive's skid plate screeched across the railroad tracks. He eased off the accelerator and searched the old buildings for house numbers. He braked hard, slammed into reverse, and studied the driveway. Weeds grew in the middle of each parallel strip of concrete. White-painted brick framed a wide porch.

James parked on the curb. The frantic beating of his heart knocked against his chest as he silently got out of the truck. Not knowing what to expect, he eased up the broken sidewalk. Dark curtains swayed in the window. A door slammed and Isaac flew down the steps.

"Daddy! Daddy! You comed to get me."

James lengthened his stride and swooped his son into a tight embrace. He savored the warmth of little arms wrapped around his neck, but the smell of sour milk oozed from Isaac's shirt. James tried to pull back to inspect his son for injuries, but the little head buried against him and sobbed. "Don't leave me no more."

The rip in his heart cut deep. James blinked back tears and pushed away the guilt. "I love you, Isaac. And I swear, I won't ever leave you again."

Isaac lifted his head and wiped his nose on the back of his dirty hand. "I love you too, Daddy."

"Let's go home." James was halfway to the truck when Isaac stiffened in his arms.

"Where do you think you're going with that baby?" The booming female voice preceded a second slam of the screen door.

James hurried Isaac into the truck, shut the door, and pressed the lock button on his keyless entry. He turned toward rushing footsteps. A large woman with red hair barreled down the sidewalk. James stood between the threat and Isaac. "I'm taking my son with me."

"You ain't going nowhere." Wrinkled hands propped on ample hips. "Kathy's 'sposed to pick him up, and she owes me. Cash only. No food stamps."

James clenched his jaw. "Food stamps? Really?" He reached for his wallet.

One hand fell from her hip. "All that partying going on…" Her head bobbed and swayed as she spoke.

"Somebody's got to pay the piper." She stuck out her neck and her eyes widened. "And it ain't gonna be me." A palm turned up.

He laid a hundred dollar bill in her hand.

She tucked the money into her bra. "Nice doing business with ya. You bring the little fellow back to Granny's anytime."

James swallowed his disgust. "I don't think so."

She laughed on her way back to the porch. "Oh he'll be back, if I know his momma." Her cackle plucked at his nerves. "And e'rybody knows his momma."

James slid behind the wheel of his truck and drove west on Houston Street. Surely Isaac's abandonment proved Kathy unfit. He stopped in the road and snapped a picture of Cindy's house with his phone. Evidence of neglect was the only thing standing in his way of filing for full custody.

Isaac's bare feet dangled. He needed to be in a car seat, but James didn't know where it was. Reaching over, he tightened the middle seatbelt. It would have to do until they got home. Stains splotched Isaac's jeans and a rip was in the sleeve of his shirt. "Are you okay?"

Little blue eyes widened. "I was ascared."

James ruffled his son's greasy hair. "No way. You're the bravest boy I know."

Isaac shook his head. "Nuh-uh, Daddy, I was ascared bad."

Swallowing the lump in his throat, James kept his voice light. "Did anyone hurt you?"

"No, sir. But Granny yells louder than Momma does."

"She didn't bathe you either, did she? You smell like a little piggy." James wrinkled his nose and snorted.

Isaac's giggle lifted a heavy burden from James.

"How long since you changed clothes?"

"Yesterday."

James smiled for the first time in hours. To Isaac, everything in the past happened yesterday and everything in the future was tomorrow. "I think we'll put you in the tub first."

"Okay, Daddy." For once Isaac didn't argue about bath time. He snuggled close to James's side.

"Are you hungry?"

Isaac shook his head.

At least the mean, old woman had fed him. James blinked against the knot in his throat. He silenced the questions churning in his mind and concentrated on the Sunday afternoon traffic. He unlocked his phone and dialed his sister's number. She would be worried about Isaac, and James wanted to check on Joni. Would she forgive him for dumping her at church?

Sara answered on the second ring. "Did you find him?"

"He's fine. One of Kathy's friends was babysitting." He didn't dare tell the truth. "We'll come over tomorrow for supper."

"Good idea. Let's meet at Mom's. She's a better cook."

"How's Joni?"

"We dropped her off on University Boulevard."

James cringed. "Did she survive church?"

"She enjoyed it. Aunt Sandra had an interesting conversation with her after the service. Did you know Joni played classical piano?"

"Of course." Uncertainty pretzeled his stomach. He didn't want Joni to enjoy church and he certainly didn't like her talking to Aunt Sandra. "What did they do to her?"

"Nothing much." Her chuckle boasted a new convert.

His fingers tightened around the phone. "You were supposed to take her home, not drag her to an altar."

Feminine laughter had him grinding his teeth. "No need to get upset. Nothing that horrible happened. Although, Joni agreed to attend Wednesday night prayer meeting."

"She's not going." Isaac slumped in the seat and James adjusted his sleeping son next to him.

Sara sighed in his ear. "Do you hear yourself?"

"Yes. My meddlesome sister is ruining the perfect girl. I don't want you to change Joni. Leave her alone. She doesn't need your churchy ways. She's fine the way she is."

He braked hard for the sudden red light while holding on to Isaac. He swore and ended the call. He should've known better than to introduce Joni to Sara.

Chapter Three

Joni strolled up to the Kappa house at three o'clock Sunday afternoon. Candace and five other girls squealed and hugged her outside the common room. "We were so worried."

She shuffled through the door and perched on the burgundy sofa. "Where's my phone?"

"Girl, you're over twelve hours late and all you can say is 'where is my phone'? Trent has called four times asking if you were back yet."

Joni frowned at the girls surrounding her. "Why would he care?"

"Duh, he had a flat tire and by the time he made it to the party, you'd left with James."

"Kathy is livid."

Joni's head spun. Which one of the girls said that? "She is?" She shook her head. "That can't be right. She's the one who introduced us."

"Trent is soooo disappointed he missed out on your maiden voyage."

From another, "Girl, you was supposed to take a three-hour tour. And instead you went on a cruise."

The questions and comments came from every side. "Where'd you get them clothes?"

Finally, a question she could answer. "Sara, James's sister."

"His sister!" Over a dozen girls stared, bug-eyed.

Joni held up a hand. An explanation was in order. "Last night, after Stephanie and Marla left the party, Kathy said Candace told her to help me out, but she put something in my drink. The next thing I remember was waking up in the back of James's truck."

Candace wrinkled her nose. "He left you passed out in a nasty truck bed?"

Joni smiled at the memory of her pillow. "No. He slept beside me, and it wasn't nasty."

"Oh, yeah."

"Now, we're talking."

Stephanie's stiff smile caught Joni's attention. "I'm glad someone enjoyed their experience. I'm going to take a shower."

Candace rolled her eyes and caught Stephanie's eye. "Not yet. You've already had four today, and with Joni back we need to have our meeting."

Joni wanted a bath too, but she'd wait until she got back to her parents' house. The other girls crowded into the mauve-colored room. "Where's Marla?"

Stephanie sat in the center of the sofa. "She didn't make it."

Marla only rushed at Joni's urging. If anything happened to her, Joni wouldn't forgive herself. Despite the rivalry their mothers imposed on them, the pianists encouraged each other through losses, and celebrated victories with sleepovers, movie nights, and trips to the mall. "What do you mean by that?"

"She didn't finish the game. Walked to a truck stop and called someone to pick her up. This morning she came by and got her stuff. By the way, here's your purse."

Joni cradled her handbag and sank into the cushions beside Stephanie. "I guess I didn't make it either."

Candace smiled from a flowered wingback chair. "Of course you did. So what if you're a few hours late? As long as the deed was done."

"But James—"

"Has a live-in girlfriend." Candace raised a perfectly waxed eyebrow. "Believe me. You won't hear from him again. And don't tell Trent you spent the night. He won't like it."

Congratulations came from every side. They thought she slept with James. Well, she did sleep with him, but she didn't *sleep* with him. Joni bit back a squeal. They didn't need to know she failed. She now had sisters.

Candace shared the rules and schedule for the upcoming four weeks. There were eleven new girls. "Ya'll can now move into the house; we'll have the initiation after four-weeks probation. And don't forget, your big brother or big sister must know where you are at all times. We don't want anyone marring the sorority's image on campus or off. Joni, you're in with Stephanie and Rebecca. With Marla gone ya'll will have more room. The rest of you are in the suites across the hall."

Stephanie stood. "Come on, let's rearrange the furniture."

Halfway up the stairs, Joni's phone rang from her purse. She didn't recognize the number. "I'll be a minute." She connected the call.

"Hey, beautiful." James's voice sent her heart fluttering.

She brushed her hair back and caught her breath. "Hi. Did you find Isaac?"

"Yeah, I found him. Sorry to dump my sister on you."

She slipped down the stairs and out the backdoor. "No problem. How is he?"

"Asleep. Heard you talked with some relatives of mine."

Her curiosity of church returned, prompting her smile. "I did. Did you know God had a son? And a ghost?" Joni kicked a pile of oak leaves and twirled in a circle.

James's laugh was stiff. "I think you're talking about the Holy Spirit. You liked church?"

"It was interesting. And afterwards Sandra taught me a song. Well…she tried to. For some reason, I can't play churchy music. She and the bass player asked about you."

"What did you tell them?"

"That we're friends. The Street Preacher said to tell you that your running days were over and God has your number. What does that mean?"

"Nothing. Preachers are supposed to say stuff like that. I'm sorry you had to deal with it. I'll take you to dinner tomorrow night and make it up to you."

He wanted to date her? While living with Kathy? She wanted to say yes, but... "I don't know, James. Candace said Kathy was upset. I don't want to cause trouble."

"The trouble between me and Kathy has to do with Isaac. Not you."

Joni didn't want to say no. "If you're sure Kathy won't be mad...?"

"It's none of her business."

Bending down, Joni lifted a yellow oak leaf. She twirled the stem between her thumb and forefinger, and remembered the feel of his arms. It was irrational, and she knew she probably shouldn't, but the desire to see James overrode her common sense. "Where?"

"My mom lives in Daphne. She can babysit Isaac. What's your Eastern Shore address?"

Joni giggled. "I'll be here, at the sorority house. I met the requirements this afternoon."

A crackling thump scraped through her earpiece as if he'd dropped his phone. His voice hardened. "With who?"

"With you, silly. At least that's what they think. Trent arrived at the party and Kathy said I left with you. When I came back this afternoon, they just assumed that we...well, you know."

"Who's Trent?" His voice held no emotion. She didn't know if he was jealous or curious.

"He's from the affiliated fraternity." Joni sighed into the phone. "My big brother for the next four weeks. All little sisters are on probation. Isn't that great?"

He answered with a grunt. "Where do I pick you up?"

She needed to pack the rest of her things from her parents' and bring them to the sorority house. And since Candace and Kathy were friends, maybe Candace shouldn't know James asked her out. "Actually, I'll be at home." She gave him her address. "Do you know where it is?"

"Yeah, I'll see you at eight."

~ ~ ~

The grass needed to be cut and weeds overran the brick bottom of James's rental in the Quail Run subdivision. His teenage neighbor promised to mow the lawn of the three-bedroom, ranch-style house for a small fee. Tommy Addison was a good kid, a hard worker. His dad had died in the oil rig explosion a few years ago and his mother struggled to pay the mortgage and support Tommy and his sister. There was only one reasonable explanation why he quit cutting the yard. Kathy didn't pay him.

James parked in the driveway and killed the ignition. His stomach turned. From what he could see, the backyard was worse than the front. Aluminum cans and cardboard cartons trashed the tall grass. Lawn chairs were flipped in every direction. Kathy must have thrown some party.

"We're home?" Isaac lifted his head and peered over the dash. "Is Momma here?"

James hoped not but kept silent. He unbuckled his son and walked to the front door. A white piece of paper hung on the door knob. "What's this?" James read the notice from Alabama Power silently. *Services to be disconnected for nonpayment. Past due amount of $748.23 payable in money order or cashier's check before September eleventh.*

James bit back a cuss word. He'd have to pay the bill first thing in the morning.

Isaac tugged on his hand. "Is it from Momma? Is she coming home?"

The hope in his son's eyes about killed him. "No. It's not from Kathy." James unlocked the door. On the coffee table, flies lit on a half-eaten, moldy cheeseburger. The ashtray overflowed onto a wrapper loaded with dried ketchup and hard fries. James followed a sour smell into the kitchen. Dirty dishes covered every surface. "What does she do all day?"

"Stays in the bedroom with Brian." Isaac's blunt statement wasn't surprising.

James knelt down in front of his son. "Who's Brian?"

"Momma's friend that burnt me."

"Burnt you?" James forgot about the filth surrounding them and rocked back on his heels. Isaac picked up an action figure and dusted it off on his pants. Sometimes James couldn't understand what Isaac was saying, so he'd nod and smile. This wasn't one of those times.

"Where, Isaac? Show Daddy where he burnt you."

Isaac shrugged and turned. "My back."

James lifted the filthy shirt. Small cigarette-shaped circles formed a triangle in the center of Isaac's back. The hand holding the shirt clenched into a fist. The scars were deep. A vile string of words flew from his mouth as he dropped the shirt. Swallowing the bile in his throat, James covered his face with his hands. How could he have let this happen?

"Don't whup me." The whispered plea ignited a desire for revenge.

Isaac's body was stiff, his skinny arms locked close to his sides. James spun him around by hunched shoulders. His stomach twisted into a million knots as tears flowed onto Isaac's cheeks.

James loosened his grip and controlled the rage surging through him. "I'll never hit you. Daddy loves you, Isaac. I'm really…" He forced a smile. "…really mad at Brian. He shouldn't have done this." When James found the coward, he'd regret ever touching his son.

"I was bad." Isaac's head drooped.

Using two fingers, James lifted the little boy's chin. "It doesn't matter what you did, you didn't deserve this." James held his smile until Isaac nodded. "Does it hurt?"

Isaac shook his head. "Not no more."

"Okay, turn around and let me see again." James slipped out his phone and snapped several pictures. His arsenal against Kathy grew. Unfortunately, it came at Isaac's expense. "Let's get you a bath and some clean clothes."

In Isaac's bedroom, toys were strewn in every direction, but it was the cleanest room so far. The dresser held mismatched socks, two pairs of underwear, and a pair of jeans a size too small. In the laundry room, James's jaw dropped. An empty box of laundry detergent topped a small mountain of dirty clothes. The new washer and dryer he'd bought two months ago were gone.

Wordless, James backed into the kitchen. Stains spotted a month's worth of mail on the counter. A receipt from Joe's Pawn Shop lay on the top. He swore and kicked the bottom cabinet door shut. She'd pawned the washer, dryer, PC computer, and riding lawnmower.

His breath caught. His grandfather's hunting rifle? Surely she wouldn't pawn something with so much sentimental value.

He picked up Isaac, ran toward the master bedroom, and set the little boy down in the hall. Below the cracked doorframe, wood splinters lay on the floor. The brass door knob was loose and unlocked. Not the way he'd left it. His chest tight, he crossed the room and flipped the top mattress off the unmade bed. The gun was absent from its hiding place.

James's fist went through the sheetrock wall. He jerked his hand free and dropped onto the hard box springs. *Bet it was in the same pawn shop as the appliances.* Wide-eyed, Isaac trembled in the doorway. James fought for control. "Come here, Isaac. Daddy's not mad at you."

Isaac crept near the bed. James lifted him on his knee. He kissed the top of Isaac's head and then spit at the dirt on his lips. "You and me are gonna be fine. Okay?"

"'Kay." Isaac sniffed and hugged James tight.

James stood and went into Kathy's room. Maybe she moved the gun closer in case she needed it during the night.

"Bunkie!" Isaac wiggled free and ran to a pile of clothes in the corner. He cradled the stuffed monkey with long ears. He had trouble sleeping without it.

A huge pile of clothes sat in the corner on the floor. James crossed the room and lifted a shirt to his nose. It smelled clean. Digging through the laundry, he found Isaac three pairs of jeans, five shirts, and a pair of pajamas. A basket by the window had socks, underwear, and towels.

In the hall, he opened the bathroom door and gagged. Dried vomit clung to the outside of the toilet. Chunks trailed across the floor, drizzled the shower curtain, smeared the mirror, and clogged the sink. He flipped on the exhaust fan and shut out the smell. One hand covered his mouth and the other held his churning stomach as he blinked away the burning in his eyes.

Isaac clung to his leg and held his nose between two little fingers. "Eeew."

The bath would have to wait. Perhaps forever. No way in this world or the next could James clean that mess without puking.

He needed a maid. Would Mrs. Addison be willing to clean the nastiness? The thought of anyone seeing this mess heated his face. James looked down. Dirt caked Isaac's scalp.

"Come on Isaac. Let's wash you off in the kitchen and go see Mrs. Addison."

The sink was dirty but nothing like the bathroom. James pulled the empty garbage can over. "Hold it like this." He balanced the white plastic rim against the counter.

"Yes sir." Isaac stuck out his tongue and closed his teeth over it as he held the can upright.

James used the dustpan he found in the cabinet to rake everything into the opening.

Isaac faltered. "It's heavy."

James reached out and steadied the can. Gagging at the smell, he tossed in a congealed cereal bowl.

Isaac wrinkled his nose. "Decusting."

"Disgusting is right." James pulled a chair over to the sink. "Come help me."

Isaac climbed onto the chair. "Now what?"

"Throw everything in the trash." He considered keeping some of the cleaner dishes, but figured multiple directions would confuse Isaac. "We can buy more dishes later."

"'Kay, Daddy." Isaac grinned and hefted a plate filled with green macaroni. A few noodles hit the floor.

When the sink was empty, James grabbed a full bottle of dish soap and the washcloth he'd planned to bathe Isaac with. He scrubbed the stainless steel surface and counter top clean. "Go look in the basket of clothes in Kathy's room and get me another rag."

"Yes, sir." Isaac's little feet pounded down the hall.

James surveyed the kitchen. Only the counter and the sink were clean. But at least he could sponge Isaac off before begging the neighbor for help. Footsteps drummed near. Isaac skidded to a stop.

"Ready for a bath?" James peeled the shirt off his son and tossed it in the trash.

Wide-eyed, Isaac pointed to the sink. "In there?"

"Yep." The rest of Isaac's clothes followed the shirt.

"Cool."

He hefted his son into the sink. He was too big to sit, so James had Isaac stand while he hosed him down with the spray nozzle. Dirt clung to his pale skin. They needed some body wash, but James wasn't about to open the bathroom door, let alone go in there. He picked up the dry cloth Isaac had brought from the basket. The writing on the dish soap caught his attention. "Antibacterial." No telling how many germs were mixed in with the dirt on his son.

Bubbles sprang up. The little boy laughed as he splashed. He caught some bubbles in his hand and blew them across the kitchen. James grinned at his son's antics. He plugged the drain, squirted in more detergent, and turned the spray into the sink, doubling the fun. By the time Isaac was degreased, disinfected, and clean, the bottle of soap was empty. James's wet shirt clung to his chest, and an inch of bubbly water covered the floor.

Standing Isaac in the chair, James dried him and dressed him in clean clothes. Outside, he stopped by his truck and changed his own shirt before ringing the neighbor's doorbell.

When they returned from shopping hours later, five black trash bags lined the curb. Mrs. Addison had left a note in the middle of the coffee table. Isaac's birth certificate and his social security card slid out from under the slip of paper.

James, we boxed Kathy's things like you asked but I thought you might want to keep these. Just call, if you need more help.

He smiled at the legal documents. The last time he was home, he'd searched everywhere. Without them, he couldn't petition for paternity rights. He wished he'd paid Mrs. Addison two hundred instead of the one she requested.

"Daddy, I gotta pee."

James eased the bathroom door open. The smell of bleach stung his eyes, but the white tub and floor sparkled. Clear blue water filled the toilet. "Leave the door open. I don't want you inhaling fumes."

"Yes, sir."

Ray walked in through the front door and sat a twelve-pack of longnecks and a pizza box on the coffee table. "I need a place to crash until our next construction job. Deana wasn't kidding last week when she said she'd found my replacement."

James saw the hurt beneath his friend's goofy grin. "I had Kathy's room cleaned. You're welcome to it." He rescued the papers under the box.

"Uncle Ray." Isaac zoomed up the hall. Ray tossed him over his shoulder and flipped the little body across his arm. "Gotcha."

Isaac giggled and squirmed until Ray set him on his feet.

"Ooh Pizza! Is that for me?"

"Sure is."

When James returned from taking the documents to his room, Isaac had sauce on his chin and his little hands grabbed for another slice. Ray handed James a beer.

"What about Isaac? Did you get him anything to drink?"

Ray grimaced. "Forgot. I can go back to the store. What do you want, buddy? A coke? Or one of them juice things?"

Isaac shrugged and grabbed an opened beer. "Momma pours it in a cup."

"What?" James snatched it before his son could drink.

"Makes me sleepy, but I like chocolate the most."

Innocent blue eyes blinked. James imagined the satisfaction of strangling Kathy. *One.* Inhale. *Two.* Exhale. He counted breaths as Ray took the remaining bottles into the kitchen.

He returned with a Kool-Aid box. "Look what I found in the fridge." Ray stabbed the straw through the small hole and slammed the carton in front of Isaac. "No beer for little boys."

Later that night, Ray went out to a nearby bar, and James booted his laptop while Isaac lay on the floor watching cartoons. Joni had sent him a friend request. He accepted and went to her wall. Jade eyes sparkled from her page. He reached for his bottle and knocked his cell off the table. It landed with a thud.

"Whatcha doing, Daddy?" Isaac crawled over and peered at the screen. "She's hot."

James laughed. "You've been spending too much time with Uncle Ray."

Isaac scooted near. "Her eyes smile. Why you looking at her?"

"She's my friend." The green chat button lit up by her name. He patted his knee. "Climb up here and Daddy will show you how to talk on the computer."

Isaac climbed onto his lap. James pointed at the chat box. "Here's where I type the words I want to say." *Isaac thinks you're pretty.* "I told her you said hi."

Her reply was quick. *You showed him my picture? Lol. Hold on.*

As James swigged from the bottle, Isaac touched the screen. "Can she be our girlfriend?"

If only. He ruffled the silky blond hair. "How old are you?"

Isaac held up four fingers and giggled.

"And you want a girlfriend?"

Little blue eyes blinked, and then he nodded. "I want her."

In the past months, girls became friendlier whenever Isaac was around. Hungry for a mother's love, he thrived in their attention, but James sensed this was different. "Yeah, me too."

"Ask her to be our girlfriend, Daddy."

Joni sent him another message. *Looking at your photos now. He's sooooo cute.*

Isaac touched the screen. "She say yes?"

"Yep." What could it hurt to let Isaac pretend? If he wanted to claim Joni as his girlfriend, that was fine with James.

Isaac tilted his head. "Can she live in Momma's room? With Uncle Ray?"

"No." *He asks too many questions.* James softened his tone after he sent his reply. "Go finish your cartoon."

Isaac pouted his way back to the carpet but focused on the animated movie.

Little boys are supposed to.

How did she know? In her drunken chatter, she admitted she was an only child. He leaned up and reached for his phone. She answered on the second ring. "Hey, beautiful."

Joni's laughter made him smile. "Sorry, I can't talk now. I'm chatting with someone."

"Oh, yeah? With who? Someone special?" James logged off and shut down the computer.

"I can't say."

"Why not?" He propped his feet on the coffee table and drained his beer.

"We just met and I don't know how he feels."

James set the empty bottle on the side table. "He thinks you're pretty special."

Joni giggled. "Oh really?"

"Yes. And he can't wait to see you aga—"

The front door slammed. Kathy crossed her arms over her chest. She was either sober or bumped with meth.

"James?" Joni waited.

He lowered his feet to the floor and stood. He glared at Kathy, but hid his anger as he spoke into the phone. "I'll see you tomorrow night, beautiful."

At his words Kathy lifted a black eyebrow.

Joni's sweet voice floated through the phone. "Goodnight, James."

"Goodnight, Joni." James ended the call and frowned at Kathy. "Is your boyfriend Brian with you?"

She smirked. "Jealous?"

The scars on Isaac's back flashed through his mind. "I can't wait to meet him."

"Momma!" Isaac leapt off the floor and wrapped his little arms around her waist. She patted the top of Isaac's head. Why couldn't she pick him up and hug him like a real mother?

"Are you gonna stay here? Please. Joni can't. You hafta sleep in my room 'cause Uncle Ray moved in yours."

Kathy's eyes narrowed on James. "You asked Little-Miss-Perfect to move in?"

He widened his stance. "That's not any of your business. I've talked to a lawyer, Kathy."

Her lips twisted into a snarl. "I'm the mother. No judge rules against a mother."

"He does when she abandons her child and lets her boyfriends abuse him."

She barked a laugh. "You're crazy. Does Isaac look like he's been abused?"

"Yes. Were you so stoned you didn't know what was happening? Or did you not care?" James lifted Isaacs's shirt and ran a finger over the burn scars. "What is this?"

Kathy gasped, then shrugged. "Mosquito bites. He probably scratched them."

"He can't reach the center of his back. Your idiot boyfriend burnt him!" James dropped Isaac's shirt and barely refrained from shaking her.

She jumped back. "No he didn't."

Isaac stepped forward and latched onto Kathy's knees. "Yes he did, Momma. I cried."

"Stop lying! No one hurt you!" She screamed in Isaac's face.

His little lip quivered.

"Don't yell at him." James picked up his son and Isaac buried his face in James's neck. "It's okay. I believe you." The small shoulders trembled under his hand. He kissed the top of Isaac's head. "Go play in your room while I talk to Momma."

Isaac sniffed and wiggled. James set him on his feet. Pitiful, tear-filled eyes looked up at Kathy. "You wanna see how Daddy fix-ed my room?"

She rolled her eyes. "Not now."

Isaac glanced over his shoulder once, twice, and then closed his bedroom door.

James swallowed his rage. "Your box of things is on the porch. Get it and go."

"If I go, he goes."

His hand itched to slap the smirk off her face. He shoved his hands in his front pockets and stepped toward her. "There's no way he's going with you. Not ever again. Do you care what kind of filth I found him in? It was worse than this place. How can you forget about the real world around you? How could you abandon him to a bunch of skanks? And now you expect me to hand him over? No! You don't want him anyway."

She flipped her long bangs out of her eyes. "I'm his mother. He's valuable to me."

"Really? Like Pop's rifle was valuable to me? Have you smoked up the money you got from the furniture? What about the car? How much did you get for it?" Kathy stepped back and he fought for control. She wanted drugs and she needed money to buy them. "How much will it take for you to leave us alone?"

She licked her lips and shrugged. "Five hundred."

"Done." James reached in his back pocket and handed her his last Franklins, grabbed her arm, and shoved her out the door.

She didn't stop for the small cardboard box. Through the open door, he watched her strut down the sidewalk and get in a rusted-out car.

Isaac barreled up the hall. He rounded the wall and ducked under James's arm. "Momma, wait!"

Kathy waved from the passenger window of the old sedan. The driver squealed tires and peeled away from the curb.

The door clicked shut. Isaac wiped his face with the back of his hand. He sniffed once. "She forgot to say bye, again."

Chapter Four

How could a mother be so cruel? Kneeling in front of his son, James battled the sting in his eyes. "Hey. We don't need her. Tomorrow we'll go play in the park, or see that new cartoon movie like you wanted. How about the IMAX theater?"

Isaac sniffed and wiped his hand on the front of his shirt. "Is our girlfriend going?"

"If you want her to." James would convince Joni to skip class if it made Isaac happy.

"Yeah." Little arms reached up. "I hope she likes me. Momma don't."

James hugged his son close. "Don't worry, Isaac, Joni's gonna love you. Now go to bed. We need to get an early start in the morning."

Isaac wiggled down. "Can I sleep with you?"

How could he say no to such a sweet face? "Just for tonight."

"Yes." Isaac ran happily down the hall.

Knowing Ray had a key, he locked the doors and shut off the lights. In the dark, he nursed a beer, and thought of the legal documents on his dresser. He now had everything needed to file for custody. But what if Kathy was right? What if the judge sided with her? He couldn't afford to lose. Isaac had suffered enough. James tossed back his beer and trashed the empty bottle.

In the bedroom, the smell of mothballs lingered where Mrs. Addison had changed the sheets. Isaac looked small and helpless nestled in the queen-size bed. James put his phone on charge and crawled in beside him.

Not used to sleeping with a knee in his back, he scooted the little body over several inches and punched the flat pillow.

A vision of Joni's blonde hair and jeweled eyes drifted into his dreams. She demanded a goodnight kiss and lifted her face. But it was Isaac's lips that crushed her cheek. They both waved at James over a hotel railing.

Something slapped him across the mouth. The dream disappeared as Isaac cried out in his sleep. Little arms flailed wildly. James reached out and patted his back. "Shhh. Daddy's here." The whisper calmed him. "Daddy's right here."

Early the next morning, after paying the power bill, James's attorney advised him to file an abuse report and let the Department of Human Services take pictures of the burn scars.

In a refurbished building downtown, Isaac told his caseworker a four-year-old's version of Brian, Cindy, and Granny and then waved as a volunteer led him to a play area.

James leaned back in the seat and pleaded with the caseworker. "Now, will you press charges?"

"We have nothing to charge her with." Tasha Covington smiled with sympathy. "The system's not perfect." He tried to interrupt, but she shook her head. "It's designed with protecting a mother's rights."

"She abandoned him." James's feet hit the floor.

"No. According to the law, abandonment occurs when she leaves him without adult supervision or with an unwilling adult. From what you've told me, this granny person was willing to watch over Isaac. And he was well-fed."

"He was filthy." James stood and paced in front of the office window. Isaac played with some building blocks on the other side of the glass.

Tasha's red, manicured nails toyed with a manila folder. "At this moment, Isaac is in your care. We know his needs will be met and there is no reason for us to intervene."

Sitting back in his chair, he rubbed the bridge of his nose. "The guy burned him with a cigarette. Multiple times."

"You can't prove those scars on his back are the result of abuse.

Unless a child is in immediate danger we cannot act."

He scrubbed his hand through his hair and stood. "What about Kathy? What happens when she comes back?"

"She's his mother. Her parental rights have never been revoked. And I caution you strongly here, James. If you keep Isaac from her, you are guilty of kidnapping. And if you pay her again… well…that's child trafficking. Both are federal offenses."

He clenched his fist. "I'm his father."

"That's never been proven. And your name isn't on the birth certificate." She covered his hand. "James, I agree with your attorney. Petition for paternity. I'll file a report, but I'm sorry. My hands are tied."

He shook off her hand and narrowed his eyes. "I signed the papers this morning. I'm asking for full custody. Will you support me?"

"I'm sorry, but without good cause, I can't side against the natural mother."

James slammed his fist on the desk. "Good cause? What will it take to make you see the truth? Isaac's dead body in a drainage ditch?"

~ ~ ~

Joni yawned as Dr. Birchman pronounced the Federal Reserve an illegal, private entity. The professor expounded on the conspiracy theory behind the two failed assassination attempts on Andrew Jackson after he revoked the bank's charter.

Her phone vibrated in her purse. James? Joni perked up and dug out her cell. Her shoulders fell as she read the message from Trent. *Where are you? Pick up my laundry asap.*

The third such message this morning, all meaningless errands. Candace assured her this big brother thing would only last four weeks. Any longer and Joni would scream. *Sure after class.*

The students gasped and Joni jerked her gaze to the front. The eccentric professor had ripped the twenty dollar bill in half. "It was a worthless piece of paper, and I'm sure Mr. Jackson is protesting in his grave at the unpatriotic endorsement."

Her phone tickled her palm. The sigh of frustration turned to joy as she read James's text. *Isaac wants to buy lunch. What's your class schedule?*

Her heart fluttered, tickling the inside walls of her chest. To have lunch with James, she'd cut class. Fortunately, she wouldn't have to. But, what about Trent's laundry? She wasn't supposed to leave campus without prior permission from Trent or Candace. Her breath gushed out of her lungs while her fingers ran an imaginary scale on the books stacked in front of her.

She'd joined the sorority to escape her mother's rules. She didn't need anyone else telling her what to do. Tonight seemed forever to wait to see James. Besides, she really wanted to meet his son. A decisive thumb swiped across her screen. *Wake me in 20 mins. Lectures over at 11.*

While memories of Saturday night replayed through her mind, Joni listened to the professor as he droned on. "Two thousand pennies? Twenty dollar bill? Which one will be worth more in ten years?"

Joni was curious about Isaac, but James was the one she longed to see. She closed her eyes and imagined his arms sliding around her. The professor slammed his fist on the lectern. Joni flinched. A wrinkled face replaced James's laughing eyes.

"Take the coins and run!" Dr. Birchman's voice resumed its monotone flavor. "At the current market price of copper you'd triple your money." He held up the two halves of the twenty. "At the rate of inflation and deflation you'll be lucky to recoup seventy percent of your investment."

The message from James rescued Joni's confused thoughts. *Your chariot awaits. Which building?*

She quickly replied, *From University and Airport. Turn left on Old Shell. Fourth drive on right. Mitchell Center. No texting while driving. Dangerous.*

Texting at the red light. Nice to know you care. See you soon beautiful.

Professor Birchman's lecture ended at exactly three minutes past eleven. Joni flew out the door the second it was over. She hurried through the building but paused at the exit to smooth her hair and touch up her lip gloss.

Leaning against the side of his truck, dressed in jeans and a polo, James straightened as she neared. She stepped into his open arms and inhaled his cologne. Accepting his kiss was as natural as breathing. Two lifetimes had passed since yesterday morning. He hugged her tight and his heartbeat thumped under her cheek. His chest expanded and his voice echoed through her ear. "Joni, Isaac's had a few rough days."

She lifted her head. "Is he okay? Where is he?"

James's soft lips brushed across hers again. "He's fine." A blond head pressed against the passenger window and a little hand waved hello. "But, he needs…well…he thinks that you're his girlfriend." Mischief twinkled in James's smile. "Will you be nice to him?"

He was kidding. Right? She stepped out of his arms. "I'm gonna pretend you didn't just insult me."

He reached for her. "Joni, I didn't—"

She opened the truck door. Blond hair stuck out in all directions, but his smile captured her heart. "Hi, Isaac. I'm your girlfriend. Joni." She kissed his cheek and the smile widened.

"Hi." Isaac lifted his arms.

Joni hugged him as best as the old car seat would allow.

Judging by their white appearance, the shoes dangling off the seat were new and his little Levi's were crisp. His shirt, starchy. "Someone's been shopping without me." Joni finger-combed his hair.

Isaac frowned at James, who'd opened the driver's door. "Daddy made us. Said we had to look nice."

"I said you had to *be* nice and don't forget it." James held the driver's door open.

Joni shut the passenger door and walked around the truck. James took her book bag and purse. She slid under the steering wheel and scooted across the seat toward the blond angel with a heavenly smile.

"Do you need anything out of here? Or can I put these behind the seat?"

She held out her hand. "Let me get my phone." Joni dropped it into the empty cup holder.

After her things were in the cab's extension, James crowded in beside her. "Sorry about the room. Guess I need a bigger truck."

She leaned her head onto his shoulder. "I like sitting next to you, but Isaac could use a booster instead of that big hulking thing you've got him strapped in."

Isaac kicked his legs. "Yeah. I'm big enough without it. Momma says so."

James started the truck and backed out of the parking place. "Don't start, Isaac. Joni meant you need a new one."

"Kathy doesn't make him ride in a car seat?" Joni couldn't comprehend why a woman would willingly endanger her child. Especially a child as sweet as Isaac.

James ignored her question. "What do you want for lunch?"

She let him change the subject. "It doesn't matter. What do you guys want?"

A little hand touched her arm and blue eyes twinkled. "Daddy wants steak. Me and Uncle Ray like pizza."

"Isaac, we had pizza last night and again for breakfast this morning." James merged into the traffic on Old Shell Road.

"But Daddy…"

"No."

Isaac's face fell.

She wanted to beg James to reconsider. She held Isaac's little hand. "How about we drive through, get some chicken, take it to the park, and feed the ducks the leftovers?"

Isaac's smile returned. "Alive ducks?"

Joni laughed. "Yes."

The little boy leaned forward and peeked around Joni.

"Daddy? Can we feed the ducks?"

James changed lanes. "Chicken and ducks it is."

In the drive-thru, Trent texted, *Did you get my laundry?* Joni sighed. He didn't need to know she'd left campus. She replied. *Not yet at lunch.*

James shot her a funny look. In the close confines of the truck, he no doubt read the text or saw who it was from.

She replaced her phone in the cup holder and rolled her eyes. "He's texted five times today. This big brother thing is so not working for me."

James's jaw clenched. "You don't have to explain."

Why, then, did jealousy simmer behind his smile? Joni turned to Isaac. "Have you ever been on a picnic?"

Isaac shook his head. "Nope."

Joni didn't dare admit this was another first for her as well. At the park, while James carried the takeout bags to the nearest picnic table, she and Isaac followed along hand in hand.

Blue eyes peered up at her. "Do you like me?"

James's stride faltered and Joni knew he listened. She swung Isaac up on her hip and kissed his forehead. "Yes. You are the sweetest boy I know. I loved you the minute I saw you and I'll probably love you forever. Do you like me?"

He laid his head against hers. "Yeah. You smell good."

She laughed and eased him to his feet. "Let's go before your daddy eats all our food. I can't wait to try fried chicken."

Isaac ran the last five feet and climbed on the table. "Where's mine?" He dug in the box and grabbed a chicken leg.

James leaned over and kissed her cheek. "Thank you."

"Don't insult me again." She winked and spread a napkin on the wood surface. By the time she had a breast piece and biscuit arranged and her straw neatly in her drink, James reached for seconds.

"Does it taste better like that?" James's cough couldn't disguise his laugh.

"Maybe." She ignored him and broke off a piece of biscuit. "Where are the utensils?"

His mouth curled as he shook his head. "Sorry, we're on a picnic. No forks."

"Oh." The biscuit churned in her stomach. How was she supposed to eat chicken without a fork? "No problem."

James winked and her fake smile became real. He reached across the wooden table and covered her hand. "Do you want something else? We can go back and get a hamburger."

His touch and the sincerity in his voice reassured her. "No." Picnics were about roughing it. Except for the catered gala in Montgomery, where she'd performed two years ago, eating in the park was a foreign experience. Out of the corner of her eye, James stared. She lifted her head and smiled. "It doesn't matter." It was weird—this closeness she felt with him.

James lifted her hand and squeezed her fingers. All teasing was gone. "Joni, I'm sorry. Whatever you want, I'll get it for you."

Maybe that's what made him special. "It's okay." She sipped her coke with her free hand and then pinched off a bite of crust. It was good. Joni nibbled at the spicy layer one pinch at a time. Steam waved up from the chicken. Joni touched the white meat, but snatched her fingers back. Hot. Hearing a chuckle, she straightened her spine. "You're laughing at me?"

James's lips twitched, but he didn't laugh. Instead, he released her hand, picked up her chicken, and separated the meat from the bone. "Guess this means tonight's dinner plans for the American Steamer are out." His wink melted her aggravation. "At least until you learn how to peel your own shrimp."

Was he serious?

"I'm joking. Our dinner reservations include silverware and fine china, but I can't send you back to class hungry, so eat." His shoulder nudged against hers and softened his command.

The chicken was tender and juicy. Joni ate every bite. "Thank you." Although he had purchased extra, she saved the rest of her biscuit for the ducks.

When they were done eating, James swung Isaac on his shoulders, prompting a squeal and a giggle. Little hands carried a bag full of biscuits.

Using a napkin, she wiped the grease from her hands, bagged their mess, and wiped her hands again while James slam-dunked the trash in a nearby can. He led the way down the path.

Near the water, Joni stepped over a huge root covered with "evidence" from the ducks. Careful of where she placed her feet, she strolled alongside James. He stopped and reached for her hand when she lagged behind. Flocks of birds sunned themselves on a small island in the center of the pond. Isaac threw a biscuit at the two ducks on the grassy bank near them. Squawking, they flapped their brown wings and fought over the prize.

James swung Isaac down. "Break it in smaller pieces." Joni followed the directions he gave Isaac. A large white goose appeared from out of nowhere and honked. The frantic bird pecked the crumb that fell from her hand and waddled forward. She flinched and stumbled back against a solid chest rumbling with laughter. She forgave him when one arm wrapped around her and the other waved off the offensive bird. His chin rested on her head and he pulled her close. "Look, across the water."

Hoards of geese and ducks swam straight for them. Her heart tattooed against her thin sweater. Isaac continued to feed the three while more than fifty birds flapped on the shore. Joni's ears cringed at their squawking. She escaped behind James and threw her handful of broken pieces. The ducks kept coming.

"Daddy." Isaac's blue eyes widened and he ran for cover. Joni pulled him in between her and a laughing James.

James drew them close. "They're not going to hurt you. Throw the biscuits."

Isaac kicked at a goose. Joni's pulse raced to the chaotic tune of the honks and screeches surrounding them. She couldn't move. A duck craned his neck for the bag in the little boy's hands. James snatched the bag and flung the contents at the irate birds. He lifted Isaac in one arm and tucked Joni under the other.

The frenzied sounds lowered, and she peeked out from his chest. From a safe distance, the three of them watched the birds fight over the remaining crumbs.

Her heartbeat slammed against her chest. "Those ducks are ferocious."

Isaac's wide eyes looked down into hers. "And mean too."

Ripples broke the calm surface as the ducks sailed into the water. As they raced toward their island, her phone vibrated in her pocket. Trent. She blew her bangs out of her eyes. Her trembling fingers powered off the phone.

The arm holding her tightened. James lifted a brow. "Do you need to go back?"

She shook her head. No one, Trent and rabid birds included, was interrupting her time with James and Isaac.

Wide blue eyes stared at the retreating ducks. The irony of the situation hit her and a giggle escaped. "Crazy birds."

Isaac reached for her and Joni lifted him into her arms. Blue eyes blinked in amazement. "Was you ascared?"

Joni tickled his sides and they both laughed. "Of course not. Dumb birds."

Isaac twisted in her arms and yelled across the water. "Dumb ducks!" He threw the last remaining biscuit in his hand. At least fifteen birds flew out of the water toward them.

She screamed and ran with Isaac.

Laughter roared behind them and she knew they were safe. James clutched his sides in her peripheral vision. She set Isaac on his feet. "Let's go swing."

Lunch ended soon after, and she suffered through her last lecture of the day. That evening, she dressed for her date with James at her parents'. Not wanting Trent to intrude, she left her phone on her bedroom dresser. The only interruption during their dinner was a call from James's mom. Isaac wanted to say goodnight.

Typical for this time of year, the public beach parking lot was almost empty. Stars twinkled and a crescent moon winked. Joni walked out on the gray boardwalk with James and watched the surf crash against the sandy shore.

Inhaling the salty air, she rubbed her hands over her upper arms. Sea grass rustled in the breeze. "It's like music."

James stepped close behind her and wrapped them both in his jacket. "God's own symphony."

Joni turned in his arms. "I thought you weren't religious?" Her fingers plucked a thread on his sleeve. A dog barked and ran down the surf beside his owner. Her hand fell to her side and she tilted her head up at James.

The serious gleam in his eye surprised her. "I don't want to talk about God."

She climbed up on the hand railing and dangled her feet while he stared into the waves. She bumped his shoulder with hers.

He stepped in front of her and placed a hand on each side of the rail, blocking her in. The moon reflected bits of gold in his brown eyes. The emotion there didn't invite a conversation, but there was something she needed to ask. "You're the one who dumped me at church. I felt something, and I want to know what it was." She shrugged. "So, tell me."

"No." He stepped closer. "Joni, read your Bible. It'll answer all your questions."

Her hands gripped his shoulders as she continued the conversation. "I don't have one."

He leaned in and chuckled against her neck. "Download the app."

She ignored the warmth of his breath and pressed him for an answer. "I left my phone at the house."

If she hadn't been so close to him she would have missed his soft growl. "If you stop asking questions, I'll give you one of mine."

She jerked back but grabbed the lapels of his jacket as she almost fell off the other side. "Really?"

His smile returned. "If it makes you happy." He lifted her off the rail and her boots clunked against the wooden boardwalk. The pads of his fingers teased her palm as he clasped her hand. Her heart fluttered at his wink. "Walk with me." They strolled through the shifting sand to the water's edge in silence. A wave rolled in and they raced backward. Laughing, they played cat and mouse with the tide until her heel sunk in the wet sand and warm water flooded over the top.

His laughter rang into the night. "Are you soaked?"

She didn't want their fun to end. "I'm fine."

They strolled down the beach and back again. The taste of salt floated on the breeze. Words would have intruded so they kept silent.

She was content by his side until the cool night temperatures turned her wet socks into icicles. Her teeth chattered by the time she stepped on the boardwalk.

James's arms encircled her. "Joni? You're shivering."

She smiled past her trembling lips. "Only my f-f-feet are w-w-wet."

He swooped her up and carried her to the truck. "Why didn't you tell me? You're gonna have pneumonia." He set her in the seat and reached for her boots. He yanked without success.

She turned her ankle. "They z-z-zip."

He unzipped the boots and removed her socks before running around the truck and starting the engine. The flowing heat felt wonderful against her bare skin. "Give me your feet." He shrugged out of his jacket.

Gritty salt stuck between her toes. She kept them on the floor and shook her head.

With a sigh, he reached down and captured her feet, dusted them off with one hand, and pulled them into his lap. "Your jeans are wet." He rolled up her pant legs and wrapped her cold feet in his fur-lined, leather jacket. "Better?"

She wiggled her toes. "Yes."

As he caressed her ankles, the sparkle abandoned his eyes. "I've filed for custody. My attorney advised me to get Isaac out of town until the hearing. We leave tomorrow."

Joni blinked misty eyes. She didn't want him to go. "How long will you be gone?"

"Until Thanksgiving." One side of his mouth turned up. "Save me some turkey, and I'll bring you a surprise."

With her feet in his lap, the knowledge of his departure placed a certain distance between them. Not wanting to leave the warmth of his jacket but not willing to put it on the floor, Joni curled her feet under. "I'd rather have you."

His grin lit up his face. "Good. You make sure those frat boys know that."

She frowned at her wet boots and socks on his clean floor mat. "James, be serious."

A gentle hand caressed her cheek and turned her face. "I am

serious." Gold flared in his eyes as he dipped his head. Her lids fluttered closed. She waited but his lips hovered out of reach.

James straightened and rubbed a hand across the bridge of his nose. Pressing his lips together, he studied her with an emotion she couldn't distinguish. Was it jealousy? Or concern? She was still uncertain when his face transformed into a mischievous smile. "Joni, are you going to church with Sara Wednesday night?"

His abrupt change of subject confused her. He'd said he didn't want to talk about God. Frowning, she answered, "I don't know. I want to, but Trent advised me not to leave campus. I don't think sororities encourage church attendance."

His next smile made her dizzy. He pulled her tight against him and whispered, "Are you gonna let them choose? Tell you where to go? Who to see? What to do when you get there?"

He was right. She'd gained partial freedom from her mother's schedule. She didn't need anyone making decisions for her. But was knowing about God worth the chance of losing her new friends? "I'm not sure how I feel about church."

James winked and shifted into reverse. "Let's get you a Bible and then you can decide."

Chapter Five

No one would welcome visitors at this hour. It was past midnight, but the streetlight illuminated James's boyish smile as he turned into a residential community and pulled into a rose-lined driveway. Joni stared at the basketball hoop mounted above the closed garage door. "Where are we? Who lives here?"

He killed the engine. "This is my mom's current project. I don't read my Bible anymore. You're welcome to it. It's in the boy room." He opened the door and slid out of the truck.

Her mouth opened but she couldn't make a sound. In the hollow cavity of her chest, her heart raced silently, and then the words burst forth. "I can't go in your house."

"This isn't my house. Mom's in real estate. She buys foreclosures, fixes them up, and rents them out. Isaac and I rent a place in Tillman's Corner, but my real house is two hours north. Dad lives there." He held out a hand. "Come on, but don't wake Isaac. You're all he talked about this afternoon. I'm afraid he's got a huge crush." Wiggling fingers beckoned.

She unwrapped her feet and passed him his jacket. "The feeling's mutual." Her cold boots were still wet. Her warm toes protested at the thought of sliding them on.

James turned his back to her. "Jump on. I'll give you a piggyback ride."

"I can't believe I'm doing this." Her heart skipped as her trembling arms wrapped around his shoulders. She blew out a breath and pounced on his back. A giggle escaped her.

"Shhh." He grabbed her knees and laughed. "Close the truck."

With one hand, she did as he asked. "Don't drop me."

"Not a chance." Around the side of the garage, they approached a door. He hunched over to keep her from sliding as he fumbled with his keys. Short beeps sounded. "Forgot about the alarm."

The keypad glowed by her left arm. "What's the code?"

"Four, five, eleven."

She punched in the numbers. The beeps stopped. She sighed with relief as he stepped in the entrance and closed the door.

"That was close." He cupped her knees and climbed the stairs. The dim lamplight faded with each step.

"James, I can walk now." She whispered against his neck, but clung to him in the dark.

He trembled beneath her. "Shhh. Hardwood floors are freezing. Trust me, I know."

She bit her lip to keep silent. *Don't let his mom wake up.*

He stumbled and hissed. "Sorry, Isaac left a toy on the stairs."

A door opened in front of them and an outside streetlight cast a glow through the window into the bedroom. She let go and slid to the carpeted floor. Masculine cologne lingered in the air. A blue and gray comforter covered the bed while matching sailboat curtains displayed the bay window. She moved to the trophy-covered dresser. Despite the baseball glove and helmet sitting between a T-ball trophy and an MVP football, the room was sterile. Generic.

She jumped as the door clicked shut. The tempo of her pulse pounded in her throat. Not counting her cousin Paul, she'd never been in a guy's room.

James switched on the overhead light and winked. In two steps, he was by her side unzipping a large duffle bag. He tossed her a small bundle. "Put these on." He continued to the closet and dug through a cardboard box.

The socks would come to her knees. She eased down on the bed to brush the sticky salt off the bottom of her feet. "Ugh!" Sand covered the rolled cuffs of her pant legs.

A pair of wind pants dropped onto her lap. "Shhh." Gentle

fingers touched her lips and then tugged on her hand. They walked into a full bath. A second door led into a feminine bedroom. His sister's? Isaac's blond head rested on a lace-covered pillow. The little boy slept in a pink, eyelet-covered bed.

James let go of her hand and shut out the peaceful sight. The cabinet door creaked as he opened it. His steady hands snatched a neatly stacked towel from the shelf and added it to her arms. "Hurry up and change while I find the Bible."

She grabbed for the closing door. "I can't wear your clothes."

He turned and winked. "They're drawstring and yours are soaked. It's not a big deal." Cardboard flaps scraped against the side of the box as he once again dug through the closet.

Joni locked both bathroom doors. The clean, white tub tempted her sticky feet so she took her time with the warm water. Though the wind pants swallowed her, the string in the front tightened them to a manageable size. She rolled the waistband down and the legs up. After rinsing the sand off her jeans, she folded them in the sink and cleaned her mess. Quietly, she opened the bedroom door.

James lay on the bed with his feet on the floor. A black leather book rested on his stomach. He started as Joni eased down beside him and reached for the Bible. "Is this it?"

He raised himself to sit beside her and kissed her temple. "Anxious, are you?"

"A little." She accepted the book and opened it.

"Wait." He hugged her tight with one arm and closed the Bible with the other. "Promise you won't let anything you read in here come between us?"

She tilted her head and blinked. The butterflies in her stomach danced to the rhythm of her erratic heartbeat. "Is there an 'us'?"

"I hope so." His finger trailed the back of her hand. "Your fascination with God might make you hate me."

"It's just a book." She couldn't escape the intensity of his gaze. They were connected somehow, and nothing could sever that connection. But how could she explain something she didn't fully understand? "I promise."

He flipped open the pages and read from the front. Was it his deep voice or the mystical words tempting her soul?

"Your Aunt Sandra said somebody's songs are in here. Show me."

"The Song of Solomon?" Flames of gold flecked his brown eyes. His voice dropped an octave. "I can't." He glanced over his shoulder at the bed and swallowed. "Not while we're reading the Bible. God would strike me dead for sure."

What was he talking about? Is the Bible that powerful? "James?"

His body shuddered and he shook his head. Then he smiled. The golden flames were extinguished. "She probably meant Psalms." He turned to the middle of the book. "David wrote most of them."

"What are they?"

"Songs and poems. Many are sung in church today." Masculine hands gracefully flipped through the pages, stopped, and pointed. "Here. This is one of the fascinating things about the Bible." His boyish grin illuminated the love he'd once had for this book. "Whenever you read L-O-R-D in capital letters it means God's special name, Yahweh. Though His people constantly rebelled against Him, they refused to write or speak God's name out of fear."

"Like you." She poked his chest.

His head tilted back and wide brown eyes gawked. "I'm not afraid of God."

"If you're not scared *he'll strike you dead*, then show me the other song." She smirked as he stuttered. Her point had hit home.

"Joni, it's Psalms not songs, and I'm not scared."

The bedroom door creaked open. An older version of Sara wearing a comfortable-looking gown and robe stared at the Bible in Joni's lap. The intruder gasped. Moisture swelled in her eyes and spilled down her cheeks.

Joni winced and closed her eyes, pretending to be anywhere but here. Beside her, James groaned. "Mom, it's not what it looks like."

Joni swallowed the odd lump in her throat. She closed the Bible and stood. The words of apology wouldn't pass her lips.

"You're reading the Bible." The smile removed ten years from James's mother's face.

"No, Mom. Joni's just curious." He claimed her hand and pulled her toward the door.

Mrs. Preston laughed softly. "Joni? This is Isaac's girlfriend? I thought he had a play date at the park. Praise the Lord."

James tugged Joni out the door. "I'll be back later."

"Nice to meet you, dear." James's mother called behind them.

Blinking mutely, Joni allowed him to lead her down the stairs. Outside in the night air, he lifted her in his arms and carried her to the truck.

Climbing in through the driver's side, she found her voice. "I can't believe your mom saw me in your room. I feel like I'm sixteen again when Paul caught me swiping a drink of Daddy's bourbon." Trembling hands covered her face as she sunk down in the seat.

"Joni, it's okay. You're a hero in her eyes." He pried one hand away and grinned.

"What?"

"Trust me." He started the truck and backed out of the driveway.

"Oh, no." Her favorite jeans. How could she have been so careless?

He shifted gears. "I promise she's not mad. She heard me reading the Bible. It's like her dream come true. By now she's picturing a halo around your head and wings on your back."

"I don't think so." She traced the gold-embossed lettering on the black leather book.

James stopped for a traffic light and kissed her. "Why not?"

"I forgot my pants in your bathroom."

~ ~ ~

Although Isaac was four, James had been a father for less than seven months. During that time, convincing him to go to sleep hadn't gotten any easier. James glanced at the digital hotel clock on the end table. According to the schedule Mrs. Dawn insisted Isaac adhere to, bedtime was forty minutes late. Tomorrow, the millwright's wife would have to deal with his crankiness.

James tucked the covers under Isaac's chin and kissed his soft cheek. He crossed the short distance to the mini fridge and grabbed his second longneck of the night. Reclining on the empty bed, he twisted off the cap and swigged. Two beers was his limit, unless he'd had a particularly rough day, then he upped his ante to three.

Flipping through the channels revealed the same old, same old. He let the news anchor rattle on while he reached for his phone. Over two hundred miles and nine weeks separated him and Joni. Would she wait that long? Or would Trent convince her otherwise? It was late. James didn't want to wake her if she was asleep, so he texted. *Hey beautiful. I miss you.*

James. Her reply whispered in his ear as if she was in the room. *Lots has happened since you left. My big brother is a pest. Greek life is not what I thought.*

He frowned at the screen. Frat boys could be trouble when they didn't get what they wanted. He should know; he used to be one of them. *You want me to tell him to leave you alone?*

Thanks but he finally took no for an answer. Me and Marla went to your church Weds night. They werent as lively as the tent people but everyone was nice. Including your mother. She insisted we sit with her. Pretty cool, huh? Thanks for the Bible. I read it every night. I love the notations you made along the sides. Helps me to understand the meaning.

He'd forgotten about the notes he'd made during sermons. For a brief moment, his mind wandered back to the night in his room when they'd read the Bible. His arm around her. Her breath on his cheek. The one thing he missed most from his Christian days was the time he spent alone in the Word. Did Joni feel a connection with God as she read? Knowing she read his words along with God's drew James closer to her. He replied, *Glad you are enjoying it.* He tilted the bottle to his lips. It was no longer enough just to communicate.

She answered his call with a sweet giggle. "I thought we were texting?"

Eyes closed, he leaned back against the headboard and imagined her beside him. "I wanted to hear your voice. Tell me what you're doing."

Musical laughter soothed his weary soul. "Texting you and watching a movie on cable."

"Which one?" He flipped through the channels until he found the station she described. A red Camaro zoomed down the street of a small town. "I gotta get me a car like that."

A rustling sounded through the phone. "You're watching the same show?"

He kept his voice nonchalant. "There's nothing else on."

"Oh." More scuffs came from her phone.

A dude walked across the screen. "Is he the good guy?"

"Wait a minute." Crackles sounded in his ear.

"Are you okay? You sound as if you're wrestling with Isaac."

Her laugh cheered him. "I'm trying to get comfortable. Mom bought me a new pillow for college. It won't lay right and this mattress is harder than your truck's bed liner."

He gulped the last of his beer. "If you were here, you could snuggle against me. Pillow choice makes all the difference in a good night's rest, and my shoulder is always available."

Her voice softened. "I miss you."

He hugged a pillow next to him, and then flipped it across the room. Only Joni would do. "I miss you, too."

Comfortable silence reigned as the movie played. A hot girl in a short skirt sashayed across the screen. Joni asked, "Do you think she's pretty?"

"Yeah, but you're beautiful." His arms ached to hold her. Trying to relieve the emptiness, he stretched them overhead. It didn't work. He retrieved the pillow and curled up on his side.

He could almost imagine Joni's hair tickling his chin. Almost.

~ ~ ~

"Hey! Wake up!" Ray's voice interrupted a wonderful dream of jade eyes and golden hair. Fists pounded on his hotel door and the knob rattled. "We're gonna be late for work."

Wiping the back of his hand over his mouth, he dropped his phone on the bed. He must have conked out while talking to Joni. Shaking himself awake, he stumbled to open the door for Ray. "Sorry. Overslept."

Mrs. Dawn slipped in and lifted Isaac from the other bed. "How late did he stay up?"

James shrugged in answer. If she didn't wake him, Isaac would sleep for several more hours. With a frown, she carried his sleeping son out the door.

Ray gawked at the feminine commercial playing on the TV as James threw on jeans and a work shirt. "You're watching the chick network?"

Ignoring him, James brushed his teeth.

"Dude…" His friend turned off the TV and picked up James's phone. "If you want to cuddle up with a girl and watch a movie, Chloe's friend would be more than happy to crawl in your bed."

James rinsed his mouth and spit. "No thanks."

Hands on his hips, Ray glared and shook his head. "You need professional help. You know it?"

A laugh erupted from deep within James's chest and seared his lips in a smile. Ray was probably right. He grabbed his phone and his keys. "Let's go."

At the job site, his phone beeped. The battery was almost dead. He powered it off until lunch. Then he updated his social network status, scrolled down his news feed, and stopped on Joni's post. "Sooooo sleepy. Stayed up late watching movies with a friend." He clicked "like" and checked his email.

～～～

Hey beautiful. Wheres my girl? Thought we had a video chat date?

Joni's heart lurched as she read James's text. She'd tried to talk her way out of attending the Greek social, but Candace insisted on maintaining a good relationship with the guys from their affiliated fraternity. *Cant video at the movies. Brother n sister thing. How was your day?*

Long. The jerk with you?

She laughed at his jealousy and Stephanie jabbed her side with a bony elbow. "Shhh."

Trent glared over the tub of popcorn in Candace's lap. Joni had given up trying to figure out his moods. One minute he was all chivalrous and the next he was hateful and judgmental. She decided to answer James honestly. *Hes here.*

Next to you?

She had learned the hard way not to get lured in the shadows with Trent. *No. Three seats down. His hands wander.*

What? When?

Forget I said that. Time to change the subject. *Hows my little boyfriend? Asleep yet?*

James wasn't easily deterred. *Im coming down there if he bothers you again. And no, Isaac's not asleep. Cant seem to conquer bedtime.*

Trent leaned over Candace. "Joni, it's rude to text in a theater. Can't whoever it is wait until the end of the movie?"

She cut her eyes toward him and refrained from adding she wasn't here by choice. "I'm almost done." She keyed the words, *Tell him a story for me and kiss him goodnight. Ill call you when I get back to my room.* Before she could pocket her phone it vibrated in her hand.

Whos gonna kiss me goodnight?

~~~

James turned his phone around so Joni could see Isaac. He was wide-awake, but at least he was in the bed and it wasn't yet ten thirty.

Her voice reached out and caressed his son. "Are you snug as a bug in a rug?"

Isaac laughed and wiggled under the covers. "Yep."

"Then happy dreams, sweetie. Don't give your daddy any trouble tonight. No watching cartoons after he falls asleep."

Isaac frowned. "You wasn't suppose to tell."

"I want you to be safe." A smooch sounded from the built-in speaker. "Goodnight."

He blew a kiss at the screen. "'Night."

James flipped the camera view. "Hold on a minute." He set the phone on the empty bed and tugged the covers around his son. "If you go to sleep, I'll pretend I didn't hear about the TV." Isaac lifted his face and James kissed his cheek. "And no snoring."

Isaac giggled. "Goodnight, Daddy."

James crossed to the mini fridge and selected a bottle from the back. With Isaac all tucked in for the night, he could finally relax. Propping up against the headboard, he reclined on the other bed and grabbed his phone. "How was your day? Tell me everything."

Joni smiled from the screen. "I saw your girlfriend."

"Did you look in the mirror?" He kept his voice low, hoping Isaac was drifting into dreamland.

Beautiful eyes rolled upward. "I'm serious. Do you remember the house where we met?"

"I'll never forget." Unease settled in his stomach. He attempted to drown it with beer and his next question. "You didn't go back there. Did you?"

She propped up on one elbow. A green quilt lay beneath her and a red sign on the wall above her head read "Kappa." "I met Kathy there. Candace sent her a letter." His gut clenched as Joni ran a hand through her hair. "Stupid errands. I'll be glad when this probation is over."

He phrased his next question with care, sure he wasn't going to like the answer. "Did Kathy give you a letter for Candace?"

Joni folded her legs under her and sat on the bed. "No, but she sent Trent a small gift bag. He laughed when I told him 'happy birthday.'"

The glass bottle banged against the nightstand. Isaac moaned in sleep and James paused to take a deep breath. She looked so innocent in her pink and yellow fuzzy pajamas. Could she really be that trusting?

Her shoulders shrugged. "What?"

"You can't go back to that house. And you can't make any more deliveries."

Her mouth fell open.

He rubbed a hand down his face. "I'm not ordering you. It's just that…that wasn't a letter or a birthday present."

She stretched across the bed and reached for a water bottle. The sip was dainty. "I don't like being the errand girl, but I don't have a choice. Not for several weeks anyway."

How could he make her understand? "Joni, they're using you to deliver drugs."

She tilted her head back and frowned. "That's impossible. Candace has a 4.0, and Trent is president of student government."

"I can't let you put yourself in danger. If you got pulled over for speeding while running one of their errands, you could get five years to life. Not to mention the danger of a drug deal gone bad. Messengers have been killed in the crossfire. You can't do it anymore, even if you have to quit the sorority."

Tears pooled in her eyes as her shoulders rose. "You can't stop me. You're not my father. Don't tell me what I can and can't do."

He chewed his lower lip. Maybe he'd been a little harsh, but she had no idea the danger she was in. Swallowing his pride, he apologized. "I just want to protect you."

Her smile was sad. "I don't need protecting. Goodnight, James."

She ended the connection, but he couldn't let her risk her life for some stupid girls' club. He scrolled down his contacts and pressed send. Joni might hate him in the morning, but at least she'd be safe.

~ ~ ~

How could she have been so stupid? Joni slipped off the bed and walked down the hall. Somebody had some explaining to do. She'd thought something was suspicious when Kathy had been so nice to her today. She'd even asked about James and Isaac. Gullible. Naive. Well, not anymore. Joni may have led a sheltered life, but she wasn't an idiot.

Her knock on Candace's door was answered with a quick, "Come in."

Joni closed the door behind her but didn't cross the room.

Candace smiled from her writing desk. "I'm glad you're here. I've got a couple of things for you to deliver tomorr—"

"Are you and Trent selling drugs for Kathy? Because I'm not

into that and believe me, I will be checking every letter and package from now on."

Candace's lips pressed in a fine line. "I'm hurt that you could think me capable of something so despicable. And Trent... Why, he'll be purely devastated." The honey in her voice rang false.

Joni leaned her head against the door. No wonder Trent laughed at her today. "James is right, isn't he? You're selling drugs."

The phone on the dresser rang and Candace shot Joni a seething glance. "Don't move. We'll clear this up after I answer this." She turned her back and whispered. One hand landed on her hip. "He threatened to do what? Really? Well that's just freaking wonderful, isn't it?" Her voice lowered again. "If you'd kept James at home, he wouldn't be interfering now. Would he?" She ended the call and whirled around to face Joni. "Our errands are Greek business, and non-Greeks shouldn't know about them." Her voice hardened. "You've been talking to James behind Trent's back."

Joni pushed away from the door. James must've called Kathy, but she would deal with him later. "Trent doesn't own me. I've never dated the guy and I don't want to start."

Candace met her in the middle of the large bedroom suite. "Fine. You want to throw accusations around and whine about a few errands, you can forget living the easy life. From now on, you can concentrate on fulfilling our philanthropy requirement at St. Mary's Home for Children. All those snotty noses ought to make you thankful for your blessings." A finger pointed in Joni's direction. "And if you mention to anyone else about your deliveries, you are out of here, little girl. Do you understand?"

Joni hid her smile. "St. Mary's, the group foster home?"

"Three hours a week." Venom spewed from Candace. "And I suggest you play nice with Trent if you want to advance in Greek society. Now, get out of here."

Joni barely held in a squeal of excitement as she rushed back to her room. Yes. Yes. Yes. Every since Stephanie had complained about working at St. Mary's last week, Joni knew that was what she wanted to do. She loved kids, and she didn't get to see Paul's children nearly as often as she liked. Bursting through her door, she snatched up her phone.

James's sleepy voice answered after the fourth ring. "Joni, don't be mad. I care about you and I just wan—"

Her laughter drowned out the rest of his excuses. "Oh, James. Thank you." She sucked in a breath. "Don't ever do that again." The squeal of excitement she'd been holding since leaving Candace erupted. "I get to work at St. Mary's."

"Huh? What?" Rustling sounded through the earpiece. "No more deliveries?"

She smiled and rolled her eyes. James had a one-track mind. "No more errands, period." Hearing his sigh of relief, she dove onto her bed. "I'm so excited. There's no way I'll be able to sleep." She snuck under the covers and reached for the remote. "Want to watch a movie?"

Despite his loud yawn, he said, "What channel?"

～～～

Tuesday, as James read over the blueprints with the general foreman, piano notes danced from his phone. A video message from Joni. He bit back a smile and ignored it. He'd watch it later without an audience.

Cecil grinned across the table. "Is that her?"

James glanced at Ray, who grinned from beside the coffee pot. Ray was a favorite of the boss. No doubt he'd be running his own projects soon. James turned back to Cecil's question. He didn't know how to tell his supervisor the call was none of his business.

"Go ahead." Cecil straightened to his six-foot-two height. "I'm curious. The last girl you brought around disrupted the entire crew. Ended with two divorces and four busted drug tests."

Jaw clenched, James glared at the GF. "Joni isn't Kathy."

"Thank God." Cecil slapped James across the shoulder and laughed. "I didn't mean to insinuate otherwise."

With his phone still in his hand, James released a shaky breath.

"I'm gonna step over there and get a cup of coffee. Whistle when you're done talking to your pretty girlfriend."

After turning the volume low, James played the video.

Joni smiled on-screen. "Sorry for bothering you at work." She bit her lip and he wished he could reach out and smooth the fuzzy strands of her hair. Blue fabric stretched across her chest as she inhaled and continued. "I miss you." Full lips turned up into a smile. For one silent moment, jade eyes pleaded with him to hold her. "James…" She closed her eyes and shrugged. "Never mind. Have a good day."

The screen went black. Over his shoulder, Ray and Cecil saluted him with their foam cups. James couldn't make an answering video with them watching. He didn't consider himself a touchy-feely guy, but remembering the longing in Joni's eyes, the words almost keyed themselves into the message. *Sorry you're having a bad day. Wish I was there to hold you. Close your eyes and breathe deep. I'm including a hug and kiss with this text.*

He pocketed his phone and watched his boss cross the room. "Any chance I could lay out for a few days?"

Cecil smacked his lips and grinned. "No. Now pay attention."

The green pencil used to outline James's next project matched the color of Joni's eyes. Who placed the sadness in them? The sorority girls? Her mother? Or Trent? Two more weeks of Kappa's probation period. Why did she try to fit in with people around her? She needed to escape. Have a little fun.

Cecil snapped his fingers twice in James's face.

"What?"

"You haven't heard a word I've said. Are you sick?"

Ray answered for him. "He's lovesick. Nothing a quick trip to Alabama couldn't cure. You might as well give him a few days off."

Cecil shook his head but said, "Go. Be back here Thursday morning ready to work, and don't tell a soul or else everyone will beg for a day and a half off."

"Thank you, sir." He was halfway out the door before he remembered he needed a ride to the gate. He looked back.

Cecil waved his hand. "Ray can take you to the guard shack. Now, get out of here before I change my mind."

James waited until he walked through the mill gate before

calling her. "Hey, beautiful. What's our plan for tonight?"

"We have a paper due for economics. You said you'd help me."

The panic in her voice ignited his laugh. "What would your grades be without me?" She grunted in answer as he unlocked the truck and turned the key. "I'll write the paper if you meet me at the house in Tillman's Corner."

Her gasp was followed by a squeal. "You're coming home?" Her excitement zipped through the phone. "Now?"

He looked at his watch. "In six hours or less, depending on traffic. I'll text you the house address. Go to the neighbor's, the one with the big dog in the back fence, and Mrs. Addison will give you the key."

"James, I can't knock on a stranger's door and ask for a key to your house."

He laughed. "Yes, you can. I pay her to look out for the place. I'll call and let her know you're coming."

Chapter Six

Joni couldn't concentrate on the pages in front of her. A car door slammed outside. She ran and peeked out the window. Across the street, a little girl sprinted across the lawn and vaulted into a man's arms. A lady wearing potholders held the door open for the father and daughter. Farther down the cul-de-sac, four boys passed around a football.

Shoulders sagging, she returned to James's ugly sofa. Sweet Mrs. Addison had met her with the key thirty minutes ago.

Reaching with both hands, she dragged the computer to her lap. The cursor on the blank screen mocked her. The economics essay was due in the morning, but how could Joni concentrate when they would be here any minute? She pushed the computer aside and stood.

Was James color-blind, or did Kathy pick out the furniture? The plaid, mint sofa and taupe recliner clashed with the raspberry loveseat. Whoever decorated skipped the bare white walls entirely. A pool table stood in place of a dinette. The huge flat screen, bolted to the brick wall where a fireplace might have once been, was the only new piece of furniture in the great room.

She wandered into the spotless kitchen and opened the refrigerator to find three longnecks, a bottle of ketchup, two Kool-Aid pouches, and a box of baking powder. Why was everything so…clean? No swing set in the backyard? No chairs on the patio?

Joni blew the bangs out of her eyes and curled up on the sofa. She had enough problems without worrying about James's cleaning habits. Flipping her notebook open, she curled her feet under and scribbled her chaotic thoughts.

The sisterhood wasn't the circle of friends she dreamt of, and her mother threatened to cut off her credit cards if she didn't perform for Sunday concerts, which left church attendance impossible. She needed to make a choice. What she really wanted was to pack her suitcase and follow James across the country. Her mind rambled off into a wonderful dream as the front door banged open.

She turned her back against the armrest. James's gaze held her captive as he crossed the room. Her heartbeat skipped and then surged as his eyes widened and his nostrils flared. Joni reached for him, and before she could blink, he rolled over the back of the sofa toward her. His momentum propelled them both to the floor with her sprawled on top.

She rubbed her palm against the stubble on his chin. Yellow flames flicked to life in his brown eyes. "Kiss me," he commanded.

Digging her toes in the carpet, she propelled herself up his chest and pressed her lips to his. He took control of her chaste kiss and shifted their positions. With James as her teacher, she was more than willing to explore these new sensations his mouth and hands introduced.

"Why you down there?" Isaac's voice snapped her back to reality.

Warm lips hovered against her sensitive skin and his heated breath danced with the fine hairs on her temple. The door slammed shut. She flinched and opened her eyes to James's smiling face.

"We fell off the couch." He sat on his knees and stared.

She barely managed to lean against the couch before Isaac climbed into her lap and said, "Did you break your neck?"

"No." Joni stammered. "I don't." She couldn't catch her breath. "Think so."

Little hands pushed her chin right and then left. Isaac's blue eyes zoomed in on her throat. "I crashed off the bed yesterday.

Mrs. Dawn said I almost broke my neck."

James lifted his son and set him on his feet. "Don't badger Joni. She didn't break anything." He pulled her up off the floor and hugged her close. His short, rapid bursts of breaths matched her own.

They settled in the recliner and Isaac wiggled onto their laps. Content to snuggle against James for a lifetime, she listened to Isaac's chatter. Under her ear, James's heartbeat slowed with each pass his hand made through her hair.

"What's this?" He picked up her notebook and she braced herself as he read her pros and cons list. "Sorority equals Trent, no church, and no James." James frowned down at Joni. "No James in your life doesn't work for me."

She opened her mouth to tell him she'd already ruled out that possibility, but he kissed it closed and continued.

"No sorority equals living at home with Mom and piano concerts." His voice picked up an octave. "No concerts equals no credit cards?" He let out a whistle. "Concerts equals no church. Church equals singing." His arm caressed her shoulder. "Finally, something makes you smile." Another kiss landed in her hair. "Church equals…"

She cringed and waited for his reaction.

"…no sex with James." He inhaled and rubbed his hand across the bridge of his nose. "It didn't take them long to teach you the cardinal sins, did it? At least you punctuated it with a sad face." Releasing his breath, he continued to read silently.

~ ~ ~

A similar scrap of paper weighed his wallet. Although tempted to remind her of the uncompleted item on her first list, James didn't. Instead, he reached around her for the pen. Tapping it against the notebook he winked and pressed them in her hand. "You need to add a few facts. Write this down." Joni poised the pen at the bottom of the list.

"Write, 'Trent equals No James.'"

He shifted Isaac in his lap and handed him the television remote. "And you might want to put that in capital letters."

James peered over her shoulder and watched her write his request. "Now that we've established rule number one, let's take care of your other worries. Write…Joni equals James. Church equals James. Sorority equals James. Home equals James."

Her hand shook with suppressed laughter as she scribbled on the page.

"Stay focused. I can't let you make such an enormous decision without all the facts. I guess you'll have to deal with your mother on your own, but with her or without her, I'm not going anywhere. Add, James equals Isaac." The two guys bumped fists. "We're a package deal." He ran his finger down her original script. "Kathy doesn't belong on our list. As soon as I get full custody, she's out of our life for good. I don't use credit cards, but if you want something I'll buy it. Now, on to our final two notations." James cleared his throat. "Sex equals James. Put triple smiley faces next to that."

Joni's hand didn't move. Color flooded her cheeks, yet she raised her face and held his gaze as he caressed her cheek.

He stared deep into her jade eyes. "No sex still equals James." He grinned. "Although, I reserve the right to persuade your decision."

"James!" Wide eyed, she popped his arm with the pen.

He took the pen and notebook out of her hand and tossed them on the floor. "Joni, whether you join a sorority or a church, doesn't change the way I feel about you. As long as Trent isn't a factor, you and me are okay."

"I don't like him."

"I know, and if he keeps bothering you, I'll handle it." Stretching his long legs, he flipped the recliner lever and snuggled her against his shoulder. "As for the other, you have my permission to seduce me anytime you want, but it's not a requirement."

She propped up on her elbow and smiled. "What are you doing a week from tomorrow?"

"Long distance seduction doesn't work for me. I'll be back in Memphis." He lowered his voice to a whisper. "But I'm available as soon as Isaac falls asleep." She sagged against his chest and sighed.

Not the answer he was looking for. "What's next Thursday?"

"Sorority Date Night."

First-year pledges were required to attend all socials. James cradled Joni's cheek in his palm and lifted her face to his. "What happens if you don't have a date?"

Her bottom lip played hide-and-seek with her mouth. She was stalling. "My big brother escorts me."

This was the reason for the video message. "Why didn't you tell me earlier?" If he hadn't come home today, he might could've swung it by Cecil, but now...

"I couldn't ask you to drive six hours to take me on a date."

He closed the footrest. Isaac squirmed to the floor and scooted closer to the TV. James cradled Joni across his lap.

"Why do you think I'm here?"

She shrugged.

"Because you asked me to." His finger covered her protesting lips. "Yes. You did. I saw the question in your eyes during the video you sent." He grinned. "I just got the day wrong."

Her fingers tickled his whiskers. "I'm sorry. Next time my eyes will specify the day." Joni's kiss landed under his jaw.

"Is it formal?" He needed a new suit anyway.

Her eyes locked on his. "You'll come?" At his nod the sparkles returned. "Casual dress. You can pick me up at eight."

He flipped the lever again and reclined with his arms locked around her sweetness. "Isaac, give Joni the remote. We promised to let her choose the movie."

How could he convince Cecil to give him another day off? And why did the thought of Joni and Trent make his blood seethe? Enough to make him drive twelve hours, round trip, for one night? Twice come next Thursday.

She let Isaac choose his favorite animated movie. Green eyes blinked up at him. "What about my economics paper?"

"You can borrow one of mine." He winked. "Free of charge. Although, I don't understand why you won't stand up to your parents and study something you actually enjoy."

"You know my dad and uncle want me to take over the administration part of their construction business. Once I figure out what I'm doing, I'll learn to enjoy it." She laid her head on his chest. "Am I too heavy?"

His arm tightened, nestling her close while his lips grazed her temple. "You're perfect."

She snuggled against him. "Your heart is racing."

"Holding you does that to me." Gramps always said good things came to those who held out the longest. For Joni, he could wait. The only thing on her list that bugged him, besides Trent, was church. But if she joined the church, then the no-hooking-up-rule would apply to all those frat guys. Then he could return to work without worrying about being replaced on her first list.

~ ~ ~

The next morning, Joni emailed James's old college paper with her name on it to Dr. Birchman. She included a note proclaiming a fake sickness and then drove to James's house.

His truck was still in the drive. She rang the bell a second time. He opened the door and she stepped into his embrace.

The door closed behind her and he held her at arm's-length. "Why aren't you in class?"

She studied the contrast between her leather boots and his bare feet. He had beautiful toes. Her gaze traveled up his pajamas, devoured his muscular chest, and clung to his whiskered chin. There was no way she could pay attention to boring lectures when she could be kissing James. "What happened to the Joni-make-your-own-decisions speech?"

"The rules don't apply when you ditch Economics."

"But I love being with you." She watched his eyes soften. "And Dr. Birchman is crazy. It's rumored that he has one hundred million pennies in his basement."

"Most people prefer gold over copper." His lips twitched but he pressed them in a hard line. "Joni, your education is important."

Last night, she'd dreamt of his kisses. Starting at his chin, she kissed the ridge of his jaw before whispering in his ear. "It's one day. After you go back to Memphis, I promise to study and write my own papers and everything."

His lips tugged upward. "Too bad you won't fit in my suitcase."

"James!" She pivoted on her heel and left him standing alone. How could he?

"What? What did I say?"

She blew the hair out of her eyes and glared over her shoulder. "You called me fat."

His mouth fell open. "No, I—" He sprinted after her. With a squeal, she circled the couch. James was faster. He caught her easily and cradled her up in his arms. With one hand behind her neck and one on her lower back, he pressed her into the air. "I have weights heavier than you."

"James." Her stomach flipped as he dropped her into his arms and tossed her over his shoulder. A squeak sounded out of her mouth as he spun like a whirlwind. Bursts of laughter interrupted her pleas for help.

A blurry Isaac ran up the hall. "Twirl me next, Daddy." He clapped his hands while Joni's feet touched the carpet. Dizzy, she reached for the sofa. Her hands grabbed empty air and she tumbled to the floor.

"Joni?" James rushed to her side. "Are you hurt?"

She couldn't stop laughing long enough to answer. Isaac pounced on James's back. "Helicopter me, Daddy. I won't crash. I promise."

"Don't drop him."

James gasped and leaned back on his heels. One finger waved in front of her face. "I didn't drop you." The finger pointed at her chest. "You fell."

She perched on the sofa's edge and caught her breath. "Same difference."

James lifted Isaac to his shoulders. "No. Not the same at all." Isaac added sound effects as they spun in circles.

"What do you want to do today?"

Joni became a blur. "Well, I was thinking about my list from last night."

"Yeah, me too." He paused and let his swaying head whirl to a stop before twirling Isaac in the opposite direction. One day, his nightly dreams would become reality, but he wouldn't rush Joni.

"In order to make an informed decision, I need to have all the facts. I've experienced sorority life for weeks now. I need to try out my other option."

"Whoa!" One hand slipped off Isaac and James stumbled to a stop. His son collapsed on the floor in a ball of laughter. James fell back against the wall and pulled Joni against him. "I bet Mrs. Addison can babysit for a few hours." He wanted to kiss her, but his Jell-O-legs collapsed and they slid to the floor.

All three Jonis laughed and pecked his cheek. "You're dizzy, and I don't have to sleep with you to know I'll like it."

He shook the fuzz from his head and grabbed her ankles as she shrieked on the floor and tried to squirm away. James crawled over her and growled, "Bawhahaha!"

Isaac jumped on his back. "Don't let her escape, Daddy."

"Not a chance." He leered down at his captive who'd rolled to face him. "How can you try out your options without some alone-time with James?" He wiggled his eyebrows and watched the color flood her cheeks. "Oh, I see." He licked his lips. "You've been dreaming about me." Her eyes widened, revealing the truth of his statement. "Isaac, go watch cartoons."

"Ah, man. I wanted to play with Joni." Isaac slid off his back and moped around the couch.

"Me too." James took his time kissing her. When dainty fingers tickled the back of his neck, he lifted Joni in his arms and carried her down the hall.

Her dazed expression vanished as he lowered her to the bed. "James, take me to church."

Her words slapped him in the face. "Joni? Church? Seriously?"

Isaac ducked under the arm that was about to shut the door. The interloper snuggled next to her. "Let's play 'I spy.'"

James scrubbed his hand over his face and leaned against the door facing. How did this happen? Joni was in his bed, without him.

After each red thing she named off, Isaac shook his little head. Should he tell her his son cheated, or that he sometimes confused blue with purple? No, she deserved to lose. He grabbed some clothes from his duffle bag and headed for a cold shower. Wednesday night prayer meeting started at seven. That gave him all day to change her mind about going.

~ ~ ~

James answered her request for a video chat. The sight of Joni in her pajamas, reading his Bible, made him smile. Two nights ago, he's kissed her and held her in his arms. He missed her already. "Hey, beautiful, having fun?"

A tear leaked out of the corner of her eye and his heart jolted. "I can tell by your words written here that you used to love God. Now you change the subject when I want to talk about church. What happened to change your mind?"

Might as well tell her the truth. He blew out a breath. "I can't sing in church and that's what God wanted me to do."

Her head tilted the way it did before she asked a million questions. "How do you know God wanted you to sing?"

He needed to put an end to her curiosity of God. Choosing his words so as not to peak her interest more, he said, "Some things you just know. It's not important how."

Jade eyes narrowed as she sucked on her bottom lip. "You sound great and you sing with me. Why not sing for God?"

He needed to weed this out by the roots. "Joni, I'm trying to share my tragic childhood and you're interrupting."

Pink stained her cheeks. "Sorry. Go ahead. I'm listening."

How he wanted to hold her. He shook off the feeling and inhaled deep. "When I was little, my dad would give me a microphone and put me on the platform with him."

"You sang together?"

James had to laugh at the irony. "Not hardly. My mic was never on."

"That's funny." Joni's smile turned serious. "What happened to him?"

He swallowed as thoughts flooded his mind. Thoughts and feelings he wanted to share with Joni. "He left my mom and ran off with his backup singer." She gasped but he continued, needing to share the greatest embarrassment of his life. "It was a big church scandal. The woman wasn't married. My dad was. I was eleven."

"Where's he now?"

"A couple of months later he tried to come home, but Mom wouldn't let him. He lives alone at the family farm."

"I'm sorry." Joni's fingers brushed over the screen. "Do you need a hug?"

"Yes." He couldn't stop his grin. "Come hold me while I cry myself to sleep."

She giggled. "Nice try."

~ ~ ~

A few days later, Joni folded her jean-clad legs on the lilac bedspread and released an exaggerated sigh. Flipping the page of her English Lit book, she glanced at her laptop screen. What was taking him so long to reply to her chat request? She reread the page for the third time.

When he finally appeared, James's wet hair looked darker than normal and he'd yet to shave. She wished she could reach through the screen and smooth the coarse hairs on his chin.

His smile was tired. "Hey, beautiful. It's nice to see your smiling face."

"You're late. Rough day? Or did my other boyfriend not want to sleep?"

James rubbed a hand over the bridge of his nose. "Both."

Worried lines crinkled his forehead, and when he rolled his shoulders, Joni knew something else was wrong. "What?"

"I don't know how to tell you or what to do. Isaac was so excited. He wants to keep her."

Joni sucked in a breath and straightened. "Keep who?"

"Maybe I'd better show you." The picture blurred, and then

the hotel room refocused. Kathy's heavy eye-makeup smeared down her cheek, but it couldn't hide the green and yellow bruises covering her face.

"Is she dead?"

James huffed. "I wish."

"How can you say that about Isaac's mother? What happened to her?" *And why is she in your hotel room?* The unspoken question lingered.

"I don't know. Bad drug deal? Boyfriend roughed her up? It could be a lot of things."

The screen refocused again. James propped his head in his hand. "What do I do? I can't take off work until Thursday for our date, and I can't put her out on the street. Joni…"

She covered her lens with a finger and composed her features. Isaac stirred on the bed behind James. Swallowing the lump in her throat, she removed her finger. "You don't have to explain." She tried to smile. "You and Kathy have a child, and I won't come between you."

"No, it's not like that. Isaac's babysitter said she showed up early this afternoon and crashed." James blew out a breath and ran a hand threw his hair. "I haven't talked to her."

"Why didn't you wake her up?"

His stiff, straight lips twitched, and then the corners turned up. The smile sparkled in his eyes, and he looked like his old self again. "That's what I love about you most, your innocence. I can't wake her. It could be days before she is coherent again."

Joni didn't speak for fear of showing her ignorance. She waited for him to explain.

"Meth users cycle: binge, tweak, and crash. Get high, stay high for days, and finally their body shuts down. Bingers and tweakers can't rest, can't be still, can't eat. After they crash, it's best to let 'em sleep." He pointed at the screen. "Stop. Don't feel sorry for her. Remember Mrs. Dawn, the nice babysitter that let her in here. Three months ago, Kathy hooked up with her husband. I rented the house in Tillman's Corner to keep her away from the crew." He grimaced. "One of the wives threatened to kill her."

"Can't you talk her into rehab or something?"

"Joni, rehab is a social club. A place users and dealers meet. Three times she's been in and each time she meets new *friends*." James clasped his hands together and rested his chin on them. "Remember the night we first met, when I couldn't find Isaac? She'd left him with a dealer and went partying."

Joni gasped. "Why didn't you tell me?"

He shook his head. "That's not something you say to someone you want to impress." He winked at her, and then his eyes turned serious. "I don't want her to come between us."

"She's Isaac's mother."

His expression hardened. "She's only here because she's out of money or out of drugs. Probably both. I told you because she'll start trouble as soon as she's sober. Whatever she says, don't believe her. As soon as she wakes up, she's gone. I swear."

Was he telling the truth? James stole her breath, yet and still *she* was in his hotel room. Would he sleep with Isaac? Or Kathy?

Joni may be gullible, but she wasn't stupid. "I'm sorry, but as long as she's there…I can't talk to you." Trembling fingers ended the call.

Chapter Seven

Joni ignored the texts and calls, but his video message on the second day pierced her heart. Isaac and James waved an exuberant hello. James's tired eyes beckoned her and his whiskers were thicker than usual. "Joni, we miss you. Message us tonight. We'll be waiting."

While her laptop booted, she dashed into the bathroom and washed her face. Pausing to peek in her dresser mirror, she applied lip gloss and brushed her hair.

Kathy answered Joni's request. The evil smirk warned of trouble. "James is in the shower, but I'll be sure to tell him you called."

Isaac leapt on the bed behind Kathy and jumped up and down. "Hey, Joni. I told Daddy you still liked us. He tried to talk earlier, but Momma woke up and made him say the word you said to never say again. Then he took his beer to take a shower."

Kathy swatted his legs out from under him. "Sit down, you little brat."

Tears shimmered in Isaac's eyes. Joni wanted to reach through the computer and slap Kathy. "Don't hit him again."

Kathy whirled around and faced the webcam. "My family is not your concern."

"I'm her boyfriend, Momma." Isaac sniffed and resumed his bouncing. "She don't hurt much, Joni. Me and Daddy are tough guys."

"Shut up!" Kathy made a vulgar finger jester and the screen went blank.

Joni wanted to weep. How could a mother be cruel to a child as sweet and innocent as Isaac? Did James know how she treated him? How could he allow Kathy to hurt Isaac? Surely he could do something to stop it.

She wiped the dust off her alarm clock and set it for eight. She was new to praying, but she pleaded with the heavens for Isaac's safety. Wrestling with the uncomfortable pillow, she watched a movie alone.

Stephanie came in and tossed a bottle of water on the end of Joni's bed. "If you don't stop crying, you'll dehydrate."

"Thanks."

"No problem." Her roommate flashed a rare smile. "If your pity party wakes me up tonight, I'll smother you with your pillow."

Joni choked on the water as she thought of James. She silently prayed for peace. Finally, blessed sleep claimed her.

Her phone rang at two a.m. She blinked at James's number and answered.

"Don't hang up. I'm in front of the Kappa house. Come outside and talk to me."

Without a word, she ended the call. Careful not to disturb Stephanie, she crept downstairs in her pajama pants and tank top. So what if she hadn't brushed her hair?

James pushed off the passenger door of his truck and pulled her tight against him. Despite his warm embrace, she shivered in the cool night.

"Where are your shoes?"

She refused to answer. He opened the door, but she hesitated until the cold air forced her inside the truck.

"Scoot over." He slid in next to her, leaving the driver's seat empty, and shut the door.

Joni rubbed her hands in the heat flowing out of the vent. "Where's Kathy?"

Gentle fingers brushed through her bed-head hair. "Gone. I told you she would try to come between us. Please don't let that happen."

Not wanting to be hurt again, she resisted the hands tugging at her waist. Those same hands rubbed away the chill bumps on her upper arms and shoulders.

"You're freezing." He shifted and elbowed her back. "Sorry." His warm jacket swung around her front.

She pulled it against her chest like a blanket and tilted her head toward him. "Thank you."

His arm stretched across the back of the seat. If the sweet emotion swirling in his eyes hadn't melted her resolve, his next words would have. "Your pillow misses you." He patted his shoulder.

The instant her head touched his soft shirt her sobs erupted. Reassuring arms wrapped around her and rubbed her back. Kisses sprinkled against her hair. This was where she wanted to be. This was where she fit. Snuggled against James's side, lying half atop his chest. She wanted to stay here forever. How could she say goodbye to him and Isaac? She loved them both so much.

Reality dried her tears. She loved him? Was that why the thought of Kathy ripped out her heart? With a final sniff, she lifted her head and stared at the grape stain below his collar.

A callused thumb traced her lips. "Joni, I—"

"Where's Isaac?"

He tucked a wayward strand behind her ear and softly said, "With her."

Blood rushed through her head, making her dizzy. "No."

She reached for the handle and shoved. James didn't budge. "You have to save him. Kathy is mean and hateful."

He captured her hand and brought it to his lips. "Mrs. Addison promised to look after him. Kathy now has a free babysitter, and I bought her a phone so I can video chat with him every day. I'll give you the number."

Joni fell against him and choked on a moan.

"I didn't have a choice. Mrs. Dawn left her husband after she and Kathy talked. If I lose my job, the judge won't give me custody. I know it's not the best solution, but it's all I can do."

Joni sniffed against his shirt and inhaled his cologne.

"Shhh." He reached around her for his phone. "Look, you can see for yourself."

A few seconds elapsed before Kathy blew smoke into the screen. "What?"

James didn't hesitate. "Show me Isaac."

"He's asleep. Are you gonna call every five minutes? Because I'm tired of all the rules."

The muscled arm around Joni flexed. "Just do what I said or you'll be back on the streets before breakfast."

Joni cringed at the vocabulary coming from the speaker. The screen blurred and Kathy's movements crackled. Isaac's bedroom door focused. He flinched when Kathy jerked it open, but sighed in his sleep and rolled over. She slammed the door and glared into the phone. "There. Are you satisfied?"

James turned to Joni. "See. He's fine."

"Joni." Kathy yelled and cussed a blue streak before the call disconnected.

James's chest rumbled with laughter. "I don't think she likes you."

"The feeling is mutual." Joni snuggled into him and closed her tired, burning eyes.

A ringtone and James's deep baritone voice penetrated her dreams. "Hello." Her pillow shifted. "Yeah, sorry. I fell asleep outside Joni's sorority house."

A male voice blared through the earpiece. "You're in Mobile? Dude, it's almost six." She opened her eyes as the voice continued his tirade. "Cecil's gonna have a conniption."

James's warm lips nudged her fully awake. She stretched and then snuggled into his shoulder.

He winked at her but spoke into the phone. "Cover for me. I'll be there after lunch."

~ ~ ~

From his expression during their video chat, Joni guessed her date tonight with Trent was killing James.

"You look beautiful. Wish I was there with you." Because he missed half a day's work driving back from Mobile, he couldn't take off like they'd planned. His fingers drummed on the small table in front of him. He bit his lip and gave a pitiful, sad smile. "Call me when you get home." One hand trailed down his face. "Or not." His Adam's apple bobbed. "I mean, I trust you. I do. I really do."

Joni giggled at his apparent nervousness. "James. I'll call. Stop worrying." She blew him a kiss and severed the connection.

The night wasn't as bad as she anticipated. Despite the fact he was a little clingy and his hand loved to trail off her back, Trent acted courteous. The more he drank, the easier it became to avoid his groping. Around midnight, a drunk blonde stepped in between them and plastered her body against Trent's. Joni watched them disappear up the stairs and sighed with relief. She was tempted to wait a few hours before calling James to show him how it felt to wonder and worry, like she had when he was with Kathy, but Joni was too scared to walk alone in the dark. He answered her call before it rang and insisted on *escorting* her home.

The next morning, after she returned from Dr. Birchman's lecture, Trent waited in the common room. The look on his red face didn't put him in a good mood. "I don't appreciate you running off last night."

Joni inspected her fingernails and stepped into the room, keeping the settee between them. "I didn't run off. You went upstairs. I went home."

He crossed the room in two strides. "You tricked me into thinking she was you."

She sidestepped and took refuge in the flowered wingback chair. "You were that drunk?" His glare answered her question. "Did you seriously expect me to hook up with you? I don't do stuff like that."

Beefy fists swung loose at his sides until he towered over her. "You did with James."

She gripped the chair's arms to hide her trembling hands. "He's different."

"How? Did he tell you he loved you? That you were the only

girl for him? Did you believe him?" She turned her face away from his rancid breath. "What a joke. He lives with someone else and their kid. Why would he want Little Miss Virgin when Kathy sleeps in his bed?"

Tears stung her eyes, but she refused to let Trent see how his words hurt her. Thankfully, Candace walked in the door holding a beautiful bouquet of fuchsia roses. Green ivy trailed down a slender glass vase. "Roses for Joni." Trent rose to his full height. "Oh. You're here. I highly approve. These are beautiful."

The shock on Trent's face denied him as the sender.

Pulse racing, Joni hurried to the doorway and inhaled the sweetest perfume. The arrangement weighed more than she thought and she gripped it with both hands. On the way to the sofa the velvet petals caressed her cheek.

"Who sent my girl flowers?"

James. She hoped. The flowers and Candace's presence gave Joni the courage to speak out. "I'm not your girl and thank God last night ended the big brother thing."

Candace posed in the entryway and a half a dozen sisters peeked over her shoulder. "They're not from Trent? Then who sent them?"

Joni lied. "I have no idea."

"Duh, read the tag." Stephanie ducked under Candace's arm and strode into the room.

Holding her breath, Joni searched through the foliage for a card. Her heart thundered in her chest as she read it silently. Heat stole up her cheeks as she bit back a squeal.

Stephanie plucked the card from her hand. "Sorry about last night. Wished I could've been there. Dreaming of you always. James."

"Oh girl." Monica snapped her fingers in quick succession. "I gotta get a man like that."

"You know it, Sista." Stephanie and Monica high-fived and bumped hips down the hall. Their giggles faded with each step.

Joni replaced the card while holding the vase with one hand. She couldn't wait to tell James how beautiful they were.

A hairy fist snatched the card, shredding the delicate baby's breath.

"Stop it!" Joni reached for the vase now held over Trent's head.

His palm shoved against her chest. A collective gasp came from the doorway as Joni hit the floor. She shuddered as Trent crushed the delicate petals. She surged to her feet. "Give me back my roses!"

Trent froze. "You want him? Catch." The arrangement sailed through the air. Joni ducked but the vase clipped the corner of her left eyebrow. Glass shattered on the floor around her.

Tears blurred her vision as she slid to her knees beside the mangled roses. Someone pressed a napkin against her temple. Warm liquid oozed down the side of her face. Blood?

"He's gone." Stephanie swept Joni's hair behind her ear and dabbed at the cut. "You need stitches, and then you are filing assault charges."

"Stitches?" Joni cried out as searing pain sliced through her head. "Is it bad?"

"Don't be such a diva." Candace posed in the doorway. "You shouldn't have provoked him." She flounced out the door.

Hours later, Joni rummaged around her mother's cabinets for a vase to hold James's roses. She'd refused to go to the campus clinic before salvaging them. She touched the bandage on her temple. Thankfully the special surgical glue would prevent scarring. With her parents out of town, her afternoon move back home went unquestioned. Now, all she had to do was prevent James from seeing her face during their nightly chat scheduled in thirty minutes.

Back in her room, she rearranged the flowers and considered covering her webcam. James was smart. He'd wonder why she quit the sorority the night before the Second Degree Ceremony. There was only one thing to do. She had to tell him the truth.

"Why can't I see you?" The question wasn't a surprise. "And what happened to your roses? They look like they've been run over by a train."

She had an answer ready for him "I don't want you to see my ugliness."

He frowned on the screen. "You're beautiful and you're scaring me. Quit hiding behind the fern things."

She giggled at his description of the foliage, but winced from the pain her sudden facial movements caused.

"Joni?" He leaned close. "Where are you?"

"I quit Kappa."

He fell back in his chair and sighed. His eyes popped open. "Why?"

"Well…"

Sitting straight, he rubbed his unshaven chin.

She sucked in a breath and blurted. "Trent didn't like your roses."

His jaw clenched. "I want to see you. Move the vase."

She searched for a way to stall him. Maybe telling the truth wasn't such a good idea. "Promise you'll still think I'm beautiful?"

His smile was a tight line. "Promise."

Joni lifted the roses and set them on the dresser behind her. James's breath hitched as she looked into the screen. After adding concealer, she didn't think the bruise looked that bad. His expression made her rethink her makeup skills.

His groan broke the suspended silence. "Sweep back your hair."

She tucked her hair behind her left ear. The words exploding from James's mouth made her cringe. Steel entered into his eyes and his jaw throbbed.

She had never witnessed this side of him. She knew he'd be angry, but rage simmered in his eyes. "The nurse said it wouldn't scar, but if it does, my eyebrow should hide the worst of it."

He stood. One finger brushed the screen. "You are beautiful, but I have to go now."

"James, wait."

~ ~ ~

He kicked the door three times while buttoning his shirt. It was yanked open from the inside. A busty woman hid behind a disturbed Ray. His friend liked older women, so the fine lines around her mouth and eyes didn't surprise James.

"You want to ride with me? I need to run an errand."

"Now?" Ray held up his hands. "Dude, I'm busy here."

James turned toward the parking lot. "I won't be back till morning. Cover for me if I'm late for work."

"Again? Wait, give me two minutes." Ray sweet-talked the woman out of his room with promises of tomorrow while expounding on his loyalty to friends.

James counted the precious seconds ticking by while Ray grabbed his boots from by the door and a six-pack out of the mini fridge. During the drive South, James explained about the bruise on Joni's face.

Ray popped the top. "I knew you liked this girl, but even Brian-the-burner didn't get a special trip home."

"He would if I knew where to find him." James declined the offered beer, intending to stay alert on this trip.

"How are you going to find Trent?"

James barked a laugh and dialed Kathy's number. "Did you set up the meeting?"

"Yeah, and he doesn't know it's you. What's going on James? Since when do you volunteer to deliver candy?"

Joni's bruised face flashed through his mind. "Since I owe Trent a visit, and you are gonna make sure I get the right guy."

"He's one of my best customers. Don't screw that up. You should apologize for punching him that morning after Heather's party."

Didn't Kathy realize she'd confirmed his suspicions of her dealing? "We'll be at the house in a few hours. Don't call him until we get there."

"We?"

"Ray's with me." James accelerated around an eighteen-wheeler.

"It'll cost you a hundred."

"You've already agreed to fifty. Take Isaac to Mrs. Addison's. Tell her to keep him inside. I don't want him involved. And ask her if I can stop by to see him later." James disconnected the call.

Ray propped his foot on the dash. "You know man, I've been thinking. If you want to get rid of Kathy for good, all you gotta do is set her up. I could give my cousin a call."

He changed lanes to dodge a red Ford and gave Ray's suggestion serious thought. "Right now she's the only babysitter I've got. If she went to jail, what would happen to Isaac?"

"You worry too much. Believe me, if there's anything I can find…it's a woman. I'll get Isaac a sitter."

~~~

They were late for work the next morning. Cecil took one look at James's bloody knuckles and shook his head. "Where have you been? Sleeping it off?" James rolled the kinks out of his neck and kept silent. Cecil lifted Ray's left hand. A lone scratch ran above his wrist. "What? You didn't help your friend beat the crap out of whoever he was beating the crap out of?"

Ray grinned and shrugged his shoulders. "I prefer holding crazed women."

Cecil turned his attention to James. "Do you have anything to say for yourself?"

"Sorry we're late, sir. It shouldn't happen again."

Cecil shook his head and threw up his hands. "Just get busy."

Throughout the day, James had a tough time staying awake. At lunch, both he and Ray dozed inside the tool shed. After finally making it to his hotel room, he fell across the bed and slept till his alarm blared the next morning.

On his way to work he called Joni. "Rise and shine beautiful, it's almost time for class."

"James." Her sleepy voice never failed to amuse him. She wasn't a morning person. "Sunday School doesn't start till ten. Call me back at nine thirty." She hung up on him.

During the following week, James smiled during their video chats and pretended not to see her bruise while hiding his scraped knuckles under the table. He was glad Joni had dropped out of the sorority, but he worried about the three hours in between Dr. Birchman's lecture and her history class. Not to mention the long drive across the bay.

The Friday after she dropped out of Kappa, he could tell by her red, puffy eyes she'd been crying. "Did he bother you again?"

Her eyes were cold as stone. "I saw Kathy in the mall today. I asked about Isaac and she told me it was none of my business. She said you visited her at the house a week ago."

James didn't want her to know about his dark emotions or the way he'd dealt with Trent.

"So it's true." Her hand reached for the keypad.

"Wait." He rubbed both hands down the sides of his face. "Don't hang up. I was there, but not for the reason you think. I didn't stay."

Her beautiful chin lifted. "Then why'd you go?"

"I had business to settle." Her eyes misted and he felt like a jerk. "Please don't cry. It had nothing to do with her. I swear."

She blinked several times. "So you couldn't leave work for me, but you took off once to bring Kathy home and again to visit her a few days later? I don't think so James." Her voice broke. "And where is Isaac?"

"He's with Kathy."

"No! He's not!" Joni stood, knocking her chair over backward. "You find him James, and text if he's okay. Then I'm done. I can't handle this Kathy junk anymore. I won't!"

He covered his head and groaned as the screen turned blue. Why did Kathy screw up every good thing in his life? Even while hating her, he dialed her number. "Where's Isaac?"

"Did you have a chat with Little Miss Joni?"

"Cut the crap, and leave Joni out of it. Where is he?"

"He's at my sister's house."

James jumped out of his chair and yelled into the phone. "Like he was at *my* sister's! What have you done?"

"I got a job, you jerk. My sister agreed to babysit."

His room wasn't long enough for pacing. "Where is this mythical job? The drive-thru?"

"As a matter of fact it is. Now shut up and I'll give you Anna's number. I told her Isaac's crazy father would be in touch."

Calling himself every kind of fool for believing her, James dialed the number. A cheery female voice answered. He dropped to the edge of the bed. "Is this Anna?"

"It is. May I ask who's calling?"

"James Preston. Is my son there? Kathy said I could call."

"Oh yes. Yes, he is."

His shoulders relaxed and he fell back on the bed.

"My husband and I want you to know, we'll take good care of him. We love him like he's our own." Somehow her statement sent red flags up instead of assuring him.

He pulled one knee under him. "Could you...do you think it's possible to send some photos of you, your husband, and your house? With Isaac in them, of course. It may sound silly, but I need to know he's in a nice place."

"Anything to help alleviate your fears. Is this your cell number? I'll send them there."

The beer on the table was out of reach. He stood and took a quick swig. "Yeah. That'll be great. Put Isaac on the phone."

"Are you sure that's wise? I mean...here he is."

"Daddy."

James sagged against the wall. "Hey, buddy. How ya doing?"

"I always like it here. It's fun and they got a dog."

"I miss you." James tilted the bottle up to his mouth.

"When you coming back?"

The empty bottle bounced off the bottom of the trash can. "In a few weeks."

"Tomorrow?"

James laughed. "Yeah, tomorrow. Daddy loves you, Isaac."

"I love you, too, Daddy."

Anna came back on the line while he dug through the mini fridge for another beer. "Don't worry. I promise I'll take good care of him."

James didn't know how to approach his next subject. "If you have problems with anything"—*especially Kathy*—"call this number."

"Of course."

A twist released cold vapor from the next bottle. "Sometimes on the construction site, I can't hear it ring. Leave a message if I don't answer. Or text me."

"Relax, Mr. Preston. Isaac's fine."

~ ~ ~

With 304 social media friends you'd think Joni could find someone to talk to about James. But she couldn't. Ever since she'd joined the sorority, Marla had become distant. Joni missed her best friend. She scrolled down the chat box. Most were mere acquaintances, none of which she trusted to bare her soul. Her feelings were tangled and jumbled. No matter how much she loved James and Isaac, she couldn't deal with Kathy. She wouldn't.

A private chat message popped up.

Hi, girl. Saw you on here and wanted to invite you to church tonight. We would love to have you. Rachel Dixon was one of the girls James's mom had introduced her to at Bible Tabernacle. She'd been friendly enough, but Joni hardly knew her.

Joni replied. *James and I broke up. I couldn't go to his church.*

Lol! Why not? He doesn't. Come on. It'll be fun. What's your parents address? I'll pick you up and you can ride with me.

Maybe Rachel was the friend Joni was looking for. She typed in her address and headed for the shower. She needed to get out of the house before her mom came home and started in about next month's concert schedule.

Joni eased through the church's double oak doors. Across the foyer, James's mother elbowed his sister and they hurried her way. Joni turned to Rachel for help, but she was flirting with a guy who twirled a drum stick.

Breathe, smile, and pretend you belong here.

"Joni." The hug from Mrs. Preston knocked her off balance.

Sara was next in welcoming her. "It's good to see you. How's James?"

Joni swallowed the lie on her tongue and spoke the truth. "I don't know. We're not exactly on friendly terms at the moment."

"Oh dear." Mrs. Preston squeezed her hand. "James can be a bit bullheaded."

Sara's smile grew. "Bullheaded isn't the word I'd choose. Whatever he's done, you make sure he grovels sufficiently before forgiving him."

Mrs. Preston wagged a finger. "My goodness, Sara. Have pity on your poor brother."

"He's anything but poor, Mother. We better find our seats. Would you like to join us?"

Joni shook her head. "No, thank you."

Thankfully, Rachel walked up and Sara and Mrs. Preston crossed to the other side of the pews. "You could've sat with them, you know."

"No, really. I'm better off avoiding James's family." Joni followed her down to the front.

Once they were seated, Rachel leaned over and whispered. "If you ask me, you're better off without James. Period. Everyone knows he's a sinner. You deserve a godly man."

Joni's heart sank. Rachel wasn't the friend she was looking for after all.

The pianist played and Joni absorbed the peace in the song. What was it about church music that soothed her soul? The musicians left the platform and found seats in the congregation. Would they sing again? She hoped so.

The pastor stepped behind the wooden desk and spoke into the mounted microphone. "Tonight, God is looking for a friend. A best friend."

Joni jerked her eyes away from the baby grand. The man loosened his tie and lifted a cordless microphone.

"A friend who will tell Him all their heartaches, all their fears, all their insecurities. He's looking for a friend to walk with at day's end, to share His thoughts, His blessings, and His glory."

The speaker stepped away from the desk. The sincerity in his eyes held her captive.

"God sent me here with a question for you." Her heartbeat echoed in her throat. "And He sent you here to hear it." She leaned forward. "Will you be His friend?"

Joni nodded. Yes, she would be God's friend.

Chapter Eight

James flipped the turn signal to take the exit home. He'd gladly volunteered when Cecil asked for early layoffs. His next construction job was a shutdown in Georgia. He had three weeks to oust Kathy, to play with Isaac, and to plead with Joni.

The church bus parked at the truck stop across the highway prompted his U-turn. Churchy people drifted out of the convenience store and laughed their way across the parking lot. On the phone yesterday, Sara had gloated that not only had Joni accepted her invitation to the tent meeting tonight, but she and her friend, Marla, attended services on a regular basis.

Where was Joni?

He set the emergency brake and stepped out of the truck. His steel-toed boots clunked on the pavement. Feeling eyes on him, he turned as a group of giggling teenage girls whispered behind their hands. He ignored them and sauntered toward the door. His unbuttoned, long-sleeved welding shirt flapped against his T-shirt. Was she on the bus? He should text her.

The sight of her in a long flowing dress heated his blood as she stepped through the automatic glass doors. They hadn't spoken in days. He'd finally given up calling her, determined to make things right when he got home. Would she be glad to see him? Or slug him with the coke bottle in her hand? He stepped into her path.

Green eyes widened and then sparkled as she smiled. "James." The raspy echo of her voice caressed him.

His heart stopped but his pulse raced.

She lifted her arms and laughed as he spun her in a circle.

Soft arms wrapped around his neck.

He closed his eyes and breathed her in, grateful for whatever miracle changed her mind.

"What are you doing home?"

He released her and she hobbled on one foot. He held out his arm. "Hold on to me." A woman entering the store handed over Joni's shoe, which had landed by the newspaper rack. James placed the three-inch tall sandal between them. "I earlyed out this morning and I recognized the bus on my way home. You look beautiful."

She lifted the long skirt, held onto his arm, and slipped her foot into her sandal. She nodded at the bus and her face lit up. "We're going to see The Street Preacher. I told my friend Marla what I experienced the first time and we're curious to see if it happens to her. You wanna go?"

He wanted to throw Joni in his truck and take her as far away from church as he could. "No thanks. I need to see Isaac."

The wind blew a golden strand of hair across her face. "So, when are my boyfriends coming to see me?"

His fingers tucked the silken strand behind her ear. "How about Andrew's birthday party tomorrow?"

Her face fell. "Sara invited me, but I can't. Mom scheduled me to play in Pensacola tomorrow evening." She drew in a breath. "Candace told me what you did to Trent." She fingered a small hole in his denim work shirt. Her touch burned through to his skin. "Sorry I didn't trust you."

Though the bruises had faded, James traced the tiny scar on her temple. "I'm sorry I didn't protect you."

"Joni!" Mark stepped off the bus and jogged toward them.

She stepped away, but James kept an arm around her waist. "I may be in trouble."

He winked. "Trouble? Nah, I'll handle Mark."

"I forget he's your brother-in-law."

Mark wasn't happy. "The bus is waiting. We need to go."

"Sorry." Joni's smile made the scolding that was surely coming worth it. "Call me later."

Mark glared at James until she was out of hearing. "What are you doing?"

He swallowed against the outrage in the associate pastor's eyes and shrugged. "I'm talking to an old friend on my way home from work."

"Girls' reputations are ruined by looking at you, and a busload of people watched you twirl Joni around like a lost lover. She's new to church and vulnerable. Stay in her past, James, and let her build a future." Mark stormed away.

"I'd never hurt her." James kicked the yellow newspaper rack.

Mark called over his shoulder, "Then leave her alone."

~ ~ ~

Everyone stared in silence as Joni stepped down the aisle. Two girls whispered behind their hands as she claimed her seat. Heat crept up her neck. "Marla, why are people gawking at me?"

"You committed a carnal sin." She rolled her eyes in exaggeration toward Rachel. "You hugged James." Turning her head so only Joni could see, Marla mouthed, "Jealous."

"James is my friend."

Rachel smirked from across the aisle. "Friends don't cling. Isn't that right, Blaine?"

Two preteen girls stuck their heads up over the seat in front of her. "Has he kissed you yet? We heard he kisses dreamy. The way he spun you around, it was sooooo romantic."

"Uh…well—"

Phillip interrupted. "Stay away from him, or people will talk. He's bad news. No decent girl should be seen with him."

Of all the nerve. James was the best person she knew. "I am a decent girl. I don't mind being seen with him. He's a good friend, loves to laugh, and would do anything to help someone in need."

"He has a bastard son and lives with the boy's mother."

Joni stood in the aisle and sucked in her breath. If only she was with him now. "Isaac is not a b—" She exhaled. "He has a father that loves him." Her voice rose and drew attention, but she didn't care. "And I don't want to hear another word about James. He's my friend, so get over it."

Pastor Mark, who'd just stepped on the bus, raised his brows at her. "Really?"

Her chin lifted. He better not start in on her too. "Yes."

He blinked, smiled, and started laughing. He was snorting by the time he slid into the driver's seat.

Sara stood and held up a hand. "No more gossip about my brother or my nephew. You should all pray for them and invite them to church."

The bus motor drowned out the hubbub of conversations as Joni sank into her seat.

"I'm sorry. I've always liked James even though he is a sinner." Rachel smiled an apology. "I can't believe you've met Kathy. What's she like?"

Mean, cruel, and hateful were the words that jumped in Joni's mind. But she couldn't speak any of those things. "She's pretty."

"Figures. And she's your friend too."

Joni fiddled with her purse straps. "Uh, no. She doesn't like me." She sent Marla a pleading look and they exchanged seats, putting Joni by the window.

Marla nudged her and teased. "Girl, why didn't you tell me he was in love with you?"

"Hush. Someone will hear. And I told you, James is my friend." Joni's phone chimed. She unzipped her purse. It chimed again. Her pulse accelerated. James had texted her.

Hey beautiful. Marks not happy with me. Sorry I embarrassed you. Hes right. You shouldnt be seen with a bum like me.

James worked hard. He most definitely wasn't a bum.

Dont say that. Im not embarrassed. I missed talking to you.

Missed you too. Have fun tonight.

Joni blinked back tears as she reached for her purse.

"Was that James?" Rachel peered around Marla.

Joni put the phone away. "It's private."

The twins popped up in the seat in front of them. "James texted you?"

God forgive her lie. "No, it was someone else."

~ ~ ~

James sighed as he drove out of the parking lot. Was Mark right? Did knowing him give Joni a bad reputation? His family name had its black marks and Kathy did live in the rental house. For now. He should let Joni go. No more texting. Or chatting. And no more dreams of silky strands of gold.

Ray's truck was parked in the driveway but his latest girlfriend, Chloe, stood in the open door of the house, crying.

"What's wrong?"

"Kathy's stoned and Isaac's not here."

A black hand gripped his heart. Ray stood over Kathy, who was curled in a ball on the floor. James stormed in the house and snatched Kathy up by her arm. Her eyes were glazed over. "Where is Isaac?" He shook her. "Where is he?" She blinked incoherently.

He swore and fought the urge to slap her. Instead, he dragged her down the hall and shoved her into the shower. He twisted on the cold water.

"Thank you." Kathy fell to her knees but lifted her face into the icy spray.

"Ugh!" The shower door bounced open after James slammed it. The plexi-glass vibrated water onto the floor.

Ray and Chloe stopped in the doorway. "She tell you anything?"

James rubbed the bridge of his nose and shook his head. "She doesn't know she's in this world."

"Let me try," said Chloe.

"Have at it." In the hall, James slouched against the wall and kicked the sheetrock. How could he have been so stupid? How could he have believed her? "Isaac, where are you?"

"Duh, he's at the sitters." A skinny, brown-haired guy shut the front door. "Kat! Baby, I'm home."

Ray's jaw dropped.

James shook his head. "Wait." They followed the pimp into the kitchen. "Isaac is at Anna's?"

"Yeah." He turned one of the knobs on the electric stove. "Where's Kat?"

James held his hand out backward.

Ray took the hint and propped in the doorway.

"She's in the shower." The deadbolt was engaged in the gap between the backdoor and the frame. "Why is Isaac at Anna's at seven thirty on a Friday night?"

The intruder's eyes darted from James to Ray and then back to James. His hand trembled as he bent down and lit a cigarette on the red hot stove. "Look." Smoke circled his head. "I don't know who you are or what you're doing in Kat's house, but Isaac's daddy paid the sitter before he left town. Isaac's been there ever since."

James sucked in a breath as a picture of Granny demanding food-stamp money flashed through his mind. But the Todds were good people. Isaac was safe. Unless child services picked him up for abandonment. James groaned.

"What's Isaac to you?"

"I'm his father."

"Oh dude, why didn't you say so?" He switched the cigarette into his left hand and stuck out his right. "Name's Brian."

The crack of nose cartilage didn't stop James from pounding his fists into the idiot that dared to hurt his son. Brian crashed into the table and curved into a ball on the floor. His arms covered his head as steel-toed boots slammed into his ribs.

"Don't kill him." Ray's calm voice intruded on the insanity raging through James.

He dropped his knee into the center of Brian's back and struggled for control. Using his full weight, he kept the child abuser pinned to the floor. The stove eye burned red hot. He yanked Brian up by his shirtfront and slammed his back across the lit stove.

"Aaaaah!" Brian flailed wildly but James held him as long as he could. Brian collapsed on the floor. Flames licked the back of his tattered shirt. The stove's imprint imitated a six-inch cigarette burn.

Ray gagged and stumbled backward. The smell of singed flesh mingled with burnt cotton. Chloe rushed in. Her eyes widened. She covered quivering lips with a trembling hand. "I can't stay here. Please Ray. Don't make me stay here."

James used a booted foot to roll Brian over. The flames suffocated. Unmistakable agony covered his face. "Remember this the next time you think about touching Isaac."

"You're a monster." The look in Chloe's eyes would forever haunt James. "How could you do that to another human?"

He looked to Ray for help. His friend lifted his eyebrows. "It's okay, babe. The guy was a meth user. Probably didn't feel a thing."

A pitiful moan floated up from the floor.

Chloe gawked at Ray. "How can you defend him?"

Ray shrugged. "Dude had it coming." Chloe ran down the hall. With a shake of his head, Ray rolled his eyes and followed.

A sleazy girl and Heather, slid to a stop inside the doorway. She swore at James. "What have you done?" She helped Brian to his feet and pulled his arm over her shoulder. "Come on. Let's get out of this crazy house. Lauren, find Kathy. She's not safe here."

James laughed at the irony. "No, she's not. Take her stuff with you. And when she comes down, make sure she knows she doesn't live here anymore." Brian and Heather hobbled across the living room and out the front door.

Lauren's screech echoed from the bathroom. "Poor baby, you'll probably have pneumonia." She led a soaked, zombified Kathy up the hall.

Kathy tilted her head. "Bye-bye, James."

Pathetic. But he couldn't help feeling sorry for her. He held open the door and allowed them to pass. On the porch, he waited until their taillights disappeared around the curve.

While dialing Anna's number, James walked back to the kitchen. He stomped the small flames eating a hole in the linoleum as her sleepy voice answered.

"Is Isaac there?"

"James, he's asleep. Call back in the morning. You can talk to him then."

He leaned against the counter and ran a shaky hand through his hair. "But he is there? With you?"

Her sigh was short and loud. "Yes. Now, goodnight."

The phone reverted back to his home screen.

What kind of babysitter hung up on a parent? A lot of things didn't add up, but one thing was for certain. Isaac wouldn't stay with Anna again.

The stove was on. He turned it off and stepped over the charred mark on the floor. Brian's cries for mercy resounded in the back of his mind. Needing to escape the reality of his actions, James walked out of the house toward his truck. One smile from Joni would shed some light on his dark world.

~ ~ ~

At the roadside park, James reclined against his truck hood. Under the tent, a hundred yards away, The Street Preacher gave a call for repentance. James scanned the near empty seats and found Joni close to the front. Never taking his eyes off her, he slipped his phone from his pocket.

Hey beautiful. I need a hug. He sent the text and watched for her reaction.

She dug through her purse. From this distance, he couldn't see her facial expression, but she jerked her head around and stared toward him. The tension in his shoulders relaxed as he read her reply. *Where are you?*

Parking lot.

Joni slipped out of her seat and walked out of the tent while the brunette beside her fought the crowd to the altar.

His phone vibrated in his hand. *Where?*

Beside the church bus. He shoved his cell in his pocket and watched her walk into the shadows. Her phone illuminated her angelic face. He slid off the truck. His heart rate accelerated with her every step. "Joni."

Her smile and open arms welcomed him. The guilt vanished. He crushed her against his chest and swirled her around in circles. Her giggles were music to his soul. The flowery scent of her hair intoxicated him. Eyes closed, he breathed her in. "Joni." His eyes opened. Her arms were wound around his neck and her body was pressed close. She was too good for him. Reluctantly, he set her on her feet.

"Ouch." She stepped up on his steel-toed boots. "My feet."

In the dark, he couldn't see what caused her pain. "What's wrong?"

She teetered. Her hands gripped the lapels of his shirt.

His arms balanced her against him. "Are you hurt?"

The tension in his muscles eased at her giggle. "I lost my shoes mid-twirl." She giggled again. "And that gravel is sharp."

"Those flippity-flappity heels?" He bit his lip to keep from kissing her. She should be under the tent praying, but surely no one would miss her during the chaotic altar service.

"Yes." She shifted her weight against him.

They couldn't stay in their current position. After what he did tonight, he didn't deserve the angel in his arms. "Hold on to me."

"I won't let go." Her hands clenched his biceps.

"I'm gonna walk backwards. You can sit on the tailgate while I find your shoes."

"Don't drop me."

A moonbeam peeked from behind the clouds. Trust filled her green eyes. "I won't," he vowed. Without breaking eye contact, he stepped back with his right leg. "One…" The length of her dress shortened his stride. He smiled down at her. "Two…" Left foot. "Three…don't look at me like that."

"It's like dancing." She snuggled against him.

Wavering at her touch, he lost count.

"Only better." Soft arms wound around his waist.

He couldn't breathe. Reaching around her, he dropped the tailgate. She scooted onto the seat. Her hand trailed down his arm as he backed away. His arms ached at the loss of her. She released a ragged breath.

He slipped out his phone and touched the screen. Using it as a flashlight, he found one shoe halfway under the truck and the other four feet from it. "You're gonna break your neck in these things." But oh, he loved the way they looked on her.

"You sound like Isaac. Did you find them?"

"Yeah, hold this." He handed her the phone, brushed the gravel dust off one of the shoes, and knelt before her. "Left." Caressing her soft ankle, he slid the shoe over her bare foot. It fell to the ground. "What?" He picked it up and tried again but gravity reclaimed the sandal.

Joni's sweet laugh soothed his irritation. "Some prince charming you are."

He frowned up at her. "This is not a glass slipper. It's not even a whole shoe. There's no heel." A few swipes of his hand leveled the gravel where he placed both shoes.

Her laughter blossomed.

"They're half-shoes." He laid the phone on the ground so she could see to step into them. "With spikes."

With one hand on his shoulder, she wobbled once and regained her balance. "Thank you, Sir Knight." Her sweet kiss landed on his cheek.

Tonight, in his anger, he'd set a man on fire. He wasn't an honorable knight or a charming prince, but Joni didn't need to know that. "You better go. People are probably looking for you."

Her smile faded in the moonlight. "Are you coming?"

"No, and you shouldn't be seen coming from the parking lot."

"I don't care what they think." Joni wrapped her arms around his waist and tilted her face upward. "I told everyone on the bus we were friends and dared anyone to say anything about it."

Only Joni would stand up for his black soul. "Thank you." A gentle breeze caressed the gauzy fabric of her skirt. "Jesus looks good on you."

"You think so?" She held the sides of her dress and twirled.

He couldn't stop his smile. "Yeah, but those flippity-flappity shoes have got to go." A group of people walked toward the parking lot. "Get out of here before I throw you in my truck and steal you away."

She kissed the underside of his jaw before shuffling through the gravel. Once she hit the sidewalk, the sway of her hips mesmerized him and he realized why he let her go when everything in him screamed to hold her near. He loved her, and if anyone deserved to go to heaven, it was Joni. "I'm in deep trouble."

"Yes, you are."

He jerked his head around. His brother-in-law stood between the church bus and his truck. James swallowed. How long had he been listening? "Mark."

"You asked Joni to meet you out here?" The frown on his face wasn't brotherly.

James leaned against the tailgate.

"There's a name for girls who follow guys into the shadows."

His fists clenched at his sides. "Don't. Joni's not like that." He couldn't let Mark think the worst. "She's not like me."

Mark's hard gaze never wavered. "What would happen if Cole or Phillip knew she was out here with you? Would they believe she was good and innocent?"

James shoved away from the truck and widened his stance.

"Or do you suppose they'd think…they could be next?"

Chapter Nine

At one thirty, James coasted his truck into Sam and Anna's driveway. The lights were out and the house slept. A blue, child-sized bicycle lay haphazardly on the lawn. Maybe, he should have waited until morning. A dog barked in the backyard while James contemplated his choices. A light flicked on and a robe-clad Sam appeared on the porch. The decision made for him, James stepped into the night. "I know Anna wanted me to wait, but I just learned that Isaac's been here for the whole time."

The balding man led him indoors. "How could you not know? You called every day."

James knocked the dirt off his boots before stepping into the ceramic-tiled foyer. "Yes, but I thought Kathy picked him up in the evening and brought him back the next morning."

"We haven't seen her since she dropped him off."

"Where is he?"

Anna descended the stairs. Both she and her husband mirrored the pictures sent to James's phone. She crossed her arms and blocked his access to Isaac. "I told you. He's asleep."

"Wake him up." An uneasy feeling settled in his gut. Something wasn't right here.

"Follow me." Sam pulled Anna aside. "Make some coffee, honey. We're gonna need it." He led James up the carpeted stairs to a little boy's dream room.

Inhaling the fresh scent of paint, James feasted his eyes on his son. Isaac was curled up next to Bunkie on a pirate ship bed. James kissed his cheek and whispered. "Daddy loves you."

Sam shifted his feet in the doorway. "Let him sleep and come downstairs for a minute. I want to talk to you about something before you take him."

Why did they agree to keep Isaac? Judging from the expensive furnishings in the house, they didn't need the money. Sam hadn't looked James in the eye since he opened the door. What had Kathy done? "All right. We'll talk."

Downstairs, Sam flipped on the dining room light. "Have a seat."

James remained standing. "Tell me what I owe you and we'll be on our way."

"Did you know I'm an attorney?"

James's heart stopped. So they didn't do it for money. "No, sir."

"I want to offer you my legal services."

James breathed out slowly. "Why?"

Sam clasped his hands on the table. Glasses magnified the emotion swimming in his eyes. "Until a moment ago, I didn't realize you loved him. Haven't you wondered about us?"

James's gut churned. He didn't like where this conversation was going. "Kathy said Anna was her sister. I didn't believe it."

Sam shrugged and shook his head. "I can't blame you."

"How *do* you know Kathy? And why would you think I didn't want my son?" James clenched his jaw and prepared himself for the worst.

Anna balanced three coffee mugs as she walked into the room. She set them on the table and spoke directly to James. "Kathy is my half-sister."

The blow stole James's breath. "How's is that possible? She's twenty and you're…?"

"Fifty-three." She sipped from her cup and continued. "My dad had an affair during a midlife crisis. Kathy's birth broke my mother's heart. We knew she existed. Sent money every month. Dad would visit her once a year, but we didn't talk about it. He died of a heart attack twelve years ago. Mom couldn't deal with things, so she offered Kathy's mother a settlement."

James tilted his head. "Then how did she find you?"

"I don't know. She showed up about five years ago. Claimed she wanted to get to know her big sister, but she robbed us blind. She didn't have Isaac then." Her eyes shifted to the floor.

"There's more. Tell me all of it."

Anna inhaled sharply and looked him in the eye. "I can't have children. When Isaac was six months old, Kathy knocked on our door again. She agreed to let us keep him."

The earth shifted, and James longed to shut out her next words.

"She signed consent for us to adopt, but the judge required the biological father's permission as well. Kathy named you as the father, but claimed she didn't know where to find you. About a year ago, she was supposed to get your signature, but she disappeared with Isaac. We didn't see her again until six weeks ago."

"How much did you pay her?"

Sam shifted his glasses. "Child trafficking is illegal…"

James's fist landed on the table between them. "How much?"

"Ten thousand dollars."

He swore. "You wasted your money. My son is not for sale." He retraced his previous path to the room Isaac slept in. The fresh paint had new meaning given Anna's revelation.

"Isaac." He cradled him close and turned for the stairs.

"Daddy! You're home!"

Little arms clung to his neck and he swore no one would take away his son. He'd kill Kathy first. He hardened his heart against Anna's sobs and stormed out the door with Isaac.

Ray had a beer waiting when he returned to the house. "You look like you need this."

With Isaac tucked safely in bed, James drained the bottle in two gulps and reached for another. "Call your cousin."

"The one that works on the drug task force?"

"Yeah." James collapsed in the recliner and twisted the top off the bottle. "Tell him about Kathy's deliveries via the local drive-thru and whatever else he wants to know."

"Are you sure? She is Isaac's mother."

James scrubbed a hand down his face. "I'm sure."

~ ~ ~

The next morning, James stopped by a toy store and let Isaac choose a gift for Andrew. While they waited for the present to be wrapped, they bought Isaac a new toy truck.

On the drive across the causeway, Isaac chattered about the party. Guilt slammed James. Next year, Isaac would have more than a store-bought cake served with chips and beer.

Isaac dropped his truck on the floorboard and wrinkled his forehead. "Where's Joni? Is she with us?"

"She's busy. Maybe we'll see her tomorrow." Vehicles packed his sister's drive. Hopefully, Mark wouldn't say anything about last night.

Isaac unbuckled himself and hefted the blue-wrapped box. The paper ripped as he dragged it up the sidewalk, but he refused help. James opened the front door and held it for him.

"There's grandma's darling."

Isaac was snatched up in a hug and made a face. He wiggled down and propped his arms on his cousin's gift. "Where's the party? Where's Andrew?"

"Sorry we're late." James hugged his sister and kissed his mom's cheek.

"It's okay. I'm glad you made it home in time for Andrew's birthday." Sara lifted Isaac and carried him and the package toward the backdoor. "He's waiting for you out on the patio."

James's mother clung to his arm and led him to the couch. "Sit with me and tell me what's got you frowning."

"Kathy's sister paid ten grand in hopes of adopting Isaac." The words jumped out of his mouth without thought.

His mother sucked in a breath. "How could a parent contemplate such an idea? You didn't agree, did you?"

"No." James propped his feet up on a blue ottoman that matched the couch. "They can't do anything without my signature. I told 'em they wasted their money. I'll never sign."

"Thank God." She patted her hair. "James, you've been reluctant to accept my help, but that's what families are for. I know you want to be a good father, but I'm a nice grandma."

"Thanks Mom. I've got three weeks before my next shutdown. Monday, I'll call my attorney and see what's holding up the custody issue. We're moving out of the house. I don't want Kathy to know where we are. Technically, we have to stay in Mobile County, but can we stay with you until we find an apartment?"

"Of course you can. No need to ask. I pray for you and Isaac daily."

He stood and kissed his mother's cheek. "That's not necessary. I've got everything under control. Now let's go eat some cake and ice cream."

He looped his arm across his mom's shoulders as they strolled out to the party. The few people he knew, he greeted by name, and then escaped from Mark's piercing scowl to a lone chair away from the crowd. When James finished eating, he dropped his empty plate into a black garbage bag and walked to the kid table to check on Isaac. Andrew's birthday cake was smeared all over his son's fingers. A lady handed him a baby wipe.

"Hold still." Isaac needed soap and water. The wet square was a joke. He'd never be clean. James's hand halted in midair as Joni walked through the patio door carrying a frilly gift bag.

Her stage makeup was flawless. Her hair was slicked back and twisted on the back of her head. A stick of a woman in her mid-fifties followed.

Sara waved her over to the adult table. "Joni, you made it."

"I can't stay." She placed her offering with the others on the table. "But I wanted to give Andrew his gift." Joni introduced her mother to his mom while her eyes searched the crowded plastic-covered tables. Was she looking for him?

"That's our girlfriend!"

James shoved the disposable wipe across Isaac's mouth a few seconds too late. Her smile tripped his pulse. Isaac escaped and barreled around the table. She knelt and stretched out her arms.

Wanting to avoid a disaster, James said, "Be careful, he's sticky."

She lifted him into her arms anyway.

Andrew piped up. "She's not your girlfriend."

"She is too. Ain't that right, Daddy?" His son's words caused a lull in the adult conversation, and the kids' attention was keen on the argument between the two boys.

James searched for something to say. He wanted to claim Joni as his, but he'd embarrassed her enough.

She turned bright red and stepped toward the house. "Isaac, let's go wash your hands."

"Joni, dear. We don't want to be late."

"It's okay, Mom. I'll just be a minute."

Isaac wrapped his sticky hands around her neck. "Aren't you my girlfriend?"

James held his breath.

"Of course I am." She kissed his cheek and smoothed his hair.

Isaac turned back and stuck his tongue out at Andrew. "Told you."

James sighed with relief and poured himself a glass of coke. The adults stared at him, especially Mark and Joni's mother. He swallowed and abandoned his plastic cup. "Excuse me. I'd better help clean Isaac."

In the house, he followed the sounds of running water to the half bath under the stairs. His fears were confirmed when Isaac said, "Sure you can. Ray's girlfriend sleeps in his room. You can take turns sleeping with me and Daddy."

His loudmouthed son stood on the closed toilet lid, while Joni washed his face. Her cheeks resembled the red towel in her hand.

Isaac spotted James and held up his arms. "She won't live wif us."

He lifted his son and sighed at his bluntness. "No. I guess not."

"But we can look at her on the computer."

Great. James held his smile and set the blabbermouth on his feet in the doorway. "Go play with Andrew."

"But Daddy..."

"Now, Isaac."

"See you tomorrow, Joni." Isaac reached on his tiptoes and she bent and kissed him.

Isaac grinned out the door.

James shuffled his feet. "I'm sorry if he embarrassed you. He's only four."

Her giggle danced in his ears. "It's okay. That's what little boyfriends are for."

"I'm glad you're here. I thought you couldn't make it."

"I can't stay. We're on our way to Pensacola." Her smile blinded him. "But I don't play until six and I wanted to see you."

"I wanted to see you, too." He stepped into the small space and caressed her hair. A huge glob of icing clung to the silky strands at her temple. "Isaac left his mark on you." He reached around her and snagged the hand towel. "You have icing in your hair."

Her giggle made him smile.

"Hold still." He took his time removing the icing and stood as close to her as possible. With one hand under her chin, he titled her head left then right. He leaned in for a kiss.

Sara's voice interrupted from the kitchen. "Joni, your Mom asked me to hurry you along." The unmistakable suction of the freezer door followed.

Joni swallowed and exhaled a ragged breath. "I have to go. Mom's not a patient person."

"Right." James stepped aside but Joni's arm brushed his.

She glanced over her shoulder and he watched until the door hid her from his sight. Seeing Joni stirred a hunger in him. He knew he should let her go but... He brought out his phone and texted her. *Have dinner with me tonight.*

He paced the floor until she replied, *Cant. Wont get back until late.*

At least she didn't outright say no. He tried again. *Tomorrow? Sunday. Church. Come with me.*

James slapped his phone against his palm. Could he do it? What if conviction fell? He didn't want anything to do with God, but if that's what it took to spend time with her, he'd survive. *You'll sit with me and let me buy lunch afterward?*

Yes. Bring my other boyfriend with you.

James decided not to tell his mother or sister. He didn't need anyone preaching at him before the service.

After the party, on the way to his mom's, he and Isaac sneaked by the mall and bought identical suits. It had been a while, but James knew how to dress for the church crowd.

The next morning, Joni waited in the church foyer. Her smile greeted them. "There's my handsome boyfriends. I was afraid you'd changed your mind."

Isaac reached for her and she hugged him close. Walking down the aisle, James leaned near and whispered, "Where's my hug?"

Red-faced, Joni slipped in the pew. "Don't tempt me while I'm in church."

Isaac crawled into his surprised grandmother's lap. James stretched his legs and smiled as Joni bit her bottom lip. He covered her hand resting on the pew. He turned it over and traced the lines of her palm before threading his fingers with hers. "You insisted on coming here."

She smiled and shook her head. "Hush. The service is starting."

The pastor titled his message "The Unexpected Blessings of God." When he issued an invitation to pray, Joni led James down front and he knelt beside her.

For the first time in years, he spoke directly to his Heavenly Father. *You know I'm only here for Joni. If you want to bless someone, bless her. She deserves them. I don't.*

He tarried until he thought enough time had passed before he stood. Quickly walking up the aisle, he waited for her near the door.

~ ~ ~

The hostess led them through a beaded curtain to a room filled with hanging sombreros and tequila bottles. Latin music danced through the speakers hidden in the ceiling. She stopped at a middle table. "Is this fine?"

James nodded at the corner. "Actually, Isaac does better in a booth."

She smiled and gathered the menus. "Follow me."

"Would you like a booster seat?" Though the question was aimed at Joni, James answered. "No thanks, he wouldn't sit in it anyway."

Isaac climbed in beside Joni. James slid in opposite of them and removed the bottle of hot sauce from little hands. "Behave."

Joni opened the three-pack of crayons and Isaac doodled on the kids menu as James reached for his ringing phone.

"Hello?"

"James Preston?" The unfamiliar voice held no emotion.

"Yeah. Who is this?" He turned the receiver away from his mouth and gave the waitress his drink order.

"I'm calling on behalf of Kathleen Davies…" Papers shuffled in the background.

Joni caught his gaze. "Can Isaac have caffeine?"

"Hold on." He held the phone down and answered Joni. "Yeah. Order him a cheese quesadilla and get me the steak and shrimp fajitas." He lifted the cell phone to his ear and tuned out the waitress. "Who are you and what do you want?"

"I'm sorry, sir. What I'm about to disclose is confidential information. I need to make sure I have the right person."

"You have the right person. What has she done now?"

Across the table, Joni lifted a brow. James covered her hand with his and winked. He wouldn't let anything come between them.

The voice on the phone continued. "Kathleen was arrested last night for possession with the intent to distribute. I'm a local bondsman. Her bond was set at one hundred thousand dollars. You can come by my office or I can meet you at Metro. I require ten percent, cash or cashier's check only, and then I'll start the process of getting her released."

"She's in jail?" James picked up Isaac's red crayon and wrote Kathy's name on a paper napkin for Joni to see. "That's the best news I've heard in months."

The bail bondsman didn't give up. "Mr. Preston, Mobile Metro is not a pleasant place. And might I remind you, Thursday is Thanksgiving."

"I don't care. There's no way I'm paying ten thousand dollars to bail her out, but thanks for the information." He pocketed his phone with a smile and accepted his drink from the waitress. When she was gone, he kissed Joni's fingers. "Do you know what this means?"

Her eyes sparkled across the table. "Yes. God's unexpected blessings are real."

~ ~ ~

Three hours. Not enough time to shop and too much time to spend in the library dodging the unwanted advances of the super intellectuals. Joni stepped off the sidewalk as a speed demon on a bike raced past. Relaxing at the Kappa house for the lapse between classes wasn't an option since she'd moved out. Maybe she'd drive to the park and watch the ducks from the warmth of her car. With a destination in mind, her feet quickened their pace and then stumbled to a halt.

James. He jumped off her car's hood and jogged toward her. She met him halfway. Slivers of gold flamed in his brown eyes. Joni shivered as his gaze zeroed in on her mouth.

Stretching on tiptoe, Joni pressed her lips against his. His mouth devoured hers and she melted. She clung to his shoulders to stay upright. "James." She wanted another kiss, but he looped an arm around her shoulder and led her a few spaces down.

The truck door creaked open. Gentle fingers lifted her chin. "Get in before you freeze."

She mumbled something and climbed in the truck.

With a wink, he closed her door, and she turned on her phone. Trembling hands scrolled through her text messages. She smiled as she read three from James.

He slid under the wheel, started the truck, and flipped the heater on high. Scooting across the seat, she linked her arm through his and pressed her lips against his sleeve. He kissed the top of her head and shifted into reverse.

Music played softly and she was content to snuggle against his side for the next fifteen minutes. As long as she was with James, their destination didn't matter. Until he pulled into an apartment complex off Hillcrest Road.

"What are we doing?" Joni voiced her thoughts without thinking.

He parked in front of the office and shut off the engine. "Apartment shopping." The flash of his pearly whites sent her pulse dancing.

"You and me?" He couldn't be serious. "We're apartment shopping?"

"Yep."

She stared unseeing at the dashboard until he opened her door and tugged on her hand. Her shoes stuck to the concrete. James lifted one brow and studied her. "The apartment is for Isaac and me, but you can move in anytime you want."

"Oh." She breathed a sigh of relief as her hands slipped around his neck and played in his hair. "I knew that."

He dipped in for a kiss and then winked. "We are fifteen minutes from campus."

Heat crept up her face. "Stop teasing."

"Who says I'm teasing?"

They walked hand in hand into the rental office. "I'm James Preston. We have an appointment."

The lady smiled from her desk. "You're late."

He flashed his flirty smile. "Sorry, couldn't be helped. Joni's professor likes to hear himself talk."

The manager waved a ringed hand at the two empty chairs in front of her desk. "Please."

James kept Joni's hand secure in his as she perched on the edge of her seat.

"I have an apartment available the thirtieth of November. From what you've told me, it'll be perfect for you. It's across from the playground and pool. Would you like to see it?"

At his nod, the manager opened her desk drawer and selected a key. "This way."

His arm came around Joni's shoulder and a kiss landed on her temple as they followed the short-haired woman out the door and down the sidewalk.

"We have an Olympic-size and a two-foot kiddie pool." Wedge heels clicked as she moved on. "Playground."

The smell of fresh paint wafted along in the breeze. At least the maintenance was good. Joni pressed close against James's side. "I can picture Isaac playing here."

He stopped on the sidewalk and watched a woman push a toddler on the swings. "Yeah, he needs more kid time."

The manager had crossed the street. James's arm slid from Joni's shoulder and tugged on her hand. They quickly caught up and Mrs. Efficient led them up wooden steps. The maroon paint flaked but the stairs were sound. At the top, a concrete walkway led to two apartments. One on the left. One on the right. She turned to the left and inserted the key.

Joni missed James's simple touch as he released her hand and reached for the smaller door on the outside. "Is this for storage?"

"Yes." The manager smiled again and unlocked that door as well.

He leaned in and flipped a switch. A light flicked on overhead. "Hmph." He turned the light off and shut the door.

"The apartment opens to the living area. The carpets will be cleaned next week."

Joni kept silent as the lady showed them a simple floor plan. One floor of her parents' home was bigger than the entire apartment. Standing in the walk through closet between the full bath and the master bedroom, the lady addressed Joni. "There are washer and dryer hookups in here, if, you can afford to lose the closet space. Otherwise, we have a coin laundry on the backside of the pool house."

Joni stuttered a reply. "Oh, I won't be living here." The lady ignored her comment and marched up the hall. Joni blew out a breath and shrugged. "She didn't believe me."

James coughed in his hand. "I like it. What do you think? You ready to move in?"

Without a word, she walked off and left him standing alone. In the second bedroom, she opened the closet. It was tiny. James propped in the doorway.

Joni surveyed the room. "Does Isaac have a twin bed?"

"Yeah, why?"

"'Cause, I don't think you could get a full in here and have room for him to play."

Strong arms wrapped around her. "Joni, he's used to a hotel. He'll love this." He kissed her cheek. "Come on. There's one more thing I want to check before we decide."

The hall was too narrow for them to walk side by side. He let her go first. "Where am I going?"

"To the kitchen."

The tiny galley kitchen wasn't much bigger than the hall. "What are we looking for?"

"This." James reached around her and opened the dishwasher. "A new model. In pretty good shape." He latched the door and wrinkled his nose. "I hate washing dishes."

The lady peeked around the corner. "Are we done here? I need to get back to the office."

James held up a hand and flashed his smile. "One more minute."

The lady nodded and said, "I'll wait outside."

Joni turned back to James. He smiled down at her, waiting. "What?"

"Do you like it?"

She shrugged. "It's a little small, but it's clean and has all the necessities. I'm sure you and Isaac will make lots of memories here."

He caressed her cheek. "You know I'm on the road a lot."

She tilted her face upward. "Yes."

His arms looped about her waist. "Did I mention it's fifteen minutes from campus?"

She stared at the scarred linoleum. "James, we've been through this."

He tilted her chin up and flashed a boyish smile. "I'll need someone to check my mail and keep an eye on the place. You could use a quiet place to study during the day."

She swallowed the lump in her throat. He wasn't asking her to move in. She wasn't sure if she was disappointed or relieved. "You mean like Mrs. Addison did for the house?"

His smile widened. "Yes, you'll be the next Mrs. Addison." He chewed on his bottom lip until a snicker escaped him.

She laughed at the goofy grin on his face. "James, you're horrible."

He tugged on her hand and walked past the lady out the door. "We'll take it."

Chapter Ten

James knocked on Joni's backdoor at four Saturday morning. The Friday after Thanksgiving, she had abandoned him to shop with her friends. With apartment shopping, DNA testing and Thanksgiving, James had yet to hit the woods, and deer season had been in for a week. He'd missed opening day for Andrew's party.

Like a vision, she appeared in the entryway. He sucked in a whistle of admiration and shoved his hands in his jacket pockets. Form-fitting jeans, tucked into knee-high boots, rode low on her hips. "Joni, you look beautiful, but…"

Lifting one brow, he stepped into the warm house and closed the door. Heels? The flimsy knit hat and scarf wouldn't stop the wind from slicing through her, and the white shirt had to go. A deer could spot her from three hundred yards away. "That's not what I had in mind when I said old, warm clothes."

She propped a hand on her hip and looked down at her jeans. "What's wrong with my outfit? You don't like it?"

The hurt in her eyes propelled him forward. He tucked her hair behind her ear and trailed his hand down her arm. Hooking a thumb in her belt loop, he tugged her close. "I love it." His lips grazed hers once, twice. "But you'll freeze when we get in the deer stand. And if you have a darker shirt? Several of them. Maybe some sweatpants to go over your jeans?"

Her arms locked around his waist, but she shook her head. "I don't need all that. I have a leather coat."

"He's right." At the sound of the masculine voice, James froze.

She looked over his shoulder and smiled. "Good morning, Daddy."

Daddy? Oh, not good. James slowly stepped away from her. Through the blurred image on the stainless steel refrigerator, she kissed her father's cheek. James was a grown man not a teenager picking up his prom date. He turned and held out his hand. "Mr. Maher."

"Call me Bill." Her dad's grip was firm but not tight. "I've heard a lot about you." He scratched his bald head. "You know, Joni isn't outdoorsy."

"Daddy…" Joni straightened her father's flannel robe collar. Her dad was old, at least sixty. "We talked about this last night. Remember?"

"Yeah, yeah." Mr. Maher turned his daughter toward the stairs. "Go change your shirt. Wear something green or brown."

She stopped on the bottom step and looked over her shoulder. "I'll be right back."

If she didn't hurry they would be late. Mr. Maher shuffled over to the dining table and opened a canvas bag. "I dug through my old things. Afraid I don't have any gloves."

"I bought her a pair." Relieved she wouldn't freeze, James sized up the camouflage coveralls in Mr. Maher's hand. The orange vest wasn't needed. He had a ton of them. "How do I convince her to wear these?"

Mr. Maher's slippered feet crossed the kitchen. "That's your problem. Coffee?"

"No sir, we really need to get going." James glanced up the stairs. No Joni. He checked his watch and tapped his foot.

Four thirteen.

"You stalk hunting? You mentioned a deer stand."

James accepted the ceramic mug Mr. Maher thrust in his hand. "This morning. After lunch we're running dogs."

"Keep her close to you. She's never been in the woods. Her mother has spoiled her and Joni's used to being pampered."

"Yes, sir." James thought her mother locked Joni away from the world, but he was smart enough not to voice his opinion.

The coffee was strong and hot. He burned his tongue as Joni descended the stairs.

Her fuzzy green sweater hugged her curves and her sleepy smile beckoned him to her side. "I'm ready."

Mr. Maher cleared his throat behind him and squashed James's desire for a kiss. He helped Joni with the leather coat and threaded his fingers through hers. "Let's go." He lifted the bag from the table on their way to the door.

"Bye, Daddy."

"Have fun, honey."

In the truck, she shivered and he turned up the heater. "You've never been up this early before, have you?"

Joni yawned and looped her arm through his, snuggling close. "Yesterday, when I went shopping with the girls."

He backed out of the drive and drove through the town of Daphne. "Joni?"

"Yeah?"

"How old is your father?"

Her burst of laughter was interrupted by a second yawn. "Sixty-two." The hand caressing his arm stilled. He glanced down into serious eyes. "There's something I've been meaning to tell you." She shrugged against him. "But I'm scared you won't like me."

He braked for a red light and turned toward her. "Don't be ridiculous. Tell me."

"He's not my biological father. The Mahers adopted me when I was six. They never had children." Joni plucked at a loose thread on his denim sleeve.

He didn't know what to say. Her revelation explained her excessive need to fit in and why she let her mom and dad plan her life. The light turned green, but he didn't drive through. Traffic was nonexistent at this hour anyway. He took his hand from the steering wheel and tilted her face up to his. "And?"

She averted her eyes. "Well, there's a stigma with being adopted. You know. Unlovable. Undesirable."

"Look at me." Sadness lurked between her lashes. "If a woman

gives birth to a child, she has to take what God gives her. Right?"
She nodded.

"You were chosen by the Mahers because you *are* lovable and
desirable." A car honked behind them. "But this is not the place
to prove it to you." The angry driver passed them on the shoulder.
James accepted her kiss and drove through the yellow light.

On the hour-and-a-half drive to the farm, they talked about
everything and nothing. He tried to convince her to take a nap,
but she refused, saying she was too excited to sleep. She did
remove her coat and help him shrug out of his jacket after they
turned north on Highway 43.

～～～

Ten minutes seemed like hours with a full bladder on a bumpy
road. Especially since Joni had drank too much orange juice. Pine
trees towered on either side of the narrow, country road. "Is there
a store nearby? I need to visit the ladies room."

"We're almost there. Can you wait ten minutes?"

"Sure." Joni avoided using public restrooms and hoped
wherever they were going was clean. She leaned her head against
James's arm and dozed.

A bump in the road woke her. He parked under a large oak
tree next to a two-story farm house. A group of men stood on the
wraparound porch drinking coffee in the pre-dawn light. She held
tight to James's hand as everyone welcomed James by slapping
his shoulder, shaking his other hand, or calling him by name. He
introduced her to half a dozen faces on the way to the front door.
She would never remember them all.

The screen door creaked as he held it open. The interior of the
house was nothing like she imaged. Oriental rugs decorated the
polished hardwood floors. Contemporary furniture invited Joni to
make herself at home. The smell of bacon and coffee drifted from
the kitchen, as well as voices she recognized.

"Joni." Aunt Sandra pulled her into a warm hug and bopped
James on the head. "Why didn't you tell us ya'll were coming?"

He stole a piece of bacon from the platter behind his aunt.
"I didn't know you'd be awake. We only came inside 'cause Joni

needs to use the bathroom."

"For goodness sakes. Men are so insensitive. Follow me, dear." Joni smiled at Aunt Sandra's chatter as she followed her to the top of the stairs. "It's the second door on your right. Come on back to the kitchen when you're done. I'll fix you a thermos of coffee before James drags you out in the cold."

Thankfully, the bathroom was updated with the rest of the house, except for the antique claw-footed bathtub. She envisioned soaking in the deep water, bubbles up to the rim. The fluffy hand towel was trimmed in lace. She straightened it on the rack and made her way back to the kitchen.

Aunt Sandra pressed a stainless steel thermos and a brown bag into her hands. "You better hurry outside, the natives are getting restless. Make James come back for lunch. We'll talk then."

~ ~ ~

James reclined against the inside of the shooting house while Joni slumbered in his arms. Something wasn't right. Despite their late arrival, they should have seen something by now. Does. Yearlings. Something. The grass patch in front of them was lifeless. His phone read eight thirty-two. He let Joni sleep for twenty more minutes before nudging her awake.

"Hmm." Like a kitten she stretched and yawned. "What time is it?" Her hand clamped over her mouth while her eyes laughed. Earlier, she'd made fun of his no-talking-while-hunting rule.

He tugged her hand away from her face and whispered. "It's okay. I'm gonna walk around some. Do you want to stay here?"

Her eyes widened. "I'm going with you."

"Shhh." James rolled his eyes as Joni pressed her lips in a fine line. He mouthed the words "Follow me."

How Joni's dainty feet could make so much noise as she tromped along behind him he'd never know. He climbed the ridge and sat on a stump, waiting for her to catch up. She waddled up the hill in her giant coveralls. The bulky clothes gave her the appearance of a green abominable snowman. The orange hat she wore instead of the vest (because orange wasn't her color) tilted to one side of her head.

"Ooh!" She picked up an acorn and then a yellow oak leaf dripping with morning dew. A squirrel and a chipmunk played peek-a-boo around the tree trunk and Joni's eyes lit up. A few paces later, she stopped for a hickory nut. Her pockets were bulging by the time she reached him. Her eyes must have met his boots, 'cause she looked up and smiled.

The early morning sun shone through the canopy of leaves overhead and dappled her golden hair as she twirled a red leaf between her fingers. She'd never been more beautiful. "Joni." His eyes found hers. "I love you."

Cold smoke puffed out of her open mouth. "Here?" Her foot slipped and she reached for him.

He pulled her up the ridge and down on his knee. "You're supposed to say, I love you back."

Joni combed her fingers through his hair. "I have dreamed of those three words for weeks." Her eyes glazed over. "We'd be walking down the beach with the moonlight at our backs and you'd hold me tight and whisper in my ear. Or I'd be wearing a new dress and you'd reach across a candlelit table for my hand. Your thumb would tickle my knuckles and your eyes would hold mine captive. But I never imagined I'd be wearing this green lump." Her lips hovered above his. "Wait a minute." Joni stood and shed her coveralls.

He tilted his head as he looked over her jeans and tight shirt. "Nice." He hooked his thumbs through her belt loops and pulled her close. "And?"

"Even though you made me wear that quilted sack, I love you, James Preston."

"And I love you, Joni Maher. Even though you tromp through the woods in high-heeled boots, scaring away all the deer in four counties."

~ ~ ~

"Are you ready to go?" James held out his hand. "We should've been in the stand fifteen minutes ago."

Joni stood from the truck's tailgate and brushed off her jeans. The prospect of sitting in a wooden shack twenty feet in the air wasn't appealing, but she'd suffer through it to be with James.

"Why don't you stay here?" Beside her, James's cousin shifted the baby in her arms. Shelby's husband was one of the many hunters. "I need to go to town and you can keep me company."

Would James's feelings be hurt if Joni didn't go?

He didn't look like the thought bothered him. "It's up to you. The game starts at seven. I'll meet you back here then."

Joni reached up and kissed him. "Thank you. Shoot something for me." She turned and followed Shelby to a small SUV. Her hand was on the passenger door when James jogged up beside her.

"Hey." He reached in his back pocket for his wallet. "Here. In case you want to do some shopping of your own." He held out two hundreds.

"I shouldn't take your money."

He grinned and painted her lips with a kiss. "But you will. Buy us some snacks or whatever." He looked at Shelby. "Drive careful."

Joni caressed the light stubble on his cheek. "You be careful, too." His wink made her rethink the shopping trip, but he turned and crossed the yard before she could change her mind.

At the grocery store, as she and Shelby debated over how many bags of chips the men would eat, Joni's cell rang.

It was Mrs. Preston. "Joni. Thank God I caught you."

Isaac's cries rose in the background. She dropped the chips in the buggy. "Put him on." The cries grew louder.

Shelby stopped and stared at Joni. "What's the matter?"

Joni spoke softly into the phone. "Shhh, Isaac. It's Joni. It's okay. Don't cry, sweetie. Tell me what's wrong."

Isaac sniffed. "Daddy left me." Wails sounded again.

"No, baby, James didn't leave you. He's with me. We had to leave early this morning and he didn't want to wake you. Aren't you having a good time with Grandma?"

"No. I want my daddy."

She exhaled and paced the length of the aisle. "Okay, Isaac. Put her back on the phone and I'll see what I can do."

"Come get me. I don't like Andrew anymore."

"I promise. Now put Grandma on." She propped a boot on the buggy's bottom rail and smoothed the homemade quilt around the infant seat. Shelby was an excellent mother.

Mrs. Preston returned to the line. "Joni?"

"What happened? Isaac isn't a crybaby. Something upset him."

Shelby's eyes widened and Joni regretted her harsh tone.

"I'm not sure. He and Andrew had an argument at lunch and he's cried for his daddy ever since. When James didn't answer his phone, Isaac insisted I call you. I hate to interrupt your day, but even though I'm his grandmother...I'm a stranger to him. Oh dear, he's packing his toys."

Joni heard the unspoken question. "We're in the country. Right now, Shelby and I are in Jackson Walmart. It'll take us twenty minutes to drive back to Aunt Sandra's. James left his phone in the truck. Hopefully, he left the keys as well."

Shelby touched her arm. "I'll take you. The guys won't be back for a while and the game's not till seven. Holly nursed before we left the house. Her next feeding isn't for two more hours."

"Are you sure?" Joni sighed with relief when Shelby nodded. "Mrs. Preston, can you meet us halfway?"

"Is that café still there in Mount Vernon?"

"Why don't you and Shelby agree on a meeting place? Nothing around here is familiar."

~ ~ ~

The screen door screeched when he pulled it open. As a teenager he'd kept it well-oiled, but like many times, years ago when he'd tried to slip in the old farmhouse, his dad sat at the kitchen table with his open Bible. James closed out the cold night temperatures. "I need a place to sleep. Aunt Sandra kicked me out."

His dad removed his glasses. "Come in. As you like to remind me, it is your house."

James hung his jacket on the wooden coat rack. "I don't want to fight, Dad. I just want a place to crash for a few hours."

"Where's my grandson?"

"Snuggled up with Joni in Shelby's old room." His boots

clunked on the hardwood floor.

"I see. Who's Joni?"

James sighed and crossed the kitchen. He filled a glass with water and guzzled it down. "Our girlfriend."

His dad closed the Bible and grinned. "Oh, yeah? Is she pretty?"

James couldn't stop his smile. "She's beautiful. You'll probably see her at church tomorrow." He placed the glass in the dishwasher. "Don't look surprised. It's not my fault Joni likes church."

"No, I guess not." His dad's smile grated on James's nerves. "You want me to wake you for Sunday school in the morning?"

"I'll be in the woods by then." James ran a hand through his hair. He put one foot on the bottom stair and turned back. "Goodnight, Dad."

"Goodnight, Son."

As luck would have it, the next day was Fellowship Sunday, with dinner served on the grounds. James glanced at the broken plastic fork sticking out of Joni's fried chicken breast.

She cleared her throat and smothered a giggle, but he knew the reason for the laughter in her eyes. She nudged her plate a quarter of an inch toward him.

He shook his head. No way was he fixing her chicken with his family watching.

A delicate hand landed mid-thigh on his jeans. James removed it, but her fingernails scraped the inside of his palm. He squeezed a warning while Uncle Pete and his dad recounted lumber prices.

James captured Joni's gaze and whispered, "Stop."

She wet her lips and mouthed, "Please." Long lashes fluttered against her creamy skin. He would've done anything she asked. He was such a sap.

"Are you listening?" Uncle Pete pointed a chicken leg at Aunt Sandra. Mike had his head leaned toward his girlfriend, and the others were engrossed in their own conversations. James whispered in Joni's ear. "Go get another fork and some napkins."

She stood, and as all eyes turned to her, James quickly switched their plates. Keeping watch in his peripheral vision, he removed the broken fork and tore the meat from the bone. Something clattered behind him. He switched the plates back to their original positions. Joni returned and caressed the inside of his arm. "Thank you."

"Aw." Aunt Sandra eyed them both. "That was the sweetest thing I've ever seen."

He cringed. There was no way to stop what was coming. "Aunt Sandra, don't—"

"What?"

Conversations stalled around them and everyone tuned in to Aunt Sandra, who told everyone within hearing how James doctored Joni's chicken.

"It's not a big thing." He looked to his dad for help.

Suppressed laughter twinkled in his brown eyes. "You want to borrow my pocket knife so you can cut mine up too?" He guffawed and slapped his knee.

James drank his tea and squirmed in his seat.

Isaac piped up and said, "Daddy breaks Joni's chicken all times."

Joni's tinkling laughter joined in with the rest of the table.

James glared at her. "Traitor."

Her smile erased his frown. "But, I love you."

"You better." Though he knew everyone was staring, he couldn't stop his smile or tear his eyes away from hers.

His cousin Travis came to his rescue. "Enough mushy stuff. You're making me lose my appetite."

~ ~ ~

The first sunrays peeked through peppermint curtains. Joni dressed quickly, layered her shirts, and grabbed her jacket. Yesterday, James had moved into the apartment, but she was stuck performing in Bay St. Louis.

Traffic was heavy, but despite morning commuters and some patches of fog, she made it to Hillcrest and smiled at the glowing "Hot. Donuts. Now." sign at James's favorite donut shop. She bought a spilt dozen, glazed and cream-filled, two coffees, and chocolate milk for Isaac.

Seeing James's truck parked in front of building Y thrilled her. Her heart pounded as she balanced the drink tray and the box of donuts up the wooden stairs. Through the window, Isaac laughed at cartoons while wearing only pajama bottoms.

She tapped on the window with her elbow.

"Joni!" He scrambled to the door.

A scrape sounded and the door opened to Isaac standing in his miniature rocking chair. Little arms wrapped around her neck. Joni clutched the donuts and drinks. "Just a minute, sweetie." She maneuvered around the unpacked boxes to the scarred coffee table and relieved her arms of their burden.

Isaac laughed when Joni lifted him high in the air and tickled his sides. She shut and bolted the door. "Where's your shirt? You're gonna freeze."

"Shirts choke me and Daddy when we sleep." A wet kiss landed on her cheek. "Hugs are better real. I miss-ed you."

Joni held the little boy tight. "I missed you, too. Where is your daddy?"

Isaac frowned. "Sleep."

"I brought donuts for breakfast."

"Yummy." Isaac wiggled and Joni set him on the floor.

In the kitchen, she rummaged through the boxes, looking for dessert plates. Nothing but plastic bowls and spoons. The cabinets were empty. James needed to do some serious shopping.

Thankfully, she found a roll of paper towels on top of the microwave. Trying not to focus on the awful furniture, she knelt on the floor beside Isaac. The sugary pastries were still warm. "Which kind do you want?"

Isaac reached in and grabbed a donut in each hand. Joni hid her smile as he bit off a chunk out of each one. She placed a small brown jug in front of him. "Look what I bought you."

"'Kay." Isaac ignored the milk and slurped from Joni's lukewarm coffee. She blinked down at him. "James lets you drink coffee?"

"Yep." Isaac focused his attention on the television.

Joni shook her head. To think she'd worried about feeding him too much sugar. So much for nutrition. She ate a glazed donut and stared down the hall. She wanted to wake James. Did she dare go into his room?

She rinsed her hands in the kitchen sink and tiptoed down the hall. Her breath caught as she peeked at his bed from the doorway. The quilt covered him from the waist down, leaving his torso bare. Heat flushed her face. His muscled chest rose and fell in a deep rhythm. She hoped, like Isaac, he at least wore pajama bottoms.

Her prince charming snored softly and broke the spell. She swallowed a giggle and moved to the edge of the bed. "James." Her whisper didn't stir him. Maybe he really was her sleeping beauty. Leaning down, her lips nudged his.

~ ~ ~

The sweet taste of donuts invaded his dreams. Wanting more, he opened his mouth and reached for Joni's unique scent.

"James."

He shivered as flames danced over his skin. A hunger surged through him and his lips devoured hers. Something restrained him. He blinked. Joni lay beneath him. The sheet wrapped around him held her captive. "Am I dreaming?"

Dainty fingers played along the stubble of his jaw. Jade eyes smoked over. "I must be dreaming too."

"Daddy, you s'posed to eat the donuts, not Joni."

James froze. Isaac stood in the bedroom door. Each hand held a glazed donut. This wasn't a dream. Joni was in his bed. Her shirt had risen slightly and his hand lay on her bare midriff. His heart slammed against his chest as her long lashes fluttered closed. Without taking his eyes off her, he said, "Isaac, go eat your breakfast."

"But Daddy, Joni's here."

"I know." James couldn't stop his smile. "I need to talk to her. Now go watch TV."

Isaac huffed. "For how long?"

"Three shows. And save me some breakfast."

"Yes, sir." Isaac turned and moped up the hall.

James brushed her warm mouth with his. "Joni?" Her eyes remained closed. He kissed her again and smacked his lips. "You taste like donuts."

Her giggle sparked his laughter. He propped up on his elbow and stared into her green eyes. "What are you doing in my bed?"

Joni's fingers smoothed the whiskers on his jaw. "My prince charming slept. I kissed him awake, and before I knew what was happening…he captured me."

He turned his head and pressed a kiss to her open palm. "He's awake now."

Jeweled eyes sparkled up at him. "I missed you." Her fingers tickled the back of his neck.

"I missed you, too." He dipped his head and kissed her again. Silken hands stroked his back and bliss waved through him. Until dainty hands came between them and shoved. He lifted his head. "Joni?"

Her voice wavered. "I-I shouldn't be in here."

He buried his face in her hair. No other smell compared to her sweetness. He left a kiss on her neck before smiling down at her once more. "Let's go see if Isaac saved me some breakfast." He pulled her by the hand and led her up the hall. The green and white box on the floor near Isaac lured him over.

He looked up from his donut and caught Joni starring at his naked chest. He winked but her eyes avoided his.

Breathless, he said, "I love you."

Her shaky smile squeezed his heart. "I love you, too."

Wrapping his arms around her, he fell back into the recliner and claimed another searing kiss. He pulled back and searched her eyes. They sparkled with love for him. Content, he smiled and reached around her.

Joni's musical laughter was priceless. "Do you love me or my donuts?"

"Both. The best breakfast in the world is the taste of donuts on your lips."

The flaky pastry melted in his mouth. He swallowed and kissed her again. "Hmm, delicious."

She giggled against his neck and he shivered, hugging her close. "I do love you, Joni."

Isaac climbed up James's legs and wiggled between them. Joni stood and disappeared into the kitchen. The microwave beeped a minute later and she brought him a cup of coffee.

"Hop down, Isaac. I don't want to accidentally burn you."

Joni caressed his cheek. Her forceful kiss shocked him, but he loved it.

As he drank his coffee, she bit her lip and stared at him from the couch. Her smile hinted at something he couldn't quite grasp. Her smile was different, deliberate.

Her words were playful. "Did I mention I love you?"

Ah. James grew up with Sara. She'd smile at Dad like that and Dad would give her anything she wanted. It used to drive James crazy. Didn't his dad know he was being manipulated? "Joni, that look doesn't work with me."

"Oh." Her smile fell and she rose from the couch. "Never mind then."

His intention wasn't to make her sad. He set his cup down and hooked an arm around her waist as she came near. "What?"

"Nothing."

He pulled her across the armrest onto his lap. "Tell me."

"Well." The pads of her fingers trailed down his throat. "Monday, I stopped by the library to study. You know how Mom drives me insane at the house, especially since she followed me to church. Anyway, there was this guy there and he kept staring at me. I couldn't concentrate."

His hand fisted in her hair. "You don't have to worry about creeps like that anymore. I made you a key. You can come here to study."

She looked around the room and frowned. "That's the thing. Your furnishings don't exactly produce a learnable environment."

What? She didn't like his furniture? He'd had this recliner since his freshman year.

Her finger traced his bottom lip. "The gallery down the street has the most amazing mahogany square table with barstool-type cushioned chairs." Her fingernail scraped his chin and he shivered. "And since you stored the pool table above Sara's garage, the dining area is empty. You and Isaac need a place to eat. So... would you mind if I made some changes in here? I saved some money from—"

"Whoa. Hold up a minute." He flipped the wood handle and kicked in the footrest. "You've picked out a table for the apartment?"

She wet her lips and stared at the blank wall. "Kind of."

For the past week, he tried to think of a way to convince her to move in. If buying new furniture made her feel more at home here, he'd buy rooms of it.

Devouring her words, he kissed her and stood. Gently, he lowered her feet to the floor. He cradled her head in his hands and studied her while his pulse danced through his veins. "Let me take a quick shower."

She had Isaac dressed and ready to go before James finished shaving.

He drove her car to the furniture store. She showed him the table and delivered her own sales pitch. She didn't realize he'd buy her whatever she wanted.

Corralling Isaac, he sat on a recliner sofa and waited for the salesman to write up the transaction. "I'm paying. You can buy dishes and stuff with your money. I want this too. Our old one isn't nearly this comfortable."

Joni cringed and wrinkled her nose.

"What?"

She shrugged her shoulders. "It's beige."

"And?"

She tilted her head down. "And the carpet's beige."

"But I like it."

Joni lifted her brows. "And the walls are beige." She perched on the arm of the couch and kissed him. "We need to add some color to our living area, and our lease says we can't paint."

He didn't miss her choice of pronouns. Buying furniture was working to his advantage.

Her cheeks reddened. "It's your apartment. You can buy whatever you want."

"No." He threaded his fingers with hers. "Not if you don't like it."

Isaac flipped down a center armrest and revealed a storage bin with cup holders. "Cool."

The returning salesman grinned. "This set also comes in charcoal and periwinkle."

James squeezed Joni's hand. "How about blue?"

Her smile returned. "Can I spruce up the place with accessories?"

He kissed her palm. "While you're decorating, don't forget the bedroom."

Chapter Eleven

A Sunday school book lay on the new table. Scented candles gave the apartment spice and yellow pillows rested on the new couch, but the bedroom was as James left it two weeks earlier. How could he convince her to move in?

The problem plagued him as he drove across the bay. He dropped Isaac off at Sara's and returned to the apartment to wait for Joni. When she arrived, she insisted they take her car for their day of Christmas shopping, but he claimed the keys. The Honda's bucket seats prevented her from snuggling. They should have taken his truck.

Joni yawned. "Studying for finals and practicing with the praise team on Saturdays is getting to me."

"Why don't you stay at the apartment during the week? It will save you an hour and a half round-trip commute."

Her eyes widened. "I can't sleep in your bed."

"Why not? I'm never there." He winked over at her. "You can sleep beside me too, but only if you say please."

"Sara said it wouldn't look right. For some reason, the younger girls look up to those of us on the praise team. I don't want to set a bad example."

He braked for a light and made a mental note to tell his sister to stay out of his business. "I worry about you driving across the bay at night. Sara means well, but when I'm hundreds of miles away…?" He kissed her palm as the light turned green. "What difference does it make?"

At the mall, the smell of cinnamon and peppermint lingered in the festive air. The hum of shoppers drowned out the carol floating from the ceiling speakers while lights twinkled in every window display. Joni was jostled into James's side by a big man burrowing his way through the mall. "It's two weeks until Christmas. All the procrastinators are panicky."

He laughed and pulled her into an electronics store. "Like me."

Remote-controlled vehicles of all shapes and sizes were arranged in the center aisle. Joni selected a truck design with a simple remote control. Forward. Left. Right. Reverse. She studied the box. Recommended for ages five and up. She turned to James.

He had a complicated remote in his hand and a little-boy sparkle in his eye. "This thing tops out at 55 miles per hour and can be controlled from a hundred yards away."

The controller had two throttles and at least a dozen buttons. She suppressed a smile at his excitement. "Don't you think that's a bit advanced for a four-year-old?"

"Isaac's smart. I'll teach him how to handle it."

A young salesman pointed to the far wall. "Demos are set up along the back."

"Come on."

Joni couldn't resist as he tugged on her hand and pulled her through the crowd. A clear plastic wall separated the consumers from the dirt track. Half a dozen vehicles zoomed over small mountains, ramps, and puddles of water. One vehicle climbed halfway up the wall, flipped over, and raced in the opposite direction.

A young boy, probably about twelve, turned and pressed his control in James's hand. "I've got to tell Mom to buy me one of these."

Joni stood on tiptoe and peeked over James's shoulder. His whole body turned with the controller. It took her a minute to figure out which vehicle he controlled. James swerved through a pool of water and avoided a head-on collision. "Yes!"

She squeezed his elbow. "James?"

His eyes never left the track. "Yeah."

"I'm gonna look around a bit."

"What?" He shook his head. "Where're you going?"

"I saw something near the door I want to buy for Isaac. I'll meet you there."

He leaned down and she barely had time for a quick kiss before he turned his attention back to the track. "I want to see how well this thing holds up in a crash. Isaac's pretty rough with his toys."

Joni walked away, smiling. Isaac would never touch the controls. James wanted the jeep for himself. She hesitated at the price but purchase the jeep for him and the smaller truck for Isaac.

A Yamaha keyboard near the window caught her eye. She fought her way through the throng and ran her fingers down the full-scale keys. She'd always wanted a portable piano, but her parents insisted the baby grand at home was sufficient. The giant bag rested at her feet while she toyed with the variety of instruments and sounds. Unable to resist the urge, she played Bach with the violin option and Yiruma through the piano. The sound was great. The stand was secure and the foot pedal easy to access. She lifted the price tag. Ouch. Ever since her first concert at fourteen, she'd been saving for her own place, but she'd already spent more than she intended on the apartment. The keyboard would have to wait.

Strong arms wrapped around her and James kissed her neck. "Find something you like?"

"Not really. I was just passing time."

His strong fingers danced across the keys, producing a familiar tune. "Are you sure? Santa wanted me to keep an eye out for anything that interests you."

"I'm sure." She pressed up the volume and gasped as she recognized the rhythm in his song. "You can play church music. Teach me how."

His hands disappeared behind them. "That's ridiculous. You're a concert pianist." He whispered near her ear, "I can't read music."

"Which means, you're not bound by a sheet of paper." She turned into his arms and snuggled into his side. "I wished I possessed that kind of freedom."

"You think one of these will help break the chains?" He shook the keyboard with one hand. "Get rid of all that polished wood and ivory. Wouldn't that be considered slumming it in the concert world?" He gathered their bags.

Laughter bubbled and escaped her. "Probably. Although I doubt anyone but you would have thought of it that way." She cast a backward glance as they walked out of the store. James caught her gaze and winked. "You never know. Santa may surprise you." He tugged her close and whispered. "Unless you're on the naughty list?"

"Behave, or you might find a lump of coal in your stocking."

His deep laughter tickled her neck before he straightened. "Fine. I promise to be good. Where to next?" He lifted both their shopping bags in one hand. "With this, and what we bought at the toy store earlier, we can cross Isaac off our list."

"After I pick up some lotion for Marla, I'm done." She turned them in the right direction, but James drug his feet.

He stalled out ten feet from the entrance and shook his head. "I can't go in a girly store." He nodded at the men crowding the nearby benches. "I'll wait out here."

She giggled at his expression. You'd think she'd asked him to walk into a lingerie department. "Body wash and perfume insult your manly ego?"

He leaned down and whispered next to her ear, "My manly ego loves those girly scents against your skin." He sniffed against her neck and Joni shivered.

She nodded at a drink vendor. "You need something to cool you down."

"Uh-uh. You shivered. We need some more heat. You want a double mocha?"

"No, I'll just have a sip of yours."

He kissed her cheek. "Take your time. I'll wait near the fountain."

Joni lingered in the shop. She bought four tubs of body butter for gifts and two for herself. James wasn't at the fountain, so she entered the bookstore and purchased her dad the latest hardback from his favorite author. When she exited, James walked from the direction of the electronics store. She smiled. He'd been playing monster trucks again.

~ ~ ~

The clear tape tangled between his fingers, tearing the paper underneath James's thumb. Joni giggled as she walked past him and placed another perfectly wrapped gift under the tree.

Rising on his knees, he looped a red ribbon around her and pulled her close. "I admit it. I'm better at opening gifts." He tied a loose knot at her waist.

The colorful lights on the tree reflected in her eyes. Her hands rested on his shoulders. "Maybe, you should put Isaac's truck together and leave the gifts to me."

His knuckle traced the ribbon's curl near her zipper. "I'm tired of waiting. I want to open a present now." Her gasp drew his attention to her mouth. He stood. "I've been a very good boy this year." He tasted caramel on her lips. "Isaac's with Sara until we finish the gifts."

Dainty fingers toyed with the buttons on his shirt. "James, you know there can't be any of that kind of unwrapping until…"

Her cheeks turned the color of a conch shell. Would he be a good husband? Or would he turn out like his own father? He pushed those thoughts aside. Lifting her left hand, he pressed kisses on her ring finger. "Until…?"

She rolled her eyes and huffed out a breath. "James, you know."

He rested his forehead against hers and closed his eyes. "When I was a kid, I'd use my pocket knife and slice the tape on my presents." He tugged on the little ribbon and it fell to the carpet. "After peeking inside, I'd rewrap my gifts and no one ever suspected a thing."

Her voice was so low he barely heard. "Weren't you disappointed Christmas morning?"

He grinned as her eyes clouded over. "Uh-uh. Knowing what was inside those packages made me more eager to claim them."

Long lashes fluttered against her creamy skin. "James."

He lowered her to the carpet. Gift wrap, bows, and ribbons scattered with a wave of his hand. He relinquished her mouth long enough to pull her sweater over her head. The hem of her silky red camisole was bunched in his fist when his phone rang. He froze. What if Isaac needed him? The ringing persisted. James snatched up the phone. "Yeah!"

Joni's eyes opened and she sat up with her back toward him.

"Hi." Sara's cheery voice intruded on his thoughts. "I know you wanted Isaac home tonight, but it's late and he wants to sleep over. What do you say?"

James grinned into the phone. "Sounds great. I'll pick him up in the morning." He ended the call and reached for Joni. His hand landed on her shoulders. The thin straps couldn't hide their nakedness and his lips followed the path of his hands. He turned her in his arms and dipped his head.

Her phone rang across the room.

James stilled. "Let it ring. It's probably Sara again." He kissed the curve of her neck.

The ringing persisted. Joni crawled away and hurried toward her purse. As she answered, his eyes glued to the rise and fall of her chest. The lacy shirt dipped low in the front. He followed her and recaptured her waist as she said goodnight to Isaac. "Hang up, Joni."

"Is James there with you?" Sara's voice was loud enough for him to hear.

"Yes." Joni flinched from his touch.

He caught his shirt, which she threw at him, and growled in protest. "Come back."

Joni spoke into the phone. "No, he's fine. Just aggravated with the *some assembly required* thing." She waved him toward the door, grabbed her sweater, and disappeared down the hall. The bathroom door shut a few seconds later.

His sister ruined everything. If only she hadn't called? James stomped outside and let the frigid air cool his heated blood. Isaac's big truck was in the storage room. It needed to be put together, but first he had to sneak Joni's gift out of the car.

He shivered in the night air. The keyboard had barely fit. He may never get it out of the trunk. After maneuvering the box a hundred different ways, it was finally freed. His frustration wasn't helped by either the inflexible cardboard or the stubborn lock on the storage room. By the time he had Joni's keyboard safely hidden away and Isaac's truck parts in the living room, James was ready to throw both gifts over the banister.

The bathroom door creaked open.

The ribbon on Joni's shirt was laced tight and secured in a double knot. Her eyes traveled over him and then shifted to the gift wrap littering the floor. "We can't do that again. It's dangerous."

He released a sigh and got to work assembling the ride-on toy. After she finished wrapping Isaac's gifts, she helped him with the stickered headlights. She yawned and collected the excess paper. "I'd better get going."

James glanced at his watch. After midnight. "Stay. I worry about you driving this late."

Her condescending frown made him laugh. She disappeared into the kitchen with the trash and came back empty-handed.

He opened his arms. "I'm serious." Hugging her close, he rested his cheek against her head. "You can sleep in Isaac's room. There will be a locked door between us."

She lifted her eyes and gave an exaggerated gasp. "I can't believe you'd lock me out."

"Never." He tucked a strand of hair behind her ear. "I love holding you while you sleep." She lifted a questioning brow. "The night we met." Memories assailed him and he gulped a steadying breath. "The night in front of Kappa House." His lips brushed hers. "Stay."

She stepped out of his arms. Her eyes wouldn't meet his. "It's not the same now and you know it." She shrugged into her coat and reached for her purse.

Frustration welled up inside him. He refrained from beating his head against the wall and followed her to the door. "I'm walking you downstairs." He shoved his arms in his jacket. "Call me when you get home." He stepped into his shoes and clasped her hand. "I love you."

She leaned up and kissed him. "Stop pouting."

"What?" The cold sliced through him as she opened the door. "I'm not pouting." He shut it behind them and they walked side by side down the stairs. "I'm concerned."

At her car, she giggled and kissed him again. "I promise to drive the speed limit, stop for every yellow light, and I'll be on the lookout for wacko drivers."

He knelt in the open door as the seat inched slowly forward. "Be careful." She started the engine and turned on the heater. He cherished her smile and leaned into the hand caressing his whiskers. He turned and kissed her palm. "Don't forget to call me. As soon as you get home. If you get sleepy, call before then. I'll keep you awake."

"I promise." She shivered and he leaned in for one more kiss.

Two hours later, he paced the floor as he listened to her voicemail greeting once again. He left another message and willed his pulse to slow. She was probably sleeping peacefully and forgot to call. He reached for the TV remote. His generic ringtone sounded from his phone, prickling the back of his neck.

The caller ID displayed William Maher. He breathed easy. Her battery must be dead and she was calling from her dad's line.

"James Preston?"

His dread returned at the sound of the deep male voice. "Yeah, this is James."

A sigh floated through the earpiece. "I'm sorry to bother you, but I should've called as soon as the paramedics said Joni asked for you. A father doesn't like sharing."

Joni? Paramedics? James grabbed his keys on his way out the door. "What happened? Is she okay? Where is she?" His feet flew down the stairs. "Ugh. I begged her to sleep here." He was almost to his truck by the time her dad answered.

"The airbag saved her life, but unfortunately her left hand is injured. She's in x-ray."

"Which hospital?" James turned the key and shifted into reverse.

"Mobile Infirmary."

He gassed the engine. "Sir, tell Joni I'm on my way and thanks for calling." On the ride to the hospital, he ignored the speed limit and ran three lights. After parking in a handicap zone, James raced by the triage desk to the treatment rooms.

"You can't go back there."

He ignored the warning. "Joni!"

"James." Her voice was weak. Glancing in all the curtains, he ignored the nurses until he found her midway down the hall. The bed swallowed her. He ran a hand through his hair and caught his breath. A machine beeped beside her. He sat on the bed and lifted her hand.

A bruise marked her forehead and her lip was busted. A second bruise decorated her chin. He kissed the delicate fingers peeking from the white bandage. "You're never leaving me again."

A nurse sighed behind him. "Oh, forget it."

"James." Droopy eyes smiled from the bed. "I didn't fall asleep. Some idiot blindsided me."

Gently, he kissed the unblemished side of her forehead. "You scared me. No more late driving. You're staying at the apartment. I'll move out if I have to."

Her good hand brushed across his cheek. "I can't. What would the church people think?"

"Who cares about those self-righteous hypocrites?"

Her right hand plucked at the covers.

"Joni, you'll be safe."

"Where is this apartment?" Her dad stepped around the curtain, followed by her mother.

"Off Hillcrest." If he could convince her dad, Joni would go along with it. "Sir, I work industrial construction. I'm home maybe one weekend every two months. During those weekends, she could stay with you, or I could stay at my sister's."

"I can't put you out of your own apartment. What about Isaac?"

James ignored her protest and spoke with her father. "It's fifteen minutes from campus. She takes care of the place during the week as it is. Checks the mail and whatever."

"Bill, please." Joni's mother spoke for the first time. "I don't want my daughter shacking up with some construction bumpkin."

"Mother!" Joni rose up in the bed and winced.

James kissed her forehead while Mr. Maher glared at his wife. "I was once a blue-collar worker."

She had the grace to blush. "Yes, but you were destined for a better life."

After much debate they agreed. Joni would "share" the apartment, but only when he was out of town. To ease her mother's conscience, James agreed to let them pay half the utilities.

~ ~ ~

Mr. Maher glared as he untied the rope securing Joni's wooden dresser. James drummed his fingers against the bedrail as a police cruiser parked one building down. "A city cop and a sheriff's deputy live in the complex. You won't have to worry about Joni staying here alone, sir."

Mr. Maher loosened the final knot and threw the rope at James's chest. "My daughter staying here *alone* isn't what I worry about."

James untangled the rope in his arms and placed it in the truck. "Sir, I love Joni. I'd rather shoot myself in the foot than hurt her."

Her dad's hand paused on the tailgate. "I won't be aiming that low."

James heeded the warning in Mr. Maher's eyes and kept his mouth shut. He didn't know how to deal with Joni's dad. The sooner her parents left, the better.

Without another word, they carried the antique furniture up the stairs. Joni and her mother stood at the new dining table unpacking a box labeled "Fragile. Grandmother's china."

Her smile relieved the tension in his shoulders. "What took you guys so long? I was beginning to worry that you dropped it." Horror covered her face. "You didn't, did you?"

Her dad answered. "No. James and I had a chat. I needed to lay some ground rules."

A hand went to her hip. She frowned at her father. "Daddy, I told you not to do that." She looked at James. "Did he threaten you?"

Although her protective streak was cute, he didn't need her to fight his battles. He winked and asked, "Where do you want this?"

"Oh." She became animated. "Put it against the wall at the foot of the bed."

"But that's where my weights are."

She fluttered down the hall. "I had Daddy move them out of the way. We put them in Isaac's closet." She glanced over her shoulder. "That's okay with you, isn't it?"

Her dad snickered and then covered with a cough.

Before James could stutter a reply, Isaac barreled out of his room and hugged his knees from behind. "Daddy, guess what? Joni gets to live here."

Mrs. Maher playfully swung his son in her arms. "Oh no you don't, little munchkin. You're daddy's carrying a family heirloom."

He could only stare as Isaac playfully kissed Mrs. Maher's cheek.

"James?" Joni peeked out their bedroom door. "Hurry up. I want to have everything settled before you leave."

He ignored Mr. Maher's gloating smirk as they placed the dresser where Joni indicated. From Mrs. Maher's arms, Isaac reached for him. James claimed his son and escaped to Isaac's room. The master bedroom wasn't meant to be shared with parents. With one hand, he opened the closet and pulled out Isaac's duffle bag.

The little boy wiggled to the floor and packed his tote with toys. "Where we going?"

James rolled up Isaac's little jeans and shirts. "A shutdown in New Orleans."

"When we coming home?"

"Four days."

Little hands threw in some building blocks. "Is that the short tomorrow or the long?"

James chuckled. Isaac got smarter every day. "The short one."

"Excuse me." Mrs. Maher stood perfectly poised in the doorway. "Might I have a word?"

James shoved Isaac's pajamas into the duffle and stood. Whenever someone asked permission to ask a question, it required more than a simple answer. He leaned back against the chest of drawers and kept his tone light. "Sure. What can I help you with?"

The knots in his stomach tightened as Mrs. Maher entered the room and closed the door. Her hands fisted under her chin and her shoulders lifted. "Joni is very much loved by her father and me. She's been sheltered from the depravity of the world and, as a result, I'm afraid she's naïve to dangerous consequences."

This wasn't the right time to point out that any danger Joni faced as a result of her sheltered life was because her mother kept her in a bubble.

Mrs. Maher twisted a ring on her finger. "Joni refused to keep her appointment with my gynecologist. Although I do not agree with this move, I will respect her father's wishes, as per our agreement to her upbringing. However, this places me in a delicate situation where I find myself having to depend on you to protect her future."

James held perfectly still as his mind raced to keep up with the woman's jargon.

Joni?

Woman's doctor?

Protection?

Duh. James felt like slapping his forehead. Now who was the naïve one? Wait. If Mrs. Maher wanted Joni on birth control then that meant... "Are you saying that it's okay for..."

Her eyes widened and her lips parted. "Absolutely not." Her arms crossed over her chest. "Keep your filthy hands off my daughter." She held up one finger. "But, should a lapse in judgment arise…" Her shoulders rose and her chin lifted. "Wear a glove."

Words failed him. Chaotic thoughts ran rampant in his mind as Mrs. Maher continued her lecture with statistics of pregnancy rates and STDs in college students. "I see I've offended you. Well, no matter. If you're embarrassed to procure the necessary items, I can visit the drug store on my way hom—"

"Joni!" He needed help. "Can you please come in here? Uh, now would be good."

The door snatched open and he breathed easy. Joni appeared behind Mrs. Maher in the hall. "James, are you okay?" She crossed the room, stepped in between them, and faced her crazy mother. "What's going on in here?"

Isaac snapped the lid on his tote. "Grandmother wants to buy Daddy some gloves, but he already has some in his truck. Don't you, Daddy?"

Mrs. Maher lifted a bow-shaped brow. "Does he?"

"Mother, what James wears or doesn't wear isn't any of your business." As Joni defended him, the reality of the situation cleared.

Her stuck-up mother had offered to buy him condoms. James erupted into laughter. Ray would never believe it. His arms circled Joni's waist, hushing her defense of him. "Mrs. Maher, I promise, I'll keep Joni protected."

"Then it's settled."

Mr. Maher appeared behind his wife. "What's settled?"

"Nothing."

"Nothing." James and Mrs. Maher were both quick to answer. Isaac pulled his toy box along the carpet. "I'm packed, Daddy."

Mr. and Mrs. Maher disappeared into the hall, whispering fervently to each other. Joni turned and wound her arms around his neck. "Was that something I need to know about?"

Careful not to bump her bandaged hand, James pulled

her close. "Uh, no." He brushed her lips with his. "That was something I didn't want to know about."

She giggled. "You're scared of my mother?"

"Terrified." Laughter prevented him from claiming the kiss he wanted. So he held her while the shock wore off.

Isaac's exaggerated sigh echoed through the room. He bumped his heels against the plastic tote. Sitting on the lid, he propped his chin on his fist. "It's not fair. Joni just got here, and we have to go to work."

The bandage on her hand scratched his cheek. "James?"

He recognized the smile in her eyes. She wanted something and he'd give anything to make her happy. So when Joni asked if Isaac could stay the week, he couldn't say no.

~ ~ ~

Sunday morning, Joni waited outside the preschool class. Isaac barreled out the door holding a fist full of coloring pages. "Did you have fun?" She smoothed his baby-fine hair.

"Yeah, that was cool. This guy found money inside a slimy fish."

She cringed. "At least you were paying attention."

Holding his little hand, they walked into the sanctuary. The praise and worship team warmed up instruments while people in the pews chatted among themselves. In the back, Pastor shook hands and welcomed newcomers at the double doors.

Joni walked over to the piano where Marla played the opening music.

"Who's this?"

"Isaac."

Rachel turned up her nose. "James's son?"

"I'm babysitting."

Marla smiled warmly at Isaac. "Well, I'm glad you came to church."

Isaac grinned. "Me too."

Joni held her friend's gaze and whispered, "I can't sing this morning?"

"Why not?"

Joni tilted her head toward Isaac. "Mark and Sara are on vacation and Mrs. Preston wasn't in Sunday school. I'm scared to leave him by himself in the pews. I doubt he'll sit still."

A hand landed on her shoulder. Joni jumped. Pastor knelt in front of Isaac and held out his hand. "It's good to have you in service with us today."

Isaac lifted one brow and frowned up at Joni. "Who is this man?"

She stifled a giggle. "This is the pastor. Be nice and say hello."

"Hi."

Pastor shook a reluctant hand. "And what's your name?"

"Isaac."

Pastor tilted his head and a slow smile crept up his lips. "It's nice to meet you, Isaac." He lifted the little boy and placed him in the chair reserved for a guest speaker. "Can you sit here quietly while Joni sings a few songs?"

Isaac smiled. "Yeah. Me and Daddy like when she sings."

Heat crept up her cheeks.

"Problem solved." Pastor crossed the stage and greeted Cole and Philip.

Remembering how James's dad gave him a microphone, Joni wondered if she should do the same for Isaac. "Don't move unless I say you can."

"Okay." His serene smile put her on guard. She never knew when a burst of energy would hit him.

The music began. She pictured Isaac dancing all over the platform and took a deep breath. "Sit right there."

Isaac blinked with innocence. "Okay."

"And don't wiggle." Joni said a quiet prayer and lifted her microphone. Isaac was a perfect angel. Until the middle of the second song.

"Grandma!" He jumped off the platform and ran toward James's mom who'd walked in the church. Halfway to Mrs. Preston, he skidded to a halt. Joni stumbled over her words as Isaac raced back to her.

Somehow, she managed to force the lyrics from her mouth.

Isaac whispered. "Can I go sit with her?"

Joni quickly nodded.

He dashed up the center aisle. Thankfully, his grandmother caught him by the waist and hauled him into her pew.

After service, Isaac chatted nonstop while Mrs. Preston hugged Joni. "I'm sorry if we embarrassed you."

"It's okay. I survived." Joni smiled at Isaac.

"Where's James?"

"He's in New Orleans. I'm, uh…" A deep-gutted feeling told her not to mention where they were staying. "I'm keeping Isaac for a few days."

Isaac held up his hands and Mrs. Preston lifted him in her arms. "Joni moved in my apartment, but she sleeps in Daddy's room."

Mrs. Briggs, the church gossip, smiled maliciously and sashayed toward the pastor.

Chapter Twelve

James had every intention of driving to his mom's house, but Joni had been upset when he called to tell her he was on the way home, and she wouldn't tell him why. He decided to stop by the apartment and check on her, even if it was after midnight.

Needles of worry pricked his tired eyes as he hurried up the stairs. He opened the front door, and the sound of her weeping clenched his heart in a vise grip. He abandoned his duffle bag by the Christmas tree in the living room and hurried down the hall. Kneeling by the bed, he wiped her cheeks with his thumb and whispered, "Joni."

Her gasp caught him off guard. She shrieked and sat straight up on the mattress. "James? What are you doing here?"

"You're crying. What happened?" He settled on the bed beside her.

Her eyes widened and she scooted away from him. A trembling finger pointed at the door. "Get out. You can't be in here. Especially now. Go, James. Leave."

The light coming from the closet illuminated the tissues littering the bed. The lace hem of her nightgown barely covered her thighs. The covers were quickly snatched to her neck as fear entered her red, swollen eyes. "Joni, you know I'd never hurt you."

Wet lashes fluttered against her cheeks, creating a new river of tears. The rapid rise and fall of her shoulders slowed. She nodded and relaxed her death grip on the blanket. "Please, James. I'm fine. Now, get out."

He stood and she sunk into the mattress. For some reason, his presence agitated her. He thought back to the days of living at home with his sister. Stopping at the door, he turned toward her. "Is this a bad time of the month?"

"No!" She laughed, sniffed, and laughed again. Her gaze held his. "Come back in the morning. I missed you."

"I love you, Joni." He shut the door on her soft cries.

In the hall, Isaac rubbed his fist over his eyes and held up his arms. "I wanted you to come home yesterday. Joni's sad."

James lifted his son and retreated to the living room. "I see that. Do you know why?"

"That man at church said she couldn't sing."

He placed his son on the couch and sat beside him. Joni had a beautiful voice. Who would dare tell her such a thing? A few women at church might be jealous of her talent, but... "What man?"

"The one I was supposed to be nice to."

Bending, he unlaced his boots. In his mind, he reconstructed the arrangement of church pews. Most people sat in the same row every Sunday. None of the men would criticize the singing. Unless he was new. Maybe that's why she wanted Isaac to be nice. But not to like her voice and to tell her she couldn't sing were two different things. "Wonder why someone would do that?"

"Cause that mean girl is jealous."

James toed off a boot and sighed. Whoever she was, she probably couldn't carry a tune in a bucket. "Did Joni tell you that?"

"No, Miss Marla did. We don't like gossips. Do you?"

"Nope." The other boot clunked to the carpet. For Joni to be crying after midnight there had to be more to the story than Isaac knew. James fell against the couch cushions, but sat up as a random thought hit him. "Did Joni slap anyone?"

Little blue eyes narrowed. "No sir, but I kicked that man's leg."

"Good." James grinned and ruffled the little blond head. "Go back to bed. Joni will be okay. She just had her feelings hurt."

Isaac scrambled off the couch. "If you don't cry, you can sleep with me in my room."

"That's okay. I'm gonna bunk on the couch tonight." James grabbed a couple of throw pillows and stuffed them against the padded armrest.

A sweet kiss landed on his cheek. "Is Joni the momma, now?"

What happened while he was gone? Innocent blue eyes blinked, waiting for an answer. "Not yet, but hopefully one day she will be."

"Good. That means you can sleep with her."

James choked. "What?"

Isaac tilted his head. "Uncle Ray sleeps with girlfriends, but you don't sleep with Momma. When I grow up, I'm gonna be like him. Mommas are bad."

Pulling his son in his lap, James did his best to explain about girlfriends and why he was sleeping on the cold couch instead of in a warm bed next to Joni.

~~~

The smell of bananas and pumpkin woke him. James smiled as Joni hummed in the kitchen. On the floor by the coffee table, Isaac sat in front of a half-empty bowl of oatmeal. Stretching fully awake, James tossed the blanket-thing covering him and swung his feet off the couch.

Isaac smiled. "Good morning, Daddy." Oatmeal ran down his chin.

"Don't talk with your mouth full."

Joni walked out from the galley kitchen with an apron tied around her waist. One hand parked on her hip, but a playful smile graced her lips. "It's Christmas Eve, and since we have to be at the farm for lunch, we'll skip the argument concerning sleeping arrangements. Don't let it happen again."

"My damsel was distressed. What kind of prince charming leaves his lady without wiping her tears?"

"The prince was forbidden to enter the castle. He wasn't supposed to hear the distress." Her smile grew. "You have to stick with the rules. No cohabiting."

He bit his bottom lip. "Yes, ma'am." He stood and walked

in front of her. There was no sign of tears. "Good morning, beautiful." He dipped his head and tasted pumpkin on her lips. "Hmm. Pie for breakfast?"

She snuggled against him. "It isn't pie. It's a pumpkin roll with a cream cheese center."

He sniffed the air above her head. "And the bananas?"

She giggled near his heart. "Pudding. It's my grandmother's recipe. It doesn't come from a box. I hope everyone likes it. Some people would rather have instant."

"Good." He kissed her temple. "That means more for me." Holding her shoulders, he searched her eyes. Happiness sparkled back at him. "Are unwanted guests allowed shower privileges?"

She smiled and returned to the kitchen. "You were never unwanted. Just not allowed." She stuffed her hands into oversized mitts and removed a pecan pie from the oven.

"Is that breakfast?"

She pointed to a bowl of dreaded oatmeal. "If you want a shower, you need to hurry. I don't want to be late. Aunt Sandra said your family eats at twelve thirty."

"Trust me, by the time the women get the ham cooked it will be closer to one. Everyone will be starved to death and won't mind the dried-out meat."

~ ~ ~

Lunch was exactly as James described, but Joni was surprised to see both Mr. and Mrs. Preston there.

James whispered near her ear. "Don't look so shocked. My family is good at pretending." He winked and swiped a piece pie off her plate.

"Wait until you meet my family tomorrow."

"Good thing we're not eating chicken, eh James?" These words came from one of the uncles near the television.

"Don't be jealous." James landed a quick kiss on her lips. "Yum, better than chicken."

Heat crawled up her cheeks. "James, people are watching."

Despite the frowns aimed at them, his smile was contagious. "I know."

Across the room, Aunt Sandra cleared her throat. "Joni, how was the Christmas Cantata? I'm sorry we couldn't make it."

The thought of never singing in church again stung her eyes. She smiled through the hurt as she remembered Pastor's words.

James caressed her cheek. "You okay?"

She leaned into his palm and whispered, "I'm fine." Turning to Aunt Sandra she said, "There were some last-minute changes, but I heard it was nice." Catching Mrs. Preston's gaze, Joni silently begged her not to elaborate.

~~~

James cornered his mother at the sink. "What happened at church? I came home last night and found Joni crying."

The hardness in her voice matched the wet plate she pressed in his hand. "James Isaac Preston. Have you lost all sense?"

He glanced around the busy kitchen to see if anyone overheard. He hadn't been scolded by his mother in years.

She nodded to a dish towel. "Dry."

"Mom, I didn't do anything. I'd never hurt Joni."

"You caused this mess." Her hands stilled in the soapy water. "How?"

"Oh, for goodness' sake." She scrubbed the bottom of a stainless steel pot with a vengeance. "You can't expect to move her in without someone gossiping in the church. She can't sing in choir from your bed of sin."

The plate clattered into the empty sink. "God, Momma. Don't talk like that."

She pinched his arm. "Don't take the Lord's name in vain."

"Ouch. That hurt."

"Good." His mom returned to her scrubbing.

Through the window above the sink, James watched Joni push Isaac in the tire swing. What did her sharing his apartment have to do with her singing?

"James, I need your help out in the barn." His dad walked out the backdoor without glancing in his direction.

His mother mumbled under her breath. "Maybe he can get through to your hard head."

Circling through the living room, James lifted his jacket off the back of the couch. Uncle Lawrence, the probate judge, stretched out his feet. "Let me know if you need my services."

"Or my shotgun." Male laughter from his other uncles rose above the football announcer on the television. James obviously didn't get the joke. All day his family had been acting strange. They treated him like a leper and Joni like a queen. What could his dad want in the barn? There was nothing out there but the tractor. He walked through the double doors and looked up in time to see his father's fist.

James found himself on the cold dirt floor. He touched his burning lip and then stared at the blood on his fingers.

His dad bolted the door. "Get up."

He hadn't seen his dad this angry since Uncle Tommy, the sheriff, busted James and his friends for drinking beer down by the pond when they were sixteen. Up until today, his father had never punched him.

"What's it gonna take to penetrate that thick skull?" His dad circled.

Ignoring the ringing in his ear, James came to his feet. "What's wrong with you? Why'd you hit me?"

"What's wrong with me? I'm not the one who ruined a young girl's reputation. Why, James? She's not one of those girls you picked up off the street. Did you buy her a wedding band for Christmas? Is that what you're waiting for?"

"No, Dad. I bought her a keyboard." A second blow landed on his chin. James staggered back into the tractor. His temper ignited. He worked his jaw and glared at his father. "You do that again, old man, and you'll regret it."

"Who's gonna make me? A wet puppy like you? A real man steps up to his responsibilities. He doesn't hide in some apartment. Your mother and I raised you better than to treat Joni that disrespectful."

Laughter erupted from James. "Of all the sins I've been guilty of, you choose to go ballistic over this? Joni's innocent. Not that it's any of your business, but last night I slept on the couch."

All the bluster went out of his dad. His shoulders sagged with his sigh and he dropped his fist. "You expect me to believe you? With your reputation?"

"My reputation? Don't forget about yours. You know, the sins of the father…" James's words hung in the air. He upturned an empty five-gallon bucket and sat, careful to stay out of swinging distance. "Dad, Joni and I haven't…" He rested his elbows on his knees. "It's not my first choice, but she keeps me in line. I love her. I couldn't do anything to hurt her."

"You love her?" At James's nod, his dad continued, "Then why don't you marry her?"

Pulling his jacket closed, he fumbled with the buttons. "She needs to finish school."

His dad nodded his head. "I agree. But you can't live together without making her your wife. You've put the cart before the horse. Why?"

James sighed and peeled the yellow paint from the bucket. "I was there when you left. Mom cried herself to sleep for months." His father groaned, but James didn't look up. "What you did, it destroyed her. Everyone says I act just like you. I love Joni too much to hurt her like that. I mean, how do I guarantee something like that won't happen?"

Tears shimmered in his dad's eyes. "Son, there are consequences to sin that outlive forgiveness. Learn from my mistake. I wanted things my own way. Not God's. That's where I went wrong. If you stay with Him, life's road is a lot less bumpy."

Isaac's wail echoed through the thin barn walls. James raced out the barn toward the swing. By the time he reached them, Joni cradled his son in her arms and wiped blood from his mouth. "He fell off the tire swing." Her eyes widened. "What happened to you?"

Isaac sniffed and reached for James. He held him with one arm while Joni's gentle fingers traced his own bottom lip. "I'm fine. A little mishap in the barn."

She kissed the place between his lip and chin. When Isaac leaned down, she kissed him too. "Like father, like son?"

~ ~ ~

That night, as James drove her new Honda down the country road, Joni closed her eyes and thought back to the events of the day. After Isaac fell off the swing, James acted different. Although his eyes caressed her from across the room as the family sang carols around the piano, the kisses and hugs stopped. Why? She reached for his hand, but it was on the steering wheel. Her fingers rested on his jeans. "James?"

He braked at the stop sign and signaled right. "Yeah, Joni?" He was studying the oncoming traffic and didn't look her way.

She unbuckled and crowded his space. When he turned his head, she covered his mouth with her own. He returned her kiss and the air sizzled between them. Joni felt the jolt when he placed the car in park. His arms came around her and the steering wheel pressed against her spine. A horn blew. She scrambled back into her seatbelt. The heat in James's eyes was brighter that the headlights that zoomed around them. "What was that for?"

She licked her lips and smiled. "Just checking to see if you still love me."

James's laugh stirred a sleeping Isaac in the backseat. "Are you convinced? Or do you need another demonstration?"

Content with the knowledge that James was his old self again, she leaned against the seat. "I'm convinced." Her eyelids drifted as he pulled onto the highway.

"Joni." Warm, soft lips kissed her hand. "Joni."

Slowly, she stirred and smiled. "Hmm."

"We're home." He pressed the apartment key into her palm. "Open the door and I'll carry Isaac."

She blinked and yawned. "Okay."

He followed her up the red-stained, wooden stairs. She fumbled with the keys and opened the door. James entered with Isaac.

In Isaac's room, she pulled back the sheets. James laid his son on the mattress and stepped aside allowing Joni to remove Isaac's little sneakers. He curled under the covers as she kissed his cheek and whispered, "Goodnight, sweetie."

He never opened his eyes. "'Night, Joni."

In the hall, she stepped into James's waiting arms and snuggled against his chest. His heartbeat was strong. His arms comforting.

"Don't go back to sleep."

As if she could sleep standing up. "Why not?"

He led her to the master bedroom. She remembered Pastor's words on keeping your distance and untangled herself from his arms. With a flourish, he opened the closet and flung back the sheet that hid Isaac's Christmas gifts. "Because, Mrs. Claus, it's time to play Santa."

"Joni! Wake up! Santa came! He was here!" Isaac's voice intruded on her wonderful dream. She opened her eyes to stare into his excited face. "Get up! Get up! Wait till you see what he brought you."

He bounded off the bed and she rose up on her elbows. James reclined against the bedroom doorframe with a mug of coffee in his hand. His lips tugged upward as she scooted out from the covers. She felt his gaze and was glad she wore her new pajamas instead of a nightgown. Although James agreed the bedroom was off-limits during his overnight visits, she had to admit her dream of him lying beside her was fresh on her mind. His habit of not wearing a shirt wasn't helping the situation.

"Good morning, beautiful. Ready to open presents?"

She smoothed a hand through her hair and crossed the room. "Good morning." Ignoring the desire to snuggle against him, she kissed his cheek and ducked under his arm into the hall.

Isaac raced back from the living room and snatched her hand. "Hurry."

She stifled a yawn and quickened her pace. Her breath caught. Between the colorful, lit tree and a mountain of gifts, the keyboard she'd admired in the mall called to her. "James." A big red bow shined from the middle of its keys. Ribbon trailed down to an amplifier hidden behind the tree. Isaac jumped in his battery-powered truck and promptly drove into the wall. She should scold him. Slowly, as if in a dream, she weaved a path through the gifts and trailed her fingers down the weighted keys. James reached around her and turned on the power. A kiss landed on her neck. "Merry Christmas."

She turned into his arms. "I love you."

He tucked a strand of hair behind her ear. His lips twitched once. Joni glanced over her shoulder and then back at the man she loved. "Thank you." She leaned her head back and laughed. "I love it, and I love you. Now, teach me to play church music."

He groaned playfully against her neck. "Forget church. How about heaven? It's the first song I can remember singing."

The look in his eyes had nothing whatsoever to do with God's home, but Joni turned and placed her hands on the keys. "Show me."

Strong arms came around her. "All right. Put your hands on top of mine. I can't tell you the notes, so close your eyes and feel the music."

She did as he asked, and he sang about the desire to experience heaven. Though the rhythm of his song was similar to that heard in church, his sultry voice reminded her of last night's dream of forbidden pleasures. Warm breath tickled her ear and Joni shivered with sensations that were everything but godly. She opened her eyes and removed her hands. "James, your music feels different. Are you sure this song is about Jesus?"

He turned her in his arms and she saw the danger in his eyes. His lips teased her to a state of breathlessness and skimmed across her neck. He whispered, "Heaven can be found on earth."

The knock on the door snapped her out of his spell. James stepped back and rubbed a hand down his face. "Who visits on Christmas morning?"

She giggled at his frustration as he snatched open the door.

Isaac looked up from his truck, which had plowed a row through the presents. "Grandpa. Grandma. Look what Santa got me."

～～～

His mother scooped Isaac up while his father closed the door and glared a hole through James's chest. Derision dripped from his voice. "Put some clothes on, son."

Without a word, James headed down the hall. After shrugging into a blue T-shirt, he hurried to the recliner and smiled as Isaac shredded through paper, ribbon, and bows.

Joni walked from the kitchen balancing a cup and saucer in one hand and a mug in the other. "James, you want coffee?"

"Yeah." He couldn't help but admire the view as she bent over the coffee table and placed a cup in front of his mother. The green, shimmery fabric of her pajamas clung to her backside. He sucked in a breath as his pulse drummed in his ear. She stood and turned. Gold bells dangled just below her waist from each end of the drawstring belt. He swallowed and clenched his hands in his lap.

"James." Her voice penetrated the fog surrounding his brain.

His gaze traveled upward. Gold paint splashed "Merry Christmas" across her chest. He thought about the lyrics in the song he sang for Joni and wanted to explore some golden streets of his own.

Fingers snapped. "James." He blinked. Her lips pressed in a tight line. Face crimson, her eyes cut to the couch were his parents sat and then narrowed on him. "Your coffee?"

He snapped out of his fantasy and accepted the mug. His thumb caressed the inside of her wrist during the exchange.

She wet her lips and addressed his parents. "Excuse me."

His eyes followed her down the hall until she disappeared behind the bedroom door. Isaac was busy playing with the remote-controlled car Joni had bought him.

James's mom balanced her cup and saucer on her knee. "I thought you said yesterday that you and Joni aren't living together?"

"We're not. It's Christmas, so Joni let me sleep on the couch again."

His dad lifted the folded blanket and pillow and raised one brow. "She *let* you sleep on the couch?" James nodded. "In your own apartment?"

"Yeah." His jaw ached from yesterday. He didn't have any intentions of repeating the fight with his dad. "Joni moved in because the apartment is close to campus. She takes care of the place while I'm working out of town."

His mother turned her attention to Isaac, but James knew from experience that she had eyes and ears in the back of her head. Doubt clouded his dad's eyes, but James refused to cower under his father's questions. "And when you're in town, you sleep on the couch?"

The bedroom door opened to reveal Joni fully dressed. Hopefully his father would drop the subject. He didn't want her embarrassed by his parents. She was halfway to the living room when Isaac came to his defense. "Daddy has to sleep on the couch, Grandpa. We don't want Joni to be a momma yet. Ain't that right, Daddy?"

James choked on his coffee, and Joni froze in the hallway.

His mother's sharp hiss of breath was followed by, "Isaac? Where did you hear that?"

Innocent blue eyes glanced around the room. "Me and Daddy talked about it, yesterday. We gotta wait till after Joni's school is finished. If you marry them, mommas ain't bad."

His mother stammered while his dad said, "At least we know he slept on the couch."

"James?" Tears shimmered in Joni's eyes. "Can I see you in the kitchen?"

Isaac continued to shock his grandparents with a four-year-old's philosophy of why girlfriends were better than mommas. Without a word, James rose from the recliner and followed Joni behind the wall separating the galley from the living area. With each step, he wrestled with the perfect words of apology.

She stopped in the small space between the refrigerator and the stove with her back toward him. His hand slid across her shoulder. He stepped close and whispered, "I love you."

"Did you tell Isaac that you wanted to—?" Her shoulders rose. "That after I graduate, we would...?" A delicate hand waved in front of her. "About the whole marriage thing."

His arms wrapped around her. He kept his voice low so his parents couldn't overhear. "We talked about this last week. Remember? The night of your wreck?"

She turned and slowly shook her head. The tears were gone. Her tongue peeked out and wet her parted lips. "I thought you were just saying that to get me to spend the night."

James swallowed and shook his head. "No." Her lips curled slowly and her eyes traveled the length of him. His body shivered as if her caress was real. Then it was. Intoxicated by her kiss, he moved closer, crowding her against the wall.

"Your mother and I can't stay for breakfast."

James lifted his head and the kitchen refocused. Heavy footfalls sounded on the other side of the wall. In one swift move, James released Joni, stepped back, and opened the refrigerator door to shield her from his dad's knowing eyes.

"James?"

Glancing over his shoulder at his father, James fought for breath. "Yeah, Dad?"

"We need to make our way to Sara's and see what Santa brought Andrew. We can't stay for breakfast."

As James struggled to conceal his desire, Joni grabbed the orange juice and pivoted on her heel. Facing the cabinets, she said, "Sorry, Mr. Preston. We'll be right there."

His father disappeared around the corner and James fell back into the refrigerator, closing the door in the process. He released a breath and opened his eyes to find Joni's mischievous stare. Her teeth scraped across her bottom lip.

After one step, he tasted sweet oranges. He whispered urgently into her hair. "Don't ever do that again." His mother's voice called his name from the living room and he added, "At least, not while we have company."

Chapter Thirteen

"What's up with you this morning?" Cecil waved his pen in front of James's face. "Pay attention."

James pushed Joni from his thoughts. "Sorry, sir. Late night."

Cecil cocked his head. "Ray talk you into going out partying?"

James shook his head.

"Snuggled up to your phone again?" Cecil put the pen down. "What's got you distracted?"

James took a deep breath. "I was wondering if the prefab shop has any openings."

"It's that girl, isn't it?" Cecil laid his hard hat on the drafting table. "You want to settle down? Start a family?"

James pulled up a chair and met his boss's stare. "Yes, sir. I do."

"Dang, boy. I need you out here in the field." The older man slurped coffee from a white mug. "You know, at home there's little overtime pay and no per diem."

The check from the sale of timber on his land could pay the rent for two years. His dad called yesterday to say he'd deposited it into James's account. "I know."

The general foreman propped his feet on the table. "We're working five, tens here. You've been home every weekend since New Year's."

James tapped his boot heel against the table leg as he thought of the lonely drive to Sara's every Friday and Saturday night. Sunday mornings, he met Joni and Isaac for breakfast and then suffered through a long-winded sermon. Isaac's custody-court date was in a few weeks. James wanted to make them a real family.

He couldn't allow Joni to quit school, but he could be there to help her study every night. "It isn't enough."

Cecil sighed and frowned. "I'll see what I can do."

~ ~ ~

James Isaac Preston is excluded as the biological father of Isaac Steven Davies.

The piece of paper trembled in James's hand. Excluded? That would mean that… This couldn't be right. The return address was from the clinic where he and Isaac gave blood samples for the court-ordered paternity test. He flipped back to the letter and skipped the comparison chart. He read the conclusion again. *James Isaac Preston is excluded as the biological father of Isaac Steven Davies.*

He ripped open the letter from his attorney, and then the one from Isaac's Guardian ad Litem. A court hearing was scheduled for Monday morning.

James sank into the chair. Isaac lay on his stomach watching cartoons on the hotel flat screen. Blond hair curled around the collar of his Diego pajamas.

A roaring in James's ears blinded him. Isaac wasn't his son? Resting his elbows on his knees, his head hung in limbo. How could Kathy do this? She swore Isaac was his and he believed her.

His college career. His dreams. He traded them all to be a dad. Only now he wasn't. He cursed and slung an empty bottle across the room. The vanity mirror shattered into a million pieces, like James's heart.

"Daddy." Little hands tugged on his leg. "You make me sad and funny inside."

"Isaac." He lifted the little boy he loved so much. He couldn't lose him. It didn't matter what a DNA test said. No one would take him away.

"Daddy, you squishing me."

Easing his hold on Isaac, James covered his inner turmoil with laughter. "You want to go see Joni tomorrow?"

The little boy grinned. "Yeah. Can we? Can we, please?"

He nodded. "In the morning, after we pack up."

Isaac danced in front of him, chanting, "Joni. Joni. Joni."

Someone knocked on the door. "You guys okay in there?" Ray must've heard the crash.

Shattered glass covered the floor. James lifted Isaac before his son stepped on a sliver of glass and then carried him to the door. He held him out to Ray. "Hold him a minute, will ya? I need to clean up this mess."

Ray's brows shot up and he set Isaac down outside the opened door. With shaky hands, James passed his friend the envelope. Ray read the package contents as James picked up the glass fragments.

"Man, I don't know what to say."

"It doesn't change anything. I still have custody and on Monday, I'll make it permanent."

"James, be reasonable. I don't think the judge will rule in favor of a single guy who travels like you do. They're not—"

"Shut up!" James clenched his fist. A triangle of glass sliced through his palm. Blood poured down his arm. The pain made it real. He swore and threw the shard on the carpet.

"Is Daddy okay?" Isaac asked Ray.

"He's fine. Let's go find Lorraine."

The door closed and Ray and Isaac were gone. Chunks of glass swam in his vision. Blood flowed from his palm. What would it be like to bleed out and give into the numbing pain? How easy would it be to finish the job? Then he'd feel nothing. He picked up the triangular prism and touched its tip.

"Don't even think about doing something stupid." Ray helped him stand and settled him in the chair. He threw the glass into the garbage can.

"Where's Isaac?"

"With Lorraine." Ray poured amber liquid from a bottle into a plastic hotel cup and placed it on the table. "Drink it."

Numb with pain, James swallowed liquid fire while Ray picked the bits of glass from his right hand. "Stupid, moron. Did you think I'd let you do it?"

"I wouldn't have."

"You got that straight. I would've whooped your butt all the way to hell and back." He wrapped a hand towel around James's palm. "Hold this and don't move." Ray stepped out on the sidewalk and flagged down a maid. "Hi there, sweet thing. Baby Ray needs a favor."

James drank two cups of whiskey while the cute maid cleaned up the glass. "Bob will probably charge you for the mirror. But don't worry, they've been broken before."

"Thanks." Ray winked at the girl and closed the door.

How did Ray do that?

His friend laughed. "One day, I'll tell you my secret. Until then, drink up my friend." Ray filled a second cup placed there by the maid moments ago and toasted James's misery.

When Ray's image blurred before him, James mumbled, "Thanks."

"That's what friends are for, dude. That's what friends are for."

The next afternoon, James declined Ray's offer to ride with him. He texted his mom and sister and reminded them about the court date. The paternity results weren't mentioned.

On the road home, he called his attorney. "Nothing's changed. I still want custody. Do you think it's possible?"

"Only the judge knows, but it's probable unless a suitable home is found. The county is usually given supervision in cases like this, but unless a blood relative files, I don't see any reason why the state wouldn't grant you guardianship. Tasha Covington knows you."

Later, James stopped for a burger and let Isaac run off some energy in the play place. He'd forgotten to tell Joni he was coming home. He dialed her number. "Hey beautiful, you miss me?"

Her laugh tickled his ear. "Of course I miss you."

Isaac's eyes lit up. "That Joni? I wanna talk."

James tuned out Isaac's chatter and waved him down in his seat. "We have a court hearing Monday morning."

"Daddy, I want to talk!"

Joni laughed. "I remember, but maybe I should talk to my other boyfriend first."

"Don't hang up. I have something important to tell you."

"Sure."

James passed the phone to Isaac.

"Joni, will you take me on a date?"

James laughed and nearly choked on a french fry.

Isaac smiled at whatever Joni was saying. "Tomorrow." Then he frowned. "Does Daddy have to go?" Little blue eyes rolled. "Yes, but he cried when he cut his hand."

"Isaac. That's enough. Give me the phone."

"I'm talking to Joni," he whispered. In the phone he said, "Uncle Ray gave him some whiskey to make it better."

Not good. James snatched the phone from Isaac. "Go play."

Isaac ran to the tunnel and crawled in. James held the phone up to his ear. "Joni?"

"What happened to your hand?"

He flexed his wrapped hand. "A scratch."

"You were drinking whiskey?"

"Alcohol can be used as an antiseptic." He cleared his throat. "I took off work for court Monday." He wanted to tell her about his transfer to the prefab shop off Dauphin Island Parkway.

"Are you okay? You sound distracted."

The paternity results were locked in his truck, but the words on the pages swam in his head. Joni loved Isaac more than his own mother did. If they lost him…"I'll be fine if I can convince my son to come down from the slide and eat his kid's meal."

Her laughter had healing properties. "Good luck with that. I love you, James."

"Goodnight, Joni."

Hours later, James yawned and turned into his apartment complex. He drove past the office and the pool. The truck's headlights illuminated the back of her Honda.

Joni was here.

In his apartment.

In his bed.

He was sick of playing by the rules. Tired of sleeping alone. He needed Joni's smile to remind him of innocence. He needed her kiss as proof of her love. He needed her arms around him to steady his shattered world. He wanted to hear her whisper that everything was all right. That Isaac was theirs, regardless of what a piece of paper claimed.

He needed her.

He shut off the ignition and eased out from under the wheel. He reached in the truck-bed and slung Isaac's bag over his shoulder. Rummaging through his own bag, he dug out the box he'd purchased two weeks ago and shoved it in his front pocket.

James held his breath and opened the passenger door. Nimble fingers unbuckled the sleeping child. *Don't wake up. Don't wake up.* He lifted Isaac against him. Using his hip, he bumped the door shut. Isaac stirred and James shifted him against his shoulder. "Shhh. Daddy's got you." He pressed the remote lock and eased up the stairs.

Balancing Isaac, he inserted the key into the lock. The duffle bag slipped off his shoulder and landed with a thud. James froze and held his breath. He relaxed when Isaac remained asleep. Stepping over the bag, he opened the door and eased down the hall. The bathroom light was on. Was Joni scared of the dark? Isaac slept on while James tucked him into the bed.

He retraced his steps. A cat ran into the night when he retrieved Isaac's bag. Stepping back in the apartment, he closed the door. Joni's keyboard glistened in the light coming through the window. He left his shoes and socks by the door.

His heart thumped in his throat as he moved down the hall. He froze in the bedroom doorway. Joni slept on her side, facing him. One arm rested on top of the quilt. The bathroom light streamed in through the walk-in closet and her golden hair shimmered. James's smile grew.

He moved to stand beside the bed. Green silky straps crossed Joni's bare shoulders. James swallowed and placed the box on the side table.

She shrieked and snatched the covers to her neck.

"It's me." James suppressed the urge to reach for her.

Her wide eyes blinked. "James?"

"Yeah." A shaky hand ran through his hair. "I'm sorry. I didn't mean to scare you."

She reclined against the headboard. "What are you doing here?"

He knelt beside the bed. "I told you I was coming home for court."

"I thought you meant tomorrow."

"Nope."

"It's late." She dropped the quilt. "I guess you can sleep on the sofa."

The lacy front of her nightgown dipped low. His whole body quivered. "I love you."

She smiled. "I love you, too."

He reached for the box on the side table and flipped it open. A princess cut diamond ring glistened against the black felt. Joni gasped and her hand trembled at her throat. "James?"

"I wanted to wait until after court because I didn't want you to question my motives. But…" He removed the engagement ring and slid it on her finger. "You need to plan our wedding."

"Are you proposing?" Joni tilted her hand toward the light and stared.

He waited until she looked at him, and then he smiled. "I'm not asking. I can't take the chance you'll say no. Especially after tonight."

Her ringed hand caressed his cheek. "What's so special about tonight?"

James stood and shrugged out of his shirt. Joni swallowed as he tossed it on the carpet. The metal button on his jeans released with a flick of his fingers.

She wet her lips. "James?" Color crept up her cheeks. "What are you doing?"

"I'm not sleeping on the couch." He stepped near the bed and held his breath. The final decision was hers.

Joni lifted the covers and he slid in beside her.

~ ~ ~

James whistled as he flipped the omelet onto a plate and

turned off the stove. Joni's arms wrapped around him and a soft kiss landed between his shoulder blades. He turned into her embrace and gathered her close to his heart.

Her head buried against his chest and she whispered, "James, I love you."

He lifted her chin and captured her gaze. "Don't do it, Joni. Don't feel guilty."

"But we—"

"Love each other." He threaded his hand through hers and kissed her ring. "Didn't Abraham go into Sarah and make her his wife? They had no ceremony. Isaac and Rebekah? No. What's the difference between them and us? Last night, you became my wife in the biblical sense and soon we'll make it legal."

"Joni!" Isaac barged up the hall and wiggled between them. "You're here. Wait, I gotta get something." He ran to his duffle bag near the door.

James recaptured Joni's gaze. "I love you." He bent to kiss her lips.

"Daddy, I can't find 'em." Isaac yelled from the living room.

Their lips curled at the interruption. James rested his forehead against hers. "Look in the side pocket."

Isaac held out a piece of construction paper with two stick figures drawn on it. The girl had yellow hair the same color as the small boy holding her hand.

One blink and her tears were gone. She hefted Isaac in her arms. "Is it me?"

"That's me and you." Isaac touched the paper. "Daddy's at work."

"Thank you." She hugged him close. "I love it."

James leaned against the cabinet and breathed easy. His son snuggled close to Joni and told her all about his new school. James leaned down and kissed her full on the mouth.

"Daa-dee!" Isaac pushed him away.

James winked at Joni. "Is there a parade today?"

"Yes." She smiled down at Isaac. "You'll love it. We'll catch beads and eat MoonPies until we're sick."

"Can we go, Daddy?"

"Whatever you want, Isaac. Today is a special day."

"Why? Is it Christmas?"

James ruffled Isaac's hair. "No. It's better than Christmas. Joni and I are engaged."

He wrinkled his forehead. "What's 'gaged?" Joni laughed beside them.

"One day. *Soon.*" James captured her smiling gaze before he looked down at his son. "Joni will marry us."

Isaac grinned at Joni. "You'll be the momma. Will you go to work too?"

"Yes."

"No." James interrupted. "After court Monday, I'll be working at the shop in town. You can't sacrifice your education to be with us."

Isaac wiggled down and ran toward the bathroom.

Joni stretched on her toes and James leaned down to meet her halfway. Her arms slipped around his neck. "I want to be with you, wherever you go." Her kiss left him winded.

He winked. "You'll have to persuade me later."

Chapter Fourteen

A knock landed on the bathroom door and the knob rattled. She shut off the hairdryer.

"Joni, we need to get in there."

She snatched the plug from the wall and unlocked the hall door.

Isaac ran in. "Me first, Daddy."

Ducking through the walk-through-closet, she rushed to find an outlet in the master bedroom. James hooked his thumbs in the belt loops of her jeans and pulled her against him.

She laughed. "James, I'm late for class and I have to finish drying my hair before I can straighten it."

"It's already straight."

She turned and wiggled out of his arms. "The straightener smoothes the frizzy strands." She unplugged the clock. It was no good setting the alarm when James turned it off after the first beep. Joni'd slept through it. She plugged in her dryer and perched on the edge of the bed.

"I like the fluffy parts." He lay behind her and propped on an elbow.

Flipping her head upside down, she dried the rest of her hair. She could feel his eyes on her. Peeping through the curtain of her hair, she smiled at his wink.

She turned the dryer off and set it on the floor. "What time is it?"

"Don't know. Someone unplugged the clock."

"James…"

He laughed and picked his phone up off the end table. "Eight twenty-nine."

"Ugh! I've got to go." Brushing her hair out, she caught his gaze in the dresser mirror. "It's your fault I'm late."

"Because somebody wouldn't stay on her side of the bed."

Her fingers pulled her hair through a scrunchie. Heat climbed the sides of her neck. "I like to snuggle."

"And I like it when you snuggle."

Her eyes found his in the mirror. "If I skipped class, we could snuggle for another hour."

He lifted her under the arms and half-carried, half-dragged her up the hall. Joni laughed the whole way to the front door. "What are you doing?"

"Bawhahaha. I'm throwing you out." He kissed her cheek. "Leave now or stay forever."

"Both."

Isaac looked up from his cartoon. "If Daddy don't want you, you can sleep in my room."

Laughing, Joni turned to James.

"I don't think so."

Joni broke his hold. She crossed the room, bent down, and kissed Isaac's cheek. "I'll see you in a little bit, okay."

"'Kay, Joni."

She slipped on her shoes while James held the door. Rising on her tiptoes, she kissed him again. "See you at eleven." She slipped out of his arms, walked three steps on the concrete porch, and spun around. "Wait."

She wrapped her arms around his waist and snuggled close against his chest. Strong arms tightened around her. His heart thundered under her cheek. She held him until his heartbeat slowed to a steady pace. Lifting her face to his, she said, "You are the best daddy in the world, and I'm sure the judge will realize it."

James dipped his head and brushed his mouth across hers. "Thank you. I needed to hear that." He kissed her again and Joni put all her love in her response. A few moments later, he smiled down at her. "You're late."

She massaged his tense shoulders. "I know, but you need Isaac's booster seat."

James turned. "Isaac, stay here. I'll be right back."

"Okay, Daddy." Lying on his stomach with his legs crossed, his little feet swayed in midair.

She waited on the landing while James grabbed his keys and pulled the door to. They walked down the stairs side by side. At her car, he switched Isaac's booster to his truck.

He turned toward her and dipped his head. She rose on tiptoe, anticipating his kiss. His gaze landed somewhere over her shoulder. He pulled her arms from around his neck. Instead of kissing her lips, he lifted her left hand and kissed her engagement ring. "I love you."

Joni turned to follow his gaze, but when his lips met hers, the world around them faded. Holding her hand, he stepped aside and she slid in the driver's seat. "Drive safe." Kneeling down, he leaned in and brushed his lips over hers again. "Learn something for me."

With a turn of the key, the car hummed. "If I have to walk out in the middle of an Andrew Jackson impression, I'll be there."

With a nod and after one more kiss, James stepped back and closed her door. Thankfully, Joni was in such a hurry she didn't see their visitor.

The concrete sidewalk chilled his bare feet, but James held his ground against the temper in Pastor's eyes. The messenger of God closed the distance between them, and a cool February breeze brushed over James's naked chest.

"I hope that was a wedding band on her finger?" The look on his face reminded James of the church volleyball game four years ago when he'd punched sissy Billy for cheating.

James lifted his cold toes and rocked back on his heels. "Joni and I are engaged." He swallowed. "Come on up to the apartment and congratulate me."

~ ~ ~

Maybe he should've told her about the results of the paternity test and warned her of today's outcome, but he couldn't diminish the sparkle in her eyes. As James turned right on Stanton Drive, his cell rang. "Out of class already?"

"Kathy's here."

His heart stopped as his eyes darted to the little boy beside him. This wasn't good. How did she get out of jail? He ran a hand through his hair and breathed deep. "Has she seen you?"

"No, I'm in my car. She just walked through security."

Ray's prophetic words of doom breezed through his mind. James had to protect Isaac. No matter the cost. "Don't go in. Meet me at Tricentennial Park."

"I'll be there in two minutes."

He curved down Lake Drive and parked the truck near the entrance.

Isaac craned his neck to see the park area. "What we doing here? I want to see Joni."

"She's coming." James wished he could be as innocent as Isaac. Would he see him again after today?

The little boy pointed and said, "Look, ducks."

"Isaac, Daddy loves you." James blinked against the sting in his eyes.

"Are you gonna be sad again?"

"I hope not." James propped his hands on his head and breathed. He couldn't lose Isaac. He couldn't.

"Are you ascared?"

The wave of dizziness passed. He shook off the feeling of helplessness and smiled at his son. "A little bit."

A small hand covered his larger one. "Joni says when we are ascared we talk to God."

He ran a hand down his face. "Joni would say that."

"She's here!" Isaac reached for the buckle release.

"Isaac, wait here." James leapt out of the truck. Joni met him outside her car.

"What's wrong?"

"I think—I know—Isaac isn't…" He couldn't say the words. "Joni, will you trust me?"

"Yes." She caressed his cheek and kissed him. "I love you."

James wrapped her in his arms and held on until the fear eased. He lifted her chin and kissed her hard. "Take Isaac back to the apartment. Pack up our things. All of them. I don't have time to explain, but if Kathy's there…"

Her eyes widened. "The judge? Doesn't Isaac have to be there?"

"No. It wasn't mentioned in the papers. If they ask, I'll say he's with a sitter." He grabbed her and held her tight once more. "Joni, I love you. Don't forget it."

"James?" Her gaze captured his and he didn't disguise the fear crawling in his gut. "Oh, no. We could lose him? Why didn't you tell me?"

He turned her loose and lifted Isaac, booster seat and all, out of the truck.

"Wahoo! Look, Daddy, I can fly."

Joni opened her backdoor and James strapped him in.

"Where'm I going?"

James kissed Isaac's cheek. "Joni'll tell you on the way."

"Are we going to work?" Isaac gasped. "Can Joni go with us?"

"No."

"Yes." She lifted her chin. "If this is what I think it is, I'm going too."

"Joni…"

"You will not leave me behind." Moisture gathered in her eyes. His love for her grew as she blinked them away. "I love you both."

"You don't understand. I couldn't find the words to tell you."

She caressed his cheek. "I'm not stupid. I understand exactly what's happening here."

James turned into her palm and brushed a kiss on her wrist. He couldn't let Joni quit college to be with him and Isaac, but he didn't have time to fight about it now. "We'll talk about it later." He opened her car door. "I'll meet you at the apartment."

"Call me and let me know what's happening."

~ ~ ~

He was out of his mind. James placed his keys and loose change in a box and stepped through the metal detector.

He should be on the road. Pocketing his things, he checked in with the officer in charge. But he wanted to be a real family with Joni and Isaac, and he couldn't do that traveling across country.

A blue pen marked through his name. "Where's the minor child?"

James swallowed. "With a sitter."

The officer cut his eyes to his partner. "Note that in the file."

"James." His attorney crossed the tiled floor and held out his hand. "How you doing?"

"Ready to get this over with."

"They're ready."

His mom and Sara waved from the waiting area. "Give me a minute."

His mother looked around behind him. "Where's Joni and Isaac?"

He whispered, "Home." He ran a shaky hand through his hair. "Mom, if things go bad..."

His mother's smile faded. "Are you expecting trouble?"

"Pray, Mom." He kissed her cheek. "Pray." Sara paled at his words.

James strode with his attorney in front of a bulletproof glass door. A guard entered a code and it opened. The attorney stopped on the other side of the glass. He waited for the click and lowered his voice. "There's been a new development. This morning, Kathy filed for return of custody."

"What? Why isn't she in jail?" James scrubbed a hand down the bridge of his nose. "I can't let that happen."

"If the judge rules in her favor, you can't stop it."

He rubbed his forehead and breathed. "You're saying I don't have a chance?" He should leave now, take Isaac, and run.

"I don't know. With the paternity results...I don't think your role as primary caregiver is going to amount to much." The attorney slapped his shoulder. "Let's pray this works out."

Pray? James had sneered at Pastor's suggestion of prayer this morning. Now it wasn't laughable. The room had one long mahogany table. Kathy and a suit sat on one side. He and his lawyer sat opposite of Kathy. A plain-clothes detective sat on the end, his gun visible on his side. Detective Simmons. Ray's cousin? He nodded at James.

A sheriff's deputy guarded a second door. He tapped on it. A robed judge entered and sat at the head of the table. "All interested parties are present?"

"Yes, Your Honor."

"Where is the minor child in question?"

James's attorney answered for him. "There was no indication his presence was required. My client chose to protect the child from an ugly court scene."

The judge removed his glasses and stared down the table at James. "Commendable, but as the child's welfare is no longer your concern, unwarranted."

James sucked in a breath. He opened his mouth to speak, but his attorney cut him off.

"Although my client has been excluded from the minor child's parentage, he wishes to continue with his petition for custody."

"I'm afraid this court rules his suit unacceptable in light of a recent filing."

Kathy couldn't have him. She couldn't. James rose from the table. He had to get to Isaac and Joni.

"Retain your seat."

He obeyed the judge's command and lowered himself to the chair.

"This court hereby revokes your custody of Isaac Steven Davies and orders you to present him to the J. R. Strickland Youth Center within two hours."

Kathy smirked across the table.

"No." The roaring in his ears drowned out the warning from his attorney. His chair fell back. Kathy would never find Isaac. He promised.

The detective blocked the door.

One of the suits spoke about flight risk and begged for restraint. When their intentions soaked through the fog in his brain, James's fist connected with the detective's jaw. He lunged for the door and ran toward the glass. Four deputies swarmed him and he fought them off. Stars danced before his eyes. Fire pierced his side. "Isaac!" Darkness overtook him.

~~~

Joni rocked Isaac in the recliner and sang softly. What was taking James so long? She knew the youth center didn't allow cell phones, but court should have ended hours ago. Isaac's eyes drifted shut. She kissed his brow and held him a little while longer. When he was awake, he usually wasn't still long enough for her to cuddle. "God, be with James, wherever he is. Protect Isaac from the cruelness of this world. And please let me stay in their life."

Silence answered her prayer. God seemed so far away.

By the door, two duffle bags and a suitcase were packed and waiting. One for each of them. The arm supporting Isaac went numb. She lifted him, walked to his room, and tucked him in.

A knock sounded at the door.

She hurried to answer before the noise woke Isaac.

A pretty black woman in her fifties, dressed in a suit, appeared in the peep hole. Joni slowly opened the door. She gasped. A uniformed sheriff's deputy and a plain-clothes cop stood on either side. "Joni Maher?" the lady asked.

"Yes, can I help you?"

The lady smiled. "My name is Tasha Covington. I'm with the Department of Human Services. This is Detective Simmons and Deputy Johnson." She waved her hand to the officers in turn. "We're looking for a minor, Isaac Davies. Do you know the location of this child?"

She wiped her palms on her jeans. "Where's James?"

"Mr. Preston was incarcerated for assaulting an officer and contempt of court. If Isaac isn't found soon, he will be charged with first-degree kidnapping."

Joni fell against the doorframe. *Oh God, what do I do? James will hate me if I give Isaac away, but I can't let him go to prison. Help me, Jesus. Help me.* "Wait. You can't charge a parent with kidnapping. James has custody."

"James Preston is not Isaac's biological father."

"What?" The floor spun under her feet. Little snippets of conversation from yesterday and this morning came back to her. He knew. He'd asked her if she would love Isaac if he wasn't his. The fear in his eyes this morning was real. How long had he known? "What will happen to Isaac? Where will you take him? To Kathy?" Her throat hurt and she sniffed several times. "She doesn't take care of him."

"Miss Maher, I'm sorry I can't divulge—"

"The mother tested positive for methamphetamines." The detective had the makings of a black eye and his lip was swollen. "Mobile County has retained protective custody of the child."

"Are you sure? How do you know this?"

His smile was kind. "I was in the courtroom, but I'm also a father. Where is he?"

Joni choked on a sob. "What will they do with Isaac?"

He shook his head. "I've said too much."

"Yes, you have." The social worker frowned at the officer. "Miss Maher, if you kno—

"Joni, I'm thirsty." Isaac rubbed his sleepy eyes behind her.

She slammed the door and slid the deadbolt in place. "Oh God, help me."

The pounding began immediately.

She swept Isaac up in her arms and held him close. The pounding continued.

"Oh God, help us." Joni ran through the living room. Her feet skidded to a halt in the hall. She was on the second floor.

She raced back to the door.

"Open up!"

Please God, make them go away. Joni turned to the kitchen. Glass rattled in the living room as the officer knocked on the windowpanes.

She was trapped. Nowhere to go. Joni heaved a sigh and ran to the bathroom. With both doors locked, Isaac trembled in her arms.

"Did they come to get me again?"

"Oh Isaac, I'm sorry. We should've left. We should've gone to the country. I should've known something was wrong when your daddy didn't call." Joni buried her face in Isaac's stomach. "I'm so sorry."

Little arms clung to her. "I'm ascared."

Joni breathed deep. The panic raged, but a defense of Isaac surged. Her kiss landed on his cheek. Shaky hands framed his face. "Isaac, look at me." Her eyes burned and her throat hurt, but Isaac needed her reassurance. "Don't be scared. I love you. Daddy loves you."

His pale eyes darted from the bathroom door back to her.

She hugged him close. "We'll find you. I promise, Isaac. Me and Daddy will find you."

Footsteps grew louder in the hall. "Miss Maher?"

Isaac flinched in her arms. Joni smoothed his hair. "It's going to be okay. Daddy and I will find you."

The bathroom door crashed in. Joni's heart lurched. Isaac clung to her as strong fingers pried him away. "Nooooo! I don't want to go. Joni! Joni!"

"Please don't take him." Fire pinched her fingers and her arms emptied. "Isaac!"

Little arms and legs flailed against his captors. "Nooooo!"

She collapsed on the bathroom floor. Isaac's cries faded up the hall. A surge of adrenaline surfaced. Leaping off the floor, she rammed the muscled officer blocking the door. "Isaac!" She slapped the detective's unwavering shoulders. "Move! Let me go!"

"Miss Maher, it's for the best."

She slapped his face. "Best for who? Isaac? His daddy loves him. Feeds him. Clothes him. And you gave him to a crackhead mother who doesn't care about anything but her next fix." Joni slapped him again. "You took him from people who love him. Who's going to feed him? Who's going to read him Bible stories? Who's going to wrestle with him?"

The officer grabbed her arms. "Calm down."

Over a beefy shoulder the uniformed officer whispered, "They're gone. The child's safe."

Chapter Fifteen

The thin mattress did nothing to soften the concrete floor. James stared at the stained ceiling through the dim light peeking from the cardboard box taped around the light fixture. Like a caged animal, he stood and paced. Where was Isaac? Did Joni leave the apartment before the authorities arrived? He scrubbed a hand down his face. Why would she? He told her to wait. He'd been so confident. How did Kathy post bond?

He scratched his thumbnail down the steel bars. Blue paint flaked to the floor. One of his four cellmates stirred behind him. "You got a smoke?"

"No." James rubbed the lump on the back of his head. He had to get out of here and find Isaac. Joni must be panicked by now.

"Hey, you the guy that punched Detective Simmons?"

James flexed his sore hand. "Yeah."

"You deserve a reward. How can Frankie help?"

Maybe idle talk would keep James from losing his mind. "Make someone disappear."

A match struck and sulfur scented the stale air. "They call me the life-giver. I don't deal in murder." The end of a cigarette glowed. "But if you ever need a new identity, I'm your man."

"Preston!" The jailer turned the corner and rattled his keys.

A bony hand reached from behind and snagged James's sleeve. "You can find me at the old docks, in an abandoned red railcar. Eight grand a person."

James stepped out of the man's grip as the jailer opened the door. "Your mommy posted bail. Ain't that sweet?"

The stars in the sky had never looked as bright as when he stepped out of his mom's car in front of the apartment.

"Thanks for the ride, Mom."

"James, I know it's hard to let Isaac go, but you need to remember, God knows best."

He bit back a sarcastic retort. "Mom, Joni's waiting."

"Please take her home. People talk, and when they find out you're living here…"

"Mom." He held up his hands. "Look, I'm sorry my life is an embarrassment, but I love Joni and Isaac. They both belong to me and I won't let either of them go." He slammed the door on his mother's pleas. Taking the stairs three at a time, he raced into the apartment.

Joni paced the living room with her phone to her ear. She turned toward the door as he walked in. She ended the call and threw herself into his arms. "James, you're home." He held her close and kissed her temple. Somehow, while holding her, he felt hope.

"They said you had to stay overnight."

His hand stroked her silky hair. "Ray's cousin pulled some strings."

She leaned back and tugged him by the hand to the dining table. Ten different lists were spread out on its surface. "Candace and Trent told half a dozen people that Kathy is networking, so I'm pretty sure she's in rehab. No one has seen Isaac. All I got from the authorities was that he's in protective custody. I've called everyone I know. Can you think of anyone I've missed?"

James scanned her lists and kissed her hard on the mouth. "Have I told you I love you?"

Her smile gave him hope. "Not lately."

"I do." He kissed her again and searched the charts. "How do you know these people?"

She gave him a cheeky grin. "I was once a delivery girl."

Isaac could be in serious danger. "Don't remind me. Have you called Anna and Sam?"

"Who?"

"Kathy's sister." At her blank look, James snatched up her keys. "We'll have to take your car. My truck is impounded with my phone in the front seat, but I know where she lives."

Joni was unusually quiet once they turned into the subdivision. James reached between the bucket seats for her hand. His thumb rubbed across the diamond on her finger. In Sam and Anna's driveway, a gentle squeeze brought her eyes to his. "We'll find him. If he's not here, we'll keep looking. I won't give up until he's safe again. I swear."

The light from the streetlamp illuminated her sad nod. On the sidewalk, he reclaimed her hand. She hugged his arm and kissed his bicep as he rang the doorbell. The volume of a sitcom lowered and Anna opened the door. Surprise was evident in her smile. "You've changed your mind? You'll sign the papers?"

"No." James stepped into the foyer and pulled Joni in after him. His eyes searched for signs of Isaac's presence. "Is he here?"

Sam appeared at the end of the hall with a book in one hand and reading glasses in the other. "We haven't seen Isaac since the night you stormed out of here. Why isn't he with you? I know Judge Baker granted you custody last December when Kathy was arrested."

"Things changed."

Sam narrowed his eyes. "If you'd sign the papers, we could protect him from Kathy."

An ironic laugh escaped James. "My signature won't do you any good." He turned toward the door. "If you see Isaac, or hear from Kathy, call me."

Joni held out a business card as they walked out into the empty night. "Sam gave me this. Do you want it?"

James shook his head and she put the card in her purse. "What papers were they talking about?"

He waited until they were out of the subdivision before answering. Choosing his words carefully, he told her of the Todds' attempt to adopt Isaac. Caught up in frustration at his failure to protect Isaac, he blurted. "What kind of monster gives a child to strangers? How could they want me to consider—?"

Joni's sharp gasp interrupted his tirade.

He'd forgotten she was adopted. "I'm sorry. I didn't mean to sound insensitive."

She stared out the window. One hand swiped under her eye and he cringed from the guilt.

He pulled over in a parking lot. "Hey." He tugged on her hand, but she ignored him. "I'm sure your father loved you. Maybe he didn't know you existed. Please look at me."

Misty eyes glistened as her chin lifted. "You're wrong. My father didn't want me anymore than Kathy wants Isaac. Allowing the Mahers to adopt me was the most loving thing my parents did for me."

He couldn't believe his ears. "Are you saying the best thing for Isaac is adoption?"

She faced the window once more. "I don't know. Maybe."

His fist landed on the dash. "You and Kathy may not want him, but I do."

She whirled around in her seat. Daggers flashed in her eyes. "That's not fair. Were you there when they pried him out of my arms? Did you hear him begging me not to let go?"

He couldn't ignore the tears flooding her cheeks.

"I couldn't fight the authorities, James. Unlike you, I have no delusions. What happens when we find him? When Kathy comes down and needs more money and drugs? I'll tell you what happens. She'll use Isaac to get what she wants. He's nothing more than a means to an end. A pawn in her sick game. He deserves better. He deserves a family that loves him."

"I love him! I'm his family!" Suppressing the urge to hit something, he got out of the car and slammed the door. Pain shot up his foot as he kicked the tires. He hobbled onto the trunk. Grabbing his head with both hands, he fell against the back glass as traffic hurried down Airport Boulevard. Why wasn't his love enough?

The car shifted beneath him as Joni opened and shut the passenger door. He pushed off the glass and pulled her up beside him. With his arm around her shoulders, they silently watched the traffic for a few awkward moments. "I love you."

She snuggled close. "I love you, too."

He kissed the top of her head. "Let's go home and get some sleep. Neither one of us is thinking straight right now."

"Sleep sounds wonderful."

The next day, James called every friend of Kathy's he could think of while Joni contacted St. Mary's Home and asked for the locations of children's safe houses. Adoption wasn't mentioned again. They confirmed the rumors that Kathy attended a seven day rehab, but found no sign of Isaac.

Ten days after Isaac was taken, James broke down and begged God for help. Later that same night, he dragged his feet through the glass doors of a convenience store. A small boy stretched his arm and a grimy hand slid a candy bar onto the counter.

The guy with him turned. "Go put that crap back. I ain't wasting good money on junk." He winked at the cashier. "Give me two boxes of Marlboro reds."

"I'm hungry." The little boy sounded familiar. James stepped for a closer look. It couldn't be this easy.

"Your momma didn't give me no money to feed you."

James swallowed the knot in his throat. The dirty jeans and plaid shirt was identical to the ones he'd dressed Isaac in the morning of the court hearing. His heart stopped. "Isaac?"

The little boy's eyes lit up as he swiveled around. "Daddy!" He flew into James's outstretched arms. "Joni said you would find me. And you did. She was right. I was ascared, but Joni promised."

James lifted him up and held him tight. The skinny arms clinging to his neck felt like heaven. "I missed you so much."

"Hey. The kid belong to you?"

James faced the sorry joker who'd dared to mistreat Isaac. Flames of rage burned out of control. One arm held Isaac safe in his arms. The other snagged the coward by the throat and pinned him against the energy-drink display. Wide-eyed, the punk's cigarette shook in his hand.

The customers in the store froze. James reined in his strength and kept his voice calm. "Did he hurt you, Isaac?"

Isaac buried his face in James's neck and whispered. "No, sir."

"Where's Kathy?"

Small bottles rained on the floor as the captive shook his head. "I don't know. She asked me to keep an eye on the brat for an hour. That was three days ago. I haven't seen her since. She don't answer my texts or calls."

"The next time you hear from her, tell her Isaac is with me." James released the coward who then ran out the door. He paid for the candy bar and a chocolate milk.

As he stepped onto the sidewalk with Isaac in his arms, Joni leapt out of the car and ran toward them. Isaac reached for her and tears mingled with her laughter. "Thank you, Jesus. Oh, thank you."

James blinked against the sting in his eyes as Isaac clung to Joni. "I prayed. Like you said. I asked God to help you and Daddy find me." His smile outshined the sun. "And He did. God helped Daddy find me."

Her watery gaze met James's. "Take us home."

He kissed them both and held open the rear passenger door.

Joni buckled Isaac in his booster seat and then climbed in beside him. James didn't blame her for wanting to be close to the precious little boy. If someone didn't have to drive, he'd be in the back with them too. He cherished their laughter as he slid under the wheel. *God. I don't deserve it, and I know you didn't do it for me, but thank you for answering Isaac's prayers.* He glanced at the miracle in the backseat. The candy bar had been devoured. "You still hungry?"

"Yes, sir."

James drove up to the menu board and ordered a cheeseburger kid's meal for Isaac, a grilled chicken salad for Joni, and a twenty-piece chicken nugget meal for himself. He paid at the first window and pulled to the next. He almost dropped the bag of food at Isaac's words.

"...then Daddy grabbed Eric by the neck like this." Isaac held his throat with both hands. "And threw him at the stuff. Then he squeezed real tight and—"

"Isaac." James shook his head and reached for their drinks. "I'm sure Joni doesn't want to hear all that."

Isaac reached for his fries, crammed a fistful in his mouth, and mumbled, "But you rescued me."

~ ~ ~

Rain drizzled off the tin roof and pooled in the dirt below the eaves of the farmhouse. Beside him on the porch swing, Joni shivered, and James pulled her closer while Isaac pushed a Tonka truck across the wooden boards near their feet. The yellow dump truck carried a load of blocks to the potted plant beneath the living room window.

"Vrmmm." Isaac smiled as he filled up another load with sticks this time and pushed the steel-framed truck across the wide planks.

Joni snuggled close. "What are you thinking about?"

James kissed the top of her head. "His father."

She stiffened in his arms. "Do you know who he is?"

He shook his head. "I'm trying to figure it out."

"He looks so much like you. Maybe the lab made a mistake."

"No. They did the test twice. Once, they swabbed the inside of our mouths. They said Kathy's DNA shouldn't matter. The first test was inconclusive. The last time they drew blood."

"How could that happen?"

"I don't know. Maybe someone has DNA similar to mine."

She lifted her head from his shoulder. "What if he was related to you?"

"Joni? Seriously? A long-lost cousin turns out to be my son's father? I mean, come on."

Her eyes narrowed. "Not long-lost, but maybe a cousin. Has Travis ever meet Kathy?"

She was grasping at straws, but James decided to humor her. "Once."

"What month?"

"It was Thanksgiving."

"And when is Isaac's birthday?"

"August nineteenth." James sat up straight. His foot held

the bench mid-swing. "Joni, I get what you're saying, and if it was anyone other than Travis, I'd be suspicious. But our dads are twins. He's like my brother. I'm sure Kathy wouldn't have minded, but Travis would never sleep with someone I was seeing."

Her hard gaze never wavered. "Yes, he would."

"No, he wouldn't."

"James, I know different."

"Whoa! Wait a minute." James scrubbed his hands through his hair. "Are you saying you and Travis...?" He swallowed the bile in his throat.

She slapped him across the chest. "No."

He pushed off the porch with his toe, putting the swing into motion. "Then what makes you sure he's capable of doing it?"

Joni bit her bottom lip the way she did when she was nervous and swallowed. "Back in the fall, before you made it to the church..." A pink tongue wet her lips. She sucked in a breath and blurted, "There was an incident."

Acid churned in the bottom of his stomach. He didn't like where this was going, but he had to find out the whole story. If Travis hurt her, he was a dead man. James tried to keep the anger out of his voice. "Did he ask you out?"

She shook her head. "Not exactly."

"Then what?" He kissed her hand. "Joni, tell me."

She stared at her hands. "When Aunt Sandra introduced us, I was floored at how much he resembled you. Well, other than his blond hair. After she left the room, he said he could imagine my loneliness while you were out of town. He offered to...uh...stand in for you."

James stood and paced the length of the porch. He turned and knelt in front of her, his hands on either side. "Did he touch you?"

Her fingers traced his jaw. "No."

"You should've told me sooner." He half rose and gave her a lingering kiss before walking out into the rain.

"Where are you going?"

He called over his shoulder. "While Dad is gone on vacation

with Mom, Travis is working the lumber yard."

~ ~ ~

The next day, Joni wrapped supportive arms around James as he called Tasha Covington on speakerphone. Again, the caseworker defended the abandonment accusation against Kathy because the sitter was willing.

James tried to convince Joni to go back to school, but their time with Isaac was almost up. She couldn't leave them. Surely Kathy would crash soon. Late at night, they'd whisper ideas to each other about how to keep Isaac. One night, he came to a conclusion. "Sam and Anna paid her ten thousand. We'll offer her double, triple. I can't let him go again, Joni. I can't."

Greed wasn't Kathy's only motive. For some reason, she hated Joni. "I don't think she'll sign the papers for any amount of money."

Unfortunately, three days later, during Isaac's nap, her theory was proven correct when the sheriff knocked on the door with official papers.

James held it open. "Uncle Tommy, come in."

She accepted a hug from James's rotund uncle. "Would you like a glass of sweet tea?"

He shook his head. "Can't." He folded the papers and slipped them inside his pocket. "James, I have no intention of honoring this warrant for your arrest. You have twenty-four hours to produce Isaac or you're guilty of child abduction. Find a way to appease Kathy. I don't want you in Mobile County Jail."

"Yes, sir."

James's uncle tipped his hat in her direction. "Hope to hear you sing in church soon, Joni. Maybe when all this settles down, you'll do me the honor."

"I'd love to. Thanks for not taking James to jail."

Wrinkles appeared at his eyes. "You're welcome. Keep him out of trouble."

"I'll try."

Sitting once again at the kitchen table, James dialed Kathy's cell and turned on his phone's speaker. He pulled Joni into his lap and kissed the side of her neck. The call went to voicemail. "I got your message. What do you really want? Call me and we'll talk." He pressed the end button.

Joni turned into him and kissed his brow. "You look tired."

His arms locked around her. "I'm exhausted."

She kissed him and tried to take away his worries. "It'll be over soon."

He held her close and she listened for his heartbeat. "I hope so." His pulse accelerated when the phone rang.

He put the call on speaker. "How much?"

Kathy laughed. "You've got to be joking. I don't want a lump sum. I want everything. The land, the house, the money."

His shoulder muscles tightened beneath Joni's hands. "I'll sign it all over, if you'll give me and Joni consent to adopt Isaac."

"No."

He swore and slammed his fist on the bar. "You don't want him and you know it. Give him to me."

"You want him and I find myself in need of a babysitter. You pay me five hundred a week and you can be Isaac's new live-in nanny."

"You're crazy."

"That's my offer. Take it or leave it. But if Isaac isn't here in twenty-four hours, guess who goes back to jail? Then who will look after the brat? Little Miss Perfect?" Kathy snorted. "I don't think so. I want things the way they were before that home wrecker showed up."

"Joni is not a—"

"Tomorrow, James. Isaac better be here with or without you."

Joni sagged against him as the call dropped. "What are we going to do?"

Isaac ran into the kitchen. "Are the cookies ready?" He climbed up in the chair next to them. "I'm hungry."

Without a word, James walked out. The screen door slammed as Joni rose to pour Isaac a glass of milk.

She held her sorrow at bay until hours later when Isaac slept beneath James's grandmother's quilt. What would happen to him?

If James went to jail, Isaac's abandonment was a matter of time. Kathy only used him as a ploy to bend James to her will.

The shower cut off down the hall and Joni knew she only had a few minutes. She knelt by Isaac's bedside. Holding his hand against her lips, she quietly prayed. "Please, Lord. Protect him. Keep him safe. I believe in your redeeming love. Save Kathy and change her into a loving mother. Isaac deserves a safe childhood. Whatever your will, Lord, I won't stand in your way. I know loving James is wrong, but please don't punish Isaac for my sin."

Joni sucked in a ragged breath. "Help me to let them go. Help me to say goodbye."

Strong arms lifted her from the hardwood floor. "No. Isaac needs you. I need you. Joni, we won't leave."

~ ~ ~

"We're home." Isaac ran down the hall of the apartment to his room.

James memorized the layout, Joni's new furniture, the rug under the coffee table, the huge portrait of him and Isaac on the wall. He wouldn't give up. He'd waited too long and fought so hard to have Joni in their life.

Her fingers trailed down the keyboard. "I don't know if all of my things will fit in the car. I didn't realize I'd moved in this much stuff. I'll have dad come back for the dresser."

He pulled her into his arms. "No, Joni. This apartment has always been yours. I swear, she will never step foot in here."

"But James—"

His gentle kiss silenced her words. "We'll go, but only until I find another way."

The hopelessness in her eyes sliced through him. "There isn't a way."

"Yes, there is. I met a guy in jail. He can help us." James blinked back his emotions and did what had to be done. "There's money in our account. Use it to pay bills and whatever. If you need more, call me." He didn't look at Joni as he spoke. He couldn't.

He placed her suitcase against the wall while Joni explained to

Isaac why she couldn't go with them.

James claimed a few more things from the apartment that he needed for work and slipped downstairs to stow them in his truck. He slammed the passenger door and glared into the dark heavens. "Joni loves you and she's taught Isaac to love you. How can you do this to them?" Without waiting for an answer, he forced his feet to climb the stairs and walk down the hall.

Joni lay on Isaac's bedroom floor. Two blond heads blended together. Why couldn't she be Isaac's mother? Why couldn't they be a family?

The buzzing of his phone interrupted his thoughts. It was Kathy. *Thirty minutes or I'm calling the cops.*

"Come on, Isaac."

Isaac jumped off the floor and his building blocks tumbled down. "We going to work?"

"No." James couldn't look at Joni as he answered. "We're going to Kathy's."

"But I want to stay home."

With a sniff, Joni rose and hugged Isaac to her. "Don't argue with your daddy. Your momma wants to see you."

Isaac rolled his eyes and huffed. "Yes, ma'am."

"Have fun. And remember that I love you." Joni turned Isaac toward the door. Her wet eyes met James's. "You'd better go."

The tightness in his chest threatened to explode. His feet refused to move. She stepped near and caressed his jaw. He turned his face into her palm and closed his eyes. "I can't."

"Shhh." Her soft kiss spoke the words neither of them could say. Joni led him by the hand up the hall and opened the door.

He rested his forehead on hers. "I don't want to do this."

Her bottom lip quivered, but her words gave him the strength to do what was necessary. "Isaac needs you."

"I love you." He tucked her hair behind her ear, and then trailed his knuckle down her jaw, over her chin, and across her lips. "Don't ever forget, Joni."

Tears spilled down her cheeks. "I love you, too. Take care of him."

James crushed his mouth to hers and drank from her sweetness. Then he whispered, "If you need me, call. I'll be here."

"I know."

He broke away while he had the strength. "Let's go, Isaac."

Joni lifted his son and kissed his cheek. "I love you."

Little hands wiped her cheeks. "Don't cry, Joni. We'll come home soon."

She choked on a sob and James peeled Isaac from her arms. He didn't trust himself to look back. He was afraid he'd never leave.

~~~

The address Kathy had given him, led them to the old wood house that belonged to Cindy's granny on Houston Street.

Kathy waved from the porch swing as James and Isaac got out of the truck. She nudged her friend. "Told you he'd be here." She stood and met them at the steps. "Come to Momma."

Isaac buried his head against James's neck. "Leave him alone. He's had a rough night." James glared at Cindy. "Where's your grandmother? I don't think she'll want me here."

The tip of her cigarette burned bright as she inhaled. "She died. The house now belongs to me."

James glimpsed the sadness hidden beneath Cindy's tough exterior. "I'm sorry for your loss."

She shrugged her shoulders. "It happens."

Isaac wiggled in his arms as James asked, "What's really going on? Why am I here?"

Cindy frowned at Kathy before answering. "I'm going straight. No more dealing. No more using. But until I get a job, someone needs to pay the utilities. She owes me. You're here to pay her debt."

Nothing new. He'd paid for Kathy's sins for over a year, but if in the end he'd have Isaac, he'd give everything he had. "Where's our room?"

Kathy butted into the conversation. "There's two bedrooms. You and Isaac can share mine with me."

"No. We get our own room or we're out of here." James held his ground on the bottom step.

Cindy flicked her cigarette across the yard. "Done. She can bunk with me." The two girls stared at each other. "Unless you want to move in with Maria at Elliot's? Or work for that creep Brian again?"

Isaac shuddered. James caressed his back and whispered near his ear. "It's okay. I won't let anyone hurt you."

Kathy's hands trembled as she opened the front door.

Surprised the house was clean, he followed her to a large bedroom with an old brass bed and one dresser. Both were probably antiques. He set Isaac on the made bed. "Stay here while I get our things out of the truck."

The wide-eyed look on his son's face squashed any remaining sympathy he had for Kathy. Isaac silently nodded and scooted to the center of the bed. James grabbed her arm and pushed her out the door. "We need to talk."

"Ouch." She rubbed her arm and stared at him. "What's wrong with you?"

"We need to get a few things straight."

She fell into a torn fabric recliner and lit a cigarette. "Fine. Talk."

"I'm glad to see you're sobering up, but regardless of your plans for a bodyguard and a provider, I'm here because of Isaac. If anyone, including you, hurts him, we're gone."

Kathy blew smoke in his eyes. "You can't do that. He's my son and if you take him, I'll have you arrested." She shrank back in the seat as James leaned over her and glowered.

"Not if you're at the bottom of the river."

Chapter Sixteen

Seven sleepless nights later, Joni lifted her head from the library table and stared at her caller ID. Why would Isaac's daycare call? She ducked behind a football player and whispered, "Hello."

"Yes, I'm trying to reach Joni Maher."

"This is she." Her heart dropped to her stomach.

"Miss Maher, you're listed as an emergency contact for Isaac Davies. This is the third time his mother's been late this week, and I'm afraid she's forgotten entirely today. I can't reach Mr. Preston by phone. Do you have any way of contacting either of Isaac's parents?"

"Did you text James? Sometimes he can't hear his phone ring at the prefab shop." How could he have trusted Kathy?

"This facility doesn't have texting capabilities." The daycare director sighed into the phone. "I'm afraid my next call will be to child protective services."

"No." Joni cringed as the word echoed through the silence. She slung her purse over her shoulder and ran out the door. "I can be there in ten minutes."

"Hold please."

Joni ran to her car, tossed her books in the backseat and sped out of the parking lot.

"I've checked our records. As an emergency contact, you're authorized to sign for Isaac, but we'll need to see some picture identification, preferably government-issued. Thank you, Miss Maher. Isaac is an adorable child."

Joni disconnected the call and texted James at a red light. *On my way to Isaacs preschool. Kathy didnt show.*

Her phone rang with James's ringtone. She didn't answer. She didn't want to talk to him. How could he have abandoned Isaac to that drughead?

Isaac's face lit up when she raced through the preschool doors. "Joni!" He wrapped his arms around her. "Momma forgot me, again."

"May I have a copy of your driver's license for our records?" The harried director pointed to a binder near the door. "And please sign him out for the day."

Holding him on her hip, she trailed her finger down the list of preschoolers until she found his name. Moving across James's signature from that morning, she scribbled her name.

"Let Mr. Preston know extra charges will be added to his account. If this happens again, we will no longer be able to provide services." Thin lips turned into a semblance of a smile.

"Now that I'm aware of the situation, it can be resolved." Joni slipped her license in her purse. "Thank you."

She buckled Isaac in the backseat, but had no booster for him. James's ringtone blasted from the front. She ignored it.

"I miss-ed you, Joni. I'm glad you came to get me. I told Ms. Bozly you would. But she had to check files. I don't like it at Momma's." His smile pricked her heart. "Can I come home?"

"Yes." She brushed her lips across his forehead. "Today you can."

As she slid into the driver's seat James called again. She pressed the green button and held the phone toward Isaac. "Here, talk to your daddy. He's probably worried."

"Joni." James's voice flowed from the phone before Isaac reached for it.

"Hey, Daddy. Guess what? I'm going home."

~ ~ ~

The aroma of pizza sauce teased his nostrils as he climbed up the stairs. Pausing at the front door, James raised his hand to knock. Isaac's laugh from inside the apartment changed his mind.

He ran his hand down his face and opened the door.

"Daddy, you're home. Me and Joni made pizza." The evidence was smeared across Isaac's chin.

James stood in the doorway, not quite sure what to do. Would she invite him in? Or tell him to get out? Isaac ate at the coffee table in front of the television. Where was Joni?

"James, can I see you in the kitchen, please?"

He stepped in and shut the door. In the kitchen, her back to him, she lifted a pizza out of the oven and set the pan on top of the stove. She turned and shed her oven mitt. "I hope you're hungry."

His eyes devoured the sight of her. Her hair was pulled back in a ponytail and her shirt had small flour fingerprints on the sides and shoulders. She was beautiful. Her shaky smile begged him to pretend.

He wanted to tell her about the screaming match he'd had with Kathy over the phone. He wanted to tell her he could stay the night because Kathy was at Bayfest and wouldn't be back until tomorrow. But to speak Kathy's name in Joni's apartment would be blasphemy. He shed his boots and jacket and then crossed the scarred linoleum. He removed the thing from her hair and ran his hand through the silken tresses. "I'm starving. The pizza smells delicious." When his mouth met hers he felt as if he'd truly come home. Now, if he could find a way to stay.

The next day, James knocked off work early so he could make it to preschool on time. Mrs. Bozly tilted her head. "Miss Maher signed Isaac out at one o'clock." James pretended he forgot Joni's intentions and listened to a lecture on parental responsibility.

When he got to the apartment, Joni had dinner on the table. He ate without saying a word about the preschool and kissed her when he and Isaac left. Each morning, as he signed Isaac into daycare, he'd check the previous day's checkout time. For the rest of the week Joni picked Isaac up between one and two o'clock.

~~~

"Joni, I was ascared. You was late and they made me sleep on that stupid pallet." Isaac screwed up his face and shuddered.

If the fear in his eyes wasn't real, Joni would've laughed at his expressive nature. "I'm sorry you were worried, but I don't get out of class until four on Tuesdays."

He pouted all the way to the apartment as she tried to explain the concept of time to the grouchy four-year-old.

The preschool didn't close until six and she wasn't late. In the apartment, she went through his book bag and exclaimed over his daily papers. Since starting preschool in Montgomery, and now here in Mobile, Isaac had learned numbers and most of the alphabet.

"Joni, can I stay with you? Uncle Ray lives with his girlfriend. We saw him yesterday. And girlfriends are nicer than mommas. So can I? Can I stay here?" Sincere blue eyes blinked.

She dropped the green handprint he'd made at school on the table and knelt down in front of him. "Oh sweetie, I would love for you to live here, but your momma...well, she has custody. That's why you and James live with her."

"But we don't like it there and she yells at Daddy all the times. At dark, she laid down on our bed, but Daddy made her go away. Momma said he smelled like his horse." His little head tilted as if in deep thought. "Is Daddy a cowboy?"

She doubted horse was the word Kathy used. She would have to skimp on perfume. "Isaac, I don't know what to tell you except...there are things in life we don't like, but we can't change them. We live the best we can and pray God will help us through the tough times. Do you understand?"

He sniffed and shook his head. "No."

"I don't either." She sighed and cupped his little chin in her hand. "But, no matter where you live, I will always love you."

His smile lit up the dark corners of her heart. "I love you too, Joni."

The door clicked shut and James's eyes met hers. She hadn't heard him come in. How much did he hear?

He clapped his hands once. "Tuesday night is Joni's day off." He crossed the room and swept her up in his arms. "So what will it be, beautiful? Dine-in or take-out?"

She closed her eyes and breathed deep. It had been so long since he called her by that endearment. He twirled her around and a laugh escaped. "James."

"Three weeks, Joni." He fell back against the sofa with her in his arms. "We'll be a family again in three weeks."

"How?" Joni scrambled up in his lap and grabbed his shoulders. "Don't tease me, James. That would be cruel."

He grinned and nodded at Isaac. "You'll have to wait until little ears sleep." His kiss melted her insides, like it did before they'd lost custody.

James grilled steaks on the balcony as Joni and Isaac read a book in the recliner. After dinner, Isaac fell asleep watching cartoons and James told Joni about his meeting at the docks. "We'll have passports, social security cards, birth certificates, and driver's licenses in any state you choose." He kissed her hand. "And the best part…all three of us will share the same last name. We'll go wherever you want."

"Are you serious? Will this work?"

"Yes. They're not fakes. They're real identities of people who've died without next of kin. Will you go with us?"

She couldn't force the words past her lips. It was too good to be true.

The light dimmed in his eyes. "I know it's a lot to ask, to leave your family and friends to be with Isaac and me. If you don't want to go, I'll understand."

"No." Joni kissed him quickly and then laughed. "Yes, I'll go." She kissed him again. "I'll follow you forever, but how do we keep blabbermouth quiet?"

"We won't tell him." James sobered. "But we do have to be careful. I know you don't like to talk about her, but she's crazier than usual. I don't know if she's drugging or what, but we need to cut our evening short." His mouth claimed hers. "Three weeks, Joni. It will be over in three weeks. I love you." He kissed her again. "I love you." And again.

She forgot he needed to leave early, and it was after midnight when he carried a sleeping Isaac out the door.

Joni tinkered with the piano keys, not playing anything in particular. Three more weeks of crying herself to sleep. Three more weeks of worrying if Isaac was safe. Three more weeks of wondering if James and Kathy...

Her phone sang James's ringtone from the coffee table.

Something was wrong. He never called when he was with *her*. She snatched it up. "James?"

Isaac's trembling voice broke her heart all over again. "Joni, I'm ascared."

A horrendous crash came from the background. Kathy cussed and the commotion grew.

"Momma throwed a bottle at Daddy." Sniff. "He's bleeding. I think she broke his neck."

Her first priority was Isaac's safety. "Go to your room. Daddy's a tough guy, remember? A little scratch isn't gonna hurt him."

The fight faded to a dull murmur and a soft click ended the noise entirely. *God, help James calm Kathy down.* Joni pressed her speaker button and propped her phone on top of the keyboard. "Climb in bed, sweetie. I'll sing you to sleep."

The covers rustled. "She's loud."

"It's okay. Some people like to yell. Snuggle close to Bunkie and close your eyes." She played his favorite lullaby. After some minutes his sleepy voice interrupted. "Goodnight, Joni."

"Sweet dreams, Isaac." She sang the lullaby twice more and listened. Soft breaths echoed, making her smile. She whispered, "I love you."

~ ~ ~

James leaned on the doorframe and watched his son drift off to sleep with a smile. His fight with Kathy didn't seem to have bothered him. She was already enraged when Isaac said, "Sorry, we're late Momma. I had to take a nap before Joni could come get me." After Isaac's simple statement, it was all James could do to avoid bodily harm. Thankfully, Kathy had stormed off somewhere in the night. Cindy hadn't been home in days.

He tiptoed across the room and noticed the phone cradled against Isaac's ear. His phone. Joni's music wafted from three feet away. He crawled in the bed beside his son and stole the phone to his ear. Her sweet voice shed beams of light in their dark world. In three weeks, he could hold her forever, but until then, he couldn't see her again.

The music stopped and he absorbed her words of love.

The line clicked and James whispered into the darkness. "Goodnight, beautiful. I love you, too."

~ ~ ~

The next afternoon, the daycare director met Joni at the door. "I apologize, Miss Maher, but Isaac's mother has removed your authorization."

Joni peeked through the window at the blond head bent over a coloring page. She fought the sting in her eyes. "I see." She adjusted her purse strap. "Thank you for telling me out here." She swallowed the lump in her throat. "If something happens and Kathy forgets…will you call me?"

"I'm sorry. That's no longer an option."

She drove to the apartment in a daze. Trembling fingers texted James. *Kathy banned me. Preschool closes at 6. Don't forget.*

Two ibuprofens later, she crawled in bed and read James's reply. *Three weeks. I love you.*

Hiding under the covers, Joni cried for hours. At five, Marla's call woke her. "Hey, girl. I wanted to remind you that we have church on Wednesdays. Would love to see you tonight."

Something stirred within Joni. "Thanks, Marla. That's exactly what I need right now. I'll see you at seven."

Rejoining church activities helped pass the time, although Joni couldn't quite look the pastor in the eye during his sermons.

Why did she feel like she should apologize for loving James?

Each time she knelt to pray for Isaac's safety, Anna's face came unbidden in her mind. Was God trying to show her something? She still had the card Sam had pressed into her hand, but she couldn't contact the Todds. James would never forgive her. Instead, she helped Marla and Rachel plan Andrea's baby shower.

It had been two weeks since she'd seen James when she and the girls went to the mall looking for the perfect gift.

Joni lifted an infant sailor outfit from the sales rack. She held it up for Marla's approval. "What do you think?"

"I don't know. That's so ordinary. Let's find a unique gift. Something that won't be duplicated at the shower tomorrow."

"Joni!"

She swung around.

Isaac broke away from James's hand and ran through the maze of baby things. Joni knelt and hugged him close to her. She kissed his cheek. "I missed you so much."

"Where did you go? You didn't pick me up and now Daddy's sad."

She stood and turned to James.

His hardened stance faltered. Mouth slightly opened, he lifted his shades and turned in a half-circle. With his left brow raised, his eyes darted from diapers to baby blankets. Delicious shivers zinged up her spine as his gaze settled on her flat stomach. He tilted his head as the corner of his lips turned up. "Joni?"

The unspoken question lingered in the air. "No, James." She swallowed and shook her head slightly. "Andrea's baby shower is tomorrow."

His face fell. Sunglasses quickly hid his expression. "Right. My bad."

Rachel stepped around the wall of baby bottles. "Awkwaaaard." She smirked at James. "But…suspicions confirmed."

Marla jabbed her elbow in Rachel's side. "Let's go see what they have over there."

Joni closed her eyes and gripped the rack in front of her. The heat on her face wasn't from Rachel's statements, but rather the intense look James pinned her with. Would things be different if she carried his child?

Isaac pulled on her shirt. "Don't you love us no more?"

"Of course I do." Joni turned her back to compose her features.

Strong arms encircled her. James's whispered words were balm to her battered heart. "I love you. I need you to be strong. One more week."

Joni turned, "But Isaa—"

James claimed her mouth. Starved for his touch, Joni melted against him. Oh, what she would give to be absorbed in him. To go with him everywhere. To become part of him.

"Isn't this the nice family picture?" Kathy's voice broke them apart.

James kept his arm around Joni, but she shuddered at the venom in Kathy's eyes.

"The problem is you're stealing my family. Mine!" Kathy moved in front of Joni and sneered.

"Don't touch her." James stepped in between them.

"Or what James?" Kathy's loud voice drew a crowd, Rachel and Marla among the bystanders. "Will you cut my allowance? Take away my phone?"

"You're causing a scene." James touched Kathy's arm and Joni recoiled.

"This is nothing compared to what she deserves." Kathy snatched Isaac and slung him across her shoulder.

"Kathy." James blocked her path and reached for Isaac. "Stop it!"

Kathy swirled around, putting Isaac out of James's reach.

The little boy held out his arms toward Joni. Tears streamed down his face. "Don't let her take me. I don't want to go." Isaac cried uncontrollably.

"Shut. Up." Kathy punched the back of flailing legs and her fist rained blows on his back.

James lunged forward and captured her flying hands.

Isaac let out a wail. "Joni!" Little legs kicked the air. "Help me! I want Joni!"

Some unnamed emotion rose up within her. She grabbed Kathy's hair and slung her into the rack of clothes.

Isaac thudded against the tile floor.

Kathy swung at Joni, but James caught her arms and pinned them behind her back.

"Enough!" Joni gently lifted a crying Isaac from the floor. "Come on, sweetie. Let's get out of here." Chest heaving, she pointed at James. "Don't let her follow me." She grabbed all the cash in her purse and threw it at Kathy. "Here, go drug yourself up and leave my baby alone."

She ran toward the exit with Isaac on her hip. James called after her, but she quickened her pace. He wouldn't let go of Kathy. He'd give them time to escape because he thought Joni would find him later. But this time he was wrong. Isaac couldn't be pulled back and forth anymore. James's selfish need to be a good father clouded his thinking. Someone had to do what was best for Isaac. And that someone was her. She kissed his forehead and buckled him in the backseat. "I love you so much. She won't hurt you again. I promise."

Chapter Seventeen

In Moss Point, Mississippi, Joni gassed up her Honda using her debit card. Forging her trail west, she stopped a few miles later in Pascagoula at the nearest ATM. Confident everyone would be searching the Mississippi coast and beyond to New Orleans, she turned north and circled back to the place no one could find them.

The fight to stay awake consumed her every thought. Isaac was too precious to crash into a ditch. So at three thirty in the morning, she breathed a sigh of relief as she hid her car in the farmhouse barn. Cradling Isaac in her arms, she tapped on the backdoor with her foot.

Mr. Preston smiled in welcome. "Come in." He lifted Isaac out of her tired arms. "I've been waiting up for you. Pour yourself some coffee while I put him to bed." Joni nodded, but collapsed at the table.

The fatherly hand on her shoulder brought her back to the present. She lifted her head and faced Mr. Preston. "James is going to hate me, but I can't give him back. They're tearing him apart." Her forehead dropped to her arm and she cried her heart out.

"Its okay, pumpkin. Get it all out."

Joni wept until her eyes ran dry. She leaned back in her chair while Mr. Preston poured them a cup of coffee. "Tell me what happened."

"When Kathy hurt Isaac, I…" She sniffed. "I lost it." Trembling hands lifted the mug and she inhaled the bitter brew.

Mr. Preston took the chair beside her. "If you could have seen the way she hit him."

"I did. It was on tonight's news. The security cameras caught it all. People are outraged. Folks all over the South are praying."

"What?" She blinked at the man who would've become her father-in-law. "What happened after I left?"

"All you-know-what broke loose." He pulled her up by the hand and led her in front of the television in the den. "I recorded it on the DVR."

On the large television, Kathy hit Isaac. Joni winced at the pain etched on his little face. The Joni on-screen grabbed Isaac and ran. Kathy slapped James and struggled, but he tackled her to the floor. Marla and Rachel were frozen in the background. The scene cut to the parking lot and zeroed in on Joni's blurred license plate as she exited the mall parking lot. Kathy was led out in handcuffs. Joni's heart stopped as James likewise was shoved in the back of a sheriff's car. "Why did they arrest James?"

The news anchor answered her question. "The mother, Kathleen Miranda Davies was arrested on child abuse charges, while James Isaac Preston was arrested for assault and interference of custody."

"Assault?" Joni looked to Mr. Preston. "Who did he assault?"

"The security guard who ran after you."

Her mouth dropped. "Oh, James."

"He loves you."

She swallowed the lump in her throat. "Not for long, but Isaac comes first. Right?"

"Have you prayed about this?" He continued after her nod, "What's the plan?"

She sucked in a breath and thought of the precious boy upstairs. "Every time I pray for Isaac, I think of Anna. I don't know if it's my subconscious or God, but she and her husband, Sam, love Isaac as much as we do." Joni accepted Mr. Preston's handkerchief and blew her nose. "Anna is Kathy's half-sister. They paid Kathy ten thousand dollars to sign adoption consent, but the judge ruled the biological father must give consent as well." Joni smiled. "James refused to sign."

"But he isn't Isaac's father."

"No, he isn't. All we need is Isaac's father's consent to the adoption and Kathy can never touch him again."

"Do Sam and Anna still want him?"

"Yes, but the tricky part is finding Isaac's father. James and I discussed it. He thinks my theory is crazy, but with Isaac's looks it's got to be—"

"Travis." Mr. Preston glanced heavenward. "God help us."

"Do you think he'll sign? If he is…I mean, do you think…?" Joni didn't know how to voice her thoughts.

"This is going to kill James. Are you sure you want to do this?"

Isaac's scream had her out of her chair and running toward the living room. Her feet pounded up the stairs and into James's old room. She swept the little boy in her arms. "Shhh. I've got you."

Isaac's body trembled.

Joni cradled him in her protective embrace. She lifted her chin toward Mr. Preston, who had followed her. "I'm sure."

"Then get some sleep. We'll figure out the particulars in the morning." He kissed Isaac's cheek first and then hers. "Hopefully, James will keep his anger directed at me."

The next morning, she called her mother who begged Joni to come home, but she stood firm on her decision. After breakfast, she found some clothes for Isaac and put him in the tub.

Ugly yellow circles speckled his ribcage along with the fresh marks on his back and legs. "What did she do to you?" The soft words slipped out. Joni didn't expect an answer.

"When I was bad, Momma poked me with the broom."

Her vision swam, the blue bruises and yellow marks of Isaac's battered body merged to a puke green. Joni leaned over the toilet. She gasped for breath and threw up her breakfast.

As she lifted her head, Mr. Preston opened the door. "Joni?"

"Momma said not to tell Daddy, or I can't see him no more."

Mr. Preston turned toward the tub. His eyes glazed over. "Oh God, forgive us." His eyes closed and his features paled.

"Grandpa, are you sick too? Are you gonna tell Daddy?"

Joni plastered a smile to her face and knelt by the tub. "He's fine. I'm fine. We won't tell James. Let's get you cleaned up."

"When you're done, meet me in the kitchen."

Forcing herself to look at Isaac's battered body, she bathed him gently. Before dressing him, she snapped a few pictures with her phone. Downstairs, she turned on his favorite cartoon and found Mr. Preston in the dining room.

"I called Travis. He'll be here any minute." He brushed the hair from her eyes. "Are you ready for this?"

Joni couldn't speak. She wanted to call James and tell him about the bruises, but he'd blame himself. He would never forgive her for what she was about to do. What choice did she have? How could she live a happily ever after with James knowing the extent of Isaac's abuse? Blinking against the tears, she nodded.

The arm that came around her shoulder reminded her of James. "Joni, have you ever read the story of the two women fighting over one baby?"

She whimpered and shook her head.

"Two harlots gave birth within days of each other. One woman accidentally smothered her child and stole the living child from its rightful mother. The loving mother filed a complaint with the king. Wise King Solomon declared the living child be sliced in two, and a half given to each mother."

Joni gasped at the horror. "No."

Mr. Preston smiled. "You're like the baby's real mother. She loved her child and wanted him to live. She begged the King to stop the sword. She'd rather her child live with a stranger than die as her son."

Joni couldn't stop the river of tears flowing down her face. "W-What happened to the baby?"

"The king recognized a mother's love and returned it to his mother's arms."

With a sniff, Joni reached for a napkin. "That is not gonna happen with me and Isaac."

"No, but because of you, he will live." He sniffed and laughed in embarrassment. "I may not be a wise king, but I know a mother's love when I see it."

That afternoon, Joni told Travis her suspicions and her desire for Sam and Anna to adopt Isaac. He didn't deny the possibility of being Isaac's father.

"I didn't intend for it to happen. James was passed out near the pond and Kathy was persuasive. I'm sorry."

The next morning, Joni and Isaac rode with Travis to the local clinic for a DNA test. On the ride home, Isaac fell asleep, leaving an awkward silence. She wondered how James was being treated in jail.

"Joni, I never meant to hurt James. It just happened." Travis picked up her hand. Guilt and remorse clouded his eyes.

Despite his cavalier attitude, Joni believed him. She reclaimed her hand but turned toward him. "If you want to make it up to James…do the right thing for Isaac."

"What is the right thing?"

She sucked in a breath. "Do you want to be his father?"

"Heck, no." His exaggerated answer calmed the dancing butterflies in her stomach. "I mean, he's cute and all, but…I don't like kids." He shuddered.

She laughed at the horror on his face. "They're not that bad." She turned and stared at the blond head tilted sideways. Isaac's mouth hung open in sleep. "I wish I were his mother."

Travis's wink reminded her of James. "Then I'd keep you and Isaac for myself."

She pinned him with her fiercest glare. "You shouldn't think stuff like that, and most definitely don't say it. I'm in love with James."

"Yeah, I know." Travis jerked his head toward the backseat. "But I can give you what he can't. You'll forget about James after a while. I'm easy to love."

"Stop." She hoped he was joking. "You don't know if you're Isaac's father. For all we know, there may be a third candidate out there."

Travis mumbled under his breath. "Probably more than one."

She rolled her eyes away from him and turned the volume up.

That same afternoon, James called. "Where are you? Are you okay? Is Isaac okay? I was so worried."

"James, slow down."

"I swear I'll never leave you again. Either of you. Tell me where you are. New Orleans? I'll meet you there."

"James." Joni smiled into the phone. "We're fine, but most importantly, Isaac is safe."

"Where are you?"

She collapsed on the porch swing. Isaac's bruises had faded, but not enough to risk James seeing them. One bruise to Joni's forehead and Trent stayed in the hospital for a week. What would James do if he saw Isaac's speckled body? She couldn't risk him murdering Kathy and spending his life in prison. "I can't tell you."

"Joni, you can't do this alone. You need me. Isaac needs me." His words caused her to cry. She was tired of crying. "I love you." His voice broke. "Tell me where you are?"

Tears soaked her phone. "I have to do what's best for Isaac. He needs to be safe from the threat of Kathy ever getting custody again."

"Do not do anything stupid."

"Please don't hate me, James. I love you, but you can't protect him from Kathy. There are things you don't know."

"Joni, please. I love him."

She disconnected the call and tucked her knees under her chin. *Lord, don't let him hate me. Please don't let him hate me.*

~~~

James swore and barely suppressed the urge to throw his phone against the police station wall. He buried his face in his hands and gulped in air. Where were Joni and Isaac? What did she mean by saying he couldn't protect Isaac? Did she think she could? Her genes didn't flow through Isaac's blood any more than his.

He took a fortifying breath. One thing was certain, Joni loved Isaac. She would die trying to protect him. "Joni, what are you thinking? Where are you?"

"That's what I'd like to know." Detective Simmons stepped out from behind a bush. "But it doesn't matter. In a few moments, we'll have the location of her cell phone traced. Isaac will be picked up and returned to his mother."

James squinted against the sun. "Kathy hit him on camera."

"Yes, but she's apologized and agreed to attend therapy. Sadly, there aren't enough foster homes to place abused children. GPS tracking only works if the device is active. It would be a shame if Joni turned off her phone and denied the mother return of custody." He spit out a sunflower hull and strolled down the sidewalk.

James didn't waste any time. She wouldn't answer his call so he texted. *Turn off your phone. The cops are tracking you.*

~ ~ ~

Joni loved small town politics. James's uncles were Uncle Curtis, the circuit judge, Uncle Vincent, the judge of probate, who was currently on vacation and also Travis's father, Uncle Lawrence, one of three attorneys in the area, and Uncle Tommy, the local sheriff. Since the population of juvenile delinquents was small, Uncle Curtis also presided over family court.

Tonight, his courtroom was the Preston farm table. Uncle Lawrence read the paternity results and passed them to Uncle Curtis, who looked at Travis and shook his head. "I'll have to excuse myself from your murder trial when James sees this."

Travis had the grace to bow his head. "Yes, sir."

Uncle Curtis smiled at Joni. "My wife has got the church praying for you and Isaac. She'll be glad to know that you're safe."

"Thank her for the kindness, sir."

"You can tell her at church, tomorrow."

"Oh, we can't get out until Isaac's custody is settled. I can't take the chance of Kathy getting her hands on him again."

Uncle Lawrence opened a legal pad. "That's why we're here, honey." He scribbled on the yellow paper. "Travis, do you want to sue Kathy for full custody?"

Travis sat up in his chair. "Can I do that?"

Uncle Curtis held up the DNA results. "Unless a court revokes them or you sign them away, this gives you parental rights to the little boy asleep upstairs."

Joni gasped. "I can keep Isaac?"

"Sure, if you marry Travis. It'll strengthen his case if Kathy files for return of custody, and give James a temporary insanity plea. He could be out in five years with good behavior. Then you can live happily ever after."

She couldn't breathe. "Marry Travis? But James—"

"Isn't Isaac's father." Travis interrupted. "What do you say? You wanna get hitched?"

James's dad looked as dumbfounded as she felt. She cleared her throat and held up her hand. "No. I like you, but I could never hurt James. He and I will both help you raise Isaac."

"No deal. I don't want to be a father." He turned to Uncle Curtis, who was listening intently. "Can I sign him over to James and Joni?"

"You are free to give him up, but his mother will certainly retain custody. Unless she's proven unfit, and then the state decides his welfare. They always rule in favor of a blood relative to the fifth degree."

Joni sucked in a breath. She knew what must be done. "What about Sam and Anna?"

"Who are they?"

She told the uncles about their adoption petition and the judge's ruling about obtaining the biological father's consent.

"That's an option. It would be the easiest way to protect him, if they're still interested in becoming Isaac's parents, that is." Uncle Curtis leaned across the table toward Travis. "If you sign consent and the adoption is granted, you are forever relinquishing your parental rights. Think carefully before you do. As of now, you have as much right to Isaac as his mother. No one can force you to give him over to her care, but if she got her hands on him, she wouldn't have to release him either. Unless a court has ordered differently, it's whoever has possession of the child. As your uncle, you should talk this over with your own parents. This is their grandchild we're discussing."

Travis paled and jumped to his feet. "Every one of you are bound by confidentiality. No one tells my mother. No one!" He resumed his seat and his head dropped into his hands. "Why can't James and Joni adopt him?"

Uncle Lawrence shifted his papers into his briefcase. "They can. If Kathy signs consent."

Joni reentered the conversation. "She'll never do that. She hates me."

The adoption was discussed again. The uncles stood. The sheriff snapped his fingers in Travis's face. "I agree with Curtis. Your parents have a right to know."

Uncle Lawrence paused at the door and looked at Travis. "You have a decision to make. Become a father, or give him to these people, who by some miracle have obtained a signature from the mother." He turned to Joni. "I want to hear your beautiful voice singing my favorite song on Sunday as payment for my services."

Travis groaned and dropped his head against the table.

Joni peered up at Mr. Preston. "This is getting more and more complicated."

~ ~ ~

The bottom of Isaacs's new sneakers clipped Joni in the chin. Pausing in the play tunnel, she pressed her fingers against her face and winced.

Isaac giggled. "Follow me, Joni."

An older boy stomped on her hand as he zoomed around her in the narrow passage way.

"Sorry."

A second boy crawled over her back and hurried after his friend. Joni followed Isaac to the right. She never knew how dangerous these play-places could be. They entered a robot spaceship set on springs. Isaac twirled one of the two steering wheels. "Hurry up, 'fore somebody else gets the copilot."

There was more room in the spaceship cave. Although Joni couldn't stand, she sat at the steering wheel and looked at the patrons below eating their lunch. Kids tunneled past the opening. She swallowed her nerves and grinned over at Isaac. "Reporting for duty, sir."

"Ready to blast off?"

"Aye aye, captain."

Isaac sighed and cut his eyes at her. "That's what pirates say. You're 'sposed to count and say, 'blast off.'"

She bit back a grin and tried to look remorseful. "Sorry. Let's try it again."

Isaac straightened his stance as he stood at the steering wheel. "Ready for blast off?"

She was tempted to revert back to her pirating ways, but this could be the last time she played with Isaac. "Ready."

"Nine…seven…four…five…one…blast off!" He jumped up and down. The spaceship rocked on its loaded springs.

The smell of stinky socks drifted from the tunnel, but Isaac's carefree laughter lightened Joni's burden. She twirled the wheel and flipped the levers and gadgets with the same energy as the four-year-old beside her.

Isaac froze. His eyes widened. "Look, there's Mr. Sam." He gasped. "And Mrs. Anna too. Let's go say hi."

A quick hand stopped Isaac at the tunnel entrance. "Wait. First, tell me who they are."

Isaac tilted his head and blinked. "Mr. Sam and Mrs. Anna."

"No, not their names. Are they nice people? Or…" Joni shrugged and chose her words carefully. "Or not nice people?"

Little hands cupped Joni's cheeks. "Don't be ascared. They're not like Momma. Mrs. Anna loves me. She'll love you too."

She swallowed the lump in her throat at his revealing statement and pressed on. She had to know if he would be safe in their care. "What about Mr. Sam? Will I like him?"

His face lit up. "Oh yeah. He'll take you fishing and throw the ball. He doesn't yell when you miss or nothing." Little eyes reflected amazement. "And they have a dog."

She took a shaky breath and blinked several times. "Then let's go say hi."

By the time she scooted down the slide, Isaac was in Anna's arms. Being caught crawling out of the play-place wasn't exactly a good introduction, but it was what it was.

Sam held out his hand. "Nice to see you again, Joni." His

handshake was firm and strong. "You'll never know how much this means to us."

Anna's teary eyes as they said goodbye an hour later reassured Joni she'd made the right decision by giving them the consent form signed by Travis. While the legalities of the adoption were finalized, Isaac would remain in Joni's care. Legally, Travis had five days after the paper was probated to change his mind.

Isaac was now out of Kathy's reach, safe from her abuse, but before he moved to Sam and Anna's, there was someone who needed to say goodbye.

Chapter Eighteen

"Daddy! Daddy, you come to see us."

James leapt out of the truck and ran across the farmyard. Under the huge oak tree, he swept Isaac into his arms. Holding his son close, he blinked against the sting in his eyes. "Oh, Isaac, I missed you."

"I know." Isaac kissed him. "Joni told me."

James couldn't bring himself to look her way. He still couldn't reconcile the woman he loved with the traitor who'd given his son away.

Isaac wiggled down and climbed on the tire swing. "Push me way high, Daddy. Joni's ascared I'll fall."

Playing with Isaac was something he could handle. James ran with the swing and launched Isaac in the air. Isaac whooped as the rope tore fresh sprigs from the overhead branches. Green leaves sprinkled down. James shoved the tire higher in the air.

"James, he's four. If he fell—"

"You don't make the decisions anymore, Joni." The knife in his heart twisted. The oak leaf in her hair reminded him of the day he first brought her to the farm. The day they went hunting. The day he swore to love her forever. He pushed the memories aside. "As a matter of fact, now that I'm here, you can go back to school."

He steeled himself against her quivering lip. "James…"

His whole body flinched at her touch. "Don't."

"Look at me go, Daddy." Isaac leaned back. "Wahoo!"

James turned his back on her and pushed Isaac higher. "Midterms are next week. Go home, Joni. I don't want you here."

She sniffed behind him. "I don't want to leave Isaac."

"You should have thought about that before you sold him to the highest bidder." He turned and speared her with his eyes. "They paid Kathy ten grand. How much did you and Travis get?"

Her gasp took his breath. Her face drained of all color. James turned away and cursed himself for causing her pain. His shoulders relaxed as her footsteps faded toward the porch. He ignored the pain of her betrayal and ran with the swing. At the last moment, he stepped on the bottom of the tire. Isaac giggled as he and James sailed into the air.

Before supper and after washing his and Isaac's hands, he took the chair next to Isaac. He refused to acknowledge his father's or Joni's presence at the other end of the dinner table.

Her voice trembled as she carried on a conversation with his father. "Is Mrs. Preston arriving tonight?"

His dad forked a bite of meatloaf. "No. Tomorrow afternoon."

She rolled the peas around on her plate. "I'm sorry that I'll miss her."

James avoided his father's glare. "Where are you going?"

Joni's tight lips formed a weak smile. "Midterms are next week. I should have left this afternoon, but I need to see to Isaac's bath."

James cut his eyes from Joni to his dad and back to Joni again. "There's no need for you to wait. I can bathe my own son."

Isaac's hand smeared ketchup on James's wrist. "Joni likes to count the dots, but we can't tell you."

His dad's fork clattered on his plate and all color drained from Joni's face. She almost knocked over her tea glass. Her hand shook violently.

"What dots?"

"Don't worry, Daddy." Isaac patted ketchup into James's skin. "She only got sick once."

"Isaac, are you done?" Joni left her full plate and lifted Isaac from the table. "Let's go play in the tub."

When they were gone, James replayed the conversation in his mind. He was missing something. "Dad, what was Isaac talking about? Why is Joni sick?"

His dad's chair scraped against the hardwood floor. "Joni makes everything a game to Isaac. Maybe she counts the polka dots on the shower curtain or something."

The master bathroom had a shower stall with a door. The hall bathroom's shower curtain was solid green, but the last time James called his father a liar he'd picked himself up off the floor. He glanced at the stairs where Joni and Isaac had disappeared and decided the dots could remain a secret. Surely nothing could be hurt by a few dots. He picked up his and Joni's plates and carried them to the sink. She needed to eat more.

After helping his dad wash the dishes, he climbed the stairs and leaned in Isaac's doorway. Joni sat on the edge of the bed, head bowed as she listened to Isaac's prayers. She pulled the covers up to his chin and kissed his cheek.

James refused to move, and Joni brushed past him on her way out the door. His hand shot out and captured her wrist. He whispered near her ear. "How does it feel, knowing this is the last time you'll ever tuck him in?"

Her body went rigid before she snatched out of his grip.

James turned off the light. "'Night, Isaac. Daddy loves you."

A sleepy voice answered in the dark. "I love you too, Daddy."

He closed his eyes and listened to his son's even breathing. James had no intention of losing Isaac. The papers giving them a new life waited. In a few days, they would quietly disappear. Everything of value was packed in his truck. James was ready. He just didn't know how to leave Joni.

He moved silently down the hall. Muffled sobs came from beyond his bedroom door. His muscles tensed as he listened to Joni cry. His heart couldn't stand to hear her pain. With a trembling hand, he twisted the knob. In the moonlight near the window, she turned toward him. He stepped across the threshold and eased the door closed.

Her shoulders shook. "Will you hate me forever?"

He wished he had an answer for her question. She didn't trust him to keep her and Isaac safe. He bit his lip and shook his head. "I don't know, Joni." His chest heaved. "I don't know if I can forgive what you've done."

"James." She choked on a sob and reached out to him.

He crossed the room and gathered her in his arms. Sitting on the floor, he leaned against the windowsill and held her close to his heart. His thumb swiped at her tears. "You're too beautiful to cry." He kissed her trembling lips.

She wrapped her arms around his waist and soaked his shirt. "I love you."

His heart thundered in his chest, and he knew he could never leave her. James felt under the mattress for the manila envelope he'd hidden earlier. He held it toward her.

Her hand shook as she opened the clasp. Her mouth dropped as she shuffled through the papers. James didn't need to look to know what she saw. He'd stared at them enough this past week. She perched on the edge of the bed and waved the birth certificate. "How did you...? I thought that since...I mean...I don't know what to say."

He dropped to his knees in front of her. "Say you love me. Say you'll come with us."

"James." Her eyes pleaded with him. "Don't run. They'll catch you and you'll go to prison for a long time. In the end you'll still lose Isaac."

He pushed away and stood. Why couldn't she trust him? "If you change your mind, we'll be here for a few more days." James swooped in for one last kiss. "Goodbye, Joni." In two strides, he opened the bedroom door.

"Wait."

He didn't look back. Downstairs, he walked out to his truck and removed a fifth of whiskey from under the seat. Leaning against the oak, he drank himself into oblivion. His father's face appeared and then the couch rose up to meet him. "Joni." James whimpered her name before blessed darkness overtook him and the pain ended.

When he woke the next morning, she was gone. That afternoon, she texted him. *Im sorry for hurting you. Your last week with Isaac should be special. I wont interfere. Sam and Anna will call the farmhouse after the legalities are final. Please dont hate me. I did the only thing that would protect Isaac. Consider the consequences before making any rash decisions. But wherever you go, I will love you, forever.*

~ ~ ~

James should be halfway across the country by now, but he'd waited, hoping Joni would change her mind. He tossed the baseball and Isaac swung the bat. The ball zipped past James.

"I hit it, Daddy."

"And the crowd goes wild." He swung his son up on his shoulders in a victory celebration.

Isaac held up the bat and cheered.

"James, you have a call."

He turned toward the porch where his dad held up the cordless phone. "Joni?"

"No. It's Sam."

The adoption was final. James left Joni four more voicemails, begging her to come with them. The next morning, he loaded their things in the truck and drove east. Ray would meet them at the Atlanta airport. He promised to buy the Toyota. That would give them a little extra money until James found a job.

He pulled into a fast-food place for lunch. Isaac peeked over the dash. "Is this where Sam and Anna is?"

Carrying his son through the door, he ignored the pain Isaac's words caused. "No."

"Are you sure? This is where we saw them. Do you think Mr. Sam brought my dog?"

"Isaac, you're not going with Sam and Anna."

His face fell. "Who's gonna feed my dog?"

The disappointment on his son's face hurt. "Don't you want to see Uncle Ray?"

Isaac shook his head. "I want my dog and my cake. Uncle Ray brings beer and pizza."

James placed their order. Isaac didn't realize that staying with Sam and Anna was a permanent move. Throughout the meal, Isaac chatted about Sam building him a tree house, Anna baking him cookies, his new dog, and how he wanted to play T-ball.

James could give him all those things now. Couldn't he?

"After you work, you can come get me."

Each word spoken was like a dagger in James's gut. Sitting at the red light, he scrubbed a hand down his face and groaned. "Do you really want to live with Sam and Anna?"

"I want a dog and a pirate bed." Isaac folded his arms across his chest. "Don't be mad."

He lowered his tone. "I'm not mad. It's…well…you see that road?" He pointed to the northern exit ramp and Isaac nodded. "That's the way to work. You see that road up there?" He pointed straight ahead to the next red light. "That's the way to Sam and Anna's. We can't go both ways. You choose Isaac. Whatever you want. Which way do you want Daddy to go?"

A broad grin appeared on Isaac's face. "Uncle Ray can watch cartoons without me."

James swallowed his panic and changed lanes. He didn't know if he was strong enough to travel the path Isaac chose.

A little hand stretched across the cab. "You're the best daddy in the world."

At every exit, James slowed and wanted to turn around. He didn't know why he kept driving. For three hours, he listened to all the things promised to Isaac. James didn't blame him. If he was a kid, he'd want to live with Sam and Anna too. In the driveway, he took his time unloading Isaac's things.

At the door, his eyes burned, and his shaky hands refused to ring the doorbell. He sat on the top step and lifted his son on his lap. "Isaac, Daddy loves you."

"You told me too many times already."

He swallowed the knot in his throat and smiled. "I don't want you to forget."

Skinny arms wrapped around him. "I won't."

Memorizing Isaac's every feature, James held out his fist. "Promise?"

Isaac bumped his knuckles against James's larger ones. "I promise. Have fun at work."

The door opened behind them. Isaac ran up the steps and claimed the wiggling puppy. James dropped his head in his hands. A single tear shattered on the concrete step. A large hand landed on his shoulder and James flinched. He didn't want Isaac's last memory to be of him bawling his eyes out. He stood and rushed toward his truck.

"Daddy, wait!" Isaac ran down the steps and leapt in his arms. He whispered in a loud voice. "Take care of Joni. Love her on both sides." Two sweet kisses landed on James's cheeks.

He choked. He had to get out of here before he snatched Isaac and ran. "I'll try."

As if sensing the danger, Anna pried Isaac from his grip. James forced himself into the driver's seat. He pulled away from the curb and glanced in his rearview mirror. Isaac waved from Sam's arms while Anna wiped her eyes. The three of them looked like a real family.

Joni's words came back to him. *Allowing the Mahers to adopt me was the most loving thing my parents did.*

He turned onto the next street. His lungs burned and he couldn't breathe. He pulled to the shoulder and collapsed against the steering wheel. The tangled knot in his chest exploded as the pain overwhelmed him. Sobs racked his body.

~ ~ ~

Joni ran up the apartment stairs. It had been a month since James disappeared. She didn't know why he dropped Isaac off at Sam and Anna's, but she didn't worry about Isaac's safety anymore.

James, however, was a different story.

He wouldn't answer her calls or messages, but finally his truck was parked out front.

A crash sounded in the apartment, followed by a curse. She winced, hoping he hadn't hurt himself. She unlocked the door and flung it open. The living room was as she left it this morning before class. A thump sounded down the hall. She sucked in a breath and opened the door she'd avoided for over a month.

Unshaven, shirt wrinkled, James stood from Isaac's bed

and saluted her with a half-empty bottle of whiskey. "Heeeey, beautiful." He stumbled back against the wall and raised the bottle to his lips. "Missed you."

She eased in the door. "Where have you been? Why haven't you answered my calls?"

The lamp on an end table tilted when he jarred it as he slid down the wall. "Lost my phone." Whiskey ran down his chin after his latest swig. He stretched his feet, and a dump truck rolled across the carpet. "It's around here somewhere."

"James." She gathered the scattered toys and placed them in the closet. "How can I help?"

Powerful arms pulled her down in his lap. "Kiss me and make me forget."

The whiskey on his breath burned her lips. "No, James. You're drunk."

The edges of the square glass bottle pressed into her back as he pulled her close. "Thought you wanted to cheer me up."

"Not like this. Let go." She wasn't afraid, though even drunk he easily overpowered her.

"I know something else that would make me feel better." His hand slid under her skirt.

Her palm cracked against his cheek. "I said, no."

His hand fell to the floor. "I'm sorry, Joni. I didn't mean it. I love you."

She held on to the hope of his words. "You don't hate me?"

He cradled her against his chest. "Isaac won't let me. Keeps saying to love you on both sides. Then he waves in the mirror. He waves and waves. Then he's gone."

Joni held him tight and closed her eyes. James was lost without Isaac. How could she have done this? He was a man broken. He staggered to his feet and Joni slid onto the carpet. Losing his balance, he fell back onto the bed. Amber liquid splashed over her shirt. "I can't live without him. I went back to get Isaac." A lone tear escaped bloodshot eyes. "He was gone. You want to buy a house? It's for sale."

"No, James. God will take care of him."

"God? Screw God!" The bottle slammed onto the floor.

It was a miracle it didn't shatter into a million pieces. "Where was He when Isaac needed him? Why couldn't I keep Isaac? Why?" He reached for his keys. "I am. The. Best. Daddy. Ever. He tells me every night. I promised. I promised I'd never leave him. Isaac! Isaac. Daddy's coming, Isaac."

She pushed him against the mattress. James dropped the keys and buried his face in the pillow. "God's punishing me."

She rubbed his shoulders. "No, he isn't."

"Yes, he is. You were his and I took you. So he took Isaac. He took you both. Why Joni? Why couldn't he let me have you?"

"I'm right here." Joni wept for their loss as she snuggled against his side. While he'd been gone, God became her refuge and she wouldn't sin against him, but she couldn't abandon James either.

He babbled on about Isaac and a promise he couldn't keep. "Why did you give him away? Didn't you know I loved him?" He rolled over and shoved her off the bed. "Go away. I can't stand to look at you." Thankfully, he passed out.

Lord, why? He blames me. She choked on a sob. *It's my fault. Is this punishment for our sin? God, please help James. I'll take his punishment and mine if you save him.*

Joni sank to the carpet and did the only thing that brought her peace these last weeks. She prayed. She prayed for Isaac's happiness and James's salvation. Afterward, she emptied the whiskey in the toilet and placed the empty bottle on Isaac's floor.

In her bed, she tossed and turned.

～～～

James woke to the sound of running water. Joni was in the shower. He stumbled to the coffee pot and blinked against the pressure behind his eyes. The only pain reliever in the cabinet was for menstrual cramps. He popped four of them and eased down to his truck for a change of clothes. When he opened the bathroom door, Joni shrieked and hid behind the shower curtain.

He reached for the sink as a wave of dizziness passed. "Chill, Joni, I've seen you before."

"Get out!"

"Don't yell."

A bottle of shampoo sailed his way. He jumped in the hall and hid behind the door. Ugh! He grabbed his head and leaned against the wall. What happened to his sweet little Joni?

He eased into their room and collapsed on the bed. The ceiling swirled, so he struggled to sit upright and placed his feet on the floor. On the dresser, a note peeked from Joni's and his Bible. Despite the pain slicing his head, he reached for her list.

Baptism Service 6:00pm
No white shirt
Two towels
Change of clothes

The door between the bathroom and closet opened. Thin lavender straps peeked out from under her towel and teased his tilting vision.

The slam of the closet door jarred his aching head. What did he do last night to make her so angry? He grabbed his clothes from the dresser and the shampoo off the hall floor.

Shower first, and then maybe he could think clearly.

~~~

Joni dressed quickly as James showered. Images lingered from the nightmare. It wasn't the first time she'd been haunted by Isaac's pleas not to let Kathy take him, or his battered body smiling from the clawfoot tub. But last night added James's accusations.

"How can I love you? I can't stand to look at you."

The mirror revealed her red and puffy eyes as she wound her hair into a ponytail. She prayed as she crammed two towels and a change of clothes into a canvas bag. "Lord, help me get out of the apartment without giving in to him."

The water shut off. Joni was tired of feeling sorry for herself. She'd done the right thing for Isaac and James needed to get over it. After today, she vowed never to think of him again. So what if he broke her heart? She could live without him.

"Joni." A towel hung low on James's hips. She turned away from the hunger in his eyes. His sultry voice caressed her. "You look beautiful in that dress."

"Thank you." She didn't dare look in his direction, though he blocked the exit into the hall. "I've changed since you've been gone, but after last night, I guess it doesn't matter." In her peripheral vision, his hand grabbed his jeans off the bed. She closed her eyes and refused to look.

"Joni?" She heard the confusion in his voice. Her gaze met his. "What happened last night? Did I hurt you?"

She hated herself for allowing him to hug her close. "Not physically. I simply realized that what I did was unforgivable."

He kissed her temple and she turned in his arms. His heart thundered beneath her cheek. She waited for words that never came.

Fear squeezed her lungs. "Will you ever forgive me?"

A shudder racked his body. "You were supposed to be my wife." He spoke in past tense.

Joni crumpled against him. Her last hope vanished.

"You were supposed to be Isaac's mother. But now…every time I see you, I look for Isaac…only he's not there. I can't…"

"You don't have to explain." She stepped away, but he gripped her waist. The ring on her finger glistened against his muscular chest. The diamond mocked her. She ripped it off her hand, tearing her heart out in the process. "Here."

His arms fell to his sides.

She shoved the ring at him. "Take it."

His stance locked. His muscles flexed. His eyes closed.

She sobbed his name. "James."

His Adam's apple bobbed, but he didn't twitch.

"Fine!" Joni slammed the ring on her dresser. "I'll be gone all weekend. Take your ring and pack all your stuff. Leave the apartment key on the table."

He still hadn't budged after she lifted her canvas bag, yet she loved him despite his painful rejection. Her naked hand smoothed his whiskers and her lips stole one last kiss. "I love you."

His jaw clenched at her words.

"Goodbye, James."

~ ~ ~

He could never forgive her betrayal. James twisted the ring on his pinkie. Joni may have loved him, but she'd loved Isaac more.

Swallowing the lump in his throat, he poured a cup of coffee and called Cecil. It was time to man up. He packed Isaac's room and gathered all of his things from the apartment. Despite what she demanded, he kept the key.

The water under the causeway was choppy. The skies were overcast. He drove to his sister's and stored his things in Sara's empty garage apartment.

At six fifteen, he found a parking place in the full lot beside the church. Going in the side entrance, he slipped into the sound booth next to Cole. "How's law school?"

"Fine. It's good to see you."

James swallowed and nodded at the baptistery. "Has Joni gone through?"

Cole smacked the lollipop in his mouth and adjusted the left monitor. "Not yet. They're going by age group. She and Marla are in the second set. Her mom and aunt are in the third." He indicated a tripod on the platform. "We're recording. For a five-dollar donation, you can have a copy mailed. There's a sign-up sheet in the foyer."

James removed his wallet. "I'd prefer no one knew I was here. Could you keep a copy for me? I'll get it later."

"Absolutely."

At the front of the church, Joni stepped into the pool. Pastor spoke on Joni's sacrifice and commitment to God. As the floodlights in the baptistery haloed her hair, he thought of the night they first met. He knew then she belonged in church. His mother snapped several photos from the front pew, and James wished he was the type of man that could forgive and forget.

"I baptize you in the name of the Father, the Son, and the Holy Ghost." Pastor dipped Joni under the water. When she surfaced, James gasped at the joy radiating from her face. How could he not love her? One word whispered through his mind.

Isaac.

He turned toward the small door but called over his shoulder, "Thanks for letting me watch."

"James, I'm praying for you. If you ever want to talk, you know where to find me." Cole slapped a hand across James's shoulder.

"Thanks."

~ ~ ~

Joni stared at James's picture as she remembered their phone conversation. Last night wasn't the first time he'd called drunk and wanted her to sing. Wherever he was, did he remember saying, "I love you"? Her finger slid across her phone screen.

The Statistical Reasoning professor's lecture buzzed on. At least last year's Economics classes counted as a prerequisite toward her new goal, a bachelor's degree in social work. With her summer courses, she should graduate in three years.

Garrett, Dr. Seanbridge's graduate assistant, winked from the front of the lecture hall. Joni always knew what James was thinking when he'd winked. She blushed. Shaking her head, she pushed him out of her thoughts as her phone vibrated in her hand.

Dinner? Tonight? The fourth such invitation from Garrett in the past hour.

She sucked in a breath and replied. *No. Stop staring!*

Your address? Pick you up at 7? Cant help it.

She had never dated anyone but James. Texting someone else felt like cheating. *I can't. Quit asking.*

She scooted her chair to the right, blocking Garrett's view.

He didn't give up easily. *Dont care if you love him. I can be your rebound guy.*

Joni peeked from behind the broad shoulders in front of her and narrowed her eyes at Garrett. Ducking out of sight, she scribbled on her notepad. Her lips curled in a smile. If James still loved her, he'd take care of the unwanted invitations in a flash.

Marla texted from the seat next to her. *Is he asking you out? Dont do it. Matt is better looking and so is his friend Jeremy. We can double.*

Why did all her friends think she should forget James? She wanted to get on with her life. She really did. That's the reason she changed her major. Her parents didn't know yet, but she was slowly warming them up to the idea with her job at Twila's House, a safe home for children.

Marla's elbow nudged her and Joni replied. *I dont think I can love anyone but James.*

Didnt say anything about love. Just dinner. Next time Matt asks, say yes. You owe me.

Her friend tilted her head and Joni sent, *Ill ask Matt about his friend. But only for you. Not interested in dating.*

Marla's next message didn't surprise Joni. *James isnt a Christian. Remember what Pastor said about being unequally yoked and forget him.*

I remember. She sent the last text and put her phone in her purse. Oh, how she remembered. Everyone at church, including James's sister, told her repeatedly how proud they were of her for leaving James and recommitting her life to God.

They were wrong.

Church activities, along with school, kept her mind busy during the day. Worship music intrigued her, though the ability to play with freedom eluded her. Pastor eventually allowed Joni to sing during services again. She loved God. Loved His people, but peace was something others experienced. The apartment was her refuge. Her tear-soaked pillow was only a substitute for what her heart really desired. In her dreams, Isaac begged her not to let Kathy take him. She woke and mourned the loss of James's comforting arms.

During his few phone calls, she heard his pain in between the drunken slurs. He hurt because of her actions. Did she do the right thing? Could the three of them be living in another state as a family even now? Isaac's adoption was six months ago. Was his family everything a little boy needed? Did he have a dog?

Marla whispered, "Stop thinking about him."

Joni blinked away tears and turned her back to her friend. No one understood. She didn't know how to stop loving James.

Seven days later, Joni returned from her afternoon class and found a bouquet of fuchsia roses sitting in the middle of the dining table. "James." Her book bag slipped off her shoulder as she lifted the delicate vase. The scent of honey mingled with his cologne as the soft petals caressed her cheek. Her hands trembled as she read the card. "Happy Anniversary."

Her heart fluttered and shed the burden it had carried for months. He remembered the night they met. Where was he? She searched the apartment. Other than the roses, there was no sign that anyone had been here. She couldn't eat dinner. Couldn't concentrate on her studies.

At eleven fifteen, she gave up on James's return and went to bed. Staring at the ceiling, she tried to pray, but memories of nights long ago held her captive. The front door creaked opened. Her heart pounded in her chest. Keys rattled and then the door closed with a click. She propped up on an elbow and waited.

Two clunks sounded and she pictured his boots hitting the floor. She swallowed. He'd always removed his boots by the refrigerator. Soft footfalls landed in the hall. He stood in the bedroom door and crossed his arms.

Through the light from the bathroom, she studied him. His whiskers were wild, untamed. His normally immaculate hair was shaggy over his ears. She rose to her knees. Hungry eyes roamed over her nightgown. He crossed the room and abandoned his beer bottle on the bedside table. Silence hung on the unspoken question. Her palm caressed his jaw and her thumb brushed his unruly whiskers.

His eyes closed as he turned his face into her hand. "Joni, I need you."

She answered his plea with a kiss. In the morning, she knew he'd leave, but for tonight he was hers.

~ ~ ~

A thorn pricked her finger and blood dotted her skin.

James had disappeared sometime in the wee hours of the morning and she hadn't heard from him since. Not that she expected to.

Sunday morning, Joni trashed the dead roses and drove across the bay to church.

Guilt had her stumbling through the lyrics of the morning songs. Her jittery nerves panicked when Pastor asked what was wrong. Her chest tightened during the sermon and conviction drove her to the altar.

Oh God, I'm sorry. I swear, I won't ever do it again. Please don't leave me, Jesus. Please. I need you.

Chapter Nineteen

The redhead, he couldn't remember her name, lifted Joni and Isaac's picture from the dash of his new truck. "Who's this? You're not married, are you?"

James carefully removed the pictures from her grip. He held the photos in one hand and drank his beer with the other. In a moment of weakness, he'd visited Joni, but Isaac's picture reminded him of her treachery. "Where's Ray and your friend? They should be out here by now."

The door to the bar opened. Ray had his arm around a pretty brunette. He looked James's way and saluted before walking across the parking lot toward a compact car.

"What happened to them?" The girl nodded to the pictures.

He caressed the pictures before arranging them next to his gauges. "Look, they're really not any of your business."

She withdrew the hand trailing down his arm. "Ouch. You must still love her."

He turned the key and the engine roared to life. "You should get out now. This isn't working for me. I'm sure you can find someone more suitable back on the dance floor."

Her dark eyes turned black. "I'm sure."

The slamming door didn't surprise him. He should've known better than to listen to Ray. No one could replace Joni. The only thing that lessened the pain was large quantities of alcohol. He should be in his room, cuddled up with a bottle. Not out here stirring up old memories.

He stopped by the liquor store on his way to the hotel.

In his room, he pulled the laptop Isaac use to watch cartoons on from his duffle bag. Once it booted, he signed in as Joni on her social network. Matt Richardson had posted to her wall. *Cant wait until Friday. Hope you like oysters.*

His heart dropped to his stomach. Who was this punk? He clicked on the guy's info. A lawyer? No, worse—a want-to-be politician. Joni could do better than this jerk. He was tempted to send him a message from Joni canceling the date.

He suppressed the urge to call Cecil and request time off for a family emergency. This job had one, maybe two, days left.

Come Friday, he'd be at the apartment waiting for Pretty Boy.

~ ~ ~

Joni forced a smile as Matt led her into the restaurant. He and Jeremy sat opposite her and Marla. After months of persuasion, she'd agreed to a double date. A half-wall separated their table from the bar.

James swiveled on a stool, winked, and toasted her with a longneck bottle.

She blinked, not trusting her eyes.

James's lips curled in a malicious smile.

Not now. Why is he here? His gaze traveled to Matt. James sneered. She squirmed in her seat as his eyes met hers again, and his expression turned to one of disgust.

A sigh escaped her. Why should she feel guilty? She'd done nothing wrong.

Matt frowned at her reaction. "Sweetheart, are you okay?"

She forced herself to breath and hid behind her menu. "I'm fine."

Marla was wrapped up in Jeremy's conversation and hadn't noticed her silent plea for help.

She shot a glance over Matt's shoulder. James reached in his pocket and brought out his phone. He fumbled with it under the table.

Joni's phone chimed in her purse. He texted her! Was he crazy? She reached for her phone and read James's message. *Hes not your type. Too preppy.*

She replied. *Dont text me. Its none of your business.* Joni's heart tattooed against her chest. Please, God, don't let James come over here.

Where were you? I went to the apartment.

Joni's face flamed. It had been a while since she stayed at her parents' house, but she couldn't stand the thought of Matt or any other guy in James's apartment.

"Sweetie, the waitress is waiting."

"Sorry." She didn't look in James's direction. "I'll have the blackened seafood and penne pasta." Her phone chimed again. She ignored it.

Matt smiled. "Are you sure you're okay? You're a little pale."

Marla frowned. "Joni?"

She wiped sweaty palms on her napkin, faked a smile, and texted Marla. *James is at the bar.* She conjured up a bright smile and focused on her date. "Everything's fine."

Marla hissed as she read the text. "Oh, crap."

Oblivious to the disaster around him, Matt lifted Joni's hand and kissed it.

James's longneck slammed down on the bar. Joni flinched and snatched her hand out of Matt's grip. Remembering Trent, she whispered another prayer and shook her head. James narrowed his eyes but stalked off in the other direction.

She pretended an interest in the conversation around her. Luckily, Marla covered and all Joni had to do was sit there and listen. And watch out for James.

His ringtone echoed from her phone. She let it ring. Her face ached from forcing a smile, and her frazzled nerves could feel James's glare from somewhere nearby.

After the third consecutive call, Matt said, "Sweetie, you should answer. It may be important."

"Of course." She slipped her phone out of her purse. "Excuse me." She stepped out on the balcony overlooking the bay and answered. "Stop calling me." No one was on the line. "Ugh!" Stuffing her phone in her purse, she breathed in the cool night air and shivered.

Warm arms wrapped around her waist. "I missed you." The urge to lean back on James's strength overwhelmed. She gave in and her lids fluttered. She remembered the smell of his cologne, his touch, and his kiss as his lips scraped across her neck. Her shiver had nothing to do with the early March temperatures.

"Joni, come back to me."

With one step she was free. "*I* never left you." The blue silk of her dress flared as she twirled around to face him. Tears stung her eyes, but she refused to let them fall. She'd cried enough over him.

He reached for her. "I'm sorry, I didn't—"

She slapped his hands away. "You weren't the only one to lose Isaac. I loved him." She leaned her head back and blinked several times. "I loved his smile. His fine baby hair. The intelligence in his blue eyes." She sniffed and held up a hand. "I still love him. I dreamt one day he would be mine. Ours."

"Joni, please don't cry."

"Don't worry. I'm sick of crying for you." Inhaling the cold, crisp air, she wiped her face and stepped close to him. Her hand caressed his jaw. The whiskers she loved tickled her palm.

He rubbed his cheek against her hand. Heat branded her arm.

"James, you shut me out. I needed you. I needed your arms to hold me then." She pulled her hand back. "I don't need you now."

He kissed her. "I'm sorry."

The taste of beer lingered on her lips. "It's too late." Chin held high, she walked into the restaurant and reclaimed her seat across from Matt.

"Who was it?"

The ice in Joni's glass shook as she raised it. "Where?" Did he see her talking to James?

"On the phone." His eyes narrowed. "Have you been crying?"

She shook her head and tried to smile. "Of course not." Joni couldn't look him in the eye. Her fork clattered to her plate.

The next forty minutes seemed like forty lifetimes.

In the car, Matt leaned close.

Joni avoided his kiss by turning her head and staring out the passenger window. Moisture filled her eyes. She didn't want to kiss anyone but James.

"Jeremy and Marla are driving to Fairhope Pier. Do you want to go?" He started the Dodge Charger, and shifted into drive.

James leaned against a new Silverado. She turned in the seat to get a better look.

"Joni?" Matt tried to follow her gaze.

"I'm not feeling well. Can you drop me off at my parents'?"

~ ~ ~

With the exception of the wall photos of himself and Isaac, the apartment hadn't changed much. James inspected the montage of happier times while he waited for Joni to come home. The thought of her in Pretty Boy's arms kept him awake all night. He fell asleep sometime before dawn and awoke at noon.

She never made it home. There was only one other place she could be. He hoped. James raced across the bay. Joni's car sat in her parents' drive. He breathed easy and parked behind the Honda. Pink roses in hand, he knocked on the door.

Her mom cracked the door open. "What do you want?"

He couldn't see around her. "Is Joni home?"

"Thankfully, no."

James cut his eyes to Joni's car and several others in the driveway. "I just want to talk. Two seconds."

Mrs. Maher's arms relaxed at her sides. "I'm sorry. She and Marla are shopping. They won't be back 'til late."

Her eyes told the truth. He held out the roses. "Will you give her these? And tell her…" He rubbed the bridge of his nose. "Tell her, I'm sorry about last night."

Mrs. Maher accepted the flowers. "What did you do?"

James grimaced at her reproving look. "I never intended to hurt her."

"Who's at the door?" A booming male voice came from within the house. "If it's Frank and Paul, tell 'em to come around back."

Mrs. Maher turned and answered, "It's James."

The urge to run intensified when Joni's dad came to the door. James swallowed the dryness in his mouth under Mr. Maher's scrutiny. "Sir."

The door opened. "Come in. Watch the games with us."

The invitation was friendly enough, but James remembered Mr. Maher's warning of long ago and wondered if he kept a gun in the house. "I really can't."

"I insist." Mr. Maher waved his hand and walked farther into the house.

James lost all sense when he stepped into the foyer. "Just for a minute." Joni's mom and the lady that had gotten baptized with her walked out the door as he walked in.

Mr. Maher hefted a tray of ham and cheese. "I'm sorry about Isaac." Understanding flickered in his expression. Not sympathy or judgment, and no sermon. "Losing a son could drive a man to desperation."

James nodded. "It could."

Mr. Maher handed him the platter and grabbed another filled with sliced vegetables. "Hang in there, son. I know it hurts, but you'll make it."

"Yes, sir. I will."

James followed Joni's dad down unstained wooden stairs. The converted basement had two sets of sliding glass doors. Beyond a concrete patio he glimpsed a beautiful view of Mobile Bay.

In the room, a middle-aged man sat in one of the two recliners in front of a large TV. One of the first NCAA tournament games played on the wide flat screen.

Perpendicular to the chairs, a sofa and loveseat matched the daybed in the far corner. A bathroom door stood open along the wall. "Have a seat. You want a beer?"

James sat on the loveseat's cushioned edge and put the platter on the coffee table. "No, sir. I'm good."

"James, meet my brother, Dave." Mr. Maher picked up the tray and slid the door open with his hip. He disappeared into the backyard.

James shook Joni's uncle's hand. Though his hair was gray, Dave's grip was solid.

As they exchanged greetings, Mr. Maher returned with two empty trays. "Women. They'll never understand us." He placed them at the bottom of the stairs and dug in a closet. James caught the bag of snack mix on reflex. The second period of the game started and he settled on the two-cushioned couch.

During the next commercial, Mr. Maher passed James a beer out of a small refrigerator. The snack mix had dried out his throat. "Thank you, sir."

"Name's Bill. Or have you forgotten?"

"No, sir."

Mr. Maher entered the bathroom and closed the door.

Dave popped the top on a can. "What do you do for a living?"

"I fitted pipe, but now I hire on as a foreman."

"Same company, or different outfits?"

"Same. They keep me working. Travel a lot, but that's good."

"Ever been married? Kids?"

James swallowed, shook his head, and opened his beer. He didn't want to think of Isaac.

"I could use a good hand like you. You looking for work?"

"No, sir. I'm due in New Orleans Monday morning. Anyway, it might be awkward working for Joni's dad."

"So that's how the wind blows."

James shrugged.

"You'll work for me. Years ago, Bill agreed that I could hire the hands."

"Don't go there." Mr. Maher returned, reclined back in his chair, and tilted his can to his mouth.

"First crew he hired on," Dave laughed and shook his head. "Sorriest bunch I ever seen."

Joni's dad chuckled. "They were kinda scraggly."

Four empty cans later, James propped his feet on the loveseat. Music chimed into the basement. Bill pointed at him and then toward the stairs. "You're young. Get the door, will ya?"

"Yes, sir."

The notes sounded again while James stumbled up the stairs. He opened the door. Joni's boyfriend from last night lowered his hand.

The intruder frowned in surprise. "Who are you?"

The beer buzz must be getting to James. "The butler."

Pretty Boy tossed his head and cleared his throat. "Tell Joni that Matt is here."

Balancing against the doorframe, James couldn't stop his grin. "She's not here."

"Her car is."

"She's not."

"Do I know you?"

James crossed his arms over his chest. "Nope."

"You were at the restaurant last night." Matt's face flamed. "At the bar." His chest expanded and he bit his lip. "And in the parking lot. Forget it. I'll call her later."

James shut the door and staggered back down the stairs.

"Who was it?" Bill tossed a handful of snack mix in his mouth.

James flopped down on the loveseat. Beer splashed on his hand. He slurped it up before it could roll down onto the fabric. "Some guy looking for Joni."

Bill snickered, spewing crumbs halfway across the room.

Dave laughed. "Bet that was awkward."

"Nah." James grinned. "Not at all."

A few minutes later, the sliding glass door skidded open. Two guys in their early thirties waltzed in carrying a cooler between them. "Hey, you started without us."

Dave straightened in his recliner. "James, meet my boys Paul and Frank."

Frank, the tall one, knocked James's feet to the floor and landed beside him on the couch.

"Nice to meet you." He attempted to stand, but his vision blurred, and he sank back into the cushions. Instead, he held his can up in a toast.

Why was Paul grinning from the other sofa? "Joni's gonna bless you out."

James shook his head, leaned forward, and whispered, "She's not speaking to me."

Paul fell back laughing. "Yeah, I know. But that, my friend, will change soon enough."

Frank took possession of the remote and an NBA crowd cheered from the stands. "Toss me a beer." Paul said something about watching the fireworks. Which didn't make sense? New Year's had come and gone.

~ ~ ~

Marla's headlights illuminated a Silverado in Joni's parents' driveway. The truck James drove last night? Uncle Dave's Yukon and Paul's Camaro crowded beside the shiny rims.

"Are you okay?" Marla snapped her fingers.

"I spaced out. Sorry." Joni stepped out of the car and reached in the backseat for her bags from the outlet mall. "See you at church in the morning. I think I need to walk off all those yeast rolls on the treadmill."

Her friend laughed. "Me too, girl." With a wave, she backed into the street.

Joni circled the truck. A chrome toolbox sat on back while a duffle bag and a hard hat lay on the bed liner. No doubt, it belonged to James. He had the cleanest truck she'd ever seen. What was he doing here? And where was he?

The inside of the cab was empty.

Unease churned in the pit of her stomach. If James was in the basement with the men in her family, the term "March Madness" had new meaning.

She set her packages down in the foyer and walked through the empty living room toward the kitchen.

Male laughter surged up from Dad's den.

As an unspoken rule, Joni never ventured in The Man Cave, as mom called it, when her dad had friends over. But with James's truck out front, she made an exception.

The volume of the basketball game drowned out her soft footfalls.

Her breath caught. James constructed an elaborate house of cans on the coffee table.

"Man, what's wrong wich ya? You sippin like a lil' girl." Water rained down as Frank reached in a cooler and tossed a silver can across the room.

Paul caught it and set it on the floor. "No thanks. Ever since Nancy started to church with Joni, she's been after me to stop drinking. The less she knows, the better."

Joni froze on the steps.

Frank stretched his legs. "I refused to let Pam go. Our life is fine. Don't need no help from no God."

Uncle Dave shot a miserable look to Joni's dad. "Too late for Patsy and Martha. Wish I knew the fool who introduced Joni to church."

All heads turned to James. Frank kicked the table and James's masterpiece tumbled to the floor. James held his hands up and shrugged. "How's I 'posed to know she'd love it?" He circled his hands. "God just kinda…" He sagged against the sofa. "He stole her."

Joni gasped and clamped a hand over her mouth. She held her breath until her dad said, "You better steal her back."

James tilted a can to his mouth and then smacked his lips. "I tried to."

The conversation changed to "my truck is better than your truck." Joni waited a few minutes, hoping they'd talk about church again. None of the men noticed her presence until she stepped in front of the screen.

James struggled to his feet. "Hey, be-beau-beautiful." He blinked and swayed slightly.

"You've been drinking?"

His head jerked back and forth. She lifted a brow at his beer can, which was quickly passed to Frank. The elder of her two cousins grinned and raised both hands. "Thirsty?"

Her dad sent her a silly smile. "Give 'ames a break." Hiccup. "I like 'em."

James's stupid grin lit a fuse deep inside her. "You got my dad drunk?" She rounded on him. "How could you? First, you show up out of nowhere last night and ruin a perfectly good date. And now this?"

He wrinkled his brow. "I'm sorry?" James burped. "Excuse me."

Laughter surrounded her. "Uncle Dave, are you on his side, too?"

His bright eyes widened and he pointed a finger at her. "You should've came home sooner. James watched four games wait'n and a man needs refreshment." He cackled out a laugh and slapped the arm of the recliner. "Oh, that's good. Hope I remember to tell Patsy that one. A man needs refreshment."

Joni inhaled deeply and held on to her composure as her dad and Uncle Dave high-fived. "Ya'll are a bunch of drunks. You know that, right?"

Paul remained silent and grinned from the sofa. He acted the most sober of them all.

"*What* are you smiling about?"

He shrugged. "I think James is a pretty cool dude."

"Tank you." James stumbled forward. She caught him by the arms before he face-planted.

"Hurry up and beg forgiveness." Uncle Dave let out a long burp. "Game six is on. Turn it up, Frank."

Her dad nudged her out of the way with his foot. "Can't see TV, honey."

James kissed her hand while leaning against the metal basement support. His eyes floated in their sockets. "Pleeze? Will you love me, again?"

Her traitorous eyes blurred, but she was not having this conversation until he was sober. Without a word she stalked away.

"Joni." James staggered after her. "Joni!"

She ignored him and climbed the stairs. Something crashed behind her. James lay sprawled on the steps. Two of her mother's best appetizer platters lay in pieces around him.

He rolled to his back and moaned. "Jonaaaay!"

"Ugh." She flounced down beside him. The game consumed the others' attention. With his shirttail, Joni wiped the blood from his lip. "You are pitiful."

"Don't leave me. I do love you, Joni. I tried not to, but I can't help it."

Her heart squeezed. "What happened to your Toyota?"

He groaned. "Light pole."

Decision made, Joni dug in his front jean pockets.

Laughing, he slapped at her hands. "Not in front of your father. Ouch! Watch it."

"Quit squirming." She claimed the truck keys and ascended the stairs. Over her shoulder she called, "I'll give them back in the morning."

In the kitchen, she grabbed her packages, then ran up the carpeted stairs. Once in her room, she fell across the bed. "Lord, if you save him, I promise I will never lust over him again."

Three hours later, she removed the extra blanket and pillow from her bed. The house was quiet as she tiptoed down the two separate staircases. The backyard streetlight illuminated a path around the scattered beer cans. James was sprawled on his back across the sofa.

Her heartbeat stalled. Even in his sleep he affected her. Why? Why couldn't she forget him? What made him so special?

She removed his shoes and placed his feet on the cushions. He snuggled into the blanket and mumbled her name. Joni kissed his temple and crept away, up to her room.

~ ~ ~

Joni's scent engulfed him. He forced his eyelids open and searched for her. Her smell came from the blanket. Hers?

"James?" Bill's voice yelled down the stairs. "You awake?"

"Yes, sir." A million hammers pounded his head. "Ugh." He hated hangovers. Careful not to jostle his brain, he eased up the stairs.

"You too, huh?" Bill slid a box of headache powders across the bar. "Glasses are next to the refrigerator. Water's on tap."

James shuddered at the foul taste in his mouth. "You got any tomato juice?"

"No. We'll stop and get some on the way."

"Where are we going?"

"The girls are highly ticked. Probably more my fault than yours, and the way to appease a woman is to give her what she thinks she can't have."

James didn't understand and the sunlight hurt his eyes.

"Church, son. We're going to take back our women." Bill nodded at the clock. "Can you be ready in twenty minutes?"

"Sir, I don't know if church is the answer. We could get trapped in there." James shook his head but froze when the room spun. "And right now, I'm okay with hating God."

"That's good." Bill scratched his balding head. "You hate God. I don't believe He exists. So we make a pact. We go in. Smile at the girls and get out. No giving in. If I start to cave, you get me outta there. I'll do the same for you. And no praying."

James exhaled. "Let's do it."

The plan was to slip into a back row, but all three were filled. "Now what?"

"There's Martha up there." Bill lowered his voice. "Can you handle the fifth row?"

James ignored the stares directed his way. "If you can."

His mom and Sara gawked as he passed their aisle. The collar of his borrowed, button-up shirt choked him. Bill slid in the pew beside his wife. James followed. Joni's uncertain smile found him from the platform.

The music started and the service began. Her voice enthralled him. He'd forgotten how good she sounded. The stares multiplied as she slipped in between him and her father after the praise and worship portion of the service.

Her hand slid into his as she whispered. "I can't believe you brought Dad to church."

"Is that okay?"

Her smile tripped his pulse. "It's more than okay." She laid her cheek against his shoulder and he absently kissed the top of her head.

Pastor loosened his tie and wrapped a white handkerchief around the cordless microphone. The congregation stood as he read Samson's life story from the book of Judges.

James reclaimed Joni's hand and squirmed against the pew.

Pastor stepped off the platform and wrinkles appeared on his bald head as he smiled. "I want to talk to some Samsons today."

James rolled the stiffness from his neck. This was a bad idea.

"Before you took your first breath, God had a plan for you." Pastor threw one arm in the air. "Handsome and strong, Samson made some bad decisions."

Joni hung on the preacher's every word. James caressed the back of her hand, hoping to regain her attention from the sermon. She flinched as the messenger from God slapped the communion table.

Placing their joined hands on his knee, James covered them with his other palm.

Pastor paced in front of his congregation. He stopped in front of Joni's section. "Samson had a hindrance. Delilah was her name." He switched hands with his microphone and pointed toward them. "You have a hindrance and you know their name."

Her hand wrestled out of James's grip. He glared at the preacher and wrapped his arm behind her.

"You may love your Philistine, but…God! Loves! Him! More!" Pastor wiped his forehead with the handkerchief and paced on.

Knuckles white, Joni clasped her hands together on her lap. James weaved his fingers through her hair while trying to calm his erratic pulse.

"God knows how to save them. But you! You have to let them go!"

He reached across with his right hand, but she gripped a hymnal tight. He scrubbed a hand down the bridge of his nose while Joni's eyes followed Pastor's every step. Her lips pressed together in a tight line.

"You want the anointing? You want to live in God's blessings?" Pastor jumped on the platform and stepped behind the pulpit. "Samson, you must choose. God's Spirit or your Philistine? The altars are open."

People flooded the front.

James stood and blocked Joni's exit. He whispered, "I love you." Her sad smile triggered waves of panic. He was drowning and he didn't know how to tread these dangerous waters. "Joni? Let's go get some lunch. You choose the place."

"I need to pray first." She squeezed around him.

He grabbed for her but she was out of his reach. He swore under his breath.

Pastor grinned from the platform. He knew what he'd done, and he was proud of his accomplishment. James suppressed the urge to knock the grin off his face.

A still, small voice from long ago breezed through James's thoughts. *She's Mine. If you want her, you'll have to go through Me.*

He glared at the cross glowing above the baptistery and mumbled under his breath, "I'll never let her go."

~ ~ ~

Joni fell across the prayer bench and called out to her Savior. "Help me. Jesus, I love him, but I love you more. I love you more than this world. I love you more than James." Sobs racked her body and she cried out to Jesus unashamed. Comforting hands surrounded her as her friends labored with her in prayer.

When she was spent, she wiped her eyes and lifted her head. James winked from the back of the church. Joni prayed. *Jesus, I can't do this without your help.* His mother kissed his cheek and walked out the door. Joni smoothed her skirt and met him in the center aisle.

He squeezed her hand. "You okay?"

She smiled past the sadness and nodded once. Sara and Mark appeared at their side. Mark clapped James's back. "It was good having you in church. You should come more often."

Pastor walked toward them. Panic crossed James's face. "Joni, I'm starved. Let's go eat." He pulled her alongside him and headed toward the double doors.

The congregates stared. The ones who knew him by reputation frowned, and the ones who didn't wore curious expressions. She smiled and nodded in passing. Did everyone know the sermon was directed at her?

Outside, he held the door open to his new truck while she climbed in. "What's for lunch?"

"Mom has a vegetable casserole in the oven, but it'll be a while before she makes the sides to go with it." Joni didn't trust herself to be alone with him. "Let's go to my parents' house anyway. We need to talk about something."

"Whatever you want." James kissed her and closed the door.

Joni settled against the tan leather seat. She waited until he started the truck. "James, you shouldn't kiss me again."

Despite the warm temperatures, his wink brought chills. "I'd rather quit breathing."

She closed her eyes and leaned back against the seat. *Jesus, a little help here.*

He pulled out into traffic. "Don't worry about it. No one saw me kiss you."

"You kissed me in church."

"No, I didn't."

"Yes, you did. You leaned over and kissed the top of my head. And believe me, everyone saw." Pastor probably wouldn't let her sing tonight because of it.

"Sorry. It's kind of a reflex when I'm around you." He claimed her hand, kissed it, and held it on the console that divided the front seat.

"James?"

"Don't distract me while I'm driving." The pads of his fingers tickled her palm.

A giggle slipped out. How could she do this while he was being prince charming?

James parked beside the garage. "Your parents aren't here yet."

"That's okay. Let's walk around back." She led the way to the back lawn.

Her childhood swing hung from the massive oak in the center of the yard. He twirled the swing around and patted the seat. "Get in."

"No."

He flashed his lethal smile. "Come on. It'll be fun."

"James, we need to talk."

"No, we don't."

"James!" She propped her fists on her hips and glared. "Will you listen to me?"

He wrapped his arms around her waist and pulled her close. "I already know what you think you need to say, but you're wrong."

"Really. Why is that?" She tried not to think how perfectly she fit against him.

"Joni." He kissed her and rested his forehead on hers. "I'm not your Delilah."

Oh, how she wanted to believe him. "Prove it."

He captured her gaze. "I'm not a Philistine. I was raised in church."

Joni couldn't look away so she squeezed her eyes shut. "Knowing what to do and actually doing it are two different things. You know that. Being raised in church doesn't count."

"Delilah tricked Samson for his destruction. I don't want to destroy you. I simply want to love you. Heck, I could've preached today's sermon, I've heard it so many times. I understand your love for God and I'd never stand in your way of church." His thumbs drew circles on her sides.

Joni steeled her spine. "You have before."

"When?" Soft lips pressed against her temple.

"The day we went to the Mardi Gras Parade."

"Uh-uh. Wasn't my fault. You wanted to skip church and snuggle." Though his words were calm, his heartbeat galloped in her ear.

"See, that's what the preacher was talking about. I'll cheat on God with you."

His hands flexed on her shoulders. She felt his chest rise and fall. "That's crazy."

"No, it isn't."

James released her and she opened her eyes as he said, "I love you."

She swallowed and blurted, "He loves me more." She cringed at the words that flew out of his mouth. "Do you hear yourself? You took God's name in vain in the worst possible way."

James rubbed the bridge of his nose and paced in front of her. "Joni, I can't lose you. You are the only good thing in my life. For a time, I was crazed with grief, but I knew you waited."

Unable to speak, she shook her head.

James came near. "Joni." His breath tickled her neck. "Jesus is great, don't get me wrong, but He can't hold you." His finger painted her lips. "Touch you." He nibbled her bottom lip. "Or kiss you."

She backed away. "James, stop."

He stepped forward. "The night will come when you need real arms to hold you. Then what are you going to do? Pray? Touch me, Joni." He held her hands against his chest. "I'm a flesh and blood man and you need me."

She groaned involuntarily. "No."

"Yes." His lips smoothed across her jaw. "Think of all the donuts we could eat together."

Heat flooded her face at the memory of being in his bed. "James…"

"I leave for New Orleans this afternoon." He threaded his fingers through her hair on either side of her head. "I need to know you're here waiting."

He smelled so good. She was safe, cocooned in his arms. He kissed her hair, her eyes, her nose. Joni savored his kiss, pressed closer, and stretched on her tiptoes. Her feet left the ground as he lifted her.

"Joni?" Anger laced Matt's voice. "Who is this?"

Chapter Twenty

James glared at the same idiot from yesterday and the night before. Today, the moron hid behind a pair of shades, but he had the sense to keep his distance.

Joni paled in James's arms. Her mouth parted as she looked from him, to Pretty Boy, and back to him again.

James waited for the sissy to come within reach. He was no more than a stick. This would be like snapping a twig. Unfortunately, he stopped six feet away. The shades were now parked on his head. She would never forgive James if he started the fight, but he didn't like the shifty eyes inspecting Joni.

"Did he hurt you? Because if he did…"

"What are you gonna do?" James crossed his arms. "Sue me?"

Joni jumped between them. She spoke to the intruder. "Matt, James would never hurt me. You, on the other hand… You probably should go."

Pretty Boy shuffled his feet, but held his gaze. "So you're James. Heard a lot about you."

Mr. Maher stepped onto the patio. "James, you need some help here?"

"Daddy!" Joni swirled around and gawked at her father.

James's grin grew. "No, thank you, sir. Pretty Boy was just leaving."

Bill mumbled something about territorial rights before adding in a louder voice, "Martha's got lunch ready. You and Joni hurry in."

"Yes, sir."

The glass door screeched shut.

Jade eyes pleaded with James. "Give me a few minutes to speak with him. We work together, and I don't want Monday morning to be awkward."

"Since when do you work in a law office?"

The jewels in her eyes sparkled. "What makes you think he's an attorney?" She pressed her lips together, but her smile peeked out. "Matt's law firm provides pro bono services for the safe house where I work part-time. I'd love to tell you about it. Isaac stayed there once."

The blow of her words caused him to flinch involuntarily. He'd searched for Sam and Anna everywhere he could think of. Isaac had to be out there somewhere. One day James would find him, again. Just like he promised.

She twisted her hands. "Stand here and don't move. Unless you want to wait inside?"

"No." One wrong move and Pretty Boy would be dusting the dirt off his pants.

She bit her lip. "I didn't think so." She cupped his jaw and he looked into her smile. "James, I've loved only you."

His fists unclenched as she walked past the prissy dude to the edge of the house, a distance out of hearing. Matt followed until Joni held up a hand. She spoke and waved in an agitated manner.

Pretty Boy frowned and glared over Joni's shoulder. With a shake of his head, he disappeared around the corner of the house.

Joni tilted her face toward heaven and closed her eyes. Her lips moved, but James couldn't hear the words she prayed as he waited near the sliding glass doors. When she was within reach, he claimed her hand and led her upstairs into the dining room.

He fell in love with Mrs. Maher's baby carrots. He showered Joni's mom with praise and scooped a second helping while Joni rolled the new potatoes around on her plate. He needed to take her mind off this morning's sermon. No matter the cost. He bumped her elbow and winked. "Tell me about the safe house."

Her smile lit up the room. "I love it there. The director called me after all the publicity when the judge dropped the kidnapping charges against me. You know, on account of that 'intent to secure lawful custody' clause. Anyway, I went to Montgomery." She grabbed his hand and squealed. "I lobbied for changes in the laws protecting a father's rights, and hopefully next spring, they'll pass the Isaac's Hope Bill. It states a plaintiff must pass a drug test before the court can return custody."

Both her dad and mom interjected how proud they were of their little girl. James had to admit he too was proud—of the law, not of the loss of Isaac. When Mrs. Maher carried a pile of dirty plates into the kitchen, James leaned over to Joni and whispered, "Let's go to the apartment and finish our talk."

Sadness returned to her eyes. "We can't. I have Easter Cantata practice. But that reminds me…" She sucked in a breath. "Daddy, make James return his apartment key."

James braced himself for the ensuing battle as Mr. Maher's fork clattered onto his pie plate. "Honey, I can't ask a man for the key to the apartment when he pays the rent."

Joni's mouth gaped and her eyes rounded. "What!" She turned and stabbed James's arm with her fork. "I write checks every month for rent and utilities. Mom transferred my savings."

James and her dad shook their heads silently.

"Then who's deposited money in my account?"

Mr. Maher nodded at him, and James cowered under her explosive expression.

"Mom!"

Mrs. Maher ran into the dining room. "Joni, what's wrong?"

Joni's chest heaved. "Didn't I tell you to transfer money into my checking account for apartment expenses?"

Mrs. Maher swallowed visibly.

"Mom?"

She wrung the dishtowel in her hands. "It was for your own good."

Joni's chair fell back against the rug. James hadn't seen her this worked up since she rescued Isaac. "What was for my own good? Allowing James to pay the rent so he could visit my bed every time he passed through town?"

Bill surged to his feet. "James!"

James tripped over Joni's chair. "Mr. Maher, it wasn't like that. I swear. Joni, tell him."

Jade darts speared him. "You tell him."

He ducked behind her, but Bill backed him against the wall. The family portrait dug into his shoulders. No matter what happened, he could never hit Joni's dad. James threw up a hand for protection and closed one eye. "Sir, this really isn't necessary. You know I love her. She's the one who refuses to marry me."

Thankfully, Bill released him and stepped in between Joni and her mom.

Joni waved her arms and sidestepped her father. "I am not a baby. I have enough money saved to pay my bills without resorting to prostitution. Go get my account books."

Mrs. Maher sputtered, "Joni, I never intended for him to pay your rent. I thought when you were evicted, you'd come home."

Joni blinked once and stiffened. James recognized her struggle for control "You're not helping yourself, Mother. I want my money. All of it."

Joni's mom held her head high as she ascended the stairs.

Bill poked a finger in James's chest. "We'll talk later." Mr. Maher followed his wife.

The remaining silence reminded James of the eye of a hurricane. "I didn't deposit the money for…privileges." He massaged her stiff shoulders. "I did it because I love you. I know you value your independence. Besides, I thought you knew."

She relaxed and he turned her in his arms. He kissed the top of her head and snapped the chain from around his neck. Her engagement ring slid into his palm. He dropped to one knee and held it out to her. "Can we go home now?"

Pain flooded her eyes. "I can't. You heard what the preacher said this morning."

He fell on both knees. His voice cracked out, "Joni, please."

She shook her head and avoided his gaze. "Goodbye, James."

The crumbs on the floor mocked him as he clutched the ring to his chest. He shook himself and stood next to her. He wouldn't give up. Joni loved him. Church had her confused, but with a little time she'd come to her senses. "Joni?"

She turned her head, her words cryptic. "I'm sorry to hurt you, but I'm in self-preservation mode right now. Go to your mom's or Sara's." Joni dragged a breath in and faced him. "But don't go back to the apartment." Her hand shot out. "Give me the key. From now on, I'll pay my own rent."

James's throat tightened as he forced the lie past his lips. "I lost it."

She studied his face and clenched her teeth. He reached for her but she flinched. "Don't."

"I love you." He claimed a kiss and tasted her tears. "You're too beautiful to cry."

Her breath hitched on a sob. And then she whispered, "Go."

He'd give her time, but he'd be back. Then he'd convince her to go with them. As soon as he found Isaac.

~ ~ ~

Joni missed a step as she walked across the stage to the piano stool. For a minute, she thought she saw James in the audience, but that was impossible. If he'd been in town, his mother would have warned her. Settling against the bench, she closed her mind to everything but the melody dancing in her head. She had written this song for their wedding. Hers and James's.

The chairman of the fundraiser for abused and neglected children didn't know what this song cost Joni. Silence descended upon the audience.

Her fingers teased the keys with quick, light strokes, and she smiled at the memory of James's winks and kisses in the beginning. Her hands grew bolder, more aggressive with thoughts of stolen touches. She increased the tempo as her mind relived their nights together. The pain of losing Isaac locked her wrists.

Half notes tossed her to both ends of the spectrum and then grew desperate. Joni's hands crossed once, twice, and then parted as she said a final goodbye to James. The chorus of her favorite hymn brought joy and peace. As the last note cried, applause exploded from the audience.

Joni stood and acknowledged the real world. Again, she thought she saw James slip out the backdoor. Her heart must be playing tricks on her mind.

The next afternoon she unlocked her apartment, and a familiar cologne teased her nostrils. "James." She dropped her suitcase and went throughout the apartment, softly calling his name. In the kitchen, the coffee pot she never used was half-full of cold brown liquid. A towel lay crumpled on the bathroom floor, and his side of the bed was unmade.

She kicked off her shoes and snuggled with his pillow. It smelled like him. Reality slapped her. James had been in her apartment. Joni sprang to her feet. He lied to her. His key wasn't lost. Racing to the front door, she latched the security chain. In the bedroom, she groaned and fell across the mattress. "Lord, whatever it takes, save his soul. I can't help but love him, but I know you love him more."

A little after midnight the chain rattled. James's angry voice chased the peaceful sleep away. "Joni! Open the door!"

Heart pounding, she hid under the covers and shut out the memories and the sound of his voice.

"Joni!"

She flung off the covers and marched up the hall. "You can't come here anymore." She refused to look at him through the small opening between the frame and the door. The safety chain stretched across the small divide. She slammed the door and twisted the deadbolt.

The lock clicked and the door creaked open again. His keys protruded from the outside knob. "Joni, be reasonable." He reached through the gap and rattled the chain. "Take this thing off." His voice was calm. Soothing.

She steeled herself against the longing that grew deep inside her.

"I just want to talk."

How stupid did he think she was? "At one o'clock in the morning? I don't think so. I'm not a naïve little girl anymore. I know exactly what you want. Go away before I call the police."

His laugh sent waves of indignation through her blood. "You love me. You won't call the cops."

He was right and he knew it. Drawing in a deep breath, she glanced heavenward. "Move your hand."

He stepped back and Joni closed the door. Instead of releasing the chain, she engaged the dead bolt once more. "I do love you, but I can't let you in." Gathering her courage, she continued. "I'm going to sleep now. Goodnight, James." She straightened her shoulders and took sanctuary in the hall. There she waited.

A thunk landed on the other side of the door. "Joni, I love you." His words ripped at her heart. "I need you to help me forget. I don't want to live without you. Please, let me in."

"I can't." She knew her whispered words never reached him. She collapsed on the floor and leaned against the wall.

She prayed until keys rattled and boots stomped away.

~ ~ ~

James climbed the aluminum slide with one hand and settled on the top.

He should've been in Tuscaloosa today accepting his engineering degree from the University of Alabama. Two years of hard work were destroyed by believing one lie. But he would never regret quitting school to take care of Isaac and one day he'd find him again.

James twisted the plastic cap, breaking the seal on the square whiskey bottle as vehicles crowded the park. His heart refused to accept the mistake of leaving Isaac with strangers.

Southern gospel music drifted on the night breeze. The Street Preacher always turned one speaker so passersby could hear the service.

One side of the tent was peeled back, revealing the worshippers as they stood to their feet.

James engulfed liquid fire. He shuddered and swigged again.

Whoever played the piano stumbled over the notes. He longed to hear Joni play, but her music reminded him of Isaac and everything he'd lost. Since hearing her at Saenger Theatre, his nightmares had worsened.

Memories.

Each time James closed his eyes, he saw Isaac's smiling face. In the rearview mirror of the Toyota, little arms waved from Sam's shoulder. James couldn't escape the locked doors, nor could he drive forward or backward. He was stuck at an intersection.

The 80 proof burned a path to his stomach, yet Isaac waved and waved. His words echoed in James's mind over and over again. *You're the best daddy in the world.*

The past haunted him, but the torture had escalated during the last three weeks. James was on the verge of losing his mind.

A bottle before bedtime kept the dream at bay until the wee hours of the morning. When he'd seen the tent on his way to the hotel, he'd hoped to see Joni. No such luck. James guzzled the Kentucky brew and flames consumed the raw pain in his heart.

He took another swig and then recognized the lead singer. James's dad had once sung with this group. Small world. The worship part of the service seemed endless. While drowning his sorrows, James hummed along with the familiar songs. Piano notes drifted as The Street Preacher took the podium. James propped his forearms on his knees. He might as well see if Peter's sermons had gotten any better since they were kids playing church in Pop's hay barn.

The Street Preacher's voice was bold and sure. "'Brethren… this one thing I do, forgetting those things which are behind, and reaching forth unto those things which are before.' Amen."

James stretched his legs and leaned back against the slide. Stars twinkled through the Dogwood blossoms overhead. He cradled the fifth in the crook of his arm. He'd listen until the numbness kicked in.

"Funny thing about mirrors, they reflect the truth. What do you see when you look in the mirror?"

James closed his eyes and Isaac waved. *You're the best daddy in the world.* He scrubbed his hand down his face and shook off the illusion.

The microphone squealed. "Different mirrors reflect different images." Laughter boomed through the speakers. "Have you ever been in a funhouse? Those mirrors reflect a distorted truth. Be careful…they'll fool you."

James smiled at the recollection of his and Isaac's trip through the House O' Mirrors at Fort Conde during Mardi Gras. He could still hear Joni's tinkling laughter. Ignoring the sound, he swirled his wrist and concentrated on the slosh of amber liquid.

"There's another mirror that'll fool you. Sometime ago, when I was trying to back up a trailer… Man, I had that thing so jackknifed."

James's laughter mixed with the congregation's. He'd tried to teach him, but his cousin never could launch a boat in the river.

"Some man told me, 'Peter, those two side mirrors on your truck are used for backing up. But if you read your manual, you'd realize that mirror on the windshield is for seeing what's going on behind you. That's it.'"

James twisted the diamond ring on his pinkie. He knew this story. It was his words. He'd said them to Peter.

"He said don't look in the rearview mirror. It's gonna distract you and it's gonna give you a picture of something that isn't really true. You'll be wrapped around a tree somewhere. Up against a corner. Or in a place you don't need to be."

Despite the fire flowing through his veins, James shivered as chills covered his skin.

"That was the best advice he ever gave me. The rearview mirror is not for backing up. It's merely for viewing what's behind you."

Isaac waved from the darkness of his past and James forced his lids open.

"Each of our bodies is like a vehicle. We have a rearview mirror. It's the same inside our vehicles as in a truck. That rearview mirror you've been staring in lately, it's not for backing up. God's trying to show you where you came from, where you've been."

Liquid heat slid down James's throat and splashed through his barren dreams.

"I drive an automatic, but I was riding with my daddy on the interstate one day before he died. There was a place he needed to be. He looked in his rearview mirror and saw someone coming in close behind him in the opposite lane. You see, to get where he was going he had to change lanes."

Joni's platinum band chinked against the glass bottle.

"So, he shifted into another gear and placed some distance between him and his hindrance. Oh! I would to God that everyone here today stepped it up a notch. Surge forward! There's no need to wait for that car to catch up. No use in worrying about what's behind you. Get in a prayer closet and grab another gear!"

James slid to the ground. It was time to go.

"My friend, Jesus is saying tonight, 'I wish you'd look at Me and get your eyes out of the mirror.' He's looking through the windshield and He sees all things clearly."

James stared at the bourbon on top of the slide. How did it get up there? Isaac would like this park. Too bad there weren't any ducks. A merry-go-round spun with one shove.

"You don't want to look behind you. It hurts too much. You've thought about backing up, but God says grab another gear and go forward."

He couldn't climb the ladder again. Where was his truck?

"Somebody needs to press the clutch and look to the future. Move forward. Make your way to this altar."

James stared at the gravel under his feet. He blinked against the lights under the tent a few feet away. How did he get here? His heart pounded in his chest.

"Some trucks don't have six gears, but yours does. You can shift into sixth and surge ahead. You might even catch up with someone who's been waiting for you. Remember your blessings. Your past is tormenting you, but God says 'plan for the future.' You're gonna make it. Don't put it in reverse. Don't glance over your shoulder."

You're the best daddy in the world.

"When you look in your rearview mirror and you see that *little* car pulling up behind you – you know the one, the one that's been waving – grab another gear and surge forward. Don't worry 'bout that little car. God'll take care of 'em. You just drive on to the Promise Land."

James took one step under the tent and the whiskey fog evaporated. In an instant, he was sober. Clear eyes met those of The Street Preacher.

"Oh yeah." Compassion pooled in his cousin's eyes. "They were a blessing, but they're not for you." Peter waved him down the aisle. "Come on, James, what are you waiting for? God wants to give you a new vision."

James wiped sweaty palms on his jeans and put one boot in front of the other. He was tired of hurting.

~ ~ ~

Joni struggled with the new song she'd been working on. "Ugh." Why couldn't she get the rhythm right?

What was it about church music she couldn't comprehend? She played all the right notes. Hymns were fine, but contemporary threw her.

Disgusted with her inability, she fell into the recliner. She grabbed her phone from the coffee table and scrolled down her news feed. Sister Andrea had posted pictures of the Spring Festival. Joni hated when her hair frizzed. Maybe no one would notice. She added her "Happy Birthday" to Josh's wall and watched a funny video posted by Frank's wife. She scrolled through horoscopes and prayers requests. *Do they really pray over these needs?*

More photos, mini sermons. Joni yawned. She should go to sleep, but she clicked more posts. Gossip, somebody slamming some unknown person, event invitations, quotes…

James Preston is in a relationship.

The red heart mocked Joni as her own thumped inside a hollow chest.

Posted three hours ago. Twenty likes and three comments. Sara's read, "So proud of you." Pastor wrote, "Been waitin a long time for this day, wished I coulda been there." The last one said, "Does Joni know about this?" A smiley face punctuated Marla's comment.

Why would Marla think Joni would like James entering into a relationship with someone else?

Joni clicked on James's profile picture. She was no longer blocked. Her mouth fell open and her hands trembled.

James Preston lives in Mobile, Al. In a relationship with Jesus Christ.

Chapter Twenty-One

The concept of grace amazed him. Not only did Jesus wash him clean, but He baptized him with power to help him resist temptation. James couldn't sleep. His new life waited with the dawn and he was eager to get started. Smiling in the dark, he thanked God for salvation.

James switched on the bedside lamp. Digging around in the hotel dresser, he found a Gideon Bible and read. At three twenty, he received a text notification. He smiled as he read Joni's comment and then created a new message. *Hey beautiful. You awake? See you heard my good news. Now we can be together.*

Minutes later his phone rang. "Did you seriously pray through, or are you faking it?"

He swung his legs off the side of the bed. "Joni? How can you ask me that? I'd never fake salvation."

"You have before." Her whispered doubt stung.

He paced the length of his hotel room. "That's not true. You knew I didn't want to go to church. I made no secret that I was only there for you."

Her breath cracked in the phone. "You knelt beside me and pretended to pray. The next day you connived me into apartment shopping. A few weeks later, you tricked me into moving in. And need I remind you what happened—"

"Stop." He ran a hand through his hair. "Okay, I admit that I might have taken advantage of your curiosity of church. But." Slowly releasing a breath, he continued. "My prayers tonight were between me and God. They had nothing to do with you."

"Prove it."

"How?" He stubbed his toe against the bedrail and swallowed a curse. "I'm not perfect, but tonight I really did get saved."

She sniffed. "I hope so, but only time will tell. Goodnight, James." She hung up.

"Why is she so angry, Lord? I don't understand." James hit his knees beside the hotel bed and prayed. "Please don't take her." The words James had prayed earlier returned to him. "I give up, I'm all in. Take my thoughts, my wishes, my desires..."

But, he hadn't meant Joni. She was the best thing in his life. He didn't know if he could let her go. "Oh God, please, don't ask this of me. I don't think I can."

This was crazy. God wouldn't ask him to give up something good. He shook off his unease and crawled in bed with the Bible. The pages, crisp from unuse, fell open to the book of John. *Jesus saith to Simon Peter, Simon, son of Jonas, lovest thou me more than these?*

"Yes, Lord. I love you."

A peace he couldn't understand covered him. He opened the hotel's mini refrigerator and poured the six-pack down the toilet. The fifth of whisky under the mattress followed. When his head sunk into the pillow, a sweet presence swelled in his heart. "Goodnight, Jesus." He rolled over and fell into a blissful sleep.

An ebony-haired toddler crawled over red carpet. Smiling at James, he pulled himself up and held on to the altar bench as he teetered around the end. Pudgy hands let go and the toddler wobbled toward him. "Dada, dada." James switched his microphone to his other hand, stepped down from the platform, and swung his son in his arms. He finished the song with the warm cherub snuggled against his shoulder.

A ceiling fan twirled overhead and the baby doubled into two. Soft, chubby legs and arms roamed over James's head and chest. He laughed and created a barrier with his arms. One brave explorer scrambled over James's arm. His little head thunked against the hardwood floor. A sharp wail produced a feminine hand that soothed the crying babe.

A diamond wedding ring glistened against a delicate finger. "I told you we should've installed carpet."

"Joni?" James blinked against the morning sun streaming through the hotel window. He rolled onto his stomach and hid under the pillow. "Lord, be with her, today. And Isaac. Watch over them and protect them from harm. Go with me, Jesus. Be my strength today. And please, please let me know Isaac is safe."

~ ~ ~

The muscles bunched under James's rust-colored dress shirt as he entered the church.

Marla's words faded and Joni caught her breath. She ached to cross the room and slide her hand over his chest.

His eyes zeroed in on hers. Caught staring, Joni bit her bottom lip and held his gaze. His answering smile let her know that he knew her thoughts. He took two steps toward her, but Cole's voice stopped him midstride.

"Joni, are you okay?" Marla hadn't seen James.

"I'm fine." She listened halfheartedly as the girls planned lunch at the mall. From the corner of her eye, James shook hands with Cole and walked to the altars where most of the men in the church prayed before every service. To her astonishment, he knelt beside Cole. His voice blended with the others' prayers.

Rachel called her name and Joni turned her attention to the talk of sales and clothing accessories.

A few moments later she, Rachel, and Marla made their way toward their pew. Joni stumbled to a stop as they neared the front. She couldn't believe her ears. James was praying in the Spirit.

It wasn't possible. Was it? Yet there he lay, between the platform and the altar bench praying loud enough for anyone with ears to hear. She gulped in deep breaths and pivoted on her heel. Her long strides carried her up the aisle and down the hall. How she'd longed for the anointing power of the Spirit. Every time she'd asked James about it, he had changed the subject. Wonder what he'd say if she asked him now? Joni snatched the bathroom door open and hoped he choked on his tongue.

~ ~ ~

From the front row, James shook Pastor's hand.

"Good to see you here." The man of God stepped on the platform and raised both hands while Joni and others led the congregation in worship.

James couldn't look at her and keep his mind on the Lord. He focused on the carpet in front of him. When the music ended, his traitorous eyes followed her graceful walk to the third pew on the right side.

The pastor cleared his throat from the pulpit. "There's joy in God's perfect will."

James shook the lustful thoughts from his brain. Eyes bored in his back. He turned and smiled at Joni's flushed cheeks. She jerked her head toward the front. What was wrong with her?

He'd wanted to stop by the apartment and see her last night when he drove in, but it was late and he didn't trust himself to be alone with her. Hopefully, they'd talk at lunch.

During the altar service, he recommitted his desires to those of God's. He included a prayer for Joni to be added to his life and one for Isaac's safety. When church was over, James was welcomed back by his family and friends. Joni was nowhere to be seen.

"That blonde girl, Joni, is smoking hot." The new guy leaned on Cole's shoulder. "Is she available?"

James choked on a scathing reply.

Cole cut his eyes to James. "Blaine, Joni had a boyfriend." James narrowed his eyes and Cole corrected his mistake. "Has. Has a boyfriend... You really don't want to mess with her."

Blaine smiled. "She's experienced? Even better."

James picked up his new Bible and stepped near. "Stay away from Joni." He gripped the edge of the pew to keep from slamming said dude through the wall.

Blaine stared. "It was you."

James didn't answer.

"I see by your reaction it's true. What? Did she dump you?"

All his life James had heard "turn the other cheek," but throughout the Bible God used people as willing vessels. He rapped his knuckles on the stained wood. Right now, his fists were willing to be used by God and teach Blaine some manners.

Philip dropped a drum stick on the snare behind them. The noise reminded James where he was. "Joni isn't your concern." He walked away and conversational hum buzzed. Outside the church, Joni and a few other girls walked toward her car. He hurried over and grabbed the driver's door before she could close it. "I need to talk to you."

She turned the key and started the engine. "We're on our way to lunch. Call me later."

"This can't wait." He tugged on her elbow until she frowned and stepped out of the Honda.

She turned to the girls waiting in the car. "I'll be right back."

"Make it quick. We're starving."

James led her by the arm a few feet away.

Through clenched teeth she whispered, "Okay, since you suddenly remember me and want to talk, let's get this over with." She yanked her elbow from his hand. "Why didn't you tell me you were a jabberer?"

"What?" Her words didn't register. "Don't look toward the church, but you know that new guy, Blaine?"

"Yeah." One dainty hand shielded her eyes from the sun. "Now about the jabbering."

"Don't talk to him."

Her mouth dropped. "What?"

The anger in her eyes scared him. Joni would do the opposite of what he said. He took a breath. "Do you remember the Catalpa worms? The green squishy ones me and Isaac used for fish bait? We put them in the refrigerator at the farmhouse. I told you not to open the brown bag, but you insisted. Those icky worms crawled all over you. Remember?"

She visibly shuddered.

"This is one of those times, Joni. Don't do it. I'm right."

She giggled and his anger surged. "James, relax." She straightened his tie. "I can't stand the jerk."

He closed his eyes and breathed. *Thank you, Jesus.*

She jerked down on his tie, forcing him to look at her. "You can't tell me what to do and you can't choose my friends."

"But—"

"No buts. I decide. Now about the jabbering, you should've told me."

Marla called her name through an open window.

"I have a lot of questions, but they'll have to wait." Joni sashayed back to the car and left him standing in the middle of the half-empty parking lot. From the doorway, Blaine's eyes followed her. James stepped in his line of vision and caught his gaze. The dude propped his hands on his hips and grinned.

James relaxed as her car pulled onto the highway. What was it she'd been mad about? In his truck, he slapped his palm against his forehead. Jabbering? Because of his jealousy, he'd missed an opportunity to clarify some of her misconceptions.

Misconceptions he'd led her to believe.

There was no time to talk to her now. Cecil was expecting him in Montgomery this afternoon.

James resolved to keep his head out of the gutter and his hands to himself. God forbid she believe some false doctrine because she misinterpreted the Holy Ghost.

~ ~ ~

The argument with her mother lingered in her mind. She needed a friend. She took out her phone and scrolled through her contacts. Marla would agree with anything Joni said. No, she needed a best friend. Too bad James was off somewhere working. She should've had lunch with him Sunday. She missed him.

He answered on the first ring.

"Are you busy?"

"I'm never too busy for you. Where are you?"

"The park." Joni got out of her car and walked under the pines toward the duck pond. "Mom found out I changed my major."

"Ooh, that's not good."

"She refused to pay my tuition. I can cover the expenses with my savings, but she's using parental guilt to try to change my mind. You know my parents are retiring to Miami?"

"Yeah, my mom listed your house for sale."

Joni kicked a pine cone. "She wants me to transfer to a local university there." She climbed atop a concrete picnic table and jumped off the other side. "James, are you there?"

"Where are you exactly?"

She stopped three stage-lengths from the water. "Watching this silly duck in the pond."

"Hold on two seconds."

The duck pecked his feathers and splashed around as a mother pushed a stroller toward the swings. Joni shouldn't wallow in self-pity. "I'm sorry for bothering you. You're obviously busy."

No reply.

"James, where are you?"

"Right here." His answer came from behind her.

She squealed and swirled around. "James." Enfolded in his arms, she could conquer the world. Joni closed her eyes and leaned against him. Oh, he smelled good. She lifted her head and laughed. "How'd you do that?"

His eyes sparkled. "Your wish is my command."

She playfully swatted his shoulder. "Be serious. How'd you get here?"

"I was looking for you." Oh, how she missed his smile. "You want some lunch?"

She shook her head. "I have another class in half an hour. So, should I transfer?"

~ ~ ~

James threaded his fingers through hers and walked toward the parking lot. He was moving home to be near her, and her mother ordered her to Miami. He wanted to tell her to stay, but the mistakes of his past choked him, and he struggled with his words. "You should do whatever God wants."

She stopped and yanked on his arm. "Are you serious?"

"Yeah." He took a deep breath. "I know you doubt my conversion, but my prayers are real."

She opened her mouth but he silenced her by laying a finger against her lips.

"Let me finish." He led her to a picnic table. They climbed over the bench-style seat and sat on the concrete slab. Resting his arm around her shoulders, he prayed she'd understand his next words. "The night I went to the tent revival was the day I should've received my engineering degree."

She leaned over and kissed his cheek.

"I guess you could say I've done a lot of soul-searching since. About me. You. But mostly Isaac. I had to face the truth. Looking back, I realized that when Kathy showed up with Isaac, she wasn't looking for a daddy. She needed more drug money, and Sam and Anna needed the biological father's consent. If I wasn't so hell-bent on being a better father than my own, Isaac's adoption would have been final when he was three. But because of my stubbornness…" His voice broke and he caressed her knuckles with his thumb. Inhaling, he continued. "Isaac suffered Kathy and Brian's abuse." Though his eyes stung, he raised them to meet Joni's. "It was my fault. I'm guilty of placing a little boy in a dangerous situation."

Tears rolled down her face.

"I love him, but he never should've been mine." He forced a smile and cleared his throat. "If I'd have followed God, I'd have my degree and the ability to support a family without worrying about qualifying for a job."

Her smile spread sunshine throughout his soul. "I love you." She pressed close and kissed him the way she did in his dreams.

The afternoon heat rose and James broke contact and stood. "You're gonna be late."

Hand in hand, they strolled along the path. She pressed a kiss on his upper arm, below the fabric of his short sleeve, and snuggled close to his side. "You know, if you hadn't been at the party looking for Isaac, you couldn't have rescued me and we might never have met."

The wind whipped Joni's hair against his skin. "That's why I can't tell you to stay. What if God has someone waiting for you in Miami? Someone better than me."

A sting pierced his upper arm.

"Ouch!" He snatched his arm away and inspected the blood and teeth marks. His jaw slacked. "You bit me."

"You were talking nonsense. There's no one better for me. I know it and God knows it. That's why he sent you to that party. Enough crazy what-ifs." A gentle thumb caressed his broken skin. "What are you doing here? You said you wouldn't be home for a few more weeks."

He didn't want to spoil the surprise in case her uncle had changed his mind. "I have a job interview this afternoon."

"With who?"

"A local construction company. I'm tired of living out of a suitcase. I want to sleep in the same bed from week to week." A blue jay cried overhead.

Joni squinted. One hand shielded her eyes from the sun. "You'll be home? Every night?" She wet her lips and glanced at her shoes. "The extra bedroom is empty. I know you still have a key to our apartment."

Desire slammed him. James bent and wrapped his arms above her knees. He lifted her and stared up into her dazzling smile. "Don't. Tempt. Me."

Her giggle was priceless as he spun her around. A flip-flop flew into one of the rose bushes. He released her, avoided the thorns, and rescued the shoe.

Joni wiggled her dainty foot under the strap. "I'm serious." She crossed her arms and frowned. "Why was it okay for you to spend the night when I was the one in church? But now all of a sudden it's a sin?"

Words escaped him. "Joni…it's…ah…well…since you asked." The breeze lifted the fuzzy strands of her hair. James smoothed them behind her ear. The wheels in his brain came up empty. He slowly blew out a breath and then shrugged. "I don't know what to say."

She smothered a giggle. "You twisted the Scriptures to get what you wanted."

He picked up an acorn and aimed for a knot in a tree. Hands in his back pockets, he glanced heavenward. "I'm sorry, Joni. I was jealous of your relationship with God. Not that I wanted one with Him myself. I didn't want to share you and the simple truth is…I wanted you. I never lied." He cringed. "Except about the key. I told you partial truths to make you love me." He pulled her close and rested his forehead against hers. "Forgive me?"

When she smiled, the sparkles in her eyes outshined the sun. "I wasn't as naïve as you thought. I knew what all those nights on the sofa were leading up to. Christmas Eve night, I lay awake for hours. Waiting for you to come to bed."

He couldn't stop himself from reaching for her. He bit his lip. Oh, if he'd have only known… His mind trailed off and he shook the thoughts from his head. "Joni, stop reminding me. Do you forgive me or not?"

Her stubborn chin lifted. "If you give me the key."

He shook his head. "I might need it one day." His arms tightened around her and he kissed her temple. She drew a line across his back with her fingernail. His breath caught and his pulse ran away. Joni drew small circles on his fevered skin.

James released her and stepped away. He cleared his throat.

The flames dancing in her eyes mocked the calm in her voice. "You want to come over for dinner tonight?"

He checked the time on his phone. "You and me alone in the apartment isn't a smart idea. Anyway, I can't tonight. I have an appointment."

Her shoulders sagged. "Fine."

"How about lunch tomorrow?"

She wrapped her arms around his waist and snuggled close. "Sounds wonderful. I'll text you the address where to meet me. There's something I want to show you."

He hugged her and kissed the top of her head. "I'd better go."

"Kiss me 'bye." She stood on tiptoe and lifted her face to his.

His lips brushed her cheek, but she turned her head. Sparks ignited. His pulse thundered out of control as her mouth nibbled. Gripping the back of her head, he ended her teasing. She tasted sweeter than ever and he didn't want to let her go.

She shifted and the flames leapt out of control.

He broke contact and escaped. Desire turned into self-disgust as he stalked toward his truck and paced between it and her car.

She caught up with him there.

"Joni, I'm sorry. This is why we can't be alone. I can't control myself. No more kisses."

Her smile winked from her pressed lips. "Whatever you say, dear." She reached for him.

He held up a hand and stepped back. "Don't touch me."

A giggle escaped her.

"Joni." He glared down at her. "Stop it."

"I can't help it." She stepped forward. "You love me."

He frowned at her in confusion. "Of course I love you. How could you doubt it?"

"You haven't told me in weeks." Her voice cracked. She waved her hands in front of her face. "And you quit calling me beautiful."

He stilled her hands and raised them both to his lips. Tears shimmered in her eyes. "I love you more than anything in this world." His thumbs caressed her knuckles. "You are and will always be my beautiful angel, but when I kiss you I don't want to stop with one taste. I want you, all of you. You are my forbidden fruit, but I keep hoping and praying that one day you will belong to me again."

A lone tear slid down her silky cheek.

He dipped his head and brushed her lips with a gentle kiss. The scent of her shampoo triggered a flood of memories. "Joni, I miss you so much. Never, ever doubt my love for you."

Her soft lips parted and curled upward. Trembling hands smoothed the wrinkles from his shirt. "I should get to class."

Ignoring the desire clouding her eyes, he reached behind him and opened her car door. When she was settled in the driver's seat, he leaned in for another kiss. "Learn something for me." He jumped in front of the car before she closed the door. She narrowed her eyes as her window lowered. "What are you doing?"

He winked and shrugged. "I don't ever want to be in your rearview mirror."

~ ~ ~

The door squeaked open over a scarred wood floor. At the reception desk, nestled between the stairs and a narrow hallway, a gray-haired lady peered at James over thin glasses.

"May I help you?"

"What is this place?" From the outside, the old house looked to be another renovated business or downtown residence. There was no sign in the yard to indicate the building's purpose. If it hadn't been for the house number mounted on a porch column, he would have passed it up.

"I'm sorry, this is a private establishment." The elderly lady stood. "I'm afraid you need to leave now."

James shook his head. "Joni Maher gave me this address. I'm supposed to meet her here."

A second woman, twenty years younger than the first, walked down the narrow hall. A hand with fingernails painted the same color as her lips stretched toward him. "You must be James."

He shook her hand and looked around her. "Did Joni tell you I was stopping by?"

Her laugh was loud and hearty. "No. I've begged her for an introduction. I'm Mrs. Wendel." She dropped his hand and tilted her head. "I recognized you from your mug shot."

"Oh." The pieces didn't fit together. He had no idea why the woman would want to meet him, especially since she knew he had a criminal record. "Can you tell Joni I'm here?"

The calculating gleam in her smile put him on guard. "This way."

He followed her up the stairs toward the sound of an off-key piano.

Joni's voice was unmistakable.

So was the sound of children singing "This Little Light of Mine." Mrs. Wendel opened a door and motioned for him to go in. She closed the door behind him and left him alone with Joni and over a dozen small children.

She played with her back to him, but one by one the children quit singing and stared at the stranger among them. Joni turned.

Her smile sparked life within him.

A toddler trailed behind her as she crossed the room. "I have a few more minutes before Mrs. Grayson takes them down to lunch." She tugged on his hand. "Sing with us."

His feet were frozen. "Where are we?"

Sadness clouded her eyes. "A safe house for abused and neglected children."

An unseen hand squeezed his heart. "Joni, I can't—"

The toddler, a little girl, lifted her arms to him. "Up."

A bruise marked the little girl's cheek. Her green eyes reminded him of Joni. His throat burned, but he hardened his heart against the blond curls so like Isaac's.

"I'm sorry. They're starved for love and attention." Joni knelt and held out her hand. "Carrie, come to Joni."

Little hands clung to his pant leg. "Up."

Having no choice, he lifted the little girl in his arms. Inhaling baby shampoo, he closed his eyes as the soft body snuggled against his shoulder. He swallowed his pain and winked at Joni. "Let's sing."

James reclined on the floor against a bean bag while Joni wrestled with the outdated piano. Other children slowly edged their way to him. By the third song, he was covered in toddlers. The older children, especially the girls, eyed him with suspicion from a distance.

Joni smiled at him. "I've been replaced."

Careful not to make any sudden moves and scare the skittish children, he shook his head. "You're irreplaceable, Joni. Don't go to Miami. You have the talent to play in Carnegie Hall, but God put you here for a reason."

She turned crimson and closed the piano. "Thank you. You don't know how much those words mean to me, especially coming from your lips." She smiled away the pools in her eyes. "Now, if you can break away from my babies, it's lunch time."

James wrinkled his nose. "One of them stinks."

She laughed and pointed to a side door. "The changing room is through there."

It was a good thing she was joking, but he decided to play along. "I don't do diapers." A little boy crawled across his chest and James lifted the culprit toward her. "This one."

Mrs. Grayson clapped her hands in the doorway. "Come along, sweeties."

The kids scrambled toward the door. Joni carried the stinking toddler but turned to smile at James. "I'll meet you downstairs as soon as I take care of Ralph."

~ ~ ~

Joni descended the steps a few minutes later to find Mrs. Wendell campaigning her ideas for changing Alabama's child protection legislation to James. She waited patiently while her employer finished talking.

When they were alone outside the building, he eyed her critically. "Did you wash your hands?"

Joni laughed at his stricken expression. "Yes." She held out her hands and turned them up. "With antibacterial soap."

His wink took her breath. "Good."

They stopped at her car. "Didn't you ever change Isaac?"

Awkward silence fell. Her careless words brought a haunted look into his eyes. "He was potty-trained when I got him."

"Oh." She didn't know what to say so she kissed him instead. "I'm done for the day. I'll meet you at the restaurant so I won't have to come back for my car."

He lifted her hand and kissed her fingertips. "I'll follow you."

~ ~ ~

The waitress brought their salads and James shocked her when he bowed his head and said a short blessing over the food. "Let's eat. I'm starved."

Joni laughed. "You're always hungry."

The fork in James's hand paused halfway to his mouth. "And that's why you should be feeding me a steak instead of this rabbit food."

She giggled and caught her glass before it tipped over.

"Tell me about this safe-house thing. Does it have anything to do with changing your college major?"

Joni relaxed and told him all about her plans to get her degree and open her own safehouse one day. She told him of her trips to Montgomery and how Mrs. Wendell wanted him to speak out for a father's right to request paternity. Gone was the tension between them. The heavy weight on her heart lifted further with each smile he gave her.

Until he asked, "Is that where you met Matt?"

She swallowed a stubborn piece of pasta. "Yes. He interned for their attorneys."

His fork clattered to his plate. "I see."

"I've talked to him at work, but he, um, called me a bad name and we broke up. Sort of. I only went out with him 'cause Marla wanted to date his friend Jeremy. The night you saw us was our first and last date. But I didn't ask you to lunch to talk about that." Joni gulped her tea.

"What name did he call you?"

She shook her head. "It doesn't matter."

"It matters to me. Tell me."

"No. I've learned there are some things you should never know." Joni laughed to soften the blow of her words.

James withdrew his hand. "You'd keep secrets from me?"

She leaned over the table and captured his hand. "You explain how Trent spent a week in the hospital after you snuck into town to take care of some business and I'll tell you all my secrets."

He pressed a feathery kiss against the small scar on her temple. By way of explanation he said, "He hurt you."

"Yes, and it's your anger issues that prevent me from telling you everything."

He pushed his full plate away. "What haven't you told me? Did someone hurt you?"

"It's nothing like that." She tried to reassure him with a smile. "I intended to tell you, but there was never a good opportunity." Joni sipped her tea. "I could have been Isaac's mother."

He tilted his head slightly. "How's that possible?"

"Travis considered retaining his parental rights." Breath held, she waited for the explosion.

James frowned and stretched his legs under the table. "I've often wondered why he didn't." His lips curled into a smile. "See." He held his arms wide. "I'm calm. Tell me why?"

"Because I refused to marry him."

Dishes rattled as James's fist landed on the table. "What!"

Joni flinched and felt every eye on them. "People are staring. What happened to the calm, rational James?"

"He's trying to figure out why his girlfriend would keep this from him." He scrubbed his palms down his face. "You were tempted. Don't deny it, Joni. I see the guilt in your eyes."

"Briefly, but only because I was mad at you for leaving me and moving in with Kathy."

"I didn't have a choice. It was her or prison, and someone had to protect Isaac."

Joni recalled the bruises on Isaac's ribs. "Yeah, right. I'm not the gullible little girl you met at a party."

He leaned forward. The muscles in his jaw throbbed. "No. You're the woman who left me rotting in jail while you played mommy with Travis."

Twice now Travis had betrayed him. James didn't care about Kathy, but Joni...she was his. "Did he touch you?"

Her gaze jumped to his. "No. I wouldn't...couldn't... We didn't. Nothing like that happened. He considered becoming Isaac's father, but he knew he couldn't do it alone."

"Being a single dad is hard, but not impossible. He wasn't thinking of Isaac when he made his offer." James leaned forward. "Why did you say no?" Her love for Isaac was never questioned.

Her soft words, conquered his anger. "I'm already married to you in my heart. I couldn't call anyone else my husband."

He reached for her hand and caressed her wrist. "When they released me from jail and I called, why didn't you tell me where you were? Why did I have to learn about Travis's paternity and Isaac's adoption from my attorney? Why couldn't I hear it from you? I love you, Joni. God knows I do. But I need to understand. Why did you do it?"

"I thought if you saw Isaac's bruises, you would kill Kathy. I couldn't stand the thought of you in prison."

He wanted to believe her flimsy excuses. "I was there at the mall. I saw her hit him. I refrained from killing her then. You should've trusted me." He scraped his chair back.

On his way to the men's room, he passed the bar. The smell of hops and barley called. Getting drunk might dull the pain, but the facts would remain in the morning. He pushed through the bathroom doors and shut out the sound of whiskey splashing against the bottom of a shot glass.

When he returned to the table, she was gone. He paid the bill but waited until he reached his truck to read the message she'd sent.

His head swam as he stared at the picture of Isaac smiling from the farmhouse tub. Blue, green, and yellow patches dotted his little body. The dots Joni counted? James had suffered enough bruises to realize not all of the marks were fresh. Kathy had abused Isaac for weeks and James hadn't done one thing to stop her.

Choking on the guilt of failure, he read Joni's words: *Now you know all my secrets.*

Chapter Twenty-Two

Roses were great for apologies. James held the bouquet in one hand and knocked on his apartment door with the other. Piano notes faded and Joni's footsteps grew louder. Anticipation of seeing her curled his lips. He didn't fight the feeling and leaned in for a kiss as soon as the door opened. "I'm sorry for being a jerk."

Her fingernails gently scraped his freshly shaven jaw. One eyebrow rose and marred her face into a frown. "You shaved."

He held the bouquet towards her. "Forgive me?"

The hand caressing his jaw reached for the vase and held it under her cute nose. Lashes caressed her cheeks and her shoulders rose as she smelled the sweet petals. Jade eyes flickered open. "I love these. Thank you."

Glad that Joni had a forgiving heart, he brushed his lips over hers and smiled. "You're welcome. The florist calls them 'Dreaming of You Pink.'"

She turned and moved deeper into the apartment. His apartment. With his furniture. He stood inside the door. He was home, yet he couldn't stay.

Joni had her back to him as she arranged the flowers on the table. The table he'd bought. His arms ached to wrap around her, pull her against him, and kiss her neck. He wanted to kick back in the recliner and drag her into his lap. She'd laugh and he'd kiss her senseless. Then Isaac would squeeze between them.

James stepped over the threshold and smelled pizza.

He heard Isaac's precious giggle. "Hi, Daddy." Isaac lay on his stomach with his feet waving in the air. Sauce smeared his chin.

"Me and Joni's been waitin' for you."

James rocked back on his feet and blinked against the pain as the illusion faded.

Isaac was gone.

Unsteady hands gripped the wall. James's throat closed and his lungs burned. Darkness crowded and he struggled against a wave of dizziness.

"James?" Joni's blurred face slowly focused. "Are you okay? James?"

His lungs expanded and gulped for oxygen.

"Here. Drink this."

He pushed away the glass of water. "I'm fine." He didn't mean to sound so gruff.

Tears pooled in Joni's eyes, twisting the knife further into his heart.

He forced his feet to move past the memories. One by one they surrounded him. Tying Isaac's shoe. Wrestling on the living room floor. Watching cartoons. His footsteps quickened in the hall and passed the closed door. He escaped into the bathroom. The cold water from the sink slowly drowned out the splashes from the tub. Isaac loved to make the pirates walk the plank.

Was he sick? The bathroom door opened and James sauntered up the hall. If Joni didn't know James's strength, she would have sworn he'd almost fainted. Why?

The sweat beads were gone from his forehead and his color had returned. "You okay?"

He smiled as if nothing happened. "I'm fine." His wink erased her fears.

His brow was cool. No fever. "You want some pizza? It's homemade."

"No thanks." His strength beckoned and she snuggled close. His heart drummed an erratic beat under her ear. "I can't stay. It's late and I don't trust us to be alone."

She tilted her face upward, longing for his kiss. "Please don't go yet."

One corner of his lips curved as his eyes zeroed in on her lips. She stretched on tiptoe and met him halfway. His kiss never failed to sweep her away from this world and all the things that kept them apart. Sweet memories took her down a journey in time and she swayed in his embrace, wishing he could stay the night, but knowing that was no longer an option.

He stepped back and broke the spell. Holding her hands, his gaze raked over her and his mouth twisted into a knowing grin. "Quit distracting me. I have something important to say."

Happiness sprang up in her soul and a giggle floated into the air around them. "Do you want to snuggle on the sofa?"

"Yes. Which is why I'm staying right here." It was good to see his smile. "I got the job. Your uncle wants me to start immediately."

Another kiss muffled her squeal of delight.

"This week, I'll finish my job with Cecil, and then I promised Sara I'd help with the youth conference."

"Me, too."

"I know. That's how Sara convinced me to go along. Since she's my landlady, I figured it wouldn't hurt to be nice." He kissed her again. "Whoever dreamed I'd be a church chaperone?"

~ ~ ~

Ugh! Joni didn't want to be on the bus. She leaned her head against the window and tried to shut out the twins' obnoxious giggles coming from the seat in front of her. If she had known James was driving his truck she never would've agreed to chaperone some of the younger girls. The bus hit a pothole and her temple banged against the window.

It wasn't fair. Philip and Cole had fought over riding shotgun when she was supposed to be riding next to James. And why did he invite Blaine to ride with them? Blaine!

Twin heads popped up in the seat in front of her. "We're glad we're in your room. We're gonna stay up all night."

Joni forced a smile. "Not all night." The twins rattled on about how they wanted her to fix their hair. Sara put one adult in each room. Unfortunately, Joni got paired up with the twelve-year-olds. Marla, on the other hand, got the easy assignment. All her girls were sixteen and could take care of themselves. Amanda called from the seat in front of the twins. They turned, leaving Joni in peace.

~ ~ ~

Lint roller?

Joni smiled at James's text and set her scrunch spray on the hotel dresser. *Yeah five minutes.*

Flipping her head upside down, she styled her hair in waves. A knock sounded at the door. The twins squealed and ran to the peephole. Joni rolled her eyes and crossed the room. She unzipped the side pocket on her suitcase while the knocking continued. Patience wasn't one of James's virtues.

The twins hid in the bathroom as she opened the door. His yellow dress shirt stretched across his broad shoulders. Bare toes peeked out from navy pants.

"I told you five minutes. I'm in the middle of doing my hair." She held out the lint brush.

He flashed his killer smile. His fingers grazed hers as he removed the object from her hand. "Thank you." He lifted a strand of her hair. "Too stiff. I like it soft and fuzzy."

She hid her smile. "I didn't ask you." She shut the door. The twins bounced over to the mirror above the sink. James's voice carried through the door. "Hurry up or you'll be late."

"I can't believe James came in our room."

Joni glared at the giggly preteens. With all the busybodies at church, she had to set the record straight. "He knocked on the door. Period. He didn't come in."

"Same difference."

Joni inhaled deeply. "No, it's not the same. James doesn't need people suspecting him of inappropriate behavior. Don't spread lies about him."

One of the twins tilted her head. "I never thought about it that way."

The other shrugged. "Me either. We promise not to gossip. We like him." The three girls giggled behind their hands.

"Good." Five knocks rapped against the door. Without saying a word, she took the lint roller and shut James out.

The bus stopped in front of the small arena designated for the conference thirty minutes before service time. The place was crowded and they barely found enough chairs for their group on the bottom level. Cole and James sat close to the front. Ever since he got saved, he wouldn't sit with her in church. Why?

After some awesome praise and worship music, the evangelist admonished the crowd to seek after God's will. Chairs were moved and the people in the stands flooded the bottom level. Joni watched the girls around her stretch their hands toward heaven. It looked like they were reaching for something they couldn't obtain by their own power.

She closed her eyes and listened to the sounds around her. Individual voices jabbered. Some in shrill pitches. Others in low moans. Musical highs and lows blended together in angelic harmony. The man in the corner set the beat by jumping up and down. When he tired, a man on the other side stomped his foot. Cymbals sputtered forth from a lady propped up against a column. The chaos of over two thousand worshippers became a chorus orchestrated by someone other than the people themselves. Joni longed to play for this unseen conductor.

She closed her eyes and raised her hands. A heavy mist fell and Joni's nerve endings tingled. Tears pooled in her eyes, but she shook off the feeling and dropped her arms. Squeezing through the shoulder-to-shoulder crowd, she searched for James.

He was on the floor, jabbering. Standing beside him, Cole bounced on the balls of his feet while sweat poured down the side of his face. Her heart pounded. What if Cole stepped on James? She pushed closer. Vince staggered into her, blocking her way. She peeked over his shoulder. Tears leaked from the corners of James's eyes.

In the time since she'd known him, she had seen him cry once. In the apartment, after losing Isaac, tears rendered him weak, but now an aura of power cloaked him and joy radiated from his body. She wanted to share this new experience with him, but he was in a place she couldn't reach.

~ ~ ~

James swallowed the last of his brownie as Joni walked toward the table he shared with Philip, Cole, and Vince. "Where've you been? I haven't seen you anywhere."

A hundred questions sparkled in her eyes. "I've seen you." With a tilt of her head, she bit her lip and raised her eyebrows.

He released a chuckle and picked up his empty plate. "Come on. Let me throw this away and we'll talk about it." He tossed his trash into the nearest can. In the parking lot, Joni turned toward his truck. James captured her hand and led her into the arena. This time he was prepared for her questions.

"Why can't we talk in your truck?"

The busted streetlight cast them in the shadows. He couldn't see her face. "Because. I'd give in to temptation and kiss you. Someone would see and think the worst."

Her giggle was musical. "You're probably right."

He led her by the hand into the stadium seats. Here in the bright lights, his hands would be forced to behave, but no one could hear their conversation. He stretched out his legs across the row in front of him and leaned back on his elbows.

Joni sat on the concrete row below his knees. "How did you do that gracefully?"

That could be any number of things in Joni's mind. Speaking in tongues? Shouting? Falling out in the Spirit? What did she see exactly? "The altar service was two hours long. I get the feeling you hid out somewhere and watched my every move. Be more specific."

Curiosity sparkled in her eyes. "Start with the jabbering."

Deep laughter escaped him. A frown crossed her face and he tried to rein in his amusement. "Joni…" He pressed his lips together and held his breath until the urge to laugh passed. "I was not jabbering."

"Yes, you were, and this wasn't the first time."

He shook his head in disbelief. "You've attended church for months. Surely you've heard someone speak in tongues."

"Heard it? Yes. Understood it? No." She propped her elbows on her knees.

"Why didn't you ask someone to explain it to you?"

"I did." Her smile turned into a smirk. "And you said…" She cocked her head and mimicked him. "Joni, the Holy Ghost is for preachers, evangelists, and Sunday school teachers."

He cringed but sat up and put his feet on the floor. "Joni, you shouldn't take spiritual advice from someone who is interested in you carnally."

Her mouth fell open. And then she laughed.

"It's not funny." He rubbed the bridge of his nose. "I'm dealing with serious guilt issues."

Her laughter stopped and she leaned slightly forward. "Can I take spiritual advice from you now? Or are you still interested, carnally?"

With the way she leaned forward, the view from his elevated position distracted him from her question.

She tugged her denim jacket closed and straightened. "Never mind. I have my answer."

He couldn't hold back a grin. "I try not to be interested. Sometimes, I can't help myself."

She rolled her eyes and shook her head. "Explain the baptism of the Holy Ghost to me."

At a loss for words, he shrugged. "I can't."

She must have forgotten her loose top because she leaned over again. "Is it…scary?"

He moved beside her, blocking the view of his traitorous eyes. "Do I look scared?"

A puzzled expression crossed her face. "No, you look happy."

He lifted her hand. "Having the Holy Ghost is whatever you need when you need it. You can't label it, put it on a list, or file it away. It's a gift. Direct access to God. You can't own it or rush it. But you can choose not to accept it." Uncertainty lingered in her jade eyes.

"Hey, Romeo!" Mark called from below them. "Let's go!"

James held up his free hand. "One more minute."

"Hurry it up. Everyone is loading the bus."

James rubbed his thumb across Joni's dainty knuckles. "What's really bothering you?"

"You've seen me cry. I'm hideous. Red, swollen face. If I got the Holy Ghost I'd probably snot, slobber, and spit. That's gross."

He bit his lip to keep from laughing at her horrified expression. She snatched her hand and stood. Descending the steps, she called over her shoulder. "Go ahead and laugh. You know you want to."

He immediately sobered and ran after her. "I'm sorry, it's just, you have such a unique way of looking at things."

She stopped mid-aisle. "If I ever got it, do you promise not to watch?"

He wanted to hug her and swing her around. Joni didn't like to be left out. He recognized the hunger in her eyes. "No way. I'll be shouting beside you. Snot, slobber, spit, and all."

She backhanded him playfully across the stomach. "You will not." Her giggle sparked his grin. Hand in hand, they ran to the parking lot. She ascended the bus steps and he jogged to his truck where the guys waited on the hood.

As he drove back to the hotel, he thought about the changes in his life. A year ago, a sanctified, Holy-Ghost-filled Joni was his worst nightmare. Now, it seemed an impossible dream. He remembered words he'd spoken long ago when she had asked him why she always cried in the altar. "Joni, you're too pretty to cry. You should save your prayers for when you are alone."

The words haunted him all the way to his hotel room. He dropped his card key on the dresser and groaned. What had he done? Joni's sin was in loving him and Isaac. No wonder she couldn't let go and find truth. James had selfishly taken her hunger for God and twisted it for his pleasure. What kind of love was that? "God forgive me."

~ ~ ~

The morning speaker talked about breaking out of your box and conquering fear to worship. James turned and winked at Joni from the row in front of her. Marla elbowed her in the side. "I can't believe you're flirting in church."

"We're not flirting." Joni faced the front. "Pay attention."

During the altar service, hundreds of worshippers blocked her view of James. If she couldn't see him, maybe he couldn't see her. The singers on the platform began the song Aunt Sandra had sung long ago. She raised her hands and spoke to God the words in her heart. "I love you, Jesus. Lord, take away the hurt and pain of losing Isaac. Fill this emptiness in me, Jesus." A warmth flowed over her. She closed her eyes. The voices surrounding her faded in the distance. Joni swam in a sea of peace and love.

She lost track of time, but when coherent thought returned, a small crowd of people had gathered around her. Marla pressed tissues into her hand. Joni wiped her cheeks and eyes. Her shirt was wet. The crowd around her dispersed. James smiled from five feet away. He mouthed the word "beautiful."

Joy bubbled inside her and turned into laughter. She sniffed and wiped her nose. She was too happy to care what she looked like.

After lunch and a quick stop at the mall, she ignored Amanda and the twins and napped in her room. In the shower before the night service, she found the privacy for prayer. "Lord, I want Your power. I want Your peace. I don't care who sees me. Heal my hurt. I want to belong to You."

That night, Joni was anxious as she added her voice to the praises of the Lord.

A different preacher took the platform and read from his Bible. "Be this known unto you and hearken unto my words…This, Is That." He stepped out from the podium and paced. With his head bowed he spoke, "I know some of you are ready for the altar service. You want to get down here and feel the goose pimples. You want to cry and not be ashamed."

He pivoted on one foot and headed in the opposite direction. "Some of you just want to watch everyone else hop around on one foot. Fall out and run. Jump up and down."

Propping an elbow on the pulpit, he held the microphone adjacent to his body. "I promise, we're gonna do all that and more with the help from the Holy Ghost, but before we do, I want to echo Peter's words from the book of Acts." He slapped his hand on the wood and Joni flinched. "Listen to me! There is something you need to know!"

Joni leaned forward and waited while he drank from a plastic water bottle.

Finally, he spoke, breaking the still silence. "There are things you need to know about the Holy Ghost. One, Jesus told His disciples to tarry in the upper room until they received the power. He never told them to speak in tongues. He never told them to act like drunk men."

That couldn't be right. At another conference, a man told a young girl to open her mouth and speak her heavenly language. Joni had tried, but her tongue wouldn't function properly. She flipped through her Bible and scanned chapter two in the book of Acts.

Huh! The preacher was right.

"There's only one way to receive the Holy Ghost and that's through Jesus. And once Jesus baptizes you in the Spirit, you can't help but speak in tongues. When you allow Him to take control, you may stagger all over this building, but God will orchestrate your life in His perfect will."

Could it be that simple?

"Stand to your feet as the musicians play. You want the initial infilling of the Holy Ghost? Praise Jesus. You want the fullness and the gifts of the Holy Ghost? Praise Jesus. You want the anointing? Praise Jesus."

Chairs were moved and Joni lifted her hands where she stood. She dropped one arm and wiped her tears.

"Don't worry about yourself! Don't worry about the people around you! It's you and Jesus! Let your tears flow! Don't you know your tears are precious to him? For out of your belly shall flow rivers of living water!"

The sound of his voice faded, but somehow Joni knew he kept preaching. Light shone beyond her reach and she stretched on her tiptoes. Hands landed on her back and someone prayed. James?

The brightness dulled and the indescribable sensations faded. Joni forgot about everything around her and refocused on her love for Jesus, praising Him in an audible voice.

Nothing else mattered but reaching the place where He waited. The more she praised, the brighter the light. An explosion occurred within her and a kaleidoscope of colors merged. A deep void was filled. The final piece in the puzzle of her life connected in its rightful place.

Far in the distance, she heard her voice speaking words she couldn't understand. Amazing joy flooded her, washing away pain and confusion with peace and comfort. Time and space ceased to exist. She was invincible.

~~~

James couldn't take his eyes off Joni and he couldn't stop smiling. The others in the group had gone to eat. Sitting on the edge of the platform, he thanked God once again for his blessings.

His jacket covered her midriff. The indoor lights haloed her hair, but she wasn't the only one sprawled on the carpet. He shook his head in wonder. Only Joni would get baptized and slain in the Spirit all in one night.

Mark crossed the indoor arena. His lips curved as he tilted his head. "How can we get Joni and Marla back to the hotel?"

James had already thought it out. "We'll put them in the backseat of my truck. Sara can ride with them. Cole can have shotgun. Put Philip, Vince, and Blaine on the bus."

"Works for me. Let me tell Sara the plan and get everyone loaded up."

A few minutes later, Mark and Sara collected Marla. James threw Cole his keys. "Unlock the door." James lifted Joni jacket and all. She'd been in his arms many times, but tonight was different. As impossible as it seemed, he could feel a barrier protecting her. God killed Uzzah when he touched the Ark of the Covenant. James adjusted the position of his hands.

Sara was in the middle of the backseat with Marla leaned on her right side. James gently placed Joni on her left and cushioned her head on Sara's shoulder. His sister modestly arranged Joni's skirt as he shut the door and got in the front.

Cole slid into the passenger side. He jerked his head toward the backseat as James pulled onto the highway. "Wonder what heavenly realm they're in?"

James laughed softly. "I don't know, but I'd sure love to be there, too. Makes me want to shout all over again."

Sara yawned from the backseat. "I'm jealous and proud at the same time."

~~~

The next morning, a tall glass of orange juice sat in front of James. Joni claimed the chair. "Is this for me?"

He smiled at her "Absolutely. How do you feel?"

"Wonderful." She laughed. "I can't put it into words." She drained her glass. "Mmm, this is good. What do they have to eat?"

"You're eating before noon? Wow. You are a new girl."

She laughed again. "Shut up and show me how to work the waffle thing."

"You sit there. I'll make it for you. It's been a while since I cooked you breakfast."

She refilled her glass while James poured batter in the waffle machine. "Last night was more amazing than anything I've ever experienced."

James smiled. "Syrup?"

"Yeah, and can I borrow some earplugs for the ride home?" Joni was in such a great mood, not even four hours in chaos could dampen her spirits.

"Or you could ride with me." He better not be teasing. "I told Sara there was no need for you to ride the bus. It's not like the girls can jump out the window."

"Seriously? And that was fine with her?" She smiled as he nodded. "Thank you, thank you, thank you." She wanted to jump out of the chair, run around the table, and throw her arms around him, but she could feel people staring and she didn't want to make Jesus look bad. At the sweet bite of waffle, Joni wondered what manna tasted like. She didn't deserve God's blessings, but she'd take whatever He'd give her.

When everyone loaded up for the drive home, Blaine frowned over his shoulder before he stepped on the bus. Joni whispered across the interior of the truck, "I can't believe you let him ride with you."

"Are you kidding? It was the only way I had to make sure he left you alone."

She giggled and shook her head. "Real smooth, James." Comfortable in the front seat, she refused to complain about the hulky console between them.

"Hey, Joni." Cole called from the backseat. "Can you sing that last song?"

She half-turned in her seat. "Yeah. I've been thinking about it. Let's practice tomorrow. Can Marla pick out the notes?"

"Already got it covered. We talked about it at breakfast."

Phillip grinned from the middle of the backseat. "Unless Pastor kicks Joni off the platform again now that she's back with James."

Beside her, James's body went rigid. "What?"

She shook her head in small, quick jerks and mouthed the word, "No."

Vince and Cole got the message, but unfortunately Phillip didn't. "Sorry, I thought since she's riding with us, ya'll were back together. My bad."

James frowned at Phillip through the mirror. "As far as I'm concerned, we were never *not* together." He turned his attention back to the highway. "Tell me why they booted her."

Joni gripped his arm. "It doesn't matter. I would have told you, but I'd forgotten about it."

He squeezed her hand. "You can tell me later."

"So…" Cole leaned over the seat. "…about the song."

Chapter Twenty-Three

Practice must be running late.

James drove into the church parking lot and parked beside Joni's car. He paused in the foyer and breathed in strength and a sense of belonging. He was home and Joni waited. If he could find Isaac, his life would be complete.

She had her back to the doors while she sang on the platform. Cole played the drums. A few others played and sang too. James slipped down a side aisle and leaned back in the shadows of the second pew. Her voice blended beautifully with the music.

The second verse began and she grappled with the low notes. She stopped singing. "We've got to go up a notch. I can't reach it."

"We can't. Marla and Abigail are struggling, as it is. Try again."

Joni turned and her eyes met James's. She missed her cue but the music soon started again. Her voice lacked volume during the first two lines. "This sounds horrible."

Cole let out a shrill whistle and yelled into the pews. "Hey, quit ogling my lead singer. You're making her nervous."

James laughed and leapt out of the shadows. Joni's eyes widened as he jumped on the platform. "I'm not allowed to ogle in church."

Cole stood and slapped James's hand. "Great. Now either help or get out of here." Cole turned to Joni. "Why do you let him hang around?"

James caught the cordless microphone she tossed him.

"He'll help."

Awkward silence fell. Anticipation hung in the air.

"James doesn't sing in church." Marla's fingers danced across the keyboard.

Joni reached over and turned his microphone on.

Cole provided a drum roll. "Maybe he does now."

She whispered for James's ears only, "Sing with me."

The music began. There was nothing he wouldn't do for her. The sparkle in her eyes held him captive. His voice blended with hers. They sounded good together.

Halfway through the song, Cole held up a hand. "Marla, drop it a key. James, sing the first half of the verses, Joni back him up. Switch leads after the change." He pointed a stick at the others. "Come in at the chorus."

Are you singing for her or Me? James started at the still, small voice speaking in his heart. He dropped his eyes to the carpet. *Forgive me.* Refocusing on the lyrics, he worshipped with song.

When practice was over, Marla walked up the aisle on Joni's other side. "You guys sound amazing."

"Thanks."

"What are your plans? Where are you headed?" Cole questioned James.

"I don't know. Whatever Joni wants." James claimed her hand in the church foyer and slipped his shades on as they stepped into the evening sun.

"That's sweet." Marla bumped Joni's arm.

Joni giggled. "You choose. Dad came back from Miami to train a new employee and I promised to cook dinner. Other than that, I was just going to dream about you anyway."

James pressed his lips together to keep from kissing her in front of her friends. "What are we cooking?"

"See you lovebirds tomorrow." Cole and Marla got in their separate cars and drove out of sight as James walked Joni to her car.

"I love you." He kissed Joni's surprised lips.

"We're in the church parking lot."

He wrapped his arms around her waist and kissed her again. "Doesn't matter where we are, I still love you."

"I love you, too." Her hands slid around his neck and he dipped his head. A horn beeped. She flinched and shoved against his chest.

The pastor rolled down his window. "James. I wondered how Cole convinced you to sing with his group."

"Sir, if you'd rather I not…"

"No. No. I'm looking forward to it." To Joni he said, "Been trying to get this boy to sing in church for years." The window rolled up and the pastor's sedan merged into traffic.

Red-faced, she swatted James on the arm. "You can't kiss me in church anymore. There's no telling what the pastor thinks."

He laughed. If she knew what the pastor saw outside of their apartment last December, she'd freak. "We're in the parking lot and you asked me to."

"I most certainly did not."

"Your eyes have begged for a kiss since they saw me in the pew." He opened her door and kissed her again. "See."

Her laugh was priceless.

Later, when three steaks sizzled on the grill, he slipped into the kitchen and watched her slice vegetables for the salad. He had a vision of coming home to this scene every day. *Oh God, please, let it be so.* Sneaking up behind her, he nuzzled her neck. He couldn't keep his hands off her and they settled at her waist.

She turned and looked over his shoulder. "Hi, Daddy."

~ ~ ~

"Are you going to marry her or not?"

Joni had disappeared up the stairs to dress for their date. Her father eyed him critically. The force of Bill's question rocked him. "I hope so."

"Well, what's stopping you? You two get any closer and you'll be living together again. I may not know a lot about the Bible, but I do know premarital relations are sinful. Are you going to wait until I'm a grandfather before you propose?"

Joni obviously got her bluntness from her father. "I'm praying about it, sir."

"Pray faster."

"Yes, sir." He agreed with her father, especially when Joni descended the stairs in a shorter skirt and a pair of her flippity-flappity heels.

She stopped in front of his recliner. "Are you ready?"

"I'm waiting on you, beautiful."

Their outing failed to divert his attention from the dream of marrying Joni. After he dropped her off at her dad's house and returned to Sara's garage apartment, James prayed into the early morning hours. The sun rose and charged the air with an expectancy.

Not bothering to knock, he walked into Bill's kitchen.

"You're early. Joni's upstairs getting ready. Have some coffee."

"No, thanks." A yawn escaped him.

"Late night?" Bill shoved a mug into James's hand.

"Yes, sir. I had a prayer fest."

Bill raised his eyebrows and grinned. "And?"

"I don't know." James wanted a life with Joni more than anything, but with his past failures, he wanted to be sure.

Shaking his head, Bill stood to refill his mug. "You're the first young man I've ever known to pray before pr—"

"I'm ready." Joni gathered her Bible and purse.

The deep green dress had a half-jacket thing tied above her waist. She leaned over and kissed her father's cheek. Peach toes sparkled from spiky emerald heels.

"James?"

"Yeah." Sweet perfume teased his nostrils.

"I'm ready to go now." The frustration in her voice penetrated the fog around his brain.

Bill guffawed and slapped the table. "Boy, I feel sorry enough for you to pray myself."

Joni cut her eyes to her father as he spilled coffee. "What's wrong with Daddy?"

"Nothing." James stood. "Where's your keys? I don't want to get your dress dirty in the truck."

At the church, as they gathered on the platform, Joni whispered, "Butterflies are fluttering in my stomach."

James encouraged her with a wink and ignored the squadron of fighter jets in his own. Cole counted down the beat. Marla played the introduction. When James sang the first words, God answered his prayer. All his reservations about marrying Joni fled.

A picture of them singing together flooded his mind. He poured his thanks and his praise into worship. A cloud of glory descended and the altars flooded with worshippers. Tears streamed down Joni's face. The anointing took control and the service exploded in power.

Marla rose from the piano bench and knelt to pray with her brother. Joni stepped behind the keyboard and played in church for the first time. After singing a multitude of praises, the service quieted. The pastor spoke into the microphone. "James, come here a minute. Bring Joni with you."

He led the way while holding her hand. His body trembled with anticipation and he could feel Joni shiver. Whatever the Lord had in store for them, he wanted it all.

"When I saw you yesterday, I saw something different in you and I've seen you both plenty of times. God told me to tell you that though the devil tried to destroy you, God has a plan. The devil didn't realize who you were. He didn't know you were gonna let God's strength be your own. You may have fallen for his tricks in the past, but never again."

James held tight to Joni's hand. The pastor placed one hand on each of them. A jolt of electrical current shot through the top of James's head and ran out both of his shoes. He staggered back at the power it held.

Chills raced up James's spine as a high-pitched feminine voice gave a message in tongues. Complete silence overcame the room and a reverent hush filled the sanctuary.

The pastor interpreted. "*I*, the Lord God, have ordained you. *I* have gifted you. *I* have prepared you. *I* make this decision. It is not the whim of man but the will of God, and you will fulfill the purpose that *I* have set before you. And no man or *woman* will stop you."

Praise filled the tabernacle. Pastor leaned down and whispered in James's ear. "You don't have to fear failing any longer. History will not repeat itself. That was a scare tactic used by the devil. He didn't know who you were." Laughter flowed through him. "But God does."

The tongues of angels surrounded him and James lost himself in God's glory.

When he came to himself on the altar floor, Joni's hair fanned across the top of his leg. God reminded him of the morning after he'd met her. She blinked and stirred. Unspeakable joy swept over him. It took him a few minutes to return to reality and then he stood, pulling Joni up with him.

The congregation ignored them as people continued to pray.

James led Joni to the front pew and knelt before her. His hands trembled as he kissed hers. "I promise to search after God's will and be the husband He wants me to be. Will you marry me, Joni?"

His breath left him until she whispered, "Yes."

Joni leaned down and brushed her lips across his. He smiled. "I thought I couldn't kiss you in church."

"You didn't. I kissed you." Her smile matched his.

"Kiss me again."

Her cheeks turned pink. "Later. Right now, I want my ring back."

He'd never found a way to tell her. "I lost it the night I got saved."

Her smile faltered and her brows rose. "Really?"

"I'll buy you another one. You can pick it out. Anything you want."

She rolled her eyes but her smile returned. "I get to choose."

He'd buy her whatever she wanted as long as she married him in the end. He stood. "Let's go ring shopping, and then we'll tell our families the good news."

Joni pointed to Sara and Paul talking animatedly on their phones. "Our families know."

James laughed and pulled her to her feet. They made their way out of the sanctuary amid many well-wishes and congratulations.

In the car he asked, "Lunch or ring first?"

She laughed. "Both."

James drove toward the largest jewelry store in town. "We may have to eat a bologna sandwich after we buy the ring."

Her face paled.

He laughed. "I was joking." He parked and winked. "I've been saving up."

She swatted him in the chest and then grinned. "Did you see me playing the piano?" He nodded and she continued. "I don't know how it happened. I've tried to play church music since that first tent meeting, but I couldn't. Hymns, yes. Classical, yes. But not church music. Something just came over me and then…it was weird."

"Joni, the Holy Ghost can do in less than a minute what man can't do in a lifetime." He kissed her before he got out of the car.

A salesman nudged another as they walked in the door hand in hand. James pulled Joni to the side and caressed her cheek. "We're doing this once. Let's do it right. If they don't have what you want, we'll go somewhere else." Her eyes sparkled and he kissed her again. "And don't worry about the price. I dumped my entire savings into the checking account so we could use the debit card."

Joni's brilliant smile outshone all the gems in the store. She trailed a finger down the case and stepped over to look further. She moved to a revolving display in the center of the showroom. A saleslady followed James to Joni's side. He laid his arm across her shoulders. "See anything you like?"

The lights shimmered in her hair. "There's too many to choose."

Forty minutes later, she had her choices down to three.

His stomach growled. "I'm starved. Let's go eat, and you can think about it some more."

The saleslady tapped her pen on the glass case. "Would you like to place a deposit to hold them until a later time?"

"No, thanks."

In the parking lot, Joni leaned in for a kiss. "Sorry for being so picky. They didn't feel right. When I see the ring, I'll know."

He raised his brows.

"I can't explain it."

"You don't have to if you kiss me again."

Her eyes held a spark he hadn't seen before. Stretching on tiptoe, she slid her arms around his neck. Her lips hovered near his. "I love you."

He pulled her as close as possible and wrapped her up in his arms. "Where to?"

"How about that new Mexican restaurant in the mall? There's a jewelry store beside it."

They stopped at two different jewelers before they made it to the mall. James was starving. Across the aisle from the restaurant, she veered toward a well-known jewelry store. James moaned. "Joni, please. Feed me first and then we'll shop all afternoon. I promise."

"I won't be long."

He rolled his eyes and followed her into the store. "Five minutes."

A young salesman grinned at James's comment. "He's holding out on you, huh? No problem. Pick out your ring, tag it, and come back in a few years when he's ready."

James frowned at the way the lecher hovered near her. "Joni."

She ignored him and spoke to the salesman. "He's grumpy when he's hungry. Oh! Let me see that one."

"Nice choice. A little expensive, though." The salesman held out the ring in a baby-smooth palm. He probably never worked a real job in his life.

Joni slipped the ring on and held her hand up to the light. "Oh, James. This is it." Her smile blinded him. "This is the one."

His heart lurched at the sight of the ring glistening on her finger. His mind traveled back to the vision of babies. It was Joni's hand in his dream, wearing this ring. James kissed her knuckle and smiled. "Does this one come in a set?"

The salesman turned serious. "Yes." He brought out a black case of plain, thin bands.

Joni lifted her face to James. "Perfect."

Her lips drew him in.

"Ahem." A discreet cough, then the salesman said, "We need your ring sizes." He measured James's finger and twisted the ring on Joni's. "We need to take it down a size."

Joni nodded and slipped it off. "How soon can I have it back?"

"An hour or less."

"Not a problem." James handed over his card and the salesman keyed the purchase into the computer.

Joni leaned her head on James's shoulder. "I love you."

He kissed the top of her head and held her close. "Then feed me, woman. I'm starved." She giggled as the salesman returned. Keeping her wrapped in his arms, James signed the receipt and folded his copy into his wallet. "What time do you close?"

"Seven on Sunday."

"We'll be back by five."

Across the walk, they munched on chips and salsa. Joni reached over the table and touched his arm. "Thank you for my ring. It's beautiful. And thank you for patiently waiting for me to choose." She laughed. "I love you."

He couldn't reach her. "What are you doing way over there?" James stood and scooted in beside her. The waiter appeared with their order. When he left James said, "Eat up. I need to check on my investment."

Joni dabbed her napkin against her mouth. "What investment?"

"Your ring."

She paled. "How much of an investment?"

"You're worth every penny."

"How much?"

"I'm not gonna tell you." James held her gaze while he drank his sweet tea.

"James?"

He pictured the future. "Until I want to buy a boat and when you tell me it's too expensive, I'll tell you how much I spent on your ring." He grinned at her shocked expression.

They finished eating and returned to the jewelry store.

James slid the ring on her finger and pressed a kiss against the back of her hand. "How soon can we be married?"

Her smile was a little bit too sweet. She tilted her head and winked. "If you were in such a hurry, you should have asked me sooner."

Epilogue

"Look who just pulled up."

James tried to ignore the gossip session from the guys behind him as he wiped the sweat off his forehead with his sleeve.

"It's not every day you see the boss's daughter."

"Heard she got married."

"Lucky guy."

"Thanks." All heads turned to James. He looked past their shoulders. Out the third-story window of the hotel they were building, Joni leaned against the hood of her car.

His phone chimed with her text. *Where are you?*

He replied. *Stay put. Ill be right down*

He turned to his crew. "Lunchtime. Rest up, boys; this afternoon we need to finish this entire section."

"You're the new husband?" The four crewmen stared. "Why didn't you tell us?"

James had wanted to earn his crew's respect, not inherit it from being the son-in-law. "Would it have made a difference?"

"Yeah."

Another crew member slapped the speaker across the stomach, and he changed his answer. "No."

Sure it did, but they would've found out sooner or later. Whispers followed him down the stairs. Aware of the men watching, he swooped his head and kissed his wife sweetly.

Joni giggled and pushed at his chest. "You're all sweaty."

Sheetrock dust covered him. "You love me anyway."

"I brought your lunch." Her smile brought back memories of

the previous night. "I know you didn't have time to fix it before you left."

She stepped out of his reach and rounded the car. She brought out a towel from the trunk and removed the tag. "Lucky for you, I was saving these."

He stood still as she wiped his face and neck. Her kiss brushed his chin and she pressed the towel in his hand. "I've got a surprise for you." He wiped his hands while she fished in her oversized purse. The new tablet she'd bought for school displayed her inbox. "I received an email from a very special man this morning."

Man? He grabbed for the screen, but she held on to her end. "Let me see your fingertips." He turned his palms up.

"No grease stains. You promise not to cry?"

"Tsk." He shrugged his shoulders. "Real men don't cry."

"You will." She pressed the tablet into his hands.

Isaac smiled in a T-ball uniform. James's stomach clenched as if he'd been hit with the baseball bat. He swiped through the digital album. Isaac on the deck of a large boat. Isaac riding a bike with no training wheels. Isaac's first day of kindergarten. Isaac and a dog at his side.

His lungs failed. He gasped for breath. "Joni? Where did you get these?"

"Sam. He's invited us for a visit."

He shook his head in disbelief. Part of him wanted to race to his truck and go see Isaac, but another part couldn't dismiss the huge smile. Isaac was truly happy. His arms and legs were free from bruises.

Joni wiped her eyes with the towel. "Looks like I'm the one who can't stop crying." Her arms came around him and her head peeked around his arm.

The backpack hung past Isaac's knees and his hair was longer than James was used to seeing, but the grin on his face was the same one he had learned to cherish.

His son.

No, not his. Isaac belonged to Sam now.

James relied on the strength in Joni's arms. "Remember when

we went daycare shopping? He was so excited about his new school."

Joni's finger brushed over the photo. "I remember."

He flipped to the T-ball picture. A chuckle escaped him. "His jersey is two sizes too big."

"I think the bat is." Her arm rubbed against his. "I wonder if he hit the ball."

"Of course he hit it off the tee. He could hit my pitches when he was four." James flicked to the next picture. "Nice boat."

"He's losing his baby face. A lot can change in two years." She sniffed and locked her arms around his waist.

"Isaac grew up without us." James dropped his head. The sting behind his eyes grew. He blew out a breath, turned, and leaned against the car. With one hand, his fingers threaded through hers and held tight. The other clutched the device close to his chest. "Do you remember Andrew's party?"

She giggled. "Yes. Mother was so angry when I refused to play unless we stopped by Sara's on the way to Pensacola."

Sweet memories resurfaced. "And Isaac announced to the world you were our girlfriend."

"Yes, he did." She bumped her shoulder playfully into his. "But I didn't mind." Her eyes widened and she held up a finger. "You should have been at church when he told everyone we were sleeping together."

James sobered. "He did what?"

She laughed and continued, "Pastor kicked me off the praise and worship team. Oh, and the looks I received from Mrs. Briggs." Joni straightened. "What's wrong?"

"When? Why didn't I know this?"

The hand holding his let go and covered her mouth as her eyes widened. "I forgot who I was talking to. Everyone else knows." Delicate shoulders shrugged. "It doesn't matter. We were sharing an apartment." She smoothed her hair. "So it's not like I didn't deserve their gossip."

"Joni." He swallowed the lump in his throat. "I'm sorry." His free hand caressed her cheek. "We didn't deserve you. I never knew how much you were hurt from being with us."

She smiled. "It was my choice." Her voice dropped to a whisper. "I knew the consequences."

"I can't do this, Joni."

Her gaze met his. "Do what?"

"At Andrew's party, Isaac made me promise to one day buy us a real house. He'd never had a birthday party. Not a kid one. He'd always been in a hotel room somewhere with a daddy that took him out for pizza with a bunch of construction workers as substitute friends.

"Look at him, Joni. He's a normal kid." He flipped through the photos of Isaac and his new family. Ever so carefully, James traced Isaac's face and closed the cover. He leaned against the hood of Joni's car and pulled her into his arms. "What's your earliest memory?"

"Um." She leaned back and closed her eyes. "I'm sitting at the piano with my mom, watching a pendulum swing."

"Which mother?"

"The only one I remember. The only one I have."

"We have good memories. But what about Isaac's? The times I had to leave him to work? The long hours in a hotel room with a babysitter so he'd be safe from Kathy's neglect? Brian torching his back?"

James shut out the images and inhaled her sweetness. "I finally understand what you did. You loved him enough to give him a chance at life, regardless of your own pain." Her fingers tickled his jaw. "Tell Sam thanks for the pictures and ask him to please send more throughout the years, but I can't interfere with Isaac's new family. He deserves swings and birthday parties."

James smiled as he remembered the dog. He smoothed Joni's hair and kissed the exact spot where little hands had smeared icing so long ago.

Mischief danced in the depths of her eyes. "Isaac was right. You really are the best daddy in the world. Or you will be." Her lips twitched into a secret smile. "In eight months."

He cradled her head in his hands and prayed he'd heard right.

"Joni? What are you saying? You're expecting? I mean, we are?" As he stumbled over his words, her smile grew. He laughed as he spun her in a circle. Her flippity-flappity sandals sailed across the parking lot.

Her giggles stopped abruptly. "Ugh. Put me down before I throw up."

He lowered her bare feet onto his steel-toed boots and her complexion regained its natural color. "Your mother's gonna kill me." A vision of chubby babies returned. "Isaac made me promise to love you on both sides. I don't think he'd mind if his brothers helped me with that."

"Brothers?" Her arms locked around his neck. "Plural?"

"Yep." He brushed a kiss across her parted lips. "Twins."

Now Available
The Whatever Series
Book 2

Whatever It Takes

Preview included on the following pages.

Discussion Questions

1. Do you think James could have done more to protect Isaac? Do you know of any children that are neglected or abuse because of parental drug use?

2. Have you ever felt the presence of God as described by Joni in Chapter 2?

3. Why doesn't James want Joni to go to church?

4. Why do you think she wants to fit in?

5. How does James seduce Joni into his bed?

6. When James lost custody of Isaac, do you think he should have reacted in a different way?

7. Do you agree with Joni's decision to secure Isaac's adoption?

8. Could you empathize with James? Do you understand why he turned to alcohol?

9. Why does Joni question James's salvation?

10. Why does James feel guilty for Joni's spiritual bondage?

11. Why do you think Joni finally received the baptism of the Holy Ghost and how did He help her?

12. Did James make the right decision by letting go of Isaac in the end?

Dear Reader,

I sincerely hope you enjoyed this story. If you are like James and have forsaken your Pentecostal heritage, I urge you to return to your roots. Ask Jesus to forgive you and He'll welcome you with open arms.

Or if, like Joni, the church services depicted here, have created a curiosity to experience the presence of God, seek Him with your whole heart, and His Spirit will gently draw you into a relationship with Him. Ask the Lord to lead you to a local church, plant yourself there, and grow in God.

Wherever you are in your walk with the LORD, I encourage you to communicate with God by prayer, study the Word to familiarize yourself with the blessings that come with obeying his commandments, and seek the baptism of the Holy Ghost, for this is the power of God that can dwell in you for your help.

I am a sinner saved by grace, and I understand the temptations of this world. The Bible says we are made overcomers by the blood of the Lamb and the word of our testimony. Visit my blog to read stories of victory by myself and of others. www.bridgetthenson.com

If you have any questions, or just want to chat, I'd love to hear from you. Send me an email at bridgetthenson@millry.net.

Your friend in Christ,
Bridgett Henson

Whatever It Takes
The Whatever Series
Book 2

Chapter One

"Joni, how could you bring her into our home?"

James's angry voice woke Cindy on the first morning of her temporary freedom.

Through the window, the dark sky had turned a dull gray. She rolled in the soft comforter and stared at the locked guestroom door as Joni's whispers of hope echoed through the bedroom wall.

And then James's softened tone reached her again. "Visiting her in jail is one thing, but you're carrying the boys now. Cindy wasn't just a user. She made a living off of other people's addictions. I don't want her taking advantage of you while she's out on bail."

He was right. Cindy shouldn't stay here. In desperation to survive, she'd destroyed the lives of many.

"Her court date is already scheduled. I know you want to help her, but Cindy has to answer for her crimes."

Fully dressed, she eased out of the covers. Joni had lent her a flimsy nightgown, but Cindy hadn't worn the thing.

As she slipped into her ragged tennis shoes, her friend's singsong voice declared, "Yesterday, the doctor heard one heartbeat, James, yet you insist God promised you twin boys. Why can't you trust Him to save her? It's up to us to show her the love of Jesus, and to teach her that God wants to give her a better life. Let her stay. For me?"

James growled his consent. "Ah, beautiful, I'd do anything for you. She can stay, but lock your jewelry in the gun safe."

Who could blame James for being leery?

As she tiptoed into the hall, Joni's giggle floated under the master bedroom door. Unlike Joni, no man had ever cared for Cindy without a selfish motive, but God did love her. Of that she was certain. He had proved it in the darkest night.

She crept down the carpeted stairs. The Lord promised her a good life—one without fear. Determined to find it, she paused, her hand on the brass knob. Which way should she go?

"Jesus, I don't want to be who I was. Change me. Make me worthy of Your love. Lead me. Make me who You want me to be." She sucked in a breath. "And help me sell my stash at the pawnshop. Amen."

The deadbolt disengaged with a flick of her wrist.

She unlatched the security chain, but glanced toward the stairs. Joni had said that James would cook omelets. Cindy ignored her rumbling stomach, opened the door, and stepped into unfamiliar territory.

Unseen birds chirped in the hazy morning, as a gentle breeze flowed through the rip in her jeans, chilling her knee. Come noon, she'd crave the cool. She descended the steps.

She needed to hurry and get her stuff before the users and dealers arose and tempted her to stay. She didn't want to live in that world, but she wouldn't leave the merchandise she'd hidden away either.

The sidewalk ended, and she stepped in the fresh-cut grass. Luxury homes hid behind iron gates and tall shrubs. Would she ever have a life like Joni's? Would she ever know a love like James's? Would she ever be good enough? Maybe when she got out of prison…

Cindy shook the daydreams out of her mind. Downtown Mobile was a long walk from the Eastern Shore. Without her new friend's sponsorship, Cindy would be locked in her cell. She stumbled on a rock and wondered how Joni had talked her cynical husband into posting bail.

~ ~ ~

Cole Maxwell made good time in the early morning traffic, but the meteorologist had warned of dense fog on I-10. He crossed the bypass and took the scenic route spanning the Mobile Bay as a new voice from the radio admonished husbands to love their wives.

Cole punched the knob and silenced the voice, but the longing in his heart couldn't be ignored. Despite his earlier prayers, he consulted his savior. "Lord, is it too late? Did I miss her somehow? Is that what happened yesterday? If You show me who she is, I'll love her forever, but I'm so tired of waiting. Where's the one You promised? Where is *my* wife?"

Along the edges of the bay, the rising sun painted the oyster grass a brilliant gold. Cole passed a deserted building destroyed by a storm years ago. The causeway was a dangerous place during hurricane season, yet the beauty of the waves lured both tourists and locals to its marshy banks.

"Forgive my impatience, Lord."

A girl walked alongside the road. Sunbeams inflamed the back of her long red hair as it danced with the wind.

The Spirit within him fluttered, and Cole suppressed an urge to help her. He needed to reach his office early and prepare for his father's staff meeting.

Take her home.

His heart quickened at the sound of God's still, small voice. But he must be mistaken.

"Lord, she's a hitchhiker and I'm late."

Turn around. Take her home.

Never in his life had Cole offered a stranger a ride. Good Samaritans ended up on the five o'clock news, and he had no desire to become a statistic. He drove on.

From the cup holder, his phone sounded a drum roll. Grateful for a distraction, Cole answered James's call. "Hello?"

"Hey man, sorry to call so early, but did you see Joni's friend Cindy, on your drive across the bay?"

"Who?"

"Hold on." James's voice grew louder. "Cole didn't see her." And then it lowered. "By the way, Sara said you could have my old apartment. I'll text you her number."

Cole sighed toward heaven. "That's an answer to prayer. Thanks."

"You're welcome. See you Sunday." The call ended.

Moving above Sara's garage would cut his commute in half. Even as Cole doubted, God was good.

Turn around. Offer her a ride and take her home.

He could no longer ignore the voice of the Spirit. God had blessed Cole in abundance. He couldn't disobey a direct command. So at Battleship Parkway, Cole signaled left and waited for the traffic to clear. "Forgive my lack of faith, Lord. But please don't let her be a serial killer."

~~~

The constant wind tangled her hair, but at least it cooled the hot summer morning. She was free! After being cooped up in jail, her legs weren't used to walking. Her muscles ached, but she kept moving. Another quarter mile and she could rest on the seawall.

A horn blared, and a small hybrid zoomed past. She glanced back as a white BMW pulled alongside her. She quickened her pace.

Music drifted through the window as it lowered. "Good morning. You need a ride?"

Something in the cheery masculine voice beckoned her, but she shook her head and kept walking. She'd known girls who'd accepted a lift and were never heard from again.

"Are you sure?" A tan hand reached across the leather seat as another horn blared behind them.

He was blocking traffic. She didn't like the attention from angry drivers. One call and she'd land back in jail.

Beautiful laughter sounded as an arm clothed in grey, suit material beckoned. "Come on. Save me from angry commuters and get in the car."

An import and a blue minivan zoomed around them.

Accepting his offer was practical and time-saving.

She slung her hair out of her eyes and snatched the door open. Besides, she only had three months of freedom before her trial.

Dressed in a suit and tie, Mr. Persistent smiled across the tan leather seats. Dark waves haloed his head. "Isn't it a beautiful morning?" The light in his silver eyes sparkled.

Her heart lurched as the window crept up, sealing them in together, but the cold air from the vents felt like heaven. She ignored his question, wiped the sweat from her forehead, and then wiped her hand on her worn jeans.

The Clark Kent/Superman look-a-like drummed his fingers on the wheel in perfect time with the beat playing through the speakers. With his good looks, he probably had his choice of girls. He didn't need to pick up women off the streets. Why had he stopped for her?

"I've never offered anyone a ride before. I suppose you have a destination in mind?"

The scent of his aftershave mingled with the air freshener clipped onto one of the vents. He was too clean to enter her neighborhood.

She shouldn't have accepted his offer.

"If you lean any closer to the door, you might splatter on the roadway. I assure you, I'm perfectly harmless." After a minute of silence, he released a slow whistle. "Let's start with introductions. My name is Cole Maxwell and you are…?"

"Lulu." She spoke the nickname her brother had given her years ago. Long before he'd abandoned her.

The driver tilted his head, and deep laughter filled the car. He glanced her way several times while keeping one eye on the road. "Interesting name, Lulu. You have no idea how long I've waited to meet you." He slowed in a line of traffic and turned in his seat. His elbow propped on the windowsill, and a fist cushioned his head. Gentle eyes cherished her from her unbrushed hair to the rip in her shoe. Unlike the men in her past, the desire flickering in his eyes treasured her. Full lips curled, and his eyes closed briefly. "Thank you, Jesus."

His words intrigued her. Comforted her. Why?

Thankfully, he turned his soul-searching gaze back on the traffic. "My sweet, precious Lulu, where would you like to go? Anywhere in the world. California? New York? Italy? Name it, and I'll take you there."

Who was this guy? People didn't really help others. They used and took what they could, then abandoned you when you were left with nothing. "Why are you helping me?"

"You wouldn't believe me if I told you."

She glared until he relented.

"God told me to."

At least he was original. His was a line she hadn't heard before. She studied the hand holding the wheel. His words sounded similar to Joni's logic, but Cindy wasn't convinced. She turned toward him. In her cell, she'd felt a comforting presence, and she'd known Jesus was with her. Whispers of reassurance breezed through her mind, but the words couldn't be understood. "Tell me His exact words."

"He said to take you home. That's what I'm doing."

Really? Maybe God did talk to him. But how far was he willing to go? "Texas."

A curious smile peeked from the corner of his full lips. "Dallas or Fort Worth? Or perhaps Austin? I haven't seen my college buds in a while."

The sun broke through the haze, and two white, puffy clouds floated in the sky. If this guy were a real superman, he'd fly her to the clouds, away from the hell that waited where she had to go. "Not Texas. Downtown Mobile. Houston Street."

His brows arched. "You live in a dangerous area."

"I didn't say I live there. At least, I don't anymore. I need a few things I left behind."

He glanced her way. "Okay, but after that? Where *do* you live?"

She cleared her throat, battling against the longing she'd heard in his voice. Reality set in. She was homeless. Where could she go? It depended on how much of her life savings survived her six-month stay in the Metro jail. Her sister and her friends probably helped themselves to her possessions. No hard feelings. In her world, people did what they had to in order to survive. "Drop me off at

Houston and Government Streets. My life isn't your problem."

"We'll get your things, and then I'll take you home."

The snazzy beat of his music danced around them. Pretending an interest in the beautiful scenery of the Mobile Bay, she let the lyrics about God's mercy and grace wash over her. "Is this a CD?" She fumbled with the controls, determined to hear the entire song.

A masculine hand chased away her fingers. His soft laughter sent waves of warmth through her soul. "The driver controls the radio."

Laughter bubbled somewhere inside her. She bit her lip, refusing to let the small bit of happiness escape.

They waited at a red light for the on-ramp to the interstate. There were two ways across the bay: Battleship Parkway and I-10. The light turned green and her head lolled against the seat as he merged with the interstate traffic. She stared at his profile. Her fingers itched to touch his square jaw.

Impossible. She hated men. Feeding them the poison she cooked was her chance at revenge. She hated their touch. She hated their crude words, their foul bodies, their wicked thoughts. Was Cole any different from the others?

One hand left the steering wheel and rested on the console between them. His forearms held power. Would he hurt or protect her? Long, masculine fingers spread, clenched into a fist, and then relaxed.

Without looking at his face, she placed her pale hand beside his. The contrast was startling. His hand was strong. Hers was weak. Her nails were jagged and her cuticles overgrown.

His pinkie finger extended toward hers, sending her heartbeat into spasms as he traced the outline of her knuckle, seducing her hand to relax. Hooking around hers, his finger held her safe. She closed her eyes and enjoyed the warmth of his simple touch.

His palm rolled under hers. Her breath quickened as the hollow cavity in her chest ached. Tingles spread up her arm as her hand became weightless. With a whisper of his lips, the shell around her heart shattered as his breath danced across the back of her hand.

A whimper escaped her. She exhaled slowly as he lowered their entwined hands to the soft leather.

Reality returned with the eerie echoes of the deep, as the car entered the tunnel, submerged underneath the Mobile River. Concrete walls and rows of florescent light surrounded the West bound traffic. Tons of water and countless ships lay between her and the surface. She held her breath until the car emerged into the morning sunshine. Cole exited onto Water Street. She stared out the window as he maneuvered through the many twists and turns of downtown. She sucked in a breath as he turned onto Houston Street.

The brief dream vanished. "Which house?"

She freed her hand from his. "The green one."

~ Whatever It Takese
Now Available
www.empoweredpublicationsinc.com/our-books.html

About the Author

Bridgett Henson was raised in the Deep South by a Baptist mother and a Mormon father. During her teen years, she abandoned the Christian faith altogether. Now, she and her husband minister to a small Methodist church, while holding membership in a local Pentecostal assembly. There, they raise their three children.

When she's not writing fiction for all denominations, she attends short mission trips, youth conferences, rallies, and summer camps.

Bridgett has a special burden for the youth of today, especially those bound by sex, drugs, and alcohol. She often speaks to those recovering from these addictions.

She hopes that her readers will come to know the God who created and loves them, understand the merciful grace found in the blood of Jesus Christ, and be introduced to the sustaining power of the Holy Ghost.

Visit her website for more information. www.bridgetthenson.com

www.ingramcontent.com/pod-product-compliance
Lightning Source LLC
Chambersburg PA
CBHW072123250626
47159CB00007B/2547